A/F
JULY 2013

ALSO BY KARIN SLAUGHTER

Blindsighted

Kisscut

A Faint Cold Fear

Indelible

Like a Charm (Editor)

Faithless

Triptych

Beyond Reach

Fractured

Undone

Broken

Fallen

Criminal

eBook original

Snatched

Thorn in My Side

Busted

UNSEEN

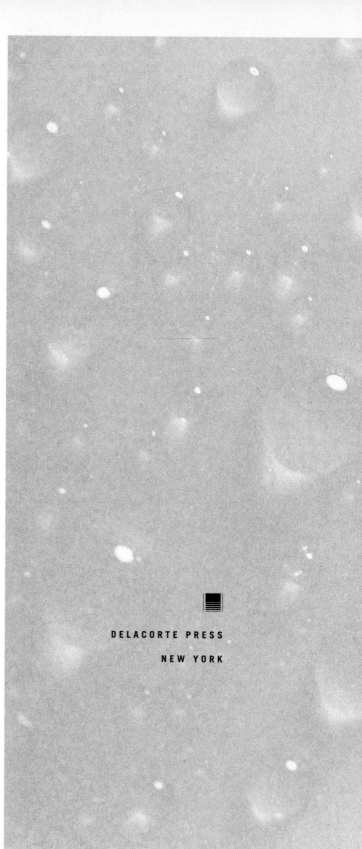

DELACORTE PRESS
NEW YORK

KARIN
SLAUGHTER

UNSEEN

A NOVEL

Unseen is a work of fiction. Names, characters, places,
and incidents either are the product of the author's imagination
or are used fictitiously. Any resemblance to actual persons, living
or dead, events, or locales is entirely coincidental.

Copyright © 2013 by Karin Slaughter

All rights reserved.

Published in the United States by Delacorte Press,
an imprint of The Random House Publishing Group,
a division of Random House, Inc., New York.

DELACORTE PRESS and colophon are
registered trademarks of Random House, Inc.

LIBRARY OF CONGRESS CATALOGING-IN-PUBLICATION DATA

Slaughter, Karin
Unseen : a novel / Karin Slaughter.
p.   cm.
ISBN 978-0-345-53947-2
eBook ISBN 978-0-345-53948-9
1. Government investigators—Fiction. 2. Undercover
operations—Fiction. I. Title.
PS3569.L275U57 2013
813'.54—dc23   2013005812

Printed in the United States of America on acid-free paper

www.bantamdell.com

2 4 6 8 9 7 5 3 1

FIRST EDITION

For Angela, Diane, and Victoria—
my champions

UNSEEN

1.

WEDNESDAY

MACON, GEORGIA

Detective Lena Adams winced as she pulled off her T-shirt. She took her police badge out of her pocket, along with her flashlight and an extra clip for her Glock, and tossed them all onto the dresser. The time on her phone showed it was almost midnight. Lena had rolled out of bed eighteen hours ago and now all she wanted to do was fall back in. Not that she'd done that much lately. For the past four days, just about every waking hour had been wasted sitting at a conference room table answering questions she'd answered the day before and the day before that— navigating the usual bullshit that came from having to justify your actions to Internal Affairs.

"Who led the raid into the house?"

"What intelligence were you acting on?"

"What did you expect to find?"

The internal investigator for the Macon Police Department had the dour, lifeless personality of a career pencil pusher. Every day, the woman showed up dressed in the same style black skirt and white blouse, an outfit that seemed more appropriate for greeting diners at an Olive Garden. She nodded a lot, frowned even more as she took notes. When Lena didn't answer quickly, she'd check the tape recorder to make sure it was picking up the silences.

Lena was certain the questions were designed to provoke an outburst. The first day, she had been so numb that she'd just answered truthfully in the hope that it would soon be over. The second and third days, she'd been less forthcoming, her level of irritation rising with each passing minute. Today, she had finally exploded, which seemed exactly what the woman had been waiting for.

"What do you think I expected to find, you miserable bitch?"

If only Lena hadn't found it. If only she could take a razor and slice the images out of her brain. They haunted her. They flickered into her vision like an old movie every time she blinked. They filled her with a constant, unrelenting sorrow.

Lena started to rub her eyes, then thought better of it. Six days had passed since she'd led her team on the raid, but her body was still a walking reminder of what had happened. The bruise fingering its way across her nose and underneath her left eye had turned a urine-yellow. The three stitches holding together the cut in her scalp itched like a rash.

Then there were the things that no one could see—Lena's bruised tailbone. Her aching back and knees. The roil in her stomach every time she thought about what she'd discovered in that desolate house in the woods.

Four dead bodies. One man still in the hospital. Another who would never wear the badge again. Not to mention the terrible memory she would probably end up taking to her grave.

Tears came into Lena's eyes. She bit her lip, fighting the urge to let the grief have its way. She was exhausted. The week had been hard. Hell, the last three weeks had been hard. But it was over now. All of it was over. Lena was safe. She would keep her job. The rat squad investigator had scurried back to her hole. Lena was finally home where no one could stare at her, question her, probe and prod her. It wasn't just Internal Affairs. Everyone wanted to know what the raid had been like, what Lena had found in that dark, dank basement.

And Lena wanted nothing more than to forget all about it.

Her cell phone chirped. Lena exhaled until her lungs were completely empty. The phone chirped a second time. She picked it up. There was a new text message.

VICKERY: u ok?

Lena stared at the letters on the screen. Paul Vickery, her partner.

She tapped reply. Her thumb hovered over the keyboard.

The distant rumble of a motorcycle shook the air.

Instead of typing out a response, Lena held down the power button until the phone turned off. She placed it on the dresser beside her badge.

The roar of the Harley-D's twin-cam engine vibrated in her ears as Jared gunned the bike so he could make it to the top of their steep driveway. Lena waited, following the familiar sounds: the engine cutting, the metallic groan of the kickstand, the heavy tread of boots as her husband made his way into the house, tossed his helmet and keys onto the kitchen table even though she'd asked him a million times not to. He paused for a moment, probably to check the mail, then continued toward their bedroom.

Lena kept her back to the door as she counted off Jared's footsteps down the long hallway. His stride sounded tentative, reluctant. He'd probably been hoping Lena would be asleep.

Jared stopped at the doorway. He was obviously waiting for Lena to turn around. When she didn't, he asked, "You just get in?"

"I stayed late to finish." It wasn't a complete lie. She'd hoped Jared would be asleep, too. "I was about to take a shower."

"All right."

Lena didn't go into the bathroom. Instead, she turned to face him.

Jared's gaze flickered down to her bra, then quickly back up again. He was dressed in his uniform, his hair twisted into a peak from the helmet. He was a cop with the Macon PD, too—a motorman, one rank below Lena and twelve years younger. Neither one of these things used to bother her, but lately, every inch of their lives was a provocation.

He leaned against the doorjamb, asking, "How'd it go?"

"They cleared me to go back to work."

"That's good, right?"

She replayed his words in her head, trying to decipher the tone. "Why wouldn't it be?"

Jared didn't respond. There was a long, uncomfortable silence before he asked, "You want a drink?"

Lena couldn't hide her surprise.

"I guess it's okay now, right?" He tilted his head to the side, forced his lips into a tight smile. He was a few inches taller than Lena, but his muscular frame and athletic grace made him seem larger.

Usually.

Jared cleared his throat to let her know that he was waiting.

She nodded. " 'Kay."

Jared left the room, but his need lingered—surrounding her, almost suffocating her. He *needed* for Lena to break down. He *needed* for her to lean on him. He *needed* her to show him that what happened had affected her, had altered her in some tangible way.

He couldn't see that not giving in was the only thing that kept her from falling completely apart.

Lena took her pajamas out of the dresser. She heard Jared moving around the kitchen. He opened the freezer door, rummaged around for a handful of ice. Lena closed her eyes. Her body swayed. She waited for the cubes to hit glass. Her mouth watered in anticipation.

She clenched her jaw. Forced open her eyes.

She wanted the drink too badly. When Jared came back, she would put the glass down, wait a few minutes, prove to herself that she could do without it.

Prove to him that she didn't need it.

Her hands ached as she unbuttoned her jeans. The day of the raid, she'd gripped her shotgun so hard that her fingers had felt like they were permanently curled. She wasn't sure why everything still ached. She should be better now, but her body was holding on to the hurt. Holding on to the poison that was eating her up inside.

"So." Jared was back. This time, he came into the room. He poured a large vodka as he walked toward her, the bottle gurgling as the liquid splashed into the glass. "You're back on duty tomorrow?"

"First thing."

He handed her the glass. "No time off?"

Lena took the drink and downed half of it in one gulp.

"I guess that's the same as when . . ." Jared's voice trailed off. He didn't have to say when. Instead, he looked out the back window. The dark panes showed his reflection. "I bet you get your sergeant's stripes off this."

She shook her head, but said, "Maybe."

He stared at her—waiting. Needing.

She asked, "What are they saying at the station?"

Jared walked to the closet. "That you've got balls of steel." He dialed the combination on the gun safe. Lena watched the back of his neck. There was a pink line of sunburn where his helmet didn't protect the skin. He must've known she was watching, but he just took his holster off his belt and stored his gun beside hers. Near hers. He didn't even let their guns touch.

She asked, "Does it bother you?"

He shut the safe door, spun the combination. "Why would it bother me?"

Lena didn't say the words, but they were screaming in her head:

Because they think I'm tougher than you. Because your wife was taking down some very bad guys while you were toodling around on your bike giving tickets to soccer moms.

Jared said, "I'm proud of you." He used his reasonable voice, the one that made Lena want to punch him in the face. "They should give you a medal for what you did."

He had no idea what she'd done. Jared only knew the highlights, the details Lena was allowed to share outside closed doors.

She repeated the question. "Does it bother you?"

He paused for a second too long. "It bothers me that you could've been killed."

He still hadn't answered the question. Lena studied his face. The skin was unlined, fresh. She'd met Jared when he was twenty-one, and in the five and a half years since, he'd somehow started looking younger, like he was aging in reverse. Or maybe Lena was getting older more quickly. So much had changed since those early days. In the beginning, she could always tell what he was thinking. Of course, since then, she'd given him plenty of mortar to build up a wall around himself.

He started unbuttoning his shirt. "I think I'm gonna go put those cabinets together."

She gave a startled laugh. "Really?" The kitchen had been torn apart for three months, mostly because Jared found a new reason every weekend to not work on it.

He let his shirt drop to the floor. "At least Ikea will know I'm still the man of the house."

Now that it was out there, Lena didn't know how to respond. "You know it's not like that." Even to her own ears, the excuse sounded weak. "It's just not."

"Really?"

Lena didn't answer.

"Right." Jared's cell phone started to ring. He pulled it out of his pocket, checked the number, and declined the call.

"That your girlfriend?" Lena didn't like the thinness in her tone. The joke wasn't funny. They both knew that.

He rummaged through the dirty-clothes basket and found his jeans, one of his T-shirts.

"It's almost midnight." Lena looked at the bedside clock. "Past midnight."

"I'm not sleepy." He dressed quickly, tucking his phone into his back pocket. "I'll keep the noise down."

"You need your phone to put the cabinets together?"

"The charge is low."

"Jared—"

"It won't take long to finish." He smiled that fake smile again. "Least I can do, right?"

Lena smiled back, holding up her glass in a toast.

He didn't leave. "You should get in the shower before you fall down."

She nodded, but couldn't stop her eyes taking in the way the T-shirt clung to his chest, followed the definition of his abs. The vodka had given her a nice buzz. Her body was finally starting to relax. There was something about the way Jared was standing that brought old memories rushing back. Lena let her mind wander to a place she usually kept blocked off—the town where she'd lived before she moved with Jared to Macon, the city where she'd first learned how to be a cop.

Back in Grant County, Jared's father had taught Lena everything she knew about being a police officer. Well, almost everything. Lena had a feeling the tricks she'd learned after Chief Jeffrey Tolliver's death would've pissed him the hell off. For all the times he crossed the line, Jeffrey sure came down hard on Lena whenever he caught her skipping near it.

"Lee?" Jared asked. He had Jeffrey's eyes, the same way of tilting his head to the side while he waited for her to answer him.

Lena finished the drink, though her head was swimming. "I love you."

It was Jared's turn to give a startled laugh.

She asked, "Aren't you going to say you love me back?"

"Do you want me to?"

Lena didn't answer.

He gave a resigned sigh as he walked over to her. She was dressed in nothing but her bra and underwear, but he kissed her on the forehead the same way he did with his sister. "Don't fall asleep in the shower."

Lena watched him go. He'd been wearing the same dirty T-shirt a lot lately. There were spots of yellow paint on the back and shoulders from where he'd started remodeling the spare bedroom three weeks ago.

Lena had told him not to paint the walls, to wait another few weeks—not because he had at least ten other projects in the house that needed to be finished first, but because it was bad luck.

Jared never listened to her.

Of course, she never listened to him, either.

Lena took the vodka bottle with her into the bathroom. She put the empty glass on the back of the toilet and drank straight from the bottle, her head tilting back. Probably not wise considering the pain pills she'd taken as soon as she walked through the front door, but Lena wasn't feeling particularly smart at the moment. She wanted the amnesia to come. She wanted the pills and the alcohol to erase everything from her mind—what had happened before the raid, during the raid, after. She wanted it all blanked out so that she could lie down and see darkness instead of that silent flickering movie that had haunted her for the last six days.

She put the bottle down on the back of the toilet. Her fingers felt thick as she pinned up her hair. Lena stared at her reflection in the mirror. There were dark circles under her eyes, and not just from the bruise. She pressed her fingers to the glass. Her face was starting to show the things she'd lost.

The number of bodies she'd left in her wake.

Lena looked down. Without realizing, she had pressed her palm to her flat stomach. As recently as nine days ago, there had been the beginning of a swell. Her pants had been tight. Her breasts had been sore. Jared hadn't been able to stop himself from touching her. Sometimes, Lena would wake up and find his hand resting on her belly, as if he was laying claim to what he'd created. The life he'd put inside of her.

But of course the life didn't stay there. His hand couldn't stop the wrenching pain that had ripped Lena from a deep sleep. His words couldn't comfort her as the blood flowed. In the bathroom. At the hospital. On the drive home. It was a red tide that left nothing but death in its wake.

And every time she walked by that fucking spare bedroom with its bright yellow walls, she was gripped by such a cold hate for him that she shivered with rage.

Lena stared up at the ceiling. She held her breath for a moment before letting it whisper out like a dark secret. Everything was getting to her today. The loss, the grief. The vodka and pills weren't helping. Would never help enough.

She searched for the cap to the bottle, but couldn't find it. Lena pulled open the door. The bedroom was empty. Jared's clothes were on the floor, exactly where they'd dropped when he took them off. Lena picked up his shirt. She smelled exhaust from the road, sweat and grease from riding all day. His pants still had his wallet in the back pocket. She took it out and put it on the bedside table. His front pockets were full. A handful of change. A small tin of Burt's beeswax to keep his lips from getting windburned. A couple of twenties, his driver's license, and three credit cards, all held together by a green rubber band. A small black velvet pouch that he kept his wedding ring in.

Lena dug her finger inside the pouch and pulled out the gold ring. Jared had stopped wearing it to work after one of his buddies had wiped out on his bike. The man's wedding ring had caught on his knuckle and ripped the skin off like a sock. After that, Lena had made Jared promise not to wear his ring while he was riding. The black pouch was a compromise. She'd told him to leave the ring at home, but her husband was romantic—much more so than any woman Lena had ever met—and he didn't like the idea of being without it.

She assumed now that he carried it around out of habit.

Lena returned the ring to the pouch and opened Jared's wallet. She'd given it to him their first year together, and he still carried it despite the fact that he'd never used a wallet before. It was really nothing more than a portable photo album. Lena thumbed past the many candid shots Jared had taken over the last five years: Lena in front of their house on the day they moved in, Lena on his bike, Jared and Lena at Disney World, a Braves game, the SEC play-offs, the national championship in Arizona.

She stopped on the photo from their wedding, which had taken place in a judge's chambers inside the Atlanta courthouse. Lena's uncle Hank stood on one side of her, Jared on the other. Beside Jared were his mother, stepfather, sister, grandmother, grandfather, two cousins, and an elementary school teacher who'd always kept in touch.

Everyone was dressed up but Lena, who was in a navy pantsuit she normally wore to work. Her hair was down, the brown curls hanging past her shoulders. She'd had her makeup done at the Lenox Macy's counter by a transexual who'd gone on and on about her skin tone. At least one woman had appreciated Lena that day. The sour look on Jared's mother's face explained why the groom hadn't insisted on a more formal affair. Somewhere right now in Alabama, Darnell Long was praying that her son would come to his senses and divorce the bitch he'd married.

Sometimes Lena wondered if she held on to Jared solely to spite the woman.

She flipped to the next picture, and her knees felt shaky.

Lena sat down on the bed.

She had seen the photo many times, just not in Jared's wallet.

It was from the shoebox Lena kept in the closet. The picture was of her twin sister, Sibyl. Lena was struck by a painful ache of jealousy, and then she felt herself start to laugh. Jared obviously thought the picture was of Lena. He'd never met Sibyl. She'd been dead ten years when Jared came into Lena's life.

She put her hand to her mouth as the laugh turned into a sob. When Lena had found out she was pregnant, the first person she'd thought of was Sibyl. There was a brief spark of happiness as Lena had picked up the phone to call her sister.

And then the loss had sucker punched her in the chest.

Lena carefully wiped underneath her eyes as she stared at the photo. She could see why Jared had chosen it. Sibyl was sitting on a blanket in the park. Her mouth was open, head tilted back. She was laughing with full abandon—the kind of happiness Lena seldom showed. Their Mexican American grandmother's genes were on full display. Sibyl's skin was bronze from the sun. Her curly brown hair was down, the way Lena wore her hair today. Though Sibyl didn't have the highlights Lena had, and she certainly didn't have the few strands of gray.

What would Sibyl look like now? It was a question Lena had asked a lot over the years. She assumed it was something all twins wondered when one passed away. Sibyl had never had Lena's hard lines and sharp edges. There was always a softness to Sibyl's face, an openness that invited people in instead of pushing them away. Only a fool would mistake one twin for the other.

"Lee?"

She looked up at Jared as if it was perfectly normal for her to be sitting in her underwear crying over his wallet. He was standing in the doorway again, feet just shy of entering.

She asked, "Who was that call from? On your cell phone?"

"The number was blocked." He looped his thumbs through his tool belt as he leaned against the doorjamb. "You all right?"

"I'm . . . uh . . ." Her voice caught. "Tired."

Lena looked at Sibyl one last time before she closed the wallet.

She felt tears streaming down her face. Her jaw tightened as she tried to force her emotions back down. No matter what she did, they kept bubbling up again, tightening her throat, squeezing like a band around her chest.

"Lee?" He still didn't come into the room.

Lena shook her head, willing him to go. She couldn't look at him, couldn't let Jared see her like this. She knew that breaking down was exactly what he'd been waiting for. Expecting.

Wanting.

But then something snapped inside of her. Another sob came out—deep, mournful. Lena couldn't fight it anymore, couldn't keep pushing him away. She didn't make Jared come to her. She crossed the room quickly, wrapping her arms around his shoulders, pressing her face to his chest.

"Lena—"

She kissed him. Her hands went to his face, touched his neck. Jared resisted at first, but he was a twenty-six-year-old man who'd spent the last week sleeping on the couch. It didn't take much for Lena to get a response. His calloused hands rubbed along her bare back. He pulled her closer, kissed her harder.

And then his whole body jerked away.

Blood sprayed into her mouth.

Lena heard the gunshot seconds later.

After Jared had been hit. After he collapsed against her.

He was too heavy. Lena stumbled, falling back onto the floor, Jared sprawled on top of her, pinning her down. She couldn't move. She tried to push him up, but another shot rang out. His body spasmed, lifting a few inches, then falling against her again.

Lena heard a high-pitched keening. It was coming from her own mouth. She scrambled out from under Jared, then grabbed him by his shirt to pull him out of the line of fire. She managed to move him a few feet before his tool belt got twisted up in the rug.

"No-no-no," Lena stuttered before she clamped her hands over her mouth to stop the noise. She pressed her back to the wall, fighting a wave of hysteria. The vodka and pills caught up with her. Vomit roiled into the back of her throat. She wanted to scream. Needed to scream.

But she couldn't.

Jared wasn't moving. The noise from the gun still rang in her ears. Shotgun blast. The pellets had scattered, penetrating his back, his head. Bright red circles of blood spread into the dried yellow paint on his T-shirt. A screwdriver from his tool belt was jammed into his side. More blood was pooling underneath his body. She put her hand on his leg, felt the lean muscle of his calf.

"Jared?" she whispered. "Jared?"

His eyes stayed closed. Blood bubbled from his lips. His fingers quivered against the floor. She could see the tan line where he'd been wearing his wedding ring even though he promised her he wouldn't.

Lena reached for his hand, then pulled back.

Footsteps.

The shooter was walking down the hallway. Slowly. Methodically. He was wearing boots. She could hear the echo of the wooden heel hitting the bare floorboards, then the softer scrape of the toe.

One step.

Another.

Silence.

The shooter raked back the shower curtain in the hall bathroom.

Lena's eyes scanned the bedroom: The guns were locked in the safe. Her cell phone was on the other side of the room. They didn't have a landline. The window was too out in the open. The bathroom was a deathtrap.

Jared's cell phone.

She ran her hand up his leg, checked his pockets. Empty. Empty. They were all empty.

The footsteps resumed, echoing down the hallway, the sound like twigs snapping.

And then—nothing.

He'd stopped outside the first bedroom. Two desks. Boxes of old case files. Jared always left the closet door open. The shooter could see it from the hallway.

He cleared his throat and spat on the floor.

He wanted Lena to know that he was coming.

She pressed her back against the wall, forced herself to stand up. She wasn't going to be sitting down when she died. She was going to be on her feet, fighting for her life, her husband's life.

The footsteps stopped again. The shooter was checking the next bedroom. Bright yellow walls. Closet door laid across a pair of sawhorses so Jared could paint balloons on it. From the hallway, you could see the thin pencil lines where he'd sketched them freehand. You could also see straight back inside the empty closet.

The shooter continued down the hall.

Lena's hand shook as she reached down to Jared. The hammer on his belt was already halfway out of its metal loop. She used her fingers to push it the rest of the way. Her hand wrapped around the grip. It felt warm, almost hot, against her skin.

Jared's eyelids fluttered open. He watched Lena as she stood up, pressed her back against the wall again. There was a glassy look to his gaze. Pain. Intense pain. It cut right through her. His mouth moved. Lena put her finger to her lips, willing him to be quiet, to play dead so that he wouldn't get shot again.

The footsteps stopped just shy of the bedroom door, maybe five feet away. The man's shadow preceded him into the room, casting half of Jared's body into darkness.

Lena turned the hammer around so that the claw was facing out. She heard the pump of a shotgun. The sound had its intended effect. She had to lock her knees so she didn't fall to the floor.

The shooter paused. His shadow wavered slightly, but didn't encroach farther into the room.

Lena tensed, counting off the seconds. One, two, three. The man did not enter. He was just standing there.

She tried to put herself in the shooter's head, figure out what he was thinking. Two cops. Both with guns they hadn't used. One was on the floor. The other hadn't moved, hadn't shot back, hadn't screamed or jumped out the window or charged him.

Lena's ears strained in the silence as they both waited.

Finally, the shooter took another step forward—short, tentative. Then another. The tip of the shotgun's barrel was the first thing Lena saw. Sawed off. The metal was rough-cut, freshly hewn. There was a pause, a slight adjustment as the shooter pivoted to the side. Lena saw that the hand supporting the barrel was tattooed. A black skull and crossbones filled the webbing between the thumb and forefinger.

One last, careful step.

Lena two-handed the hammer and swung it into the man's face.

The claw sank into his eye socket. She heard the crunch of bone as the sharpened steel splintered a path into his skull. The shotgun went off, blasting a hole in the wall. Lena tried to pull out the hammer for another blow, but the claw was caught in his head. The man staggered, tried to brace himself against the door. His fingers wrapped around her wrist. Blood poured from his eye, ran into his mouth, down his neck.

That was when Lena saw the second man. He was running down the hallway, a Smith & Wesson five-shot in his hand. Lena yanked on the hammer, using it like a handle to jerk the shooter in front of her, to use him as a shield. Three shots popped off in rapid succession; the shooter's body absorbed each hit. Lena gave him a hard shove backward into the second assailant. Both men stumbled. The S&W skittered across the floor.

Lena scooped up the shotgun. She pulled the trigger, but the shell was jammed. She tried the pump, worked to clear the chamber as the second guy climbed his way up to standing. He lunged for her, fingers grazing the muzzle of the gun before he fell to one knee.

Jared had grabbed his ankle. He held on tight, his arm shaking from the effort. The man reared back, started to bring down his fist on Jared's temple.

Lena flipped the shotgun around, grabbed it by the barrel and swung it like a bat at the man's head. Blood and teeth sprayed as his jaw snapped loose. He crashed to the floor.

"Jared!" Lena screamed, dropping down beside him. "Jared!"

He moaned. Blood dribbled from his mouth. His stare was blank, unseeing.

"It's okay," she told him. "It's okay."

He coughed. His body shuddered, then a violent seizure took hold.

"Jared!" she screamed. "Jared!" Lena's vision blurred as tears filled her eyes. She put her hands on each side of his face. "Look at me," she begged. "Just look at me."

Movement. She saw it out of the corner of her eye. The second man was inching toward the bed, trying to reach the gun. Half his body was paralyzed. He dragged himself with one arm, a wounded cockroach leaving a trail of blood.

Lena felt her heart stop. Something had changed. The air had shifted. The world had stopped spinning.

She looked down at her husband.

Jared's body had gone completely slack. His eyelids were closed to a slit. She touched his face, his mouth. Her hand shook so hard that her fingertips tapped against his skin.

Sibyl. Jeffrey. The baby.

Their baby.

Lena stood up.

She moved like a machine. The hammer was still embedded in the first man's face. Lena braced her foot on his forehead, wrapped her hands around the handle, and wrenched the claw loose.

The cockroach was still crawling toward the bed. His progress was incremental. Lena took her time, waiting until he was inches away from the gun to drop her knee into his back. She felt his ribs snap under her full weight. Broken teeth spewed from his mouth like chunks of wet sand.

Lena raised the hammer above her head. It came down on the man's spine with a splintering crack. He screamed, his arms shooting out, his body bucking underneath her. Lena held on, her mind focused, her body rigid with rage. She raised the hammer high above her head and aimed for the back of his skull, but then—suddenly—everything stopped.

The hammer wouldn't move. It was stuck in the air.

Lena looked behind her. There was a third man. He was tall, with a lanky build and strong hands that kept Lena from delivering the deathblow.

She was too shocked to respond. She knew this man. Knew exactly who he was.

He was dressed like a biker—bandanna around his head, chain hanging from his leather belt. He put a finger to his lips, the same as she had done to Jared moments before. There was a warning in his eyes, and underneath the warning, she saw genuine fear.

Slowly, Lena came back to herself. Her hearing first—the raspy sound of her own labored breathing. Then she felt the shooting pain from her tensed muscles, the singed skin of her palms where she'd grabbed the shotgun. The acrid smell of death flooded into her nose. And just underneath that, she caught the tinge of the open road, the familiar odor of exhaust and oil and sweat that Jared brought home with him every night.

Jared.

The back of his shirt was drenched, glued to his skin. The yellow spots of dried paint had disappeared. They were black now, just like his hair—darkened by blood.

Lena's body went limp. The fight had drained out of her. She lowered the hammer, let it fall to the floor.

Sirens pierced the air. Two, three, more than she could count.

A hoarse voice called from somewhere outside. "Dude, where you at?"

The sirens got louder. Closer.

Will Trent looked at Lena one last time, then left the room.

2.

THURSDAY

ATLANTA, GEORGIA

Hospital elevators were notoriously unreliable, but Dr. Sara Linton felt that the ones at Atlanta's Grady Memorial were particularly creaky. Still, like a gambling addict hitting a slot machine, she punched the button every time on the off chance that the doors would open.

"Come on," Sara mumbled, staring at the numbers above the doors, willing them to hit seven. She waited, hands tucked into the pockets of her white lab coat as the digital display showed ten, then nine, then stayed at a solid eight.

Sara tapped her foot. She looked at her watch. And then she felt her body fill with dread as she saw Oliver Gittings trotting toward her.

As a pediatric attending in Grady Hospital's emergency room, Sara was in charge of several students who—despite some evidence to the contrary—assumed that one day they would become doctors. Night shifts were particularly tedious. There was something about the moon that turned their little brains into mush.

Sara often wondered how some of them managed to dress themselves, let alone get into medical school.

Oliver Gittings was one of the better examples. Or worse, as the case tended to be. In the last eight hours, he'd already spilled a urine sample on himself and accidentally sewn a sterile cloth onto the sleeve of his lab coat. At least she hoped it was accidental.

He called, "Dr. Linton—"

"This way," Sara told him, giving up on the elevator and heading toward the stairs.

"I'm glad I found you." Oliver ran after her like an eager puppy. "An interesting case came up."

Oliver thought all of his cases were interesting. She said, "Give me the highlights."

"Six-year-old girl," he began, pulling on the exit door twice before realizing that it opened outward. "Mom says the girl woke her up in the middle of the night for some water. They're going down the stairs. The girl starts to fall. Mom grabs her arm. Something pops. The girl starts screaming. Mom rushes her here."

Sara took the lead down the stairs. She guessed, "X-ray showed a spiral fracture?"

"Yes. The girl had a bruise on her arm here—"

Sara glanced back to see where he indicated. "So, you suspect abuse. Did you order a skeletal survey?"

"Yes, but radiology is backed up. My shift is almost over. I thought I'd go ahead and call D-FACS to get things moving."

Sara abruptly stopped her descent. The Division of Family and Children's Services. She asked, "You want to go ahead and put the kid in the system?"

Oliver shrugged, as if this was nothing. "The girl's too quiet. Mom's antsy, irritated. All she wants to know is when they can leave."

"How long have they been here?"

"I dunno. I think she was triaged around one."

Sara looked at her watch. "It's 5:58 in the morning. They've been here all night. I'd want to leave, too. What else?"

For the first time, Oliver seemed to doubt himself. "Well, the fracture—"

Sara continued down the stairs. "No specific fracture is pathognomonic to child abuse. You call D-FACS and it's a legal matter. If this mother is an abuser, you want to make sure she doesn't get away with it. You need corroborating evidence. Does the girl seem scared of her mother? Does she look you in the eye and answer questions? Are there other bruises? Developmental delays? Continence issues? Is there a history of ER visits? How did she present otherwise?" Oliver didn't immediately answer. Sara prompted, "Is she healthy? Well nourished?"

"Yes, but—"

"Stop." Sara wasn't looking for a discussion. She checked her watch again. "Dr. Connor is taking over for me, but you've got all of my numbers. Order the skeletal survey to see if there are any past breaks or fractures. Notify security to keep an eye on the mom. Call the other ERs to see if the girl's ever been admitted." Sara moderated her tone, trying to make it clear she was teaching him something, not punishing him. "Oliver, sixty-five percent of child abuse cases are flagged in emergency rooms. If you stay in pediatrics, this is the sort of thing you're going to be dealing with on a weekly basis. I'm not saying you're wrong. I'm just saying you need to know all the facts before you turn this girl's life upside down. And her mother's."

"Yes, ma'am." He headed down the stairs, hands tucked deep into his coat pockets.

Sara didn't immediately follow, cognizant that Oliver's ego was fragile enough without her snapping at his heels. Instead, she sat on the bottom stair and checked her hospital BlackBerry. Sara's eyes threatened to roll back in her head as she scrolled through the administrative detritus littering her mailbox. Meetings, conferences, denied requisitions, and new procedures for requisitioning, attending conferences, and scheduling meetings.

She felt around in her other pocket and traded the BlackBerry for her personal phone. This was much better. Her father had emailed a silly joke about snails that he'd heard at the Waffle House. Her mother had forwarded a recipe that was never going to happen. There was a long email from her sister with a picture of Sara's niece attached. She marked this unread and saved it for later. The next message was a text from Sara's boyfriend. An hour ago, he'd sent her a photo of his breakfast: six mini chocolate doughnuts, an egg and cheese biscuit, and a large Coke.

Sara didn't know which one of them was going to have a heart attack first.

The door popped open. Dr. Felix Connor stuck his head into the stairwell. He eyed Sara suspiciously. "Why do you look so happy?"

"Because I can go home now that you're finally here?"

"Gimme a minute to hit the can."

Sara dropped the phone back into her pocket as she stood. Oliver wasn't the only one who wanted to get out of here. Sara had pulled several night shifts in a row courtesy of a stomach flu that was running rampant through the hospital. She was beginning to feel punished for her own good health.

Home. Sleep. Silence. She was already making plans as she walked through the ER. Thanks to her crazy work schedule, Sara had four full days of freedom ahead of her. She could read a book. Take a run with her dogs. Remind her boyfriend why they were together.

This last bit widened her smile considerably. She got some curious looks in return. Not many people were happy to find themselves at Grady, which was the only publicly funded hospital left in Atlanta. The staff tended to take on the hardened demeanor of combat veterans. If practicing medicine was an uphill

battle, working at Grady was on par with Guadalcanal. Stab-
bings, beatings, poisonings, rapes, shootings, murders, drug overdoses.

And that was just pediatrics.

Sara stopped at the computer by the nurses' station. She pulled
up Oliver's patient on the monitor. The X-ray clearly showed
where the child's right humerus had been twisted. Either the mom
was being truthful about what had happened on the stairs or she
was savvy enough to fabricate a believable lie.

Sara looked up, scanning the open-curtain area, which was
predictably filled with repeat customers. Several drunks were
sleeping off benders. There was a junkie who threatened to kill
himself every time he got arrested and an older homeless woman
who belonged in a mental hospital but knew how to game the
system so she could stay on the streets. Oliver's little girl was
curled up asleep on the last gurney. Her mother was in a chair
beside her. She was sleeping, too, but her hand was laced through
her daughter's. She hadn't yet noticed the security guard standing
a few feet away.

Not for the first time, Sara wished that nature had devised a
system to alert the rest of the world to people who were abusing
children. A scarlet letter. A mark of the beast. Some sign that let
decent people know these monsters couldn't be trusted.

Up until a few years ago, Sara had lived in a small town four
hours south of Atlanta. She'd done double duty as the county's
pediatrician and medical examiner. Her father liked to joke that
between Sara's two jobs, she got them coming and going. While
this was certainly true, too many times, Sara had been put in the
position of witnessing firsthand the awful things people could do
to children. The X-rays that showed repeatedly broken bones.
The dental records revealing teeth that had rotted from neglect.
The skin that was forever marked from burns and beatings.

Now that she was living in Atlanta, Sara had the additional
knowledge that came from dating a man who'd grown up in state

care. Sara's boyfriend didn't like to talk about his childhood. When she touched her fingers to the healed cigarette burns on his chest, or kissed the jagged scar on his upper lip where the skin had been punched in two, she could only imagine the hell he'd survived.

Still, there were far worse things that could happen to a child. The system was flawed in many ways, but it was also there for a reason.

"I wish you'd stop smiling." Felix Connor dried his hands with a paper towel as he walked toward Sara. "I gotta say, I'm still having a hard time shaking this flu."

Sara made her voice chipper. "Better sick at work than sick at home."

"Is that what you tell your patients?"

"Just the babies." Before Felix could come up with an excuse to leave, Sara started running down her cases. She was wrapping up the details on Oliver's patient when she felt a rush of heat come to the back of her neck. Sara glanced over her shoulder, feeling like she was being watched. She did a double take when she saw her boyfriend.

Will Trent was leaning against the wall. He was dressed in a charcoal three-piece suit that was nicely tailored to his lean body. His hands were in his pockets. His sandy-blond hair was damp, curving against the nape of his neck and stopping just shy of his collar.

He smiled at her.

Sara smiled back, feeling a familiar tingling in her chest. She had known Will for almost two years—met him in this very hospital—but lately their relationship had turned into something more. The depth of her feeling was an unexpected treasure. Sara had lost her husband five years ago. She had assumed she would spend the rest of her life alone.

And then she'd met Will.

Sara said, "Felix, I—" She glanced around, but he was gone.

Will pushed away from the wall and walked toward her. "You look nice."

Sara laughed at the blatant lie. "What are you doing here? I thought you were working."

"My briefing's not for another hour."

"Do you have time for second breakfast?"

Will slowly shook his head.

"Oh." Sara realized he hadn't just dropped by. She asked, "What's wrong?"

"Maybe we could go somewhere?"

She led him toward the doctors' lounge. The door was about thirty feet away, giving Sara just enough time to work up a full-on worry.

Will was a special agent with the Georgia Bureau of Investigation. He'd been working undercover for the last ten days. He couldn't—or wouldn't—tell Sara the details of his assignment, but he kept calling from strange numbers and showing up at odd hours. She had no idea where he came from or where he was going, and anytime she asked, he either changed the subject or found a reason to leave. When Sara wasn't busy feeling mildly annoyed by all this, she was consumed with fear that something bad was going to happen. Or had already happened. Sara's late husband had been a cop. He was murdered in the line of duty, and losing him had almost killed her. The thought of the same thing happening to Will was too much to bear.

"Let me get that." Will reached in front of Sara to open the door. Fortunately, the lounge was empty. He waited for her to sit down at the table before taking the chair across from her.

She repeated, "What's wrong?"

Silently, he took her hand. Sara watched as Will ran his fingers along her palm, traced the inside of her wrist. Will watched, too, his deep blue eyes tracking the movement of his fingers. There was something about the way he watched himself touching her that made Sara's skin start to tingle.

She stilled his hand. All she needed was for one of her students to walk in and find her purring like a cat. Besides, she recognized Will's stalling tactics by now.

She leaned forward. "What is it?"

He gave a half-smile. "Diversion not working?"

"Almost," she admitted.

Will took a deep breath and said, "My assignment got a little more complicated."

Sara had been expecting as much, but she still needed a moment to absorb the information.

He said, "I can't tell you why, but I'm going to be working longer hours. I won't be able to make it back to Atlanta as much. See you as much."

She wasn't so sure Will couldn't tell her about his job, but Sara didn't want to spend what little time they had together rehashing what had proven to be a fruitless discussion.

She said, "Okay."

"Good." He looked down at their hands again. Sara followed his gaze. His wrists were tan, but only to the cuffs of his shirt. His hair was streaked with blond highlights. Whatever Will was doing, it required him to spend time in the sun.

"What I wanted to say," he continued, "was that I didn't want you to think I was disappearing on you. Or that I . . ." His voice trailed off. "I mean, what we're doing." Will stopped. "What we've been doing . . ."

Sara waited.

"I didn't want you to take my not being here for—" He seemed to be looking for the right words. "Lack of interest?" He kept staring down at their hands. "Because I am. Interested, I mean."

Sara studied the top of his head, the way his hair grew in a spiral from the crown. There was going to come a point in the near future when she would no longer be able to accept his evasions. He would either have to open up to her or she would have to consider her options. The more Sara thought about it, the closer she felt to the looming crossroads.

She stopped thinking about it.

Instead, she said, "Just promise me that whatever you're doing, you're being careful."

He nodded, but she would've felt better if he'd actually said the words. Will wasn't the only detective in the relationship. The GBI was to the state of Georgia what the FBI was to the United States. Except in cases of drug trafficking or child abduction, the agency had to be specifically asked to work a case, and the local police departments didn't tend to ask unless they were desperate.

Any way Sara looked at it, whatever crime had caused Will to go undercover was too dicey for the locals to handle. Worse, being undercover meant that Will's partner wasn't there to back him up. He was completely alone, probably surrounded by men with violent histories and addictions.

Will asked, "So, we're all right?"

Sara pressed her lips together, forcing back the words she really wanted to say. "Of course we're all right."

"Good." Will slumped back in his chair, his relief almost palpable. Not for the first time, Sara wondered how a man who'd spent his entire adult life solving puzzles could be so willfully obtuse in his private life.

She asked, "How long will this take?"

"Two, maybe three weeks."

She waited for more, but in the end, Will simply looked away. The gesture was artlessly executed, as if he was going through a checklist of casual movements. Blink. Scratch jaw. Feign interest in the notices on the wall.

Sara turned to look at the posters that suddenly held his rapt attention. They were typical to a hospital: warnings about HIV and hepatitis C alongside a rudely defaced hygiene series featuring SpongeBob SquarePants.

Sara turned back around. She'd never been good at passive-aggressive game play. "Can we at least acknowledge that there's something else going on? Because I can feel it, Will. There's something else to this and I think you're keeping it from me because you don't want me to worry."

To his credit, he didn't offer false protests. "Would it make you feel better?"

She nodded.

"All right."

Sara chewed her bottom lip. She waited for more, then remembered she wanted to leave the hospital before she was old enough to retire. "That's it?"

He shrugged.

She was too tired to keep pushing the boulder up the hill. "You are driving me absolutely crazy."

"In a good way?"

She squeezed his hand. "Not exactly."

He laughed, though they both knew she wasn't kidding. He asked, "Did you hear Homeland Security arrested SpongeBob at the airport?"

"Will."

"I'm serious. They showed it on the news this morning."

Sara groaned. "Public indecency?"

"That goes without saying, but the big charge was they caught him trying to take too many fluids onto the plane."

She shook her head. "That's awful."

"He said he was framed." Will paused for effect. "But it's obvious nobody hung him out to dry."

Sara kept shaking her head. "How long did it take for you to come up with that?"

Will leaned forward and kissed her—not an apologetic brush across the lips or a quick goodbye, but something longer, more meaningful.

Briefly, Sara considered the fact that the entire emergency room was on the other side of the door, that anyone could walk in on them, but then Will deepened the kiss and none of that mattered. He was out of his chair, on his knees in front of her. He pressed closer, pushing her back against the chair. Sara started to feel lightheaded.

"Jell-O cup!" a man screamed from the ER.

Sara jumped. Will sat back on his heels. He wiped his mouth with the back of his hand.

"Sorry," she apologized, as if she could control the patients. Sara straightened Will's collar, smoothed down his tie. She could feel his pulse pounding in the side of his neck. It matched her own beating heart. "The drunks are waking up."

"I like Jell-O, too."

"Will—"

"I should probably get to work." He stood up and brushed the grime off his pants. "Remember what I said, okay? I'm not going anywhere." He grinned. "I mean, I'm leaving now, but I'm coming back. As soon as I can. Okay?"

Her mind filled with things to tell him—that she wanted him to promise that he would stay out of harm's way, that she needed him to assure her that everything was going to be all right. Sara knew these promises would be meaningless at best and a burden at most. The last thing a cop needed to think about when he was in the line of fire was whether or not his girlfriend would approve.

In the end, she told him, "Okay."

He smiled at her, but again, Sara could tell that something was off. She could see it in his eyes—a hesitation, a concern. As usual, Will didn't give her time to question him.

She caught a glimpse of the crowded hallway as he opened the door and left. The morning rush had arrived. The cacophony of beeping monitors and machinery had started to rev. Patients were already parked on gurneys in the hallway. The drunk screamed for Jell-O again, then another screamed for the first one to shut up and also that he wanted some Jell-O.

Sara clasped her hands together in her lap, silently reviewing her conversation with Will. What was he really trying to tell her? Why had he come to the hospital when everything he'd said could've been relayed over the phone? At least he'd admitted something else was going on. He could be so damn inscrutable, and Sara was not too proud to admit that she often found herself outmaneuvered.

She touched her fingers to her lips, felt where Will's mouth had been. Was that the point of his visit? Was kissing her Will's way of making sure she didn't forget him while he was gone? Or was he marking his territory before he left town?

Only one of those options was flattering.

Sara's phone rang. She dug around in her pocket, feeling for the telltale vibration. She expected—hoped—that it was Will, but the caller ID read TALLADEGA CO, AL. Over the last week, he'd called from a lot of strange places, but never from Alabama.

Sara answered, "Hello?"

There was no response, just a low humming sound.

Sara tried again. "Hello?" There was still no response, but the humming got louder, more animal than electronic.

"Hello?" Sara was about to end the call, but, unreasonably, her mind flashed up the image of Will lying on the pavement, his body rent in two. She stood from the chair. "Will?"

There was a huff of air down the line.

"Hello?" Sara pulled open the door. She ran into the hall, nearly colliding with a patient. This was ridiculous. Will was fine. He'd just left less than two minutes ago. She could still feel his mouth on hers.

"Hello?" Sara pressed the phone to her ear. "Who is this?"

"S-s-s-ara?" The woman on the other end could barely speak.

Sara put her hand to her eyes, relief washing over her body. "Yes?"

"It's . . . it's . . . I'm sorry, I . . ."

"Nell?" Sara quickly put together the pieces, recognizing the voice of her husband's high school sweetheart. He'd had a child with Darnell Long, but not much else.

"Nell?" Sara repeated. "Are you okay?"

"It's Jared!" the woman wailed. "Oh, God!"

Sara leaned back against the wall. Jared, her stepson. Sara had only met him a few times. He was a police officer, just as his father had been.

"I didn't—" Nell's voice caught. "I should've—"

"Nell, please. Tell me what—"

"I should've listened to you!" she cried. "She's got him . . . oh, God . . ."

"Listened about—" Sara stopped. She knew exactly who Nell was talking about.

Lena Adams.

Sara's husband had trained Lena fresh out of the academy, had taken her under his wing and promoted her to detective.

And in return for Jeffrey Tolliver's trust, Lena Adams had gotten him killed.

Nell sobbed, "Oh, God, Sara! Please!"

"Nell," Sara managed, her breath catching around the word. "Tell me. Tell me what happened."

The woman was too hysterical to comply. "Why didn't I listen to you? Why didn't I forbid it? Why didn't I . . ." Her words dissolved into a heart-wrenching moan.

Sara forced air into her lungs. She could feel her chest shaking, her hands shaking. Her whole body vibrated with dread. "Nell, please. Just tell me what happened."

3.

Will Trent stood in his boss's office on the top floor of City Hall East, looking out at the city. Atlanta was just waking up, the sun sparkling between the skyscrapers, commuters in BMWs and Audis honking their horns. Across the street, dozens of men were lined up outside the Home Depot shopping center. Will watched as, one after another, trucks pulled up and taillights glowed red. Hands shot out, fingers pointed, and two, three, sometimes four men at a time would jump into the back of the truck to begin the day's work.

Will could've had that life. There hadn't been much career advice at the Atlanta Children's Home. When Will turned eighteen, they'd given him a hundred dollars and a map to the homeless shelter. He'd spent the next several months jumping in and out of trucks, working construction or whatever jobs he could find. Will had been very lucky that the right kind of people had intervened. Otherwise, he never would've become an agent with the GBI. He wouldn't have his house or his car or his life.

He wouldn't have Sara.

Will turned away from the windows. He took in Amanda Wagner's office, which hadn't been altered much in the almost fifteen years that he'd worked for her. The location had moved a few times and the electronics had gotten sleeker as she worked her way up to deputy director of the GBI, but Amanda always decorated the same. Same photos on the wall. Same Oriental rug under her behemoth desk. Even her chair was the same squeaky old wood and leather contraption that looked like it belonged to George Bailey's nemesis in *It's a Wonderful Life*.

The flat-panel TV was one of her few concessions to modernity. Will found the remote and checked all the Atlanta news channels to see if they had picked up on what had happened in Macon last night. Less than a two-hour drive from the state capital, Macon was a fairly significant city, with more than 150,000 residents and a thriving university system. Because it was geographically at the heart of the state, the city served as a compromise for people who found Atlanta too busy and smaller towns too slow. In many ways, Macon was a better representation of Georgia than Atlanta. Art museums sat alongside junk stores. A handful of respected tech colleges were blocks away from expensive private schools that taught creationism. The visitors' bureau touted both the Tubman African American Museum as well as Hay House, an eighteen-thousand-square-foot antebellum home built by the keeper of the Confederate treasury.

Apparently, the Atlanta news stations didn't find Macon as interesting. Will turned off the television and put the remote back on Amanda's desk. He should be careful what he wished for. It was probably just a matter of time before all the channels were filled with the gory details about the attack on Jared Long. The Atlanta news producers probably hadn't yet gotten wind of the story. Sometimes it took a painfully long time for phone calls to be made, people to be told that their lives had been irrevocably changed.

Will had been sitting in his car outside of Grady Hospital when Sara's call came through. He'd never been anyone's first phone call before, but when something bad happened, Sara evidently thought of him. She was crying. She had to stop a few times before she could tell him the story, though she had no way of knowing that Will already knew. Could fill her in on some of the missing details.

Jared had been shot.

His life was hanging by a thread.

Lena was somehow involved.

Will had stared blankly out the windshield as he listened to Sara try to get the words out. His mind conjured up the image of Lena in that tiny bedroom. Half-naked. Covered in blood. Will had been panicked as he rushed down the hallway, careening off the walls. He felt as if he was watching a video moving in slow motion. Lena jammed her knee into the guy's back, arced the hammer high above her head. The slow motion got even slower as the hammer dropped down the first time. The hallway got longer. Will could've been running up a mountain of sand. He was moving closer, yet somehow every step seemed to take him farther away.

But Sara didn't know any of that. She just knew that Jared had been shot. That yet again, Lena Adams had been standing by while another good man had been targeted. It had happened to Sara's husband five years ago and now it had happened to her husband's son.

It wasn't a stretch for Sara to think it might happen to Will, too.

The frustrating part was that Will had specifically gone to the hospital this morning to come clean. He was going to tell Sara that he'd lied to her about his undercover assignment because he didn't want to worry her, and then he'd had to lie about where he was working so she wouldn't figure it out, and then he'd had to lie again and again until he'd realized that it would've been easier just to tell her the truth in the first place.

But then Will had seen her standing at the nurses' station and lost his nerve. Actually, he'd lost his breath. This was nothing new. Lately, every time he saw Sara Linton, Will literally felt like she had taken his breath away. That couldn't be good for his brain. He'd been oxygen-deprived. Obviously, that was why instead of confessing, he'd ended up on his knees kissing her like they were never going to see each other again.

Which might end up being the case. Will was painfully aware of the tenuous hold he had on the situation.

On Sara.

"You're late," Amanda Wagner said, scrolling through her BlackBerry as she entered her office.

Will didn't address the comment, which was automatic, something she generally said in lieu of hello. He told her, "I sent my report an hour ago."

"I've read it." Amanda's thumbs started working as she stood in the middle of the room responding to an email. She was dressed in a red suit, the skirt hitting just below her knee, white blouse neatly tucked into the waist. Her salt-and-pepper hair was in its usual helmet. Her nails were trimmed, the clear polish gleaming.

She looked well rested, though Will knew Amanda hadn't gotten much sleep last night. The Macon chief of police. The director of the GBI. The GBI crime scene unit. The GBI medical examiner. The GBI crime lab. They each had to be read in or sent out or relayed orders. And yet Amanda had managed to call Will back three more times before the sun came up. He could tell she was worried by the calmness of her tone, the way she spoke to him as if he'd gotten a flat tire on the side of the highway instead of walked into a bloodbath. Usually, Amanda took a certain joy in making Will miserable, but last night was different.

It was also fleeting.

"So." She finished the email and moved on to another. "Quite a mess you've gotten yourself into, Wilbur."

He wasn't sure which mess she was talking about.

"I don't have to tell you that we're not out on the limb anymore; we're on the thin part of the branch. The twig."

"Yes, ma'am."

"Whoever these men are, they don't mind going after cops."

Amanda glanced up at him. "Try not to get yourself killed, won't you? I don't have the patience to break in someone new."

"Yes, ma'am."

She turned her attention back to her email. "Where's Faith?"

Faith Mitchell, Will's partner. "You said meet at seven-thirty." He checked his watch. "She's got six minutes."

"How wonderful. You've learned to tell time." Amanda continued reading as she went to her desk, sat in her chair. The old cushion made a sound like a pig snort. "I looped the director in on your midnight escapades. He's keeping a close eye on this."

Will didn't know how he was expected to respond to this information, so he took his seat, waiting for the next shoe to drop. Just recently, Will had come to accept that Amanda Wagner was the closest thing he would ever have to a mother—that is, if your mother was the type to lock you in a refrigerator or strap you into the back seat of her car and roll you into a lake.

She put down her BlackBerry and took off her reading glasses. "Anything you need to tell me?"

"No, ma'am."

Uncharacteristically, Amanda didn't press. She turned on her computer, waited for it to boot. Will guessed Amanda was in her mid to late sixties, but there really was no way of knowing her exact age. She was still in good shape, still capable of running circles around men half her age—or Will's age, to be exact. And yet watching her try to work a computer mouse was like watching a cat try to pick up a pebble.

She slapped the mouse against the desk, mumbling, "What is wrong with this thing?"

Will knew better than to offer his help. He brushed a speck of dirt off the knee of his trousers. It made him think about Sara. She was probably in her car by now, heading down to Macon. The drive was about an hour and a half. Will should've offered to take her. He could've confessed the whole sordid truth along the way.

And then Sara would've given him a choice: walk back to Atlanta or walk the rest of the way to Macon.

Amanda said, "You're brooding."

Will considered the description. "Don't you need the moors for that?"

"Clever." Amanda sat back in her chair, giving Will her full attention. "You investigated Lena Adams last year?"

"A year and a half ago," Will corrected. "Faith helped me. Lena's partner was stabbed. He practically bled out in the street. And then she arrested the suspect and he died in her custody."

"Reckless endangerment, negligence?"

"Yes," Will answered. "She was formally reprimanded, but she left Grant County a week later and joined the Macon force. They didn't seem to mind the taint."

Amanda picked at the stem of her glasses. Her voice got softer. "She was Jeffrey Tolliver's partner when he was murdered—what?—five, six years ago?"

Will stared out the window. He could feel her eyes lasering the side of his face.

She said, "There's an Eric Clapton song about telling the truth. Something about how the whole show is passing you by. Look into your heart. Et cetera."

Will cleared his throat. "It makes me very uncomfortable to think about you listening to Eric Clapton."

Amanda's sigh held a tinge of sadness that he didn't want to dwell on. "How exactly do you think this is going to end?"

He indicated the gray clouds that were suddenly crowding the sun. "I think it's going to rain."

"There's definitely a storm coming." Her tone quickly changed. "Ah, Major Branson. Thank you for making the drive."

Will stood as a woman wearing a dark blue police uniform came into the office. Ribbons and commendations filled her chest. A heavy-looking leather briefcase was in her hand. She was short and stocky, with her curly black hair shaved close to her head. She seemed about as happy to be here as Will.

Amanda made the introductions. "Special Agent Trent, this is Major Branson with the Macon Police Department. Denise is our liaison on the Jared Long shooting."

Will felt his bowels loosen. "I'm doing the investigation?"

A smile teased at Amanda's lips before she said, "No, Faith will take the lead."

"Already got it figured out?" Branson's temper sounded poised to uncoil. "I'm gonna be honest with you, Deputy Director. I'm not real happy with the idea of your people stomping around my patch like you own the place."

Amanda's tone stayed light. "Yet your chief sent you two hours north expressly to turn over all of your files."

"An hour and a half," Branson corrected. "And I may work for the man, but I don't always agree with him."

"Fair enough." Amanda indicated the chair in front of her desk. "Why don't we get our little pissing contest out of the way while Agent Trent fetches us some coffee?"

Branson sat, her briefcase clutched in her lap. Without looking at Will, she said, "Black, two sugars."

Amanda smiled her cat's smile. "Just black for me."

Will wasn't happy to be the designated fetcher, but he knew better than to linger. Outside the office, Caroline, Amanda's secretary, was sitting at her desk. She smiled at Will. "Cream. Two Sweet'N Lows."

Will saluted at her request as he walked into the hallway. His shoes sank into the padded carpet on the floor. He felt the chill of air-conditioning. City Hall East was housed in an old Sears building that had been built in the 1920s. When the city took over back in the nineties, only the important parts had been renovated, namely the executive suites. Three stories down in Will's shoebox of an office, the air was stale and likely toxic. The windows were rusted closed. The cracked asbestos tiles on the floor were scuffed red from the Georgia clay that had traveled in on nearly a hundred years of wingtips.

It wasn't just the air that was better on the top floor. The kitchen was a showplace, with dark cherry cabinets and stainless steel appliances. The coffeemaker looked like something a Transformer would shake off its leg. Will guessed the machine was the fancy kind that required pods. He checked the cabinets and found two boxes. He assumed Amanda drank the pink and orange Dunkin' Donuts high-test. The other box contained purple and yellow pods with flowers and vanilla beans emblazoned on the foil. Will took out three hazelnuts and shut the cabinet door.

After a few false starts, he figured out how to load a pod. Another minute passed before he managed to pry open the lid of the water tank and fill it to the line. He took three mugs off the hooks and waited for the water to boil.

Out of habit, Will opened the refrigerator door. There were a couple of paper bags in the fridge, but no old takeout containers or rotting food that smelled like it belonged in the morgue. Before Will started dating Sara, everything he ate was an on-the-go type of meal, whether it was a bowl of cereal he downed while standing over the sink or the hot dogs he bought at the gas station on his way home.

Now when Will went home, that usually meant Sara's apartment and something for dinner that didn't roll under a heat lamp all day.

Or it meant that for the time being.

Finally, the red light flashed on the coffee machine. Will pressed down the handle on the pod and watched the hot liquid squirt out. The smell reminded him of the cloying perfume some women wear in an attempt to hide the odor of cigarettes.

He refilled the water tank for another round. The hazelnut scent wafted into his nostrils as he stirred powdered creamer into the first mug. Will had never liked the taste of coffee, but he made

Sara's for her every morning. She liked it strong with no fancy flavoring. He'd started to associate the smell with her.

Will put down the spoon and stared at the machine.

There was no use fighting it anymore. He gave in completely to thinking about Sara, letting his mind consider all the things he was going to lose. Feeling her long auburn hair tickle his face. Tracing his lips along the freckles at the small of her back. Watching her chest blush bright red when he touched her. Then there was the way she would sometimes kiss him, showing him with her mouth what she wanted him to do.

"Will?"

He looked up, surprised to find Faith Mitchell standing in the doorway.

She asked, "What's wrong? You look sick."

The red light was flashing. Will loaded another pod. "You want one?"

"If I have any more caffeine today, my head will explode."

"Emma keep you up?"

Emma was Faith's ten-month-old daughter. Will knew the baby was with her father this week, but he listened to Faith like it was the first time he was hearing the news.

"Anyway." Faith rounded out the litany of complaints about her baby's daddy by asking, "What do you think about coincidences?"

Will recognized a trick question when he heard one.

She said, "Like, you're working an undercover case one minute and the next minute you're sucked into another Lena Adams shitstorm." She held out her hands in an open shrug. "Coincidence?"

"We always knew it was possible I'd run into her."

"We *did*?" She raised her voice high on the last word, like she was questioning a toddler.

Will turned his attention back to the coffee machine. He slowed down his movements, feigning uncertainty so that Faith would take over.

Instead of taking the bait, she told him, "Sara called me about fifteen minutes ago."

Will concentrated on filling the water tank precisely to the mark.

"She knows the state investigates officer-involved fatalities."

He loaded up the next pod.

"She wanted to know what was going on with Jared." Faith paused a moment, then added, "She didn't want to bother you with it, but we both know she's terrified of you getting mixed up with Lena, so . . ." Faith shrugged. "I told her I'd look into it."

Will cleared his throat. "That should be easy. Amanda's putting you in charge of the investigation."

"Well, great, but I didn't know that when I told Sara. I was lying to her. Just like I was lying when I agreed that it's a good thing you're working undercover God-knows-where and you're not going to get sucked into this, because I'm not sure if you know this, but Sara is terrified of you being around Lena."

Will checked the kitchen drawers for sweeteners. He found two pink packets and tore off the tops.

Faith said, "You know Sara thinks Lena's responsible for her husband's murder. I pretty much agree with her, by the way."

Will tapped the sweetener into the mug.

"She's also going to think it's Lena's fault that Jared was shot, which, considering her history, is a real possibility." Faith paused again. "Actually, it's a pattern now. I saw it back when you were investigating Lena Adams a year and a half ago. People who get close to her end up dead. Sara's right to be scared. Jared's just the latest casualty."

Will tossed the trash into the garbage can. Stainless steel, just like the appliances. He wondered if Amanda had used her own money.

Faith needled, "Jared, Sara's stepson by her dead husband who she thinks Lena got murdered."

The red light started flashing on the coffee machine. Will

pressed down the handle on the pod. He tried the weather thing. "I think it's going to rain today."

Faith groaned. "You're a dumbass, you know that?"

He grimaced, mostly because he couldn't contradict her.

"It's not the case that's going to piss Sara off, it's the cover-up." Faith paused, but only for breath. "Actually, it won't piss her off. It'll hurt her. Devastate her. Which is a hell of a lot worse than her being mad. People get over being mad."

Will scooped up the three mugs in his hands. "Amanda's waiting."

Faith trailed him out of the kitchen. Will hunched his shoulders against the disappointment radiating off her, but she was blissfully silent as she followed him to Amanda's office. He knew better than to think this was over. Faith was probably itemizing in her head all the different ways she was right about this.

Sadly, there was nothing Will could say, because Faith *was* right. Sara wouldn't be angry. She would be hurt. She would be devastated. And then she would probably inventory the steaming load of crap Will had brought into her otherwise normal life and decide it wasn't worth it. His Dickensian childhood. What had happened to his family. His ardent desire not to discuss either topic no matter how gently Sara pressed. There just wasn't much to recommend him. Will had almost been kicked out of high school. He'd been homeless. He'd barely graduated from college. And this didn't even touch on Will's hateful wife, who had evaporated off the face of the earth the minute he'd filed divorce papers, yet still somehow managed to leave the occasional nasty message tucked under the windshield wiper of Sara's car.

Caroline was still at her desk. She helped Will move the mugs around, taking the one with cream. He realized he'd screwed up the orders at the same moment he realized he didn't care.

Unbelievably, the tension in Amanda's office was thicker than when Will had left. Amanda's jaw was set. Denise Branson's body was rigid, her hands clenched into fists. The pissing contest was far from over.

Amanda's tone could've cut through steel. "Major Branson, this is Special Agent Mitchell."

Oddly, Denise Branson smiled warmly at Faith. "I worked with your mother when I was a rookie. I hope she's enjoying her retirement?"

"Yes." Faith shook the woman's hand. "I'll tell Mama you asked after her."

Branson continued, "Evelyn was always the consummate professional." She still didn't look at Amanda, but they all took her meaning. "I'm sorry I don't have time to look her up while I'm in town."

Faith's perfunctory smile and lack of response made it clear she wasn't going to be so easily charmed away from Amanda's side.

To break the awkward moment, Will passed out the coffees. Amanda held the mug to her lips, then recoiled when the smell hit her. Branson noted the gesture and placed her mug on the desk.

Amanda said, "Let's try to keep this brief. We all have work to do."

Will waited for the women to sit, then leaned against the windowsill, feeling—literally—like the odd man out. He was used to being surrounded by women, but there was something about this particular group that made him feel the need to cross his legs.

Amanda began, "All right, let's start with this officer-involved . . ." She searched for the appropriate word. ". . . hammering." She smiled on this last bit, though Will had seen firsthand why the observation wasn't funny. "Denise, any leads on why Adams and Long were targeted?"

"We have some theories."

They all waited, but Branson didn't share them.

"All right," Amanda said. "We'll need to review all recent case files, talk to their partners and team members and see if they can come up with any—"

"We've already done that," Branson interrupted. "No one stood out. They're police officers. They don't get thank-you notes for arresting people."

Amanda did not demure. "And yet they were targeted for a reason."

"We've reviewed all of Adams's cases going back twelve months. Same for Long. They've been doing mostly routine stuff. No dangerous work. Nothing that would draw this kind of attention."

Amanda smirked. "Fascinating you were able to reach that conclusion in less than six hours."

"We're a crack team down in Macon."

Amanda analyzed the woman. So did Will. Branson obviously relished the game, but her lips quivered at the corner when she was hiding something. It was almost as if she was fighting a smile.

Amanda asked, "You've met Charlie Reed?"

"That's your forensics guy?" Branson shook her head. "Didn't have a chance. Per your request to my chief, the house was sealed immediately after Jared Long was taken to the hospital. It didn't seem like a good use of my time to drive over there and wait for your boys to mosey on down."

"Thank you for your cooperation, Major. I'm sure it will help our investigation run more smoothly. Too many cooks and all that." Amanda stopped to offer a canned smile. "The lab knows to rush any trace Charlie finds. He'll report directly to me, and I'll share anything relevant with your department. Faith is taking point on the investigation." She told Faith, "Let's be sure to keep Macon in the loop."

"Yes, ma'am." Faith took out her notebook and turned to a fresh page. "Major, what can you tell me?"

Branson had obviously come prepared. She told Amanda, "Go ahead and pull up those photos on the zip drive."

Amanda raised an eyebrow at the order, but she still complied, moving the mouse around, looking at the TV set as if she expected something to happen. The screen stayed static. "Why isn't this working?"

Will kept silent, but Faith asked, "Is it on?"

"Of course it's on." Amanda picked up the remote and pressed the red button. The screen flickered on, then a photograph came up. Will guessed he was looking at Jared Long's employment photo. He'd met the young man once before. Long was a handsome kid with the kind of charming self-confidence that made him a natural leader. From all reports, he was a lot like his father.

Branson provided, "Jared Long, Lena Adams's husband. He's a motorman, been on the Macon force seven years. Good at his job. Likes being on the bike. No red flags. Stellar officer."

Faith mumbled, "Unlike his wife."

If Branson heard the comment, she chose to ignore it. "Long is out of surgery as of half an hour ago. It's touch-and-go, but that doesn't change anything on our end. An officer was shot. Another was almost murdered. Someone put the hit out. Next picture, please."

Amanda clicked the mouse. She stared at the screen, waiting for the image to change. "Oh, for the love of—"

Faith said, "Hit the space bar."

"That won't work." Amanda tapped the space bar. The picture changed. The new photo showed an older man with a pockmarked face and squinty eyes. He was dressed in an orange prison jumper. There was a placard under his chin with his name and inmate number.

Branson supplied, "Samuel Marcus Lawrence, the first assailant who entered the house, DOA shortly thereafter. He's our first shooter. Mid-level thug with a couple of assaults that put him inside for two and three years, respectively. Early parole for good behavior, times two. He told anyone who'd listen that he was an ex–Hells Angel but there's no evidence he ever patched in."

Faith kept writing in her notebook as she asked, "Drugs?"

"Meth. He had more sores on his face than a backseat whore."

Amanda said, "Either way, he's dead now." She tapped the space bar again. Another mugshot came on screen. The man was about the same age as the first, with gray hair and the faded tattoo of a cobra's head folding into the turkey gizzard of his neck.

"Fred Leroy Zachary," Branson provided. "He did eight years for assault with a deadly, then pulled a full dime off a kidnap and rape. Known around town as a muscle for hire. He's alive, but just barely. His jaw was broken. Spine fractured. Ribs broken. Whole body's in a cast. Mouth's wired shut. He can't talk, and even if he could, his lawyer won't let him."

Amanda said, "Well, you can't accuse Adams of not being thorough. What did she have to say for herself?"

Branson turned cagey again. "Not much. Doctors said she was in shock. They had to treat her at the scene. She sketched out the highlights—one armed male breached the house. Long was shot in the back. Sawed-off shotgun, so the pellets spread. Adams took the hammer out of Long's tool belt and defended herself. A second armed male came at her. There was a struggle, but she managed to neutralize both intruders."

Branson seemed to be finished. Amanda asked, "That's it?"

"Like I said, Adams was under medical care for severe shock. She saw her husband get shot. Fought for her life. His life, too, come to that. We'll go back at her later, but from where I'm sitting, she's earned some breathing room."

Amanda silently steepled her fingers together underneath her chin. Faith kept writing in her notebook, but Will could practically see her ears perk up. There was a big piece missing from the end of the story. Either Lena had lied about Will being at the house or Branson was lying about what Lena had told her.

Amanda said, "Faith will go back at Adams. She's had enough breathing room, I think. We need to know exactly what happened last night. You may not like it, but it's our case and that's how it's going to be."

Branson's jaw tightened, but she gave a single nod of agreement.

Faith broke the tension this time. "Major, maybe you can fill in some basic details for me?" She turned to a fresh page in her notebook. "We're talking a residential area?" Branson nodded. "A shotgun goes off in the middle of the night. Anybody see anything? Hear anything?"

Branson apparently shared Amanda's habit of answering questions she didn't like in her own sweet time. She paused a moment longer than necessary, then said, "The neighbors weren't sure at first. It's a fairly rural area. Just past midnight, you hear a shot, maybe it's poachers, a car backfiring. The area's heavily wooded. Houses are on five-acre lots. We're not like y'all here in the city, stacked up on top of each other like rats."

Faith nodded, ignoring the dig, or maybe agreeing with it. "Who called the police?"

"A neighbor who lives four doors down. You've got her name and statement on the zip drive if your boss can figure out how to open it." She glanced Amanda's way, then turned back to Faith. "There's two other cops on that street. One's married to a paramedic, the other lives with a firefighter. That's the only reason Long didn't die at the scene. His heart had stopped by the time they got there. They took turns working on him until the ambulance arrived. Took almost twenty minutes."

Amanda said, "If Long comes around, Faith will interview him to see if his statement matches his wife's."

Branson waited another long moment. The corner of her lips quivered, then curved into a smile. "Aren't you curious how I know for a fact that your boy over there was in that house last night right when the murders went down?"

Will supposed he was the boy in question. He thought about the hammer, the way the blood was still warm when he grabbed the metal with his bare hand. The sworls of his fingerprints in the dried blood would've been like a neon light to a cop as seasoned as Denise Branson.

Amanda breathed out a heavy sigh. "I think we can call Will a man, since he's the only thing that stopped your detective from hammering a suspect to death. A second suspect, that is."

Branson snapped, "You think so?"

Amanda made a calculated guess. "I gather that despite my orders to keep your people out of my crime scene, you ran finger-prints?"

Branson straightened her shoulders, as if bracing herself for a fight. She'd probably sent a team to Lena's house the minute Amanda gave the order to lock it down. Will could only imagine the major's rage when his GBI file popped up on her computer. He couldn't blame the woman. Nobody liked realizing they'd been fooled.

"All right." Amanda turned to Will. "Our turn to share. Run down your evening for the major, please."

Will hadn't been expecting to contribute, but he said, "Last night, I was approached by a contact I've been working as part of an undercover operation. He told me he needed a lookout on a house robbery. No violence involved, the occupants weren't home. Obviously a lie on both counts. It looked like a good way to get inside the group, so I said yes."

"You just happened to be in Macon?" Branson smirked when no one answered. "This contact got a name?"

Amanda supplied, "Anthony Dell."

Branson didn't acknowledge the answer. She prompted Will, "So, Dell said he had a job. What next?"

"We went to the job. Dell dropped me at the end of the street and told me to call on his cell if anyone approached. He drove down and parked in front of a house with a steep driveway. A light gray van was already parked on the street. Two males got out—I assume Zachary and Lawrence. They entered the house. Dell stayed outside by the van. I didn't see that they were armed, but I was about fifty yards away."

"That's half a football field," Branson noted. "Did you get the plates on the van?"

"It was midnight."

"Full moon."

"No streetlights. All I could see from where I was standing were shadows."

Branson kept studying him, like she was trying to suss out a lie. Finally, she said, "The Kia that Dell was driving was still on scene when our units rolled up."

Will felt his stomach drop. He had forgotten all about Tony's car.

Branson continued, "We woke Dell up at his house this morning. He seemed real shocked that his car was missing from his driveway. Wanted to file a stolen vehicle report ASAP. We checked him for gunshot residue, ran his sheet, which was packed with low-level bullshit—but I'm sure you know that."

"You let him go?" Amanda asked.

"What am I gonna hold him on? You gotta witness puts him at the scene?"

Will saw Amanda's nostrils flare.

Branson continued, "I noticed Dell's car's got a sticker on the windshield—Macon General employee parking. Now, that rang a bell for me, because we did an investigation last month on some pills missing from the hospital pharmacy. Never did get any solid leads, but I know the GBI gets a copy of all reports pertaining to the theft of controlled substances. I made a trip to the hospital this morning to check out Dell's co-workers." She asked Will, "How do you like your job at the hospital?"

Amanda managed to sound both irritated and bored. "Yes, Major, excellent work. Bully for you. Where is Dell's Kia now?"

"It's in our garage. You told us to seal the house, not the street." She seemed to take great pleasure in telling Amanda, "I'll make certain to share any relevant information with your department."

"How kind. Thank you."

"You're welcome." Branson turned her attention back to Will. "Two males went inside the house, you and Dell stayed in the street. What next?"

Will had to think a second before he could pick back up where he left off. "I heard the shotgun go off. I ran toward the house."

"Half a football field away," she noted. "And then?"

"Dell tried to stop me from going in. We struggled for a while. I don't know how long, but he's stronger than he looks, and he was obviously freaked out. Several more shots went off while we were fighting."

Branson gave him the once-over. "You don't look like you've been in a fight."

"He was trying to stop me from going inside, not knock me out."

"Nice guy."

Will shrugged, but in the criminal world, Dell had been doing him a solid. He'd been trying to get Will to leave instead of running into a firestorm.

Will continued, "By the time I made it into the house, both men were neutralized. Lena Adams recognized me, or at least it seemed like she did. I got her to drop the hammer, then I went back outside. Dell was gone. The police were close by. I could hear the sirens. I went behind the house, jumped the fence into the woods, and walked away."

Will tucked his hands into his pockets as he leaned against the window. Technically, he hadn't walked, but they didn't need to know that Will had bolted through those woods like the hounds of hell were at his back.

Branson asked, "Have you had any contact with Lena Adams since you and your partner investigated her a year and a half ago?"

Will told the truth. "Neither one of us has laid eyes on Lena since the investigation ended."

"Have you talked to her since last night?"

Will shook his head, his mind flashing on the image of Lena's face when he'd put his finger to his lips, told her to be quiet. She'd apparently taken it to heart.

Branson said, "I find it interesting that without any coordination, Detective Adams chose to maintain your cover."

Faith pointed out, "It makes her look good, doesn't it? Instead of Will stopping her from braining guy number two, she stops herself."

Branson wasn't about to publicly pile onto one of her officers. "I'll put a BOLO on the gray van and get it out to the news stations."

"Late model," Will supplied. "Probably a Ford. No windows on the back or sides. Light gray, not dark."

Branson took her BlackBerry out of her briefcase. "And nothing on the license plate, even though you were right up on it before you went into the house." She started thumbing the information into an email.

Amanda asked, "You didn't search for vehicles registered to Lawrence and Zachary?"

Branson kept typing. "Of course I did. They've both been living in the same trailer park off I-16. Zachary rides a Harley. Lawrence drives a truck. Both were parked outside their respective shitholes. Neither one of them have a gray van registered to their names."

"They're from Macon?"

"Born and raised."

"Family been notified?"

"Lawrence has an ex who seemed real happy he was gone. Zachary has a brother waiting for the needle over in Holman. Killed a gas station attendant during a robbery. Murder runs in the family."

"It usually does." Amanda was obviously ready to end the meeting. "Looks like we've got work to do." She turned to Faith, saying, "Priority number one when you get to Macon is talking to Lena Adams, making sure she knows to keep her mouth shut about Will. You'll need to review her recent cases. I'm sure the major won't mind another set of eyes on the good work her people have already done. Talk to Adams's team, get some idea of what she's been up to. I wouldn't be surprised to learn she's been working off-book. See if anyone will talk."

Branson dropped her BlackBerry into her briefcase. "You'll have to interview her at the hospital. She won't leave Long's side. Said we'd have to take her away in handcuffs."

"That can be arranged," Faith offered. She'd worked behind the scenes on the previous Lena investigation and couldn't quite get past their inability to make the case stick. "Adams did attempt to murder a man."

Branson glared at her. "Are you not familiar with the Castle Doctrine, Agent Mitchell? The state guarantees a citizen's right to protect his or her home from an intruder. To my thinking, this episode is the very reason the law was passed in the first place."

Faith couldn't argue with the legalities, but she'd never been one to let go of a grudge. "Be that as it may, Major Branson, the way Lena Adams lives her life, she's gonna end up looking out from the wrong side of a cell eventually."

"I think the only thing Lena's looking at right now is how to get her husband to wake up. We all feel that way. Jared Long is a good cop. So is Lena for that matter, and it worries me, Agent Mitchell, that you're going into this thing thinking otherwise."

Faith bristled. "I'll go where the evidence leads me."

"Regardless," Amanda said. "We need to pin Lena down on protecting Will's cover. There's still a play to be made at that hospital, and given last night's events, this just got a hell of a lot more dangerous. Major, I expect you'll honor our request for confidentiality. We've spent too much time on this thing to have it blow up in our faces."

"This *thing*," Branson echoed, giving careful weight to the words.

Amanda was silent. She wasn't buying time; she was making Branson wait. For her part, Denise Branson looked ready to roll out a sleeping bag if that's what it took.

Finally, after what felt like a full minute, Amanda said, "Will?"

He looked her in the eye, wondering how much she expected him to reveal. She made an open gesture with her hand, as if to say he should hold nothing back. Of course, what she indicated for Branson and what she actually meant were two different things.

Will carefully bent the truth. "Several days ago, we got a tip that a high roller was making a move into Macon. Street name is Big Whitey. We ran him through the system and got a ping out of Florida, but not much else."

Branson asked, "Which part of Florida?"

"Sarasota."

"You got a picture?"

Will hesitated a moment too long. Amanda made a great show of opening one of her desk drawers, pulling out a surveillance photo. She slid it across her desk, saying, "This was taken four years ago."

Branson leaned over, making a point of studying the grainy image.

Will could describe the picture in his sleep. Big Whitey wore a Marlins baseball cap with the brim pulled low. His jacket was bulky, hardly what you'd expect in the Florida heat. Mirrored sunglasses wrapped around the top part of his face. His beard was dark and dense, showing very little skin. His hands were in his pockets. Big Whitey knew how to pose for a closed-circuit security camera. There was no way to tell how tall or short, white or not white, the man was.

Will explained, "Florida never laid eyes on him personally. This photo was taken off CCTV at a chicken joint on Tamiami Trail."

Branson asked, "Florida's sure this is Big Whitey?"

"One of the fry cooks gave him up. Said he recognized him from his local pill shop."

"Gave him up for what?"

Will pointed to the photo. "About half a minute after that image was captured, Whitey stepped back from the camera, shot a cop in the head, and escaped through the back exit, where a car was waiting."

Branson sounded dubious. "And Sarasota didn't go balls to the wall looking for a cop killer?"

"The fry cook didn't know much more than his street name. They were gonna go back at him the next day, but he was shot dead outside his house later that night."

"Sarasota let their only material witness go home?"

"They didn't know Whitey had made him, and they couldn't legally hold the guy without cause."

Amanda chimed in, "And Sarasota didn't put the pieces together on Big Whitey until the FDLE came in and did it for them." Her tone dripped with sarcasm as she needlessly explained, "The Florida Department of Law Enforcement works much like the GBI. They coordinate cases across county lines. They're very good at providing the whole picture, the kind of details the local force is too myopic to register."

Again, Branson took a moment before asking, "Do you have any more details on this Big Whitey?"

Will said, "Nothing recent. FDLE thinks he was originally ganged up with the Palmetto Street Rollers. They were a Miami-based group, mostly Cuban, some Caucasian. The FBI put membership around twenty thousand running up and down the East Coast." Branson nodded, so Will continued, "The gang broke up into sets after some turf wars. Florida believes but isn't certain that Big Whitey took over from Sarasota down to the Keys. We're guessing two years ago, he moved up the coast into Savannah and Hilton Head."

"Guessing based on what?"

"Both Savannah and Hilton Head kept hearing his name come up. Snitches, mostly, but nothing concrete. At first, the locals thought he was an urban legend, a kind of go-to bogeyman. 'Play it straight or Big Whitey will get you.' 'Wasn't me, Officer, Big Whitey did it.'" Will added, "Savannah's convinced he's real, but Carolina disbanded the Hilton Head task force six months ago. Put the money on coastal trafficking instead, figured it was a wider net."

"What persuaded Savannah that this Big Whitey's not some kind of urban legend?" Branson obviously couldn't resist adding, "Other than the excellent counter-myopic services of the great GBI?"

Will ignored the sarcasm. "They started to see a pattern. The junkies and cons were suddenly more sophisticated. Crime went up but prosecutions went down. The bad guys had more money for lawyers—usually the same lawyers from the same firms. Better cars, better clothes, bigger guns. Somebody took a bunch of low-level thugs and turned them into businessmen."

"Ergo, Big Whitey is real," Branson summed up. "All the bad guys in town played along?"

"Unless they wanted to end up face-down in the sand." Will didn't tell her that in their own way, many of the cops had played along, too. The detectives who didn't request transfers asked for early retirement. "Most of the criminals complied. They didn't become drug dealers to lose money."

"And now you think Big Whitey's trying to set up the same type of organization in Macon because you got a tip," Branson concluded. "I'm assuming Whitey specializes in pills, which Tony Dell was swiping from the hospital pharmacy?"

Will said, "That's a chunk of his business, but heroin is his end game. Whitey moves into the suburbs, branches out into the rich white neighborhoods. They start with pills, he moves them into heroin."

Branson asked, "How'd you target Dell in the first place?"

Amanda quipped, "Confidential source."

Branson didn't look at Amanda. "Same source who turned you on to Big Whitey?"

Amanda said, "That's how it usually works."

Branson kept ignoring her, asking Will, "And that's why you agreed to play lookout on the so-called robbery last night, to build your bad-boy cred with Dell?"

Will nodded.

"Well, that all makes sense. Thank you for your time." Branson picked up her briefcase from the floor and held it in her lap again. "You know how to get in touch with me, Deputy Director."

Amanda was seldom thrown, but Denise Branson had managed to surprise her. "That's it?"

"You're obviously not going to tell me anything else and I'm sure as shit not going to share anything with you." Branson stood. "If I'd wanted to get fucked around with this morning, I would've stayed in bed with my vibrator."

The woman knew how to make an exit. She kept her head held high as she left the office, her briefcase gripped close to her side.

Will looked at Amanda, who silently stared at the empty doorway.

"Wow." Faith broke the silence. "That was quite a show."

Amanda played with the stem of her reading glasses again. "She knew Lawrence fired the shotgun that took down Long. I expect we'll find she ordered some tests."

Will had picked up on that, too. "She was in the house at some point before it got locked down. She knew Lawrence had meth sores on his face, but he doesn't have them in the booking photo. She called Dell Tony, not Anthony."

Amanda said, "She had about two hours before Charlie and his team got to Macon. She's obviously running a parallel investigation." Amanda shot Will a pointed look. "And hell will freeze over before she tells us what—if anything—she finds in Dell's car."

Will nodded at the rebuke, which was deserved.

"I doubt the car will be useful." Faith flipped back through her notes. "Branson obviously fingerprinted the bodies to get their IDs. Zachary and Lawrence weren't stupid enough to go in with their wallets. They probably left them in the van."

Will said, "Dell's probably sold their credit cards by now. He'll keep the licenses for his own use. The van's probably been stripped for parts." Leaving the Kia at the scene had been a risky move, but Tony Dell wasn't the type to pass on an easy score.

Amanda asked Will, "Dell's criminal record is petty—am I correct?"

"Yes," Will answered. Tony Dell had been very lucky up until now. "He's done jail time off some misdemeanors, but he's never made it to the big house."

"What's your story when you see him?"

"I'm angry. Why did he lie about the job? What did he tell the cops? Should I leave town? Do I still get paid?"

"Good. Don't oversell it."

Will nodded again.

Faith sat back in her chair. "Why didn't Lena tell Branson you were there?"

"I have no idea," Will admitted. "I buy that she was in shock. Her pupils were blown. She was dripping sweat. She'd just killed one guy with her bare hands and was about to take out another."

"Yes, how about that?" Amanda asked. "Let's keep in mind she was fully prepared to commit cold-blooded murder."

Will said, "Branson's right about the Castle Doctrine. Two people came into Lena's home and tried to kill her. She thought her husband was dead. She feared for her life. You could take it to trial, but there's not a jury on earth who would convict her." This was the problem with Lena Adams—or at least Will's problem.

He didn't condone her actions, but at a gut level, he understood them.

Amanda's tone was brisk. "I said let's keep it in mind. I didn't tell you to lock her up for it." She told Faith, "See if you can get Will and Lena in the same room together. She might talk more openly with him."

"That should be easy with Sara right down the hallway." Faith stared her displeasure into Will. "And don't forget who we're dealing with. In case it's not obvious, it still rankles me that Lena got away the last time. It wouldn't surprise me a bit to find out this time around that she knows exactly why this happened and who ordered it. Maybe she skimmed cash from the wrong bust. Took kickbacks from the wrong bad guys. That could be why Major Branson's doing her own investigation. Lena's one of her team. Branson doesn't want to look like the idiot who didn't realize she had a dirty cop on her hands."

"Lena's not working the other side," Will countered. He'd spent a lifetime dealing with damaged women like Lena Adams. Their motivations were easy to read once you knew what to look for. "She'd never take a bribe. She does bad things, but she always thinks she's doing them for the right reason."

"Whatever." Faith had never been a fan of nuance. "Major Branson thinks the hospital pharmacy theft is the reason you ended up in Macon. She's not going to stop until she finds out who your informant is."

Amanda stated the obvious. "She'll only know if someone tells her."

Will said, "Don't you think it's strange she asked if we had a photo of Big Whitey?"

"Yes," Amanda answered. "A picture isn't the first thing I would ask about."

Faith said, "She didn't do that weird thing with her mouth when she saw it, but who the hell knows?" She closed her notebook. "What else do you think she's not telling us?"

Amanda said, "More than we're not telling her, which I find highly annoying." She raised her voice. "Caroline, get me Gil Gonzalo at the FDLE."

"He's on central time," Caroline shouted back. "Give it another half hour unless you want to talk to a junior officer."

"I guess they work when they please down there," Amanda grumbled. "Will, your report said Dell approached you around eleven-thirty last night. He took you straight to the job?"

"I was just coming off my hospital shift. He stopped me in the parking lot." Will hadn't considered the timing until now. "Maybe he needed me to fill in for someone else."

Faith asked, "How did Dell pitch the job?"

"He asked if I wanted to make five hundred bucks cash for keeping my mouth shut and my eyes open."

Faith said, "Five hundred bucks is a lot of money for being a lookout. You could get a guy killed for less than that."

"You're right." Will was beginning to think he'd missed a lot of things last night. Adrenaline and sheer panic had never enhanced anyone's short-term memory.

He said, "I noticed when they were outside Lena's house that they all shook hands. Not the shoulder-bump bro thing, just a formal handshake, like they didn't know each other well."

Faith twisted her lips to the side as she considered the situation. "So, the plan was thrown together at the last minute. They didn't have a crew in place."

Will said, "Dell hangs out at a place called Tipsie's just about every night. It's a strip joint off the highway, caters mostly to bikers and ex-cons. I went with him a few times to build a rapport."

"A rapport?" Faith echoed.

Will ignored her sarcasm. "If you're looking for a guy to help you kill a couple of cops in Macon, Tipsie's is the place to go."

"I'll check it out," Faith said. "Hopefully, Macon PD will be more helpful than Major Branson. There's something a little too go-getter about her for me. Who wears all their ribbons for a downtown meeting? And what was that snickery smile on her lips?"

Amanda told them, "This sounds like a character-building exercise. Attempted murder on two cops, one man dead, another critically wounded, and the chief sends her to brief us? That's not a plum assignment."

"Especially if she's been up since one-shitty in the morning," Faith pointed out. "For what it's worth, Branson sounds to me like she's on-side with Lena. Could be an 'us against the world' thing, like they're both the same kind of bad."

"Maybe," Amanda allowed. "Misery loves company."

Will tuned out their voices. He thought about last night, the drive to Lena's house. Dell had been fidgety, but that was pretty much his default. He'd played with the radio, tapped his fingers on the dash, the steering wheel, his leg, as he drove one-handed toward what they both thought was an easy score. Dell had talked the entire time: about the weather, his ailing mother who lived in Texas, a woman at the hospital he was dying to sleep with. All Will had to do was nod occasionally to keep him going. Dell didn't need any more encouragement. He actually talked too much for his own good. Major Branson had been fed the story backward. Tony Dell was the original target of Will's investigation. His first day undercover, Dell would not shut up about a big-time dealer named Big Whitey.

Will realized that Amanda and Faith had gone silent.

Faith asked, "What is it?"

Will shook his head, but he still told them, "Big Whitey."

"It can't be coincidence," Amanda said. "You're down there for Dell. Dell turns you on to Big Whitey. Big Whitey kills cops. A little over a week later, two police officers are attacked."

Will said, "It's the timing that's bothering me. If I'm going to kill some cops, I don't do it on the fly. I plan it out. I follow them around. I figure out what their habits are. It would take several days, maybe a week, to get a team together. There must've been a clock ticking on the hit, otherwise they would've never used Dell and they sure as hell wouldn't've hired me sight unseen."

Faith asked, "You think some of their original crew chickened out?" She answered her own question. "It would make sense that they wouldn't tell you and Dell what they were really up to after their first choice walked away."

Will said, "That would explain the five hundred dollars. You overpay to keep the questions down and buy an easy yes." He went back to the timing. "Bad guys don't play the long game. This was something recent. The hit was put out in the last two weeks, maximum. So, we figure out what happened in the last two weeks."

"Macon is in Bibb County now." Amanda tapped some keys on her computer. "That's region . . . ?"

"Twelve," Will supplied.

Amanda raised her voice again. "Caroline, get me Nick Shelton on the phone."

Will said, "I've been reading the Macon paper every day." He ignored the surprised looks they gave him. "About a week ago, two cops were hurt raiding a shooting gallery that was selling mostly meth and pills. The details were sketchy. One's still in the hospital. The other's taking disability."

"Anything else?" Amanda asked.

"They netted some cash under the drug seizure rule. Paper didn't give an exact number, but Macon PD was talking about using it to buy new cruisers, some AKs for SWAT." Will shrugged again. "The rest was just the usual blotter stuff—missing teenage girls, pot bust at the school, a guy died on the toilet."

Amanda clasped her hands together on the desk. She was obviously done with talking. "All right. We have a plan?"

"My hospital shift starts at eleven." Will told Faith, "You'll have to figure out a way to get me and Lena in the same room without blowing my cover."

"I'm sure she'll cooperate." Faith sounded skeptical. She asked

Amanda, "Do you think it's worth me going to the trailer park where Zachary and Lawrence lived?"

Amanda shook her head. "Branson's probably flipped the place upside down by now. Give it a day or two. Go in soft so there's a nice contrast."

"All right," Faith agreed. "Speaking of Branson, I'll double-check the information she gave us, run down the records on Zachary and Lawrence, make sure there's nothing she's leaving out. Might as well run Adams and Long while I'm at it. I'll send everything to data analysis so they can track down bank accounts, mortgages, known associates, family members, whatever else pops up."

Amanda said, "That's going to be a lot of information to sort through. Pull some help from the field office. Make them do the bulk of the work on Jared Long so we have a long paper trail if this goes to trial. We don't want to be accused of prejudicial thinking."

"You mean again?" Faith pushed herself up from her chair. "I'll call the cell phone company and get a list off the towers near Adams's house. Midnight in a rural area, there can't be that many active calls."

"Let me know if they give you any push-back," Amanda said. Cellular providers were getting stingy about data mining lately. "If we need a warrant, it'll take a few days."

"Amanda?" Caroline yelled. "Nick Shelton's on line two."

Amanda picked up the receiver, but she put it to her shoulder instead of her ear. "Will, be careful. Keep your phone on you at all times so we know exactly where you are."

"Yes, ma'am." He followed Faith toward the door.

"Also—" Amanda waited for them to turn back around. "Will's right about the timing. Whatever set this off had to be recent. Faith, put together a timeline. Start with last night, then go backward day by day, minute by minute if you have to. Find out whatever the hell it is Lena Adams did to put all of this into motion."

4.

SEVEN DAYS AGO—THE DAY OF THE RAID

Dawn turned the morning light a cobalt blue as the raid van roared down a gravel road. There were ten cops in back, five on one side, five on the other, all jammed shoulder-to-shoulder so that every bump of the tires made them jerk in unison. The radio speakers were blaring Ice-T's "Cop Killer." The air inside the van vibrated with the raging beat.

Cop killer. Better you than me.

Lena Adams steadied her shotgun as they hit another rut in the road. She checked the Glock strapped to her thigh, made sure the Velcro held the gun tightly in place. The voice in her head screamed along with Ice-T's as they got closer to the target. She took a few quick breaths, not to clear her mind but to make it spin, to amp up the adrenaline and the absolute high that came from knowing she was a few moments away from the biggest bust of her career.

And then everything stopped.

The music snapped off. The red light came on over their heads.

Silence.

Two minutes until arrival.

The van slowed. Gravel crunched under the tires. Guns were drawn, magazines checked. Helmets and protective glasses were adjusted. The smell of testosterone got thicker. Nine men and one woman. All of them suited in Kevlar vests and black fatigues, loaded up with enough ammo to take down a small army.

Lena breathed through her mouth, tasting the fear and excitement circling inside the van. She took in her team. Eyes wide. Pupils the size of dimes. The anticipation was almost sexual. She could feel the exhilaration building around her, the way everyone shifted in their seats, gripped their guns tighter in their hands. They'd been staking out the house for the last two weeks, had planned their attack even as the junkies and whores streamed in and out like ants on a mound. There would be piles of money. Percocet. Vicodin. Hillbilly heroin. Coke. Guns.

Lots of guns.

Overnight surveillance told them that four men were inside the house. One was a low-level thug on parole off assault charges. The second was a junkie scumbag who would suck off a dog to feed his Oxy habit. The third was Diego Nuñez, an old-school enforcer who enjoyed getting his hands dirty. The fourth was their leader, a bastard named Sid Waller who'd been questioned on a rape and two different murders but somehow managed to skate on all of them.

Waller was their main target. Lena had been tracking him for eight months, doing a masochistic hokeypokey—locking him up, letting him go, locking him up, letting him go.

Not this time.

The drugs and guns would put Sid away for twenty years, minimum, but Lena wanted more than that. She wanted him to know for the rest of his miserable life that a woman had cuffed him, jailed him, convicted him. Not that he would have a long life once Lena was finished. She wanted Sid Waller on death row. She wanted to watch them jam the needle in his arm. See that last flicker of life drain out of him. And she was betting her career on making that happen.

For two weeks, she'd been fighting the brass, pushing them to keep the operation going, pleading with them to extend the overtime, authorize the manpower, spend the money, and pull in the favors for the snitch who'd brought them all to this house in the middle of the woods.

Sid's crew wouldn't last long behind bars. Diego Nuñez would hold out, but the other two were junkies, and with Sid Waller out of the way, getting high would trump being loyal. In less than twenty-four hours, they'd both be scrambling to make deals, and Lena had a DA who was ready to hand them out. Sid Waller had killed a nineteen-year-old kid. He'd raped his own niece and slit his sister's throat when she'd called 911. Every cop in this van wanted to be the one to take him down.

Lena didn't bother with wanting it. She was actually going to do it.

She looked up at the ceiling, staring at the red light until it flickered off and then on again.

One minute.

Lena closed her eyes, going over the plan. They had pulled the records on the house. It was a foreclosure, one of many on the outskirts of town. Brick, which was good because it would stop bullets. The single-story structure was in the middle of two point-five acres bordered by a national forest on one side and a rural route on the other that bisected Macon and fed into Interstate 75, heading north into Atlanta. Searching the tax commissioner's office had netted them a builder's diagram: den, bathroom, and two bedrooms in the back. Dining room and kitchen in the front, with a set of stairs opposite the sink that led down into the basement.

They'd rehearsed the raid so many times that Lena saw it like a tightly choreographed dance. DeShawn Franklin and Mitch Cabello would breach the side door with a Monoshock Ram. Lena would take the front of the house with Paul Vickery, her partner for the last year. Eric Haigh and Keith McVale would clear the bathroom and two bedrooms in the back. DeShawn and Mitch would secure any prisoners. The remaining men would guard the perimeter of the house and make sure no one slipped out through a window or door. Lena had wanted at least eight more bodies on the team, but the operation was already pushing the million-dollar mark and Lena knew better than to ask the brass for more.

They always worked in twos; no one entered a room alone. The layout of the house was choppy, each room walled off with nothing but a door in and out. Back at the station, they'd taped off the garage, mapping the rooms to scale. Lena and Paul had two doorways to contend with before they reached the basement: den to dining room, dining room to kitchen. Each opening represented a new opportunity to get shot.

The basement was going to be the trickiest part. The builder's diagram showed a wide-open space, but that had been drawn in the fifties, when the house was built. Sometime in the last sixty years, the basement had been finished. There would be walls they didn't know about. Closed doors and closets. There was no door to the outside, only two narrow, boarded-up windows that a grown man couldn't fit through. The basement was a deathtrap.

Back at the station, they had drawn straws to see who would go down first. Lena's team had won, but that was only because she had been holding the straws.

The van downshifted to a crawl. There were no windows in the back, but Lena could see past the driver's head. The sun winked underneath the visor. A thick stand of pine trees arced around the side of the house. Aerial photos showed a straight shot to the rural route less than two hundred yards through the forest. If the bad guys decided to run, that was the direction they'd take, which was why two cruisers were assigned to patrolling that stretch of road.

The van stopped. Overhead, the red light flickered again, this time staying off.

Lena pumped her shotgun, loading a cartridge into the chamber. She checked the Glock again. Her team followed suit, checking their weapons. The driver, an old-timer named Kirk Davis, whispered into the radio, letting the brass know they'd arrived. The mobile command center was parked a mile away in the Piggly Wiggly parking lot. If history was any indication, Denise Branson would wait until Lena's team had secured the house, then roll in and take credit for everything.

So be it.

Lena's credit would come when she had Sid Waller on the ground, her foot on his neck, thick plastic zip ties cutting into his fat wrists. It was the only thing left in her life that she wanted to do—could do. It got her up in the morning and it went to her empty bed with her every night.

Lena grabbed the door handle, then looked back at the group, stared each man in the eye to make sure they were ready. There were nods all around. She pulled open the door.

And the dance began.

Lena jumped out first, heading toward the house at a fast trot. She heard footsteps pounding behind her—nine guys armed to the teeth and ready to break some heads. She kept her shotgun tight to her chest as she ran toward the carport. Her Glock tapped against her thigh. She scanned the woods around the house, took in the trash littering the ground, the broken bottles and cigarette butts.

The perimeter team swarmed into position. Lena led the rest of her men into the carport. They lined up two on each side. Paul Vickery jammed his shoulder against Lena's. He winked at her, like this was nothing, though she could see his chest heaving up and down underneath his vest. Inside the house, they heard the laugh track from a TV show, then music. *The Jeffersons.* "Movin' On Up."

Lena started the timer on her watch. She gave the nod to De-Shawn and Mitch, who were holding the Monoshock, waiting for her signal.

They swung back the ram twice to build up momentum, then slammed the sixty-pound metal cylinder straight into the door. The wood splintered like glass.

Lena yelled, "Police!" as they rushed in—guns drawn, ready to light up the place.

But they were late to the party.

Two men sat on a yellow corduroy couch opposite the television. Their shirts were off. Jeans slung low. One had his hand tucked into his front pocket. The other guy held a can of beer. Both had their eyes open. Parted lips showed missing teeth. An array of handguns covered the battered coffee table in front of them.

Neither moved, or ever would again until the coroner came to pronounce them.

Their throats had been cut. The skin gaped open, showing white tips of vertebrae among the dark red sinew inside their necks.

Paul checked for pulses, though even from ten feet away, Lena could tell both men had been dead for hours. Waxy skin. The odor of decay. The junkie was one of the deceased—Elian Ramirez. His bare chest was concave, the ribs standing out like toothpicks. His murderer had saved him the cost of killing himself with Oxy.

Paul checked the second man, turning the head to get a better look at him. "Shit," he cursed. His disappointment spread around the room.

Diego Nuñez, Sid Waller's right-hand man. Lena watched a fly crawl across his eyeball. Nuñez's purple-black tongue lolled out of his mouth like a chow's. According to statements, Diego had taken his turn with Sid Waller's niece once his boss had finished with her. He'd been behind the wheel during the drive-by that killed a nineteen-year-old kid who'd been stupid enough to mouth off to Waller. Lena's guess was that, as a reward for good service, Diego had joined in on the fun with Waller's sister. The woman had been brutally raped and beaten before her throat was sliced open.

Murderer. Rapist. Thug. He'd died with a beer in his hand and his eyes glued to the TV.

"Shit," Paul repeated. He had found another body behind the couch. This one had been spared the slit throat, but part of his head was missing. It was a clean cut straight across. Lena guessed the ax leaning against the wall was the reason why. Long strands of hair and chunks of scalp and white bone were caked onto the edge of the blade.

Eric Haigh's hand clamped to his mouth. Vomit spewed between his fingers as he ran out the door. As far as Lena was concerned, he could keep running. She had little tolerance for weakness. And she sure as shit wasn't going to let her team get ambushed while they stood around with their thumbs up their asses.

She snapped her fingers for attention, the crisp sound cutting through the chorus booming from the TV. Lena pointed to the three corpses, then held up her hand, showing four fingers. Surveillance had four guys in the house. Sid Waller was yet to be found.

They didn't need further prompting. DeShawn guarded the door so there wouldn't be any surprises from the rear. Mitch took Eric's place and followed Keith into the back hallway. Lena headed for the dining room, Paul behind her.

They kept at a low crouch as they walked. Trash was scattered across the floor—mostly beer cans and empty fast food bags. The carpet underneath was thick with grime. It stuck to the soles of Lena's boots as she moved toward the open doorway to the dining room. She kept her tread light, mindful of the basement. She imagined Sid Waller down there, gun pointed up, listening for a sound he could shoot at.

The *Jeffersons* theme wound down with a gospel flourish. Lena could barely hear it over the sound of blood pumping in her ears as she stood to the side of the open dining room doorway. Her shoulder was against the wall. Plaster, lath, a few studs. Easily punctured by a nine-millimeter Parabellum, which Lena knew for a fact was Sid Waller's ammo of choice.

Paul tapped her leg twice, giving her the go signal. She spun around the doorframe in a low stance and pointed her shotgun into the room. There was no dining room table, just a blood-stained mattress on the floor with the usual detritus found in a shooting gallery. Crack pipes. Scorched aluminum foil. Spent hypodermics. The sharp vinegar smell of heroin burned Lena's nostrils. Water damage from a recent rain had caused the ceiling to collapse. There were chunks of plaster on the floor. The hardwood was warped, cupping like the hull of a canoe. Lena scanned upward, making sure no one was hiding in the rafters.

The room was empty. Through the broken window, Lena saw one of the other detectives in the front yard. He held his Colt AR-15 at chest level as he scanned back and forth like a pendulum. He stopped to shake his head at Lena, indicating no one had come out of the house.

She glanced back at Paul, then pointed toward the next doorway. This one was closed. The kitchen was beyond, then the basement door.

As rehearsed, Paul took the lead. Lena kept her shotgun braced against her shoulder as she walked backward, guarding the rear.

From the bedrooms, Mitch yelled, "Clear!"

Lena tapped Paul's leg, indicating he should go. His movements mirrored her earlier ones as he kicked open the door and pointed his Glock into the kitchen. Lena swiveled with her shotgun.

Empty.

None of the cabinets had doors. Half the ceiling had fallen down. The other half was stained dark brown. The sink had been pulled out. Plaster was missing where copper pipes and electrical wire had been ripped out of the walls and sold for scrap. The stench from the open drain was nauseating. Paul pointed his Glock into the ceiling as he checked for hiding places, then shook his head, indicating it was clear.

They both looked at the basement door.

This was unexpected.

There was a wooden brace like you'd find across a barn door. A two-by-four rested on two metal U-channels that were bolted to each side of the doorframe.

Paul gave Lena an inquisitive look. She could practically hear his thoughts. They'd talked a great deal about the basement door. In all the scenarios, they had assumed two things: the door would be locked and a bad guy would be standing on the other side with a loaded gun. The plan called for them to work with their backs to the wall—use the butt of the shotgun to break off the knob, the lock, or whatever was in their way, then yank open the door and rush into the hell that was waiting for them.

The bracing changed things, but maybe not too much.

Lena stood to the side, back flat to the wall as she used the muzzle of her shotgun to try to push up the wood. The fit was too tight. There was no way to slide it out. One of them would have to use both hands to heave it away, leaving his or her body as an open target to whoever might be standing on the other side of the door.

Lena didn't think about it for long. She tossed her shotgun to Paul. He caught it with his free hand, then backed up to give her cover.

She had to put her shoulder into moving the brace, kneeling down and pushing up. The damn thing was wedged in there. It wouldn't budge. She tried again, bending deep at the knees and exploding up. That worked—sort of. The board finally slipped free, but Lena stumbled back in the process, losing her balance and falling flat on her ass.

So much for the element of surprise.

The board clattered to the floor. Her tailbone felt like it had been cracked. There was a sharp, biting pain in her scalp where her head had met the sharp edge of the laminate counter. Her helmet had tipped forward, smashing her safety glasses into the bridge of her nose. Lena put her hand to the back of her head. The hair was wet. She looked at her fingers: blood.

Paul stared at her, his brow furrowed, like he couldn't understand how she'd screwed up something so easy. Lena couldn't either, but there was no time to figure it out. She pulled herself up, keeping an eye on the closed door. She tried to shake it off. Her vision was blurry. Her nose felt like a metronome was pounding inside. She took off the safety glasses. They were cracked at the bridge. She tossed them into one of the open cabinets.

There was a low whistle from the other room: *Don't shoot.* Keith came into the kitchen. Mitch followed. They were both big guys, their shoulders so wide that they made the kitchen feel more like a closet.

Lena felt a bead of sweat roll down the back of her neck. She used her hand to wipe it away. Her fingers were sticky. It wasn't sweat, it was blood.

Paul chewed his tongue between his front teeth, a tic she'd spotted their first week working together. It meant he was about to disagree with her. He didn't do it much, but when he did, he meant it.

Lena opened her mouth to take back command, but by some silent agreement, Mitch and Keith stepped forward, pulling out their flashlights as they stood on either side of the door. They all looked at Lena, but this time it was with irritation rather than expectancy.

Reluctantly, she moved over to the sink and jammed the shotgun to her shoulder so she could at least back them up. The laugh track on the television seemed to mock her. Lena couldn't make out the words, just the low rumble of Weezy's voice followed by a high-pitched response from George.

Mitch swung open the basement door. No one shot him, so he went down the stairs. Keith followed. Paul stood at the top, Glock pointing down in case someone managed to get past the combined four hundred–plus pounds of cop.

And then the waiting started.

Time changed. Even the particles in the air floated at a different frequency.

Paul didn't move. Sweat dripped from his hands, spotted the floor. Lena held her breath as she waited for some kind of resolution—guns firing, men yelling. Her head ticked down the seconds. Five. Ten. Another roar of laughter came from the television. Weezy again. Then Lionel.

Twenty seconds. Paul still hadn't moved. He was like a statue.

Lena quietly let out the breath she'd been holding. She inhaled again.

Thirty-five seconds.

Forty.

Finally, Keith called, "Clear."

Paul's hands lowered. Lena felt her lungs shake as she exhaled.

"Do the second sweep," she ordered, propping the shotgun against the counter so she could take off her helmet. There was a string of curses from below, but Lena didn't care. Three dead men were in the house—a house that had been under twenty-four-hour surveillance. She'd spent a million bucks of the department's money on this clusterfuck. She'd managed to rip open her scalp and bruise her nose. Her ass ached like a motherfucker. Her head was pounding. Meanwhile, Sid Waller was probably on a beach somewhere sipping a margarita and wondering which woman he was going to follow home and rape tonight.

Lena looked down at her watch. The timer was still running. They'd been in the house four minutes and thirty-two seconds.

"Shhh-it," Lena drew out the word. She looked up at the ceiling. The bare rafters showed white specks of mold. A clump of plastic bags was shoved into a hole in the asphalt shingles. She heard heavy bootsteps in the next room as the rest of the team came in to see what had happened.

Lena raised her voice so it would carry through the house, ordering, "We clear out of here A-SAP. This is an active crime scene."

DeShawn called back, "Branson's on the way. Coroner's thirty minutes out."

"Great," she said. "The more the merrier."

Paul took off his helmet. He ran his hand through his sweaty hair. "You okay?"

Lena shook her head, too angry to speak. This was supposed to change things. This was supposed to make everything better. The only goddamn thing she had in her life right now that was working was her job, and she'd managed to screw that up, too.

She unstrapped the Velcro around her vest so she could breathe. Her shirt was stuck to her back. She knew her neck was covered with blood. This wouldn't stop with Denise Branson. The chief would want answers. The brass would show up. Internal Affairs. Lena would need to call her husband to bring her a change of clothes so she didn't look like she'd gotten her ass handed to her while they chewed her out. Not that Jared was answering her calls. Not that he probably even thought of himself as her husband anymore.

Lena covered her face with her hands. Shook her head. She had to get her shit together. She couldn't fall apart now.

"I'll back you up with Branson," Paul said. "Whatever you need."

Lena dropped her hands. "I need to know why that door was braced."

Paul's brow furrowed again. She could see he hadn't thought that far into it.

Lena said, "You butcher three guys and you get the hell out. You don't stick around inside the house. You don't barricade the basement." She indicated the door. "Look at the edge of the wood—somebody pounded it in." Lena wiped away the sweat pooling on her brow. The house was like a kiln. "Goddamn it. Branson's probably gonna bust me down to patrol for this."

"You and Jared can ride together."

"Go to hell."

"Hey." Paul put his Glock on the counter. His hand was on her arm, then her face. He smiled at her, trying to make everything okay.

Lena pulled away from him. She stamped her boot on the floor so they'd hear her in the basement. "Cabello? McVale? What's taking so long down there?"

"Found some money!" Keith called back. "We're rich!"

"Thank God." Lena headed toward the basement. "Please let it be a million dollars." A drug seizure like that would at least pay for all the overtime.

She told Paul, "Get everybody out of the house. Tell CSU they're gonna need to bring lights. I want to talk to the coroner when he gets here."

He gave her a curt salute. "Yes, boss."

Lena took her Maglite out of her pants pocket as she headed downstairs. She searched the wall for a light switch as she reached the bottom landing. The electrical panel was open. She could see old fuses plugged into slots. She tapped a few, but nothing happened.

As predicted, the basement had been chopped into tiny rooms. The beam of Lena's flashlight picked up buckling, cheap paneling, and busted-open bags of trash that had been tossed down the stairs. The back of the stairs was open, empty but for more trash. There was no hallway, just a series of open doors, one room leading directly into the other. There were four doorways in all, so five rooms, counting the one she was standing in.

She saw a soft glow of light in the distance, probably Keith and Mitch counting the stash of money in the last room. Lena's eyes blurred on the light. She put her hand to the back of her head, suppressing a string of curses. The blood was coming out in a steady stream. She would probably need stitches. Her head throbbed with pain. Her nose felt cracked. The day's humiliations were piling up. Her only chance of salvaging the operation was finding a mound of hundred-dollar bills that was high enough to touch the ceiling.

Lena opened her mouth to call to the guys, but something stopped her. Sixth sense. Cop's intuition. There were no voices. Keith and Mitch couldn't take a dump without narrating it for all to hear. They'd found a pile of cash and weren't joking about how they were going to spend it?

Something wasn't right.

Lena's hand wrapped around her Glock. She turned off the flashlight, then waited for her eyes to adjust to the darkness.

She strained to pick up sounds, trying to block out the noise from the television set upstairs.

Nothing.

She made her way into the next room. As carefully as Lena moved, it was impossible to not make a sound. There was too much trash on the floor—empty beer cans, glass crack pipes, aluminum foil. The carpet was thick and wet, like a suction cup against the soles of her boots. Every sound was amplified in the crowded space. She might as well start singing.

No.

What she really should do is go upstairs and get backup. You never went into a room alone. You always worked in pairs. Lena was breaking her own cardinal rule.

But she'd already fallen on her ass, cut open her head, and spent a fortune capturing three dead men and securing a crime scene that probably contained more DNA than a men's toilet at the local truck stop. She wasn't going to risk what was left of her reputation based on feeling some bad juju.

Still, Lena felt for the loose strap around her Kevlar vest and pulled it tight against her waist. She moved forward, her knees bent, her center of gravity low in case she had to dive to the ground or fight off an attacker. The closer she got to the last room, the more certain she was that something had gone horribly wrong.

Twenty feet. Fifteen. Lena was approximately ten feet away when she saw the tip of a boot. Black leather. Steel toe. It was just like the one she was wearing, only three sizes larger.

And pointing up toward the ceiling.

Lena froze. She blinked her eyes. Her vision doubled. Blood was pooling up around the collar of her vest. Her mouth was bone-dry.

She took another step. Lena could just make out the floor in front of her. The flashlights from the other room were walleyed, one pointing toward the door, the other toward the wall. There was a suitcase opposite the door. Money spilled out onto the floor. Hundreds, just like she'd prayed for.

Lena two-handed the Glock. She wasn't sweating anymore. She didn't feel any fear. All extraneous thought left her mind. She counted out her steps—one, then two, then she was in the last room and pointing her gun at Sid Waller.

He had Keith in a choke hold, the muzzle of a Sig Sauer nine-millimeter jammed into the man's neck. Mitch was flat on his back. His scalp was ripped open. Blood covered his face.

From the moment they put a gun in your hand at the academy, they taught you to always rest your finger on the trigger guard, never on the trigger. This gave your brain a few extra milliseconds to process what you were looking at, to tell whether or not you were drawing down on friend or foe. You never put your finger on the trigger unless you were ready to shoot someone.

Lena put her finger on the trigger.

"Get back," Sid Waller ordered.

Lena shook her head. "No."

He made a show of tightening his grip on the Sig. "I want a car. I want the road cleared."

"You're not getting anything." Keith's eyes went wide as Lena took another step closer. "Let him go."

"Get a negotiator."

"I'm your negotiator," she told him. "Let him go or die."

"Back up." Waller jammed the Sig harder into Keith's neck. "I'll do it."

"Do it." She took another step forward. There was no way in hell she was letting him take Keith out of this basement. "You're gonna kill him either way. Do it now so I can go ahead and kill you."

"I mean it."

"So do I."

Waller's eyes turned jittery. This wasn't the first time he'd stared down Lena, but it was the first time he'd done it with a gun pointed at his head. "You're fucking crazy."

"You're fucking right." Lena took another step forward. She felt numb, like she was watching someone else do this. A different woman held her Glock. A different woman stared down this murderer, this child rapist. "Put the gun down."

Keith let out a sob. He whispered, "Please . . ."

Waller turned the Sig on Lena. "I'll kill you, then. How about that?"

She glanced into the dark nothingness of the muzzle. "See if you make it up those stairs."

"Back the fuck up!" Waller screamed, spit flying from his mouth. "I'll do it!"

"Do it." Lena was less than two feet away.

"I will!"

"Do it!" she screamed. "Pull the trigger, you fucking pussy!"

Waller's hand moved quickly. There wasn't even a blur. One second, the Sig was pointed at Lena, the next it was pressed to his head. His finger jerked. There was a flash, and the side of his head exploded.

"Jesus Christ!" Keith slapped at the pieces of skull and brain that had sprayed his neck. "Christ!" He scrambled to get away, his feet sliding on the wet carpet.

Lena braced her hand against the wall. All the buzz left her body. "Check on Mitch."

"Fuck!" Keith pushed himself up, stumbled from the room. "Jesus!"

"Lee?" Paul trampled down the stairs, his voice filled with panic.

"Get the paramedics!" she shouted back. Lena knelt down beside Mitch, made sure he knew she was there. "Take it easy," she managed. "We're getting help."

Mitch coughed. His chest heaved from the effort. His eyes were as wild as Keith's.

"What the—" Paul took in the scene with visible shock. "What—" He didn't say anything else, just kicked the gun out of Waller's hand like a guy with half his head missing was still a threat.

DeShawn's voice came from the other side of the basement. "Y'all okay?"

"We're okay. Stay where you are." Lena sat back on her heels, slid her Glock back into the holster. She told Paul, "Waller shot himself in the head."

"No shit," Paul said. "Mitch? Are you—"

"Get me outta here." Mitch reached up, touched his fingers to the bare bone of his skull. He stared at Lena. She couldn't read his expression. Either he was terrified or impressed. She still wasn't sure when he told her, "You gotta fuckin' death wish."

"Come on." Paul folded Mitch's scalp back into place like it was a piece of cloth. "Can you stand up?"

Mitch tried, but Paul did most of the lifting, telling Lena, "Branson's five minutes out."

Lena felt something tickle her neck. She put her fingers to the spot and rubbed away the grit of Sid Waller's brain. Flashlight beams came from the other end of the basement. Lena guessed most of the team had come down the stairs when they heard the gunshot.

She shouted, "Jesus Christ, get out of here! Why do I have to keep reminding everybody that this is an active crime scene?"

There were grumbles of protest, but no one challenged the order.

Paul told her, "IA is gonna be all over this."

Lena didn't answer. She was no stranger to Internal Affairs.

"I'll talk to Keith, make sure he's on board." Paul looped Mitch's arm around his shoulders. He asked Lena, "You got your story straight?"

"Just get Mitch upstairs."

Paul practically lifted Mitch's feet off the ground as they staggered toward the basement stairs. The climb was cumbersome, but a couple of men had obviously disobeyed Lena's orders and stuck around to help Paul carry Mitch out. She heard them walk clumsily through the kitchen, then they were finally gone.

The house was silent. The wood creaked and flexed as the temperature started to change. The sun was coming up fast. There was a hint of white light seeping around the edges of the boarded-up windows.

All of Lena's energy had drained. Her vision was still hazy. The room felt off-kilter. A sense of separateness took hold. The aloneness turned lonely. She wanted Jared. She wanted him to rush into the room and put his arms around her. If she thought about it hard enough, she could almost feel his hands rubbing her back, hear his calming voice in her ear.

Lena wiped away tears. Why did she ache for Jared so much when he wasn't there, yet every time he was standing in front of her, all she could think about was how much she wanted him to leave?

She looked down. Her hand had gone to her stomach again. Her palm flat to her belly.

Lena shook her head, tried to make herself focus because Paul was right about one thing: the minute Branson got down here, she'd want a clear story. Three men had been murdered in the night while the cops were sitting in a surveillance truck less than five hundred yards away. Keith was probably still shitting himself from having a gun jammed into his neck. Mitch had almost been scalped. Sid Waller was dead by his own hand.

What could Lena say? That part of her had been hoping Sid Waller would kill her? That just about everybody in Lena's life would be better off if he had?

No. She would tell Branson that she had followed her training. You didn't leave a hostage with a madman. You didn't let them go to a second location. You took your shot when you could.

Or, you let the bad guy take his shot.

She turned her flashlight on Sid Waller. His mouth was open. She could see the titanium cap on his front tooth. There was a skull and crossbones etched into it. Lena had seen it enough times during interrogations to draw it from memory. Waller would sit at the table with his legs spread wide like his balls needed the extra room. He barely looked at Lena, but when he did, he conveyed such a sense of disgust that she felt dirty just being near him. Even with his lawyer there, he would sneer at her, spit at her, call her a stupid cunt. It drove Paul insane, but Lena just let it slide. Waller wanted a reaction. He wanted her to lunge at him so he could laugh in her face. You didn't have to be a genius to recognize a man who hated women. The bastard would rather kill himself than be taken in by one.

She trained the flashlight on the gleaming wet hole where the side of Waller's head used to be.

Wish granted.

Lena turned away from the body, shining the light into the suitcase. She'd been wrong about that—there were more fifties than hundreds. Maybe half a million dollars. Denise Branson would have to fill her chest with all her ribbons and commendations again for when they put her picture in the paper. The fact that two seasoned cops had let the bad guy get the drop on them wouldn't be part of the story.

Lena wanted the question answered, though. Mitch and Keith were better than this. At least she thought they were. She scanned the room with her Maglite, trying to figure out what had happened. There was a piece of paneling hanging crookedly off the wall. She craned her neck to see behind it. Waller's hiding place. The earth was dug out around the foundation. Like rats in a trap, Keith and Mitch had gone straight to the money, and Sid Waller had sprung out from behind the wall and taken them both down before they could make a squeak.

Mitch first, probably brained with the muzzle of the Sig. Then the next thing Keith knows, the Sig is jammed in his throat. Much more frightening than the thought of getting shot in the head. You get shot in the neck, you might live. You might never walk again, you might breathe through a tube or piss in a bag for the rest of your life, but you'd live.

Someone was on the stairs. Lena waited for Denise Branson to pick her way through the filthy basement.

"Adams? What the hell happened here?" Denise yelled. "You're gonna be damn lucky if Chief Gray doesn't bust your ass over this."

Lena had heard the threat before, and from people a lot scarier than Denise Branson. She answered, "Waller took Keith hostage. He pointed the gun at me. I pointed my gun at him. He made a choice."

Denise scowled at Waller's dead body. She looked mad enough to spit. "Who do you think is gonna give us Big Whitey now?"

Lena was so sick and tired of hearing that fucking name. "Denise, I really don't give a shit."

"You best check that attitude before I—"

She stopped.

There was a sound. They both heard it. Waller's hiding place. There was something else behind the wall.

Lena's Glock was in her hand. She couldn't even remember pulling it.

Denise moved more slowly. She stepped back, drew her sidearm.

The sound came again. Lena moved to the right, tried to use her flashlight to see behind the panel. Just like before, she had her shoulder to the wall. She knelt down, angling the light. The whole left side of the hole was obscured. All Lena saw was wet, black earth and a filthy, wadded-up athletic sock.

Lena stood back up. The two women stared at each other. Predictably, Denise nodded for Lena to take lead.

Lena waited for the numbness to come back, the autopilot to take over. It didn't—or wouldn't. All the bravado from before had evaporated away. Her body didn't want to move. Five minutes ago, she'd had a death wish, but now that the opportunity had presented itself again, she found herself unwilling.

Denise made a hissing sound between her teeth. Lena turned to look at her. The major was waiting, gun pointed low, finger resting on the trigger guard. Her eyes went wide. Her lips parted, showing her teeth.

Lena turned back around. She looked at the dirty, wet sock, the dark hole Sid Waller had crawled out of.

The sound came again.

No more thinking.

Lena pulled back the panel.

5.

Sara had only visited Macon a handful of times, but she'd always gotten the impression that the city was one forever stuck in limbo, caught between the liberal state capital less than one hundred miles north and the smaller, more conservative towns that made up the majority of the state. Most Atlantans never gave Macon a second thought, but everything about Macon seemed to strain with the need to impress its wealthier neighbor.

Macon General Hospital was a perfect example of this endless striving. Even as Sara pulled into the freshly paved parking lot, she couldn't help but notice the difference in scale between the towering monolith of Grady and the three architecturally ornate brick buildings that made up the much smaller county medical complex. Up until the 1960s, Grady had been segregated into two different wards—one for black and one for white. As with many areas in the modern South, a different sort of segregation had taken hold in Macon. It wasn't about race anymore, but class. All were welcome so long as they could afford the entrance fee.

Sara didn't realize she had driven to the back of the parking lot until she noticed the exit signs. She pulled into a space under some trees. For a few minutes, she just sat in the car, trying to decide what to do next. Then her brain took over and made her hand open the door, her feet hit the asphalt, her legs move as she walked toward the hospital. The large fountain in the middle of the circular drive sent up a wet mist as she passed by. The rhythmic lapping of water was probably meant to calm visitors, but to Sara, the sound only managed to further set her teeth on edge.

She felt time roll back as she walked toward the front doors of the main hospital building—not by decades, but by years. Just like that, she was in Grant County again, transported back to the day her husband had been murdered. Sara's body made the connection before her brain did. It was probably all the police officers, a sea of blue that filled the parking lot, the front entrance, the lobby.

The sight of them sent a jolt of adrenaline straight into Sara's heart. Her ears filled with a high-pitched ringing. Her head ached. Her muscles twitched. It was as if all the wires that held together her body had suddenly gone taut.

Or maybe it wasn't adrenaline. Maybe it was anger, because by the time Sara walked into the hospital, she was so angry that she could barely function.

No—she wasn't just angry. She was furious.

Furious to be here. Furious that she wasn't home taking a shower or eating breakfast or walking the dogs or sleeping in her bed or going about her normal life. Furious that yet again, she'd become ensnared in another one of Lena Adams's deadly webs.

If the wires had gone taut, it was only because Lena had pulled them.

The rage had started its slow build in the Grady ER, the moment Sara hung up with Nell. Sara had heard it humming in the background, like a song she couldn't remember the words to. She'd called Will. She'd packed the spare clothes and toiletries she kept at the hospital. She'd made arrangements with the dog sitter, her department head, her students. She'd filled up her car with gas. She'd driven just above the speed limit as she made her way out of the city. Jared needed her. Darnell needed her. That was what kept Sara moving forward. They were the only two things that mattered. Sara had a duty to be there for them. She owed it to Jeffrey. She owed it to Jared and Nell.

But by the halfway mark to Macon, the song got louder, and Sara's brain started adding words to the melody.

Jeffrey. Lena's partner. Sara's husband.

Sara's life.

She had held him in her arms as he lay dying. She had stroked her fingers through his thick hair one last time. She had touched the rough skin of his cheek one last time. She had pressed her lips to his, felt his ragged last breaths in her mouth. She had begged him not to leave even as she watched the life slowly leave his beautiful eyes.

Sara had wanted to follow him. Grief set her adrift, unmoored her from everything that mattered. Weeks went by, months, but the pain was a relentless tide that would not ebb. Finally, Sara had taken too many pills. She'd told her mother it was a mistake, but Sara hadn't made a mistake. She'd wanted to die, and when she found that she could not die, the only thing she could do was start over.

She'd left her family, her home, her life, and moved to Atlanta. She had bought an apartment that was nothing like the house she'd shared with Jeffrey. She'd purchased furniture that Jeffrey would not have liked, dressed in clothes he would never expect her to wear. Sara had even taken a job Jeffrey had never seen her do. She'd made her life into something that worked without him.

And she'd met Will.

Will.

The thought of his name smoothed down some of the sharp edges. Sara wanted so badly to be with him right now that she almost turned around. She saw herself getting into her car, heading toward the highway, retracing her steps back to Atlanta.

There was a clingy red dress hanging in Sara's closet. She would wear it with the painfully high heels that made Will lick his lips every time he saw them. Sara would brush out her hair, wear it down around her shoulders the way he liked. She would darken her eyeliner, load up on the mascara. She would wear a touch of perfume everywhere she wanted him to kiss her. And as soon as he walked through the door, Sara would tell Will that she was deeply, irrevocably in love with him. She'd never said the words to him before. Never found the right time.

Time.

A sharp, startling memory jolted Sara out of her plans. She was at her old house standing in front of the fireplace. What was she wearing? Sara didn't have to think for long. She was in the same black dress she'd worn to her husband's funeral. Days had passed before her mother managed to get Sara to take off the dress, to shower, to change into something that didn't carry the stench of Jeffrey's death.

And still, Sara had kept returning to the fireplace. She could not stop staring at the cherrywood clock on the mantel. It was a beautiful old thing, a wedding gift to Sara's grandmother that had been passed to Sara, just like the watch she wore on her wrist. That Sara had inherited two timepieces was not something she'd ever considered remarkable. What she remembered most from the days after the funeral was watching the second hand move on her grandmother's clock, hearing the loud tick of the gears marking time.

Sara had stopped the clock. She had put her watch in a drawer. She had unplugged the clock beside her bed—their bed that she could no longer sleep in. She had found some electrician's tape in Jeffrey's workbench and covered the clock on the microwave, the stove, the cable box. It became an obsession. No one could enter the house with a watch. No one could remark on the passage of time. Anything that reminded Sara that life was moving on without Jeffrey had to be hidden from sight.

"Mrs. Tolliver?"

Sara felt another jolt. She'd stopped walking. She was standing stock-still in the middle of the hospital lobby as if lightning had struck.

"Mrs. Tolliver?" the man repeated. He was older, with a shock of white-gray hair and a well-trimmed mustache.

As with Nell's phone call, Sara's memory took a few seconds to cull information from her past. She finally said, "Chief Gray."

He smiled warmly at Sara, though there was a familiar reserve in his eyes. Sara thought of it as the Widow Look—not the look a widow gave, but the one she received. The one that said the viewer didn't quite know what to say because, secretly, all he or she could feel was so damn lucky it hadn't happened to them.

He held out his hand. "Lonnie."

"Sara." She shook his hand, which felt solid and reassuring, just like the man. Lonnie Gray was an old-school cop, the type who could never really leave the job. Even during retirement, he'd taken up consulting, moving around the state to help whip various law enforcement agencies into shape. Sara hadn't seen Gray since the funeral. Or at least she assumed that was the last time. Sara had been so heavily medicated during the service that the only memories she had were the ones her mother and sister had planted there.

She said, "I didn't know you were running Macon now."

"Consulting proved to be even more boring than it sounded. I missed being a benevolent dictator." Gray smiled at the joke, which they both recognized as the truth. Despite his grandfatherly appearance, Sara couldn't see Lonnie Gray offering advice that no one had to take.

She said, "Macon is lucky to have you."

"Well, let's just say I'm glad it hasn't been put to a vote." He glanced down at Sara's hand, probably to see whether or not she had remarried. "I hear you're living in Atlanta now?"

"Yes." Sara decided to acknowledge the obvious. "You and I keep meeting under bad circumstances."

"We do indeed." Gray seemed to appreciate her candidness. "Jared's stabilized for now. The doctors are taking good care of him."

Sara was relieved to be on more comfortable footing. "Do you mind if I ask why he wasn't taken to MCCG?" The Medical Center of Central Georgia was a Level 1 trauma center, much better equipped for a gunshot wound than Macon General.

Chief Gray deflected. "I'm sorry. I called you Mrs. Tolliver. You're a doctor, aren't you?"

"Yes." Sara could only guess why he'd sidestepped the question. The ambulance crew had obviously been thinking in seconds, not minutes. Jared's injuries had necessitated rushing him to the closest emergency room.

"Rest assured, we'll find out who did this to your stepson." Gray gave her a sage nod, as if to remind Sara that they always got their man. It was so maddeningly black and white to some people. They thought vengeance made it easier, when, in fact, all it did was fester the sorrow.

Gray continued, "Jeffrey's surely been missed these past few years. I could use his skills on this one."

Sara already knew the answer, but she asked, "You called in the state?"

"Never hurts to have extra hands."

He wasn't being diplomatic. Lonnie Gray was the same kind of chief that Jeffrey had been. They weren't concerned with glory. They just wanted the bad guys caught and the good guys to go home at night.

Sara said, "I'm sure you'll figure out why this happened."

"As am I, Dr. Tolliver. That's a promise." His voice took on a practiced tone that he probably employed whenever duty called. "Jared's a good kid. Wish I had fifty more of 'em. And Detective Adams has been a great addition to the team. We'll have them back up on their feet in no time. You know we take care of our people."

Sara tried to think of an appropriate response, but Lonnie Gray was obviously not expecting one. He looked as drained as Sara felt. She'd seen Jeffrey in the same circumstance many times.

His shoulders were slumped from the burdens placed on him. His face was drawn. Policing was an occupation, but no one stayed in it long enough to become chief without feeling a true calling.

Sara followed Gray's gaze as he took in his officers. She tried not to catalogue the similarities from five years ago. The Band-Aids on their arms where they'd all given blood. The way boredom compelled them to chip off the edges of their Styrofoam coffee cups. The expectant looks in their eyes when anyone new appeared.

Lonnie Gray said, "My son passed away just recently."

Sara didn't know he'd had a son. "I'm sorry to hear that."

"Thank you." He sounded resigned. "I'm sure you know it never gets easy."

Sara nodded again. There was a lump in her throat that she could not swallow. "I should go."

"I'll walk you up."

"No," she said, almost interrupting him. "Thank you, I'm fine. Stay here with your men."

He seemed relieved. "The mother's up there. I take it there's no love lost between her and my detective. Perhaps you could . . . ?"

Despite the circumstances, Sara felt a smile come to her lips. He was talking to her the way he'd talk to any senior officer's wife. She imagined it was the same in the military, or any other male-dominated profession where the women were expected to keep hearth and home running smoothly while the men went out and conquered the world.

She said, "I'm not sure it's my place."

"Adams was your husband's partner."

"She was," Sara confirmed, though she gathered Gray didn't know about their complicated history. She paused before adding, "I really should go. Nell's waiting for me."

"Thank you." He grasped her hand between his. "And remember, if there's anything I can do for you, just ask."

Sara could only nod again, which was the response Chief Gray seemed to need. He touched her elbow before walking away. Sara watched him approach one of his detectives. The man's relaxed posture immediately took on a military stance. He nodded at Sara with a familiar, exaggerated deference she'd come to expect whenever any officer learned that she was a cop's widow.

Sara nodded back, thinking the sentiment was comforting until it became suffocating. She did not want to be tragic. She had fought the stigma for years at Grady, where a cop was generally posted outside every third room. Oddly, it wasn't until Sara had started dating Will that people had let her step down from the pedestal.

She didn't have it in her to climb back up again.

Sara followed the green stripe on the floor, knowing it would lead to the elevators, just as she knew the blue signage would direct her to the ICU. There was a reassuring sameness to private hospitals, with their bright lights and cheerful paintings that announced to the world that the majority of their patients were paying customers.

Sara pressed the button beside the elevator door. It was hard to believe that just a few hours ago, she'd done the same in Atlanta. As with the exterior, Grady's interior was different compared to Macon General. Everything here was clean and modern, befitting the clientele. Most of the hospital's money probably came from luxurious birthing suites, routine colonoscopies, and MRIs on baby boomers' knees. The paint was not chipped from the walls. Buckets were not strategically placed under leaking pipes. There was no permanent police precinct on site or a holding area for prison inmates and the criminally insane.

Frankly, Sara preferred Grady.

The elevator doors slid open with a tiny squeak. Sara got into the car. She was alone. The doors closed. She pressed the button by the blue sign. She watched the numbers flash on, then off, as the car traveled up to the fifth floor. With each burst of light, she suppressed the urge to speak the phrase that was playing over and over in her head: *I don't want to be here. I don't want to be here. I don't want to be here.*

Even before Jeffrey died, Sara had never liked Lena Adams. She was dangerous. Arrogant. Sloppy. Jeffrey constantly complained about Lena's headstrong ways, but Sara knew how her husband's mind worked. There was no sexual attraction between them— sometimes Sara wished it had been that simple. Lena was simply a challenge that Jeffrey could not walk away from. She was a destructive little sister to his all-forgiving big brother. Jeffrey loved her toughness. He loved her fight. He loved that no matter how hard Lena was hit, she always got back up after being knocked down.

And if Lena couldn't quite pick herself up, Jeffrey was always there to lend a hand. It was easy to take risks when you knew someone else would bear the consequences, which was exactly what had happened five years ago. Once again, Lena had gone off on her own, recklessly pursuing some very bad people. When they'd proven to be too dangerous for Lena to handle, she'd called Jeffrey to save her, just like she'd done countless times before. Only this time, this last time, the bad people hadn't backed down. This time, instead of making Lena pay, they had murdered Jeffrey.

Sara had no doubt that this same scenario had played out with Jared. Motorcycle cops didn't have hit squads break into their houses. Sara would've bet her life savings on Lena yet again pissing off some very bad men who'd decided just like the last bad men that the best way to punish Lena was to take away the thing she loved most.

As if Lena Adams was capable of loving anything.

The elevator doors slid open. Same crisp white. Same bright lights. Sara was on autopilot as she followed the arrows to the ICU waiting room. She walked by a tall man wearing a blue and orange baseball hat. He didn't recognize her, but Sara instantly knew Jerry Long, Darnell's husband and Jeffrey's boyhood friend. Everyone called him Possum because of a childhood accident involving illegal fireworks. He'd worshipped Jeffrey in that strange way that only straight men can. Possum had played wide receiver to Jeffrey's quarterback. He'd married Jeffrey's old girlfriend. He'd raised Jeffrey's child.

Sara kept walking. She kept her head down, passing unnoticed.

As a doctor, her life had been spent anticipating what would happen next, thinking three or four steps ahead, but for some reason, Sara's day was revealing itself in small slices. She hadn't let herself think past the mundane tasks in front of her: Leave Grady. Now drive down the interstate. Now take the exit. Now park the car. Now go into the hospital.

Seeing Possum offered a small glimpse of what was to come. They would want to reminisce about Jeffrey. They would want to tell old stories about pranks and practical jokes and loose women and angry husbands and Sara would have to sit there and listen to all of it as if her life had stopped the moment his had.

And it *had* stopped. Everything had come to a standstill. But, eventually, it had to start moving again, and Sara had built a new life for herself—a life that they would not understand.

The guilt felt like a vulture sitting on her shoulder, waiting for the right moment to devour her.

Sara could only put one foot in front of the other as she continued down the hall. She turned into the small waiting room just outside the closed double doors of the ICU. The space was empty but for an older woman whose hair was more gray than brown.

"Sara," Nell said. She was sitting on a love seat underneath a window. A pile of knitting was in her lap. Several magazines were splayed beside her.

There was only a five-year difference between them, but Nell had aged in that way good country women do—no hair color, no makeup, no laser treatments to remove sunspots or smooth out wrinkles. She looked, in fact, entirely her age, which was not something Sara was used to seeing in Atlanta.

"Don't get up," Sara told her, leaning down to pull Nell into a tight hug. Nell had always been stout and strong, but there was something fragile about her now. Helplessness had reduced her.

Still, Sara said, "You haven't changed a bit."

Nell barked a laugh. "Hell, honey, don't lie. We got mirrors in Alabama, too." She moved the magazines so Sara could sit beside her. She took Sara's hand, which was unusual. Nell wasn't affectionate. She was talkative, and sometimes abrupt to the point of rudeness, but she was also incredibly kind—the sort of woman you could call in the middle of the night no matter how many years had passed and she would move heaven and earth to come to your side.

The sort of woman Sara should be.

She tightened her hold on Nell's hand. "I'm so sorry this happened."

"I shouldn't've bothered you. I was just . . ."

"I'm glad you did," Sara told her, and in that moment, she really meant it. There was no way she could have stayed in Atlanta. This was where she belonged. "Is there anything I can do?"

Nell let out a heavy sigh. "I don't know what you can do other than wait. They're not telling me anything. Twenty-four hours, they say they might know more. What does that even mean?"

Sara knew that it meant they had no idea; it was all up to Jared now. Still, she told Nell, "It means he's young and he's strong and his body needs time to fight this."

"I hope you're right." Nell let go of Sara's hand. She tucked her knitting into a denim bag. "You were right about her, Sara. First Jeffrey and now this. That woman is nothin' but poison."

Sara felt a familiar tightening in her throat. "We should just concentrate on Jared right now."

Nell shook her head. "She won't leave the room. Just sits there in the corner like a damn gargoyle." Her lips turned into a thin white line. "I can't even stand to look at her. Takes everything I got not to spit in her face."

Sara forced back the impulse to agree. It would do no good for them to feed off each other. "Who's his doctor?"

"Shammers. Shaman. I can't remember. Something foreign."

"Is he with this hospital or did they call him over from Central Georgia?"

"No idea. He gave me his card." Nell picked up her purse to search for it. "I don't even know if this is a good hospital."

"It's good," Sara told her, though she hoped they'd called in the bigger guns from the trauma center. "How long has he been out of surgery?"

She looked at her watch. "About an hour."

"Did they give you any details?"

"Hell, Sara, I don't know that medical stuff. He was shot with a shotgun. The pellets went everywhere. His head, his neck, and back."

"Did any penetrate the skull?"

"They're monitoring his brain swelling. I guess that means it went into his brain." She turned to Sara. "They said they might have to release the pressure. Is that bad?"

Sara explained, "The skull has a fixed volume. If the brain swells, it needs somewhere to go."

"So they just saw off the top of his head?"

"Not like you're thinking. It's a very precise surgical procedure." She put her hand on Nell's shoulder. "Don't think about that until you have to, all right?" Nell reluctantly nodded. "What about his spinal cord?"

"You mean, will he be crippled?" She shrugged, a tight, jerky movement. "They're keeping him knocked out. Said it's best he sleeps, but I know my boy. He'd hate being pumped full of pain pills."

Sara knew that Nell couldn't fathom the amount of pain her son was in. "Did Jared say anything before they put him under?"

"Chief Gray told me he was unconscious when they brought him in. Do you know him?"

"Gray?" Sara nodded. "Jeffrey worked a case with him before we met. He trusted him. So does everyone else. Gray's worked all over the state, received all kinds of awards."

Nell wasn't impressed. "For whatever that's worth. Didn't stop Jared from getting shot." She started pulling things out of her purse. A hairbrush. Her pocket Bible. A tin of Burt's Bees lip balm. "Where did I put that damn card?"

Sara asked, "How has Jared been lately?"

"Healthy as a horse."

"No, not his health." Sara didn't know how to broach the subject, so she dove right in. "Has he been working a case he was worried about? Or has Lena been doing something?"

"Oh, he won't say a word against her—not Little Miss Perfect." Nell took out a blister pack of gum. She offered a piece to Sara.

Sara shook her head. "When's the last time you talked to him?"

"He calls me every Sunday and Wednesday after church. Mind you, he's not going himself. Stopped doing that once he met up with her."

Today was Thursday. Sara asked, "So, you talked to him last night?"

"Nine o'clock and he was at a bar with his friends. What does that tell you?" Nell wasn't looking for an answer. "Says something's not right, that's what it tells you. Wednesday night, he should be at home with his wife, not off somewhere drinking with his buddies."

Sara kept her opinion to herself. Jared was a grown man. Married or not, he was entitled to a night out. "Did he say anything on the phone that sounded off?"

"No. Just the usual. 'Work's good. Lena's great. Tell Daddy I said hey.' Nothing but puppies and sunshine." She snorted at the thought. "They didn't even get married in a church. Did it downtown like they were signing a contract. You've met her uncle?"

Sara nodded again. "He was the only one there on her side. That tells you everything you need to know right there. No friends. Nobody from work. Just some old piece of beef jerky looks like he belongs on the side of the road harassing people for money." She pointed to her bare arms. "Had needle tracks up and down his arms. Didn't even bother hiding 'em. God knows if they're old or new."

Sara pressed her lips together, catching a glimpse of that bottomless pit she'd barely managed to pull herself out of. "Nell, it won't do any good getting worked up like this."

Nell was obviously reluctant to let go, but finally she said, "You're right. If I keep talking about her, I'm gonna end up going in there and killing her." Nell looked down at her purse again and concentrated on digging around for the doctor's card. "He needs his pajamas. He'd hate waking up in one of those gowns."

"We'll get some pajamas for him," Sara offered, knowing there was no point.

"I want to see the house. I've only seen pictures. What do you make of that? I'm less than four hours away, but she's never invited me for Christmas or holidays or nothing."

Sara wasn't about to take up for Lena, but she doubted Nell had made things easy. "The forensic team is probably still there."

"The forensic team." Nell let the words settle. "I want to go by the house. I want to see where it happened."

"That's probably not a good idea," Sara countered. "The police don't clean up before they leave. It'll look just how it did last night."

Nell seemed shocked by the information. She recovered quickly, taking a small notebook and a pen out of her purse. "I'll tell Possum to go by the dollar store. There's one right off the exit." She clicked the pen and started writing. "We'll need a bunch of rags. Lysol spray. Trash bags. Some gloves. What else—bleach?"

Sara tried to reason with her. "There are services that take care of this kind of thing."

"I'm not gonna let some stranger clean my baby's house." She sounded appalled. "That's the most ridiculous thing I've ever heard."

Sara knew better than to argue.

"Why would anyone do this?" Nell asked. "He's always been the sweetest boy. Never said a hard word against anybody. Always helping people. Never asking for anything in return. Why, Sara? Why would someone hurt him?"

Sara shook her head, though Lena's name was on the tip of her tongue.

"His eyes are taped shut. He's got all kinds of tubes coming out of him. They got this plastic thing looks like a Connect Four sticking out of his side."

"That's probably a Pleur-evac," Sara guessed. "It helps keep his lung open to give it time to heal."

"Well, you've just told me more than anybody else has, thank you very much."

Sara doubted this was true. She'd seen the glazed look in Nell's eyes before. In traumatic situations, it was hard to understand the information being conveyed by doctors, let alone ask salient questions.

Sara told Nell the same thing she told the families of her patients. "Write down all your questions as they come. If I can't answer them, then we'll find someone who will. All right?"

"That's good. I should've thought to do that. I've just been so . . ." She couldn't finish the thought. "I mean, seeing him all—" Her words were cut off by a guttural sound. She lowered the notebook and pen to her lap, the shopping list forgotten. Tears rolled down her cheeks. Sara wondered if she was wishing her husband would return. More likely, she was praying her son would walk through the door.

Sara took Nell's hand again, but she couldn't look at her. The pain was too raw. While Sara witnessed the possibility of death almost every single day, knowing Nell, knowing Jared, made it different. She had lost her outsider's perspective.

"Well, this is useless." Nell's voice was filled with self-recrimination. "Crying never helped anybody." She pulled a pack of Kleenex from her purse and dried her eyes. "I haven't told Delia." Jared's sister, Nell's youngest child. "She's working in the Gulf. She's a vet now. Did you know that?" Sara nodded. "They got her scraping oil off sea turtles. She says the whole damn coast is still a tar pit."

"You need to tell her."

"What do I say? 'That bitch your brother married mighta got him killed'?" Nell shook her head, visibly angry. "I knew when I found out he was seeing her that nothing good would come of it."

Sara said nothing.

"He kept it from me for a full year. He knew I wouldn't approve. He knew why, too." Nell blew her nose in the Kleenex. "You warned me, Sara. You warned him, too. There's no harm in a big fat 'I told you so' right about now."

Sara didn't respond. She got no joy from being right.

"Jared just wouldn't listen. Kept saying Jeffrey knew the risk when he put on the badge. Like she had nothing to do with it. Like she didn't abandon him when the going got tough." Nell's mouth twisted with disgust. "Part of me wonders if I'd just shut up about her, maybe he woulda gone on to somebody new."

The arguments were so familiar that Sara could practically recite them along with Nell. She'd tortured herself with the same recriminations after Jeffrey had died. Sara should've stopped him from working with Lena. She should've put her foot down. She should've told him that it was too dangerous, too risky, to get involved in Lena's life.

But his focus had always been on saving other people, never on saving himself.

Sara told Nell, "You can't second-guess yourself."

"Can't I?" She indicated the waiting room. "I got all the time in the world to think about everything I've done wrong."

Sara forced a change in subject. "I saw Possum in the hall."

Nell slumped back against the couch. She didn't speak for a few seconds. "He's just a wreck. Keeps breaking down. I ain't seen him cry like that in five years. Won't listen to the doctors. Won't go into Jared's room. It's not because of Lena. He always got along with her. You know how friendly he is. The man would talk to a stump about its knots. But all this stuff—" She waved her hand in the air, indicating the hospital. "It just brings it back for him. You, too, I guess."

Sara looked past Nell at the floral painting on the wall. Unbidden, she thought about Will. Lying on the couch with him. Watching TV. His arms around her. Their dogs piled around them.

Nell said, "We all went to the hospital that night." She didn't have to say which night. "Drove straight through without stopping. Like there was any use him being at a hospital. Nothing could be done for him by then. Hell, if there was something to do, you woulda done it."

Sara felt the image of Will slip away. The vulture was back with its guilt, digging its talons into her flesh.

Nell continued, "I know we lost touch with you for a reason. It's just too painful, isn't it? And here I dragged you back down into all of it. I'm sorry for that, Sara. I didn't know who else to call."

Sara nodded. All she could manage was, "Jeffrey would've wanted me here."

Nell said, "I wish to God I'd told him about Jared sooner. Given him a chance to know his son."

"He understood why you didn't," Sara said, thinking that was only half a lie. Jeffrey had been trying to find a way to connect with Jared before he died. It was a tricky proposition. Nell could be a hard woman, and Possum deserved better than to have some other man come in and try to be Jared's father.

Nell asked, "Do you remember the first time I met you?"

It felt like a hundred years ago, but Sara said, "Yes."

"You musta thought Jeffrey was crazy drivin' you down past where Jesus lost his sandals."

Sara smiled. Sylacauga, Alabama, was the very definition of rural, but she had been so pleased that Jeffrey wanted her to meet his family, his people. "We crashed your garden party."

"You told me you were a stripper."

Sara laughed. She'd forgotten that part. Nell had prompted the response, asking Sara whether she was a stewardess or a stripper. They'd all had this idea of Jeffrey in their heads—the sort of man he was, the type of woman he dated.

And they had been so wrong.

"Anyway," Nell said. "We're miserable enough without digging up the past. I know you still deal with it every single day." Again, she took Sara's hand in her own, but this time, she smoothed out the finger where Sara's wedding ring used to be. "I'm glad you took it off, darlin'. Someday when enough time's passed, you'll find a way to move on."

Sara nodded again, forcing herself not to look away.

Five years.

She had mourned her husband for five years. She had been alone for five years. She had waited and waited for the ache to go away for five long, lonely years.

"Sara?"

Sara realized she'd missed a question. "Yes?"

"I asked could you go check on him? I know it'll be hard with Lena in there, but maybe you can do some of your doctor talk and see if you can find out anything they're not saying?"

Sara couldn't think of a reason not to. It was why she was here, after all. To help Nell. To help Jared. To be her husband's proxy as his son lay in a hospital bed. Even Chief Lonnie Gray had assumed Sara would play her part.

So she did.

Sara stood from the couch and left the tiny waiting room. She was still dressed in her hospital scrubs. The nurses' eyes passed over Sara as she pushed open the doors to the ICU and walked down the hall. The board behind the desk gave Jared's room number, but Sara would've known where he was by the cop stationed outside. The officer was standing a few yards down from the nurses' station, arm resting on his holster. There was a glass wall separating Jared's room from the hall. The curtain was half-closed. The door was open.

The cop gave Sara a nod. "Ma'am."

She didn't respond, just stood in the doorway to the room, acting as if she belonged.

The overhead lights were off. The machines provided a soft glow to see by. Jared's face was swollen. His body was still. Sara did not need to see his chart. The equipment in the room told the story. Pleur-evac connected to wall suction for the pneumothorax. Ventilator to assist breathing. Three IV pumps pushing fluids and antibiotics. NG tube to wall suction to keep the stomach empty. Pulse ox monitor. Blood-pressure monitor. Heart monitor. Urinary catheter. Surgical drains. A crash cart was pushed against the wall, the defibrillator on standby.

They weren't expecting Jared to rally anytime soon.

With great resignation, Sara forced herself to look at the corner opposite the bed.

Lena was sleeping. Or at least her eyes were closed. She was balled up in a large chair. Her arms were wrapped around her legs, knees hugged to her chest. She was wearing hospital scrubs, probably because her clothes had been booked into evidence.

She seemed much the same. A yellowing bruise arced underneath her left eye. The bridge of her nose had a linear cut that had started to scab. Neither was unexpected. Sara could not think of a time when Lena didn't have some visible bruise or mark that came from living her life so hard. The only thing different was her hair. It was longer than the last time Sara had seen her. At the funeral? Sara couldn't remember. No one in the Linton family could bear to utter the woman's name.

Sara took a deep breath, then walked into the room.

In many ways, seeing Jared was much harder than seeing Lena. He looked so much like Jeffrey—the dark hair, the tone of his skin, the delicate eyelashes. He was built like his father. He walked with the same athletic grace. Jared even had the same deep voice.

Sara put her hand to his face. She couldn't stop herself. She stroked her thumb along his forehead, traced the arc of his eyebrow. His hair was thick and surprisingly soft, like Jeffrey's had been. Even the scruff of his beard felt familiar, was growing back in the same pattern as Jeffrey's.

Lena still hadn't moved, but Sara could tell she was awake now—watching.

Slowly, Sara took her hand away from Jared's face. She would not let herself feel ashamed for touching him, for thinking the obvious thoughts, making the obvious connections.

Lena shifted in the chair. She unfolded herself, rested her feet on the floor.

Sara held Jared's hand. The palm was calloused. Jeffrey's hands had always felt smooth. His nails had been trimmed, not bitten to the quick. His cuticles weren't torn at the edges. Sometimes, Sara had caught him using the oatmeal-scented lotion she'd kept on the table by their bed.

Lena stood up from the chair.

Sara's heart hammered in her chest. She didn't know why. Just being in the same room with Lena made her feel nervous. Even with the cop outside. Even knowing that there was no way Lena could harm her, Sara felt unsafe.

And Lena, as usual, was oblivious. She stood by the bed. She didn't touch Jared. Didn't reach down to ease him or to reassure herself that he was still there. Instead of holding him, she held herself. Her arms were wrapped around her waist. She had always been so goddamn self-contained.

"Sara—" Lena breathed. It was more like a sob. Lena had never been ashamed to cry. She used it to great effect. She hissed in a mouthful of air, her body shaking from the effort. Her hand gripped the railing on the bed. Her wedding ring was yellow gold with a small diamond. Blood was caked into the setting. She was waiting for Sara to say something, to make it all better.

Automatically, the words came to Sara's mind, the advice she had given over countless hospital beds: *It's okay to touch him. Hold his hand. Talk to him. Kiss him. Ignore all the tubes coming out of his body and lie beside him. Let him know on some basic level that he is not alone. That you are here to help him fight his way back.*

Sara said none of this. Instead, she chewed at the tip of her tongue until she tasted blood. Her heart was still pounding. The fear was gone. A coldness had taken over. Sara could feel it moving through her body, its icy fingers wrapping around her torso, scratching at her throat.

"I can't—" Lena's voice caught. For Sara, it was like listening to herself five years ago. Just with those two words, she felt it all over again. The devastation. The loss. The loneliness.

"I can't—" Lena repeated. "I can't do it. I can't live without him."

Sara gently pulled her hand away from Jared's. She smoothed down the sheet, tucked it in close around his side. She looked at Lena—really looked at her straight in the eye.

"Good," Sara told her. "Now you know how it feels."

6.

Will rode his motorcycle around the Macon General parking lot until he spotted Sara's BMW. It was a stupid thing to do, but he was feeling pretty stupid lately anyway. She'd bypassed the doctors' lot and found a spot in the back under a stand of shade trees. He suppressed the desire to get off his bike and touch the hood of her car. Will told himself it was only to see how long she'd been there, but deep down he knew he wanted some kind of connection.

Which was embarrassing and pathetic enough to make him gun the engine and proceed to the employee lot at an unadvisable speed.

Fortunately, burning some rubber in the parking lot was exactly the kind of thing his alter ego would do. Will had gone undercover before. He liked to think that he was pretty good at getting into character. There were some happily retired chickens in North Georgia who could attest to his skills. While busting a cockfighting ring was not as dangerous as his current assignment, the GBI's information officers had managed to give Will an even more impressive cover this time around.

As with the day laborers outside the Home Depot, Will imagined that Bill Black, his cover ID, provided a glimpse into what could have been. The man was a con, the sort of guy who knew his way around the system. He had a sealed juvie record and a dishonorable discharge from the Air Force. More important, there were three serious charges on his adult sheet—two for knocking around various women and another for pushing a mall cop down an escalator.

The latter charge had landed Bill Black in the Fulton County jail for ninety days. He'd been paroled for good behavior, but was kept on a tight leash by a parole officer who reported directly back to Amanda. The PO had already dropped by the hospital a few times for surprise check-ins. Bill Black was a scary guy. There were other crimes that the cops were looking at him for. A gas station stickup. Some messy business up in Kentucky. An assault that left a man blind in one eye. Black was what those in the know called a person of interest.

The GBI had managed to locate a couple of snitches who were willing to back up Black's cover story in exchange for leniency. Another con told Will all the gossip floating around the jail during the time in which Bill Black was incarcerated. The guards had confirmed the lurid details, which sounded like a mash-up of *Cool Hand Luke* and *The Sopranos*. Then they had taken some unflattering photos of Will holding up a placard with Black's name and inmate number. Aside from the lack of any pathetic jailhouse tattoos, Will would've been hard-pressed to find the holes in his backstory.

Of course, there were always holes to be found, but Will wasn't about to share the biggest one with Amanda: the name Bill Black, which Amanda had proudly presented to Will as if on a silver platter, made his brain feel like it belonged in a Salvador Dalí painting.

"Bill rhymes with Will," she'd told him, handing over the dossier he was required to memorize. "And of course Black is a color."

Will gathered from her demeanor that he was supposed to be grateful. The truth was, she might as well have thrown on a leotard and acted out the name in interpretive dance.

Will was dyslexic, a fact that Amanda only trotted out when

she couldn't find a sharper knife in her drawer. He wasn't about to have an open conversation about his problem—that was what the Internet was for—but if Amanda had bothered to look it up, she would've realized dyslexia wasn't a reading disorder, but a language-processing disorder. Which was why Will had no ear for rhymes and couldn't understand how Black could be a color when the capital letter meant that it was a name.

But Will had sat in Amanda's office and thumbed through Bill Black's file like it made perfect sense.

"Looks good," he'd told her.

She hadn't been convinced. "You want me to help you with the big words?"

Will had closed the file and left her office.

He could read—he wasn't a complete imbecile—but it took some time and a lot of patience. Over the years, Will had learned a few tricks to help him pass as more fluent. Holding a ruler under a line of text to keep the letters from jumping around. Using the computer to dictate his reports or read his emails. He'd been told in school that he read on a second-grade level. Not that his teachers had formally diagnosed him with anything other than stupidity. Will was in college when he finally learned that what he had was called dyslexia, but it was too late by then for him to do anything but pray to God that no one found out.

For the most part, not many people did. Amanda seemed happy to keep it as a weapon in her arsenal. Faith had discovered it during their first case, and whenever anything involving reading came up, she took on a maternal tone that made Will want to stick his head in a wood chipper.

And of course Sara knew. She'd figured it out immediately. Will guessed being a doctor helped her recognize the signs. The weird part was that she treated him no different from before. She saw his dyslexia as just another part of Will, like the color of his hair or the size of his feet.

She saw him as normal.

And if he kept revving his motorcycle, she'd look out the window and see him riding through the parking lot.

The irony was not lost on Will that he'd spent the last ten days hiding the truth from Sara only to find himself stuck not just in the same city, but in the same building dealing with basically the same people. He would do anything to have her back in Atlanta, where the lies flowed a lot easier. In Macon, there was the constant possibility that Will would turn a corner or open a door and find Sara standing there wanting answers.

He coasted the Triumph into his usual spot by the employee entrance. The rain had accompanied him most of the trip down from Atlanta, spitting fine needles into his face. Will's helmet wasn't the wraparound kind, but a shorty, which gave his head the minimum coverage allowed by law. It was closer to a beanie. Every time a large truck crowded him on the interstate, Will wondered if he'd actually be able to see his brains on the asphalt before he died or if death would be instantaneous.

The thought was not a new one. Will had ridden a Kawasaki in his twenties because the bike was cheap and gas was expensive. And it had to be said that the sensation of sitting atop a large, vibrating machine was not an unpleasant feeling for a young man with limited dating experience. Add another decade, and the story took a considerably darker tone. His back ached. His hands hurt. His shoulders were screaming. Other areas were equally displeased. Will shook out his legs as he got off the bike. He unbuckled his helmet and peeled it off his head.

"Hey, Bud," a nurse called.

Will looked up. The woman was leaning against the building and sucking on a cigarette. He'd told people to call him Buddy because he didn't want to recall his conversation with Amanda every time he heard Bill Black's name. That his hospital colleagues had all shortened it to Bud was an unforeseen development.

She asked, "Good ride?"

Will grunted, which was a typical Bill Black response.

"That's nice." She smiled at him. Her bleach-blonde hair didn't move in the breeze. Her tight pink scrubs were covered in leaping dolphins. "You hear about what happened last night with them two cops?"

"Yep." Will pulled the bandanna off his head and used it to wipe the road from his face.

"One of 'em's in the ICU. Might not wake up." She picked something off the tip of her tongue. "Po-po's crawling all over the place."

Will grunted again. He stuck the bandanna in his back pocket.

She exhaled a long stream of smoke. "Tony says they were at his house this morning. Fools stole his car and used it for the hit. You believe that?"

Will stared at her, trying to decipher whether or not she was being rhetorical. He decided his best bet was to ignore the question altogether. "I need to clock in."

He tucked his helmet under his arm as he walked toward the door. The nurse took a last hit off the cigarette. She didn't seem to mind his gruffness. This was typical of the women in Bill Black's social circle. They expected their men to be quiet, to grunt and glare and scratch and spit. For Will, who'd been trained to put the toilet seat back down before he was even out of diapers, it was like living on the moon.

Or utopia, depending on how you looked at it.

"Take care now," the nurse said. She winked at Will as he opened the door. He didn't bother to hold it open for her. He knew the woman's type, had seen her standing in the periphery his entire life. They were at the children's home. They were out in the streets. Oftentimes, they were in the back of a squad car. They chose the wrong guys, made all the wrong decisions. The worse you treated them, the tighter they held on.

Will had always known this type of woman found him attractive. Maybe it was the scars on his face. Maybe it was some invisible mark left by his childhood that only fellow travelers could see.

Either way, they were drawn to Will because they thought he was damaged or dangerous or both. He had spent his life avoiding them. The only way to hold the interest of a desperate woman was to be a certain type of man. Will had never wanted to be that man.

"Hey," the nurse called. She stood in the open doorway, hand on her hip. "It's Cayla, by the way."

Will stared at her. He was standing outside the employee locker room. She was thirty feet away. The gray dolphins on her shirt looked like spoiled sperm.

She gave a flirty smile. "Cayla with a C."

Will didn't think another grunt would travel. He tried to be clever. "You want me to write that down or something?"

"Sure do." She laughed in a way that made him feel small. "Whatchu doin' after work?"

He shrugged.

"Why don't you come by my house for supper? I bet you ain't had nothin' home-cooked since you got out."

Bill Black's history had gotten around fast. Will had worked at the hospital less than two weeks and she already knew he'd been in jail.

She pressed, "How about it? Around seven? I can get a good scald on a chicken."

Will hesitated. He knew Cayla Martin's name from her rap sheet, which showed an arrest for drunken driving four years ago. DUIs came with expensive fines. Cayla still had another thousand dollars to pay before she was allowed to do more than drive herself to and from work. She was also a pharmacy nurse, which meant she had access to all the pills that kept getting stolen.

Cayla stamped her foot. "Come on, Bud. Let me cook you somethin' good."

Will was contemplating his options when Tony Dell came out of the locker room. The man panicked. His sneakers squeaked against the floor as he tripped over his feet trying to flee.

Con or cop—it didn't matter. When someone was trying to get

away from you, you stopped them. Will dropped his helmet on the floor. He grabbed Tony by the back of the neck and slammed him face-first into the door.

"Hey!" Tony cried. He was a little guy. Will was almost a foot and a half taller and carried at least fifty pounds more muscle. Lifting Tony off his feet was as easy as lifting Sara.

Will made his voice a growl. "What the fuck did you get me into?"

"I didn't—" Tony tried. Obviously, it was difficult for him to talk with his face smashed against a door. "Come on, Bud! I was tryin' to hook you up!"

"I'll hook you to a fucking noose."

"Bud! I'm serious, dude. I didn't know!" His toes kicked at the door as he tried to find purchase. "Come on!"

Will let him go. Tony's feet slid back to the floor. He took a few seconds to collect himself. He was breathing hard. Sweat poured from his brow, but whether that was because he was high or terrified, Will wasn't sure. Regardless, now that Tony wasn't afraid of having his neck snapped, he took umbrage with the rough treatment. "Jesus, dude. What's wrong with you?"

Will demanded, "Who set up the job?"

Tony looked up and down the hallway to make sure they were alone. Cayla had vanished. Women like that knew when to get out of the way.

"Damn." Tony rubbed the back of his neck. "That hurt, man."

"Who set it up?" Will jammed his finger into Tony's shoulder. "Tell me, you little shit."

Tony slapped his hand to his shoulder. "I don't know. Two guys at the bar came up and asked did I wanna make some money."

"Last night?"

"Yeah, after work."

"You knew them?"

"I seen 'em around." He started rubbing his shoulder. "You seen 'em, too. Them guys who hang back in the special corner."

The VIP section of Tipsie's. Will had seen it all right. It was about as welcoming as the shower room at the state pen. "How much money did they offer?"

Tony turned shifty.

Will put his hand on Tony's chest and pushed him back against the door. There was no force behind the hold, but the threat was enough to get the little man talking.

"Fifteen hundred bucks."

Will pulled back his fist. "You mother—"

"They told me we'd be safe!" Tony yelled, his hands going up. "They said we just needed to stand out in the street like we did. Nothin' to it."

Will kept his fist at the ready. "So you get a thou and I get five bills?"

"I was closest to the house." He gave a halfhearted shrug. "My spot was more dangerous."

Will let his fist drop. "You knew it was more than a robbery."

Tony opened his mouth, then closed it. He checked again to make sure they were alone. "I ain't gonna lie to you, Bud. I knew there was some people in the house might get hurt. I swear on a stack of Bibles I had no idea they was cops. No way I woulda taken that job, let alone bring you into it. We's friends, right?"

"My friends don't throw me in the shit when I'm already on parole." Will's shirt had pulled out from his jeans. He tucked it back in as he looked up and down the hall. "This better not blow back on me."

Tony wasn't as stupid as he looked. "Why'd you wanna go in the house so bad anyway? What was up with that?"

The million-dollar question. Will had figured out his answer on the ride down. "I need the money. Dead men don't pay."

"I hear ya," Tony said, but he was obviously not buying it. "You sure did run in there like a bat outta hell, though. Near about took my head off. I was only trying to help you."

Again, Will checked the hallway. "I got an ex, all right? Girl up in Tennessee. She's got a kid by me. I didn't believe her, but the test came back." Will tried to put some anger in his voice. "Bitch said she'd file on me if I don't throw down five K before the baby comes." He said the phrase he'd heard from many a con. "I can't go back to jail again, man. I can't do it."

Tony nodded his understanding. Will had gathered from various conversations at Tipsie's that the DNA tests they feared most were the ones that proved paternity. What was harder to believe was that the slang Will had picked up from watching an outlaw biker show on cable was actually working.

"I hear ya, man." Tony scratched his arm, a nervous habit that had left permanent red streaks on his skin. "You want, I could run up there with you, give her a talkin'-to."

"You wanna keep your voice down?" Will asked. "Every pig in the county's upstairs. That cop might not make it. You wanna guess what happens then?"

Tony kept scratching his arm. "So, what'd you see?" Again, he checked the hall. "Inside the house. What'd you see?"

"One dead guy, one on his way out." Will tried to fight back the bloody image of Lena straddling Fred Zachary, preparing to break his spine in two. "Some crazy chick with a hammer."

"She see you?"

"You think she'd be alive if she did?"

Tony lowered his voice. "I heard she used the claw."

"You know her?" Will clarified, "The cop. She ever bang you up?"

"Shit no. Ain't no bitch takin' me down, bro."

Will guessed an eight-pound Chihuahua could take down Tony Dell. "Why'd they wanna kill two cops? They on the take?"

"Dudes didn't say and I didn't ask." Tony backed himself against the door rather than let Will put him there. "Honest, Bud. I got no idea."

Will considered what a guy like Bill Black would be worried about in this situation. He asked, "What'd you do with the van?"

Tony was obviously not expecting the question. "It's cool. I know some guys."

"Whatever they paid you, half of it's mine."

Tony tried, "I didn't get much."

"Bullshit." Will grabbed Tony's arm to make sure the man was paying attention. "I'm only gonna ask you this one more time: Who do they work for?"

"I got no idea, dude. Honest."

"Well, you better think hard about it, because you and me are looking a hell of a lot like a couple of loose ends right now."

"You think they'll come after us?"

"You think whoever set this in motion is just gonna trust you not to talk?"

"Holy Christ." The color drained from Tony's face. "It's gotta be Big Whitey. He's the only dude I can think of who has them kind of balls."

Will tightened his grip around Tony's arm. It was a hell of a lot easier to interrogate someone when you could scare the crap out of them. "Why do you say that?"

"Because he's killed cops before. Everybody knows that. Hell, man, I heard he took out a federal agent down in Florida."

Yet another murder to look into. Will asked, "You sure you didn't tell them my name?"

"Hell no, brother. Hell no."

"If I find out you did . . ."

"I promise!" Tony's voice went up a few octaves. "Lookit, man. I ain't no snitch. I'm tellin' you straight up." He used his free hand to dig into his back pocket. "Look, all right?" He pulled out a wad of cash. "This is all I got for the van. You take it, all right? We'll call it even. Okay?"

Will took the cash. It was moist, which he tried not to think about as he counted out the bills. "Six hundred bucks. That's all you got?"

"That's more than you thought you'd get last night."

Will grunted. Bill Black would be satisfied with the amount.

"Lookit." Tony scratched his arm again. "Big Whitey's a businessman. We can go talk to him. Try to reason with him."

"There's no way I'm—"

"Just listen to me, hoss." Tony kept scratching, even though he'd drawn blood on his arm. "I told you I got a pill thing going here. You and me could double it up and—"

"No," Will said. "My PO got me this job. Who do you think they're gonna look at when a ton of pills start going missing?" He loomed over Tony again. "What'd you say to the police when they rang your doorbell this morning?"

The furtive look was back. "How'd you hear about that?"

"That nurse. She's probably told the whole damn hospital by now."

"Cayla," Tony provided. The soft way he said her name rang a bell. Cayla Martin was the girl Tony wouldn't shut up about on the drive to Lena's last night. It made sense that a pill freak would want to hook up with a pharmacy nurse.

Tony asked, "She say anything else about me?"

"No."

"Are you sure?"

Will was getting tired of this. "She offered to cook me supper."

Tony took the news harder than Will anticipated. He tucked his chin down to his chest. "Are you gonna go?"

"Tell me what you said to the cops this morning."

Tony didn't answer. "I thought you were my friend, Bud. I can't believe you're going out with her."

Will couldn't believe he was having this conversation. "What'd you tell the cops, Tony? Don't make me beat it out of you."

He still sulked, but answered, "That the car musta been stolen. They asked me to come down to the station and file a report."

"You stay out of that station," Will warned. "They get you in there, you won't ever come out."

"I ain't tellin' 'em nothin'."

"You think that matters? Two cops were almost killed. They're gonna pin this on the first idiot they can find."

"They got the idiots," Tony said. "Them two guys from last night—one's dead. The other one can't even move, and they's no way in hell he'll open his mouth. I keep tellin' you—Big Whitey, he's got reach. He'll take 'em out in the hospital. In the jail. In the prison. Ain't nowhere Big Whitey can't get to you. Trust me, man. He's a bad dude."

Will gritted his teeth. Every conversation he'd ever had with Tony Dell tended to turn down Big Whitey Way at some point. Something about that didn't feel right, and Will's instinct was to shut it down. "Whatever, man. Just keep me out of it."

Tony sensed he was losing his audience. "We could talk to him. Let him know we ain't gonna rat. Maybe get on the payroll."

"No." Will picked up his helmet off the floor. He wiped the scuffs with the back of his sleeve. He tried more biker talk. "I gotta kid to pay for, my PO's up my ass. I don't need to be looking for more trouble."

"It don't gotta be like that."

"Whatever, bro. Just keep my name out of it."

Will yanked open the door to the locker room. The space was empty. Blue lockers ran down the walls and divided the room into three sections. He waited a few seconds, wondering if Tony Dell would follow. When the door stayed closed, Will headed toward the lockers on the back wall.

Bill Black's name was written on a piece of masking tape stuck to his locker. Will had used a Sharpie to cross it out and write BUD. Three letters. It wasn't pretty—Will's handwriting had never been stellar—but it beat the locker next to his, where someone had drawn an ejaculating penis that had only one ball.

Will assumed it was an inside joke.

To secure his locker, Will had bought a luggage lock instead of a combination dial. Left and right had never been easy, but Will was good with numbers. He spun the four digits to the date he'd first kissed Sara. Or, technically, the date Sara had kissed him. The lock didn't need to know the details.

Will hung his helmet inside the locker and took out his folded work shirt and pants. Maintenance duty wasn't a bad job as these things went. Will was good at fixing things. The forms they made him fill out were designed for someone with little grasp of the English language. There were only five boxes to check or not check, and only one long line with an X beside it, which made it easy when it came time to sign his name. Not that Will signed his name. He wrote two capital letter *B*s and left it at that.

Will took off his street clothes and dressed for work. He wore Bill Black's photo ID on a lanyard around his neck. A security card and set of keys were attached to a retractable wire on his belt. A flashlight hooked through a metal loop on the side. Will transferred the still-moist cash from Tony Dell into the front pocket of his work pants, hoping the bills would be dry when he logged them into evidence later. In a blue Velcro wallet were a few of Black's credit cards, a copy of a speeding ticket that served as his license, and some receipts that indicated Mr. Black preferred to do all his shopping at the RaceTrac near the mouth of the Ocmulgee Trail.

He checked the battery on his iPhone. Will didn't use a smartphone in his real life, but Bill Black was a little more sophisticated. Not that the device was the sort of thing you had to be a rocket scientist to operate. Will had figured out most of the programs on his own as he whiled away the hours at the fleabag efficiency motel where Bill Black rented a room by the week.

Black's primary email account was on the hospital server. The secondary account was through Gmail. The inbox contained some increasingly nasty messages that appeared to have been written by an angry pregnant woman in Tennessee. There were a few mildly racist forwards from some dummy accounts, but Bill Black didn't have many friends. The bulk of his mail consisted of junk sent from mailing lists that advertised hunting gear and naked women, and coupons for things like beef jerky and Old Spice.

Black's musical tastes ran toward country, with some Otis Redding thrown in as a hat tip to the singer's hometown of Macon. There were some pictures of scenic views taken from the highway. Black was a hunter, so it made sense that he would appreciate woods and trees. Black also liked the ladies. There were several risqué photos downloaded from the Internet. Blondes and Asians mostly. Will had briefly considered putting a few redheads on there, but that felt weird because of Sara. And also because of Sara, he knew they weren't really redheads.

The tech specialist at the GBI had done the rest of the heavy lifting, adding some stealth features to the phone. The apps ran in the background and were invisible to anyone who didn't know exactly what to look for. One of them automatically erased all phone numbers and texts going in and out. Another turned the speakers into a recording device when you tapped the power button three times. Yet another provided a rolling phone number in case Will had to make a call and didn't want his location to come up. The most important app patched the device into the military's tracking system—not the GPS available to the entire world, but the real-time global positioning used for things like targeting drones and delivering bombs.

This last app was the reason Will kept checking the battery. Amanda was right about many things, but none more than the belief that there was a link between Will's investigation into Big Whitey and the attack on Lena Adams and Jared Long. Even Tony Dell had made the connection.

Will didn't want to go off the grid because he forgot to plug in his phone.

The door banged open. Will turned around. He was half expecting to find Tony Dell, but the new guy was beefy looking with a full head of hair and a jaw that was sharp enough to cut glass.

Will knew a cop when he saw one. He did exactly what Bill

Black would do—slammed his locker closed and headed toward the exit.

The cop held up his badge. "Detective Paul Vickery, Macon PD."

Lena's partner. That made sense. Will still didn't acknowledge him. He kept his beeline toward the door.

Vickery grabbed Will's shoulder and spun him around. He was a few inches shorter than Will, but he had a badge and a gun and obviously felt that gave him the right to be an asshole. "Where you going?" He glanced at the name stitched on Will's shirt. "Buddy."

Will tried to calm things down. "I don't want any trouble, all right?"

Vickery bounced on the balls of his feet, obviously spoiling for a fight. "Well, you're about to get it, motherfucker. Where's Tony Dell?"

Will shrugged, thinking Lena's partner didn't need to be face-to-face with the guy whose car was left outside the house where Jared Long was almost murdered. And Lena, too, for that matter. "I dunno, man. Ask at the front office."

"I'm asking you, fuckball. You're Bill Black, right?" Vickery wasn't looking for an answer. His eyes scanned the hospital ID hanging around Will's neck. "Your boss says you and Dell are real tight. Thick as thieves."

Will imagined Ray Salemi would've said anything to get Paul Vickery out of his office. "It's not exclusive," Will said. "We've both agreed to see other people."

"Funny, asshole." Vickery moved closer. "Where were you last night? You with Dell when him and his crew tried to take on my partner?"

Will had already arranged his alibi. "Ask my parole officer. He dropped in on me around midnight."

"I'm gonna do that." Vickery's beady eyes narrowed even more. "Something ain't right with you, asshole. I can feel it in my gut."

Will avoided the obvious joke.

"You're chest-high in this shit. I can smell it on you." Vickery sniffed, as if to illustrate the point. "Dell's a professional snitch. Just a matter of time before he rats you out. Why don't you beat him to it? Tell me what happened last night and I'll keep you outta jail."

"Sorry I can't help, Officer." Again, Will tried to leave, but Vickery's hand went to his chest, stopping him.

Vickery warned, "You got one more chance to tell me where your boyfriend is or I start taking it out on you."

"I said I don't—"

Vickery punched him in the face. Will saw it coming, but there wasn't enough time to get out of the way. Will's head swiveled. His jaw popped. He tasted blood in his mouth. Automatically, Will's fists went up.

He had to force them back down. Vickery was Lena's partner. Will didn't have to think long to consider the number of stupid things he'd do if someone threatened Faith and her family.

"Come on, Buddy." Vickery slapped Will's face with his open palm. "You wanna hit me, Buddy?" He whistled like he was calling a dog. "Come on, boy. Come on."

Will peeled his fingers from his palms to get them to unclench. Instead of beating the ever-loving shit out of Paul Vickery, he said, "You know there's a security camera in here, right?"

Vickery's eyes flicked upward to the corner. The camera was pointed straight down, its red light flashing. He seemed to be considering whether or not beating Will to death was worth losing his badge over.

Apparently not.

Vickery told Will, "This isn't over." He kicked the door open and stormed out with his hands fisted at his sides.

Will glanced up at the camera, which ran on a nine-volt battery and wasn't connected to anything because the Supreme Court had ruled that employees had an expectation of privacy when they were in a locker room.

You'd think a detective would know that.

Will checked his reflection in the mirror over the sink. Vickery hadn't done any visible damage. Will used his tongue to find the source of blood in his mouth. The inside of his cheek had cut against his teeth. He turned on the faucet and sipped some water. The wound started to sting. Will swished the water around until his spit was only slightly pink.

His phone buzzed in his pocket. He used the earbud to listen to the email from Ray Salemi, his helpful boss. Will read the words along with the tinny computer voice. He gathered Faith had found a way to get him and Lena in the same room together.

There was a leaking pipe in the ICU. Will had been assigned to fix it.

Will took the north stairwell up to the fifth floor. The going wasn't easy. His toolbox got heavier with each step. His body kept reminding him that he'd only gotten a few hours of sleep the night before. Will normally tried to run a few miles every day, but Bill Black's life didn't allow for such luxuries. By the third-floor landing, Will's arm was shaking. Level four brought shooting pains into his lower back. He set the toolbox down and used his bandanna to wipe the sweat off his face.

"Hey."

He looked up. Faith was leaning over the railing.

She looked down the open stairwell, making sure they were alone before asking, "Did you come up from the basement?"

He grabbed his toolbox and started climbing again. "The elevator opens up across from the waiting room, which is by the other set of stairs."

"Why didn't you take the elevator to the fourth floor and go up from there?"

Will watched a drop of sweat roll down his nose and splash onto the concrete steps.

"Will?"

He rounded the landing. Faith had that smile on her face that said she realized he was stupid but was being kind enough not to verbalize the observation. "I've been checking all the doors for the last fifteen minutes."

He asked, "Did you break a pipe or just pretend it's broken?"

"Water pistol. You'll see." She nodded toward the next flight of stairs. "Think you can make it?"

Faith took the steps two at a time. She had changed into her regs—black sneakers, tan cargo pants, and a long-sleeved blue polo shirt with the letters GBI written in bright yellow across the back. Her blonde hair was tucked into a matching blue ballcap with the same logo. Her Glock was strapped to her thigh.

Will dropped his toolbox by the door to the ICU. He looked through the skinny window into the ward. One nurse was behind the desk. The cop who was guarding Jared Long's room was so young he looked as if he was wrapped in plastic. Will had investigated cop shootings before. If Macon was like any other force on the planet, all the seasoned cops were out banging down doors and threatening sources.

Will headed up the stairs after Faith. The climb was remarkably easy without the added weight.

He pushed open the metal door. His eyes watered from the sudden sunlight. The rain clouds had receded, opening up a bright blue sky. Will gathered from the discarded cigarette butts in the pea gravel that the staff was familiar with the roof exit. He scanned the medical complex. The five-story hospital building was at the center. Two lower buildings flanked each side. Doctors rented the spaces. From what Will gathered, there were lots of baby doctors on hand. He'd been to the birthing suites a few times. They were more like hotel rooms. Most of Macon's industrial parks and factories had shut down during the recession, but Maconites were still making babies.

"Over here," Faith called.

There was a shed covering the exit door. Faith had walked around the back so no one could surprise them.

Will asked, "Sara?"

"She went shopping with Nell. Jared's mother. She wants to clean the house."

"The crime scene house?"

"That's the one."

Will felt his brow furrow. He couldn't imagine Sara thought that was a good idea.

Faith said, "I'll head over to the house later to make sure she's all right." She squinted at the name on his shirt. "Buddy?"

"It belonged to the last guy," Will lied. "I talked to Tony Dell this morning."

"And?"

"It's like we thought. Zachary and Lawrence found him at Tipsie's, said they needed a couple of men for a job."

"Tony knew them?"

"He says no, that he's just seen them around the bar. I believe him maybe ninety percent. They hang out in the back with the other rednecks in charge. Way above Tony's pay grade."

Faith pulled a pair of sunglasses out of her pocket and slid them on. "I verified what Branson told us this morning. She wasn't lying about the shooters. They're mid-level thugs. Nothing this violent in their histories. Certainly not murder for hire."

"What's the prognosis on Fred Zachary, the second shooter?"

"Don't ask me. I can't get near him. His lawyer's set up shop in his hospital room. Won't leave his side."

"That sounds expensive."

"The guy's part of a fancy firm out of Savannah. Vanhorn and Gresham. They just opened up offices in Macon." She glanced over to make sure he was following. "It's the same M.O. as Sarasota and Hilton Head. Big Whitey moves in, he organizes the local scumbags, he gives them fancy lawyers, and he takes out any cops who get in his way."

Will asked, "Anything off the cell towers?"

"Lena got a text from Paul Vickery around eleven-fifty. Nothing big, just checking if she's okay. Fifteen minutes later, Long got a blocked call we're trying to trace. Might take until tomorrow."

"Fifteen minutes later?"

"Yeah, about ten minutes before the attack."

Will stared out at the view, which was a depressing mix of interstate and strip malls. "Could be one of Jared's buddies just calling to check in."

"Could be."

"Have you talked to Lena's team?"

"What's left of it. DeShawn Franklin seems to think this is no big deal. Paul Vickery is a dick."

Will ran his hand along his jaw. "He's upset about his partner almost being murdered. He was here looking for Tony Dell this morning."

"Did he find him?"

"If Tony gets the crap beaten out of him, then we'll know he did."

"Vickery struck me as that kind of guy," Faith admitted. "Very self-righteous about me wasting his time when he could be out looking for whoever put out the hit on Lena and Jared."

Will said, "Vickery thinks Bill Black is involved."

"I'd probably make the same assumption. Black's a con with a violent history. Dell's car was at the crime scene. They both work at the same place."

"My boss told Vickery that Tony Dell and Bill Black are good friends."

"Nice. How's that target feel on your back?"

"Stabby," Will admitted. He'd have to be very careful around Vickery if he ever had the bad fortune to cross paths with him again. "What's the police station like?"

"They're all helpful on the surface, but the minute you start to pull at a string, they cut you off."

"What strings?"

"Incident reports. Daily briefings. They're not good at producing paperwork, which is odd for a police station."

Will noted, "It's been my impression that police officers have to write everything down."

"Mine, too. Maybe we should go work for Macon." She leaned back against the shed. "Chief Gray runs a tight ship, but he's got the press on his back—both Macon and Atlanta—plus there's talk someone saw a CNN truck heading down 75."

"Great," Will mumbled. He'd seldom worked a case where the media made things better.

Faith said, "Gray has every able-bodied cop pounding the streets, including himself. You gotta hand it to the old guy. He's got his sleeves rolled up just like everybody else. The downside is that Branson's got the whole station to herself. Her and Paul Vickery. I get the feeling DeShawn Franklin's heart isn't in it. He was handpicked by Chief Gray when he took over the force a few years ago. His loyalties have to be torn."

"You think he'll flip?"

"Not unless he's caught in bed with a dead woman or a live boy." Faith blew out a puff of air. He could tell she was frustrated. "I ran Jared and Lena's credit, checked their accounts. They pass the smell test. Lena's Celica is paid off, his truck's a year out. Low balance on their credit cards. There's a couple of thou left on Jared's student loans. Another thou in savings. No big trips or lake houses. They're a little upside down on their mortgage, but who isn't?"

"What about their cases?"

"We're covered up with cases. Jared was trying to win some kind of contest to write the most tickets. Lena's got a stack of arrests this big." Faith held her hands a foot apart. "I've got four loaners from the field office looking to kill me for drowning them in paperwork. They're gonna be working eighteen-hour shifts."

"It's easier to treat them badly if you don't know their names."

"I'll keep that in mind," Faith said. "First thing I asked for was the case file on that shooting-gallery raid you read about in the newspaper."

Will assumed she was drawing this out for a reason. "And?"

"IA has all the files. Every single scrap."

Internal Affairs. "That makes sense. Two cops were hurt during the raid."

"Keith McVale and Mitch Cabello. Don't be impressed. I only found out their names because I checked the duty roster."

"Did you talk to them?"

"One's in Florida spending his disability and the other checked himself out of the hospital this morning. He's not answering my calls and he's not at home." She pulled her phone out of her back pocket and swiped the screen a few times before showing some photos to Will. "DeShawn Franklin. Mitch Cabello. Keith McVale."

Except for skin color, there was a sameness to all the men—square-jawed, clean-cut. The same as Paul Vickery. They were more like a military unit than a detective squad.

Faith said, "There's a third guy who took off around the same time. Another detective." She held up the phone so Will could see his photo. "I don't know how he's connected, but Eric Haigh applied for administrative leave the day of the raid."

Will scanned the image, which was more of the same. He guessed, "Unavailable?"

"He won't even answer his phone." Faith said, "It's déjà vu all over again."

Will knew what she meant. The police forces in Hilton Head and Savannah had both seen an uptick of early retirements and transfer requests the minute Big Whitey started throwing his weight around.

He said, "It's the same strategy Whitey uses with the dealers. You kill or hurt one cop, it's easier to get the rest of them to either fall in line or fall away."

"And then Big Whitey corners the drug market." Faith changed the subject. "I was so desperate this morning I even tracked down your newspaper stories." She scrolled to the Web browser on her phone. The *Macon Chronicle-Herald* blotter was already pulled up. "We know about the shooting-gallery raid—at least that it happened. The two runaways were party girls; they straggled home the next afternoon. The school pot bust was a known offender who will be heading to rehab for his billionth time. The guy on the toilet had a heart attack. He was described as a forty-three-year-old entrepreneur." Faith looked back up at Will. "I wish I was better at making puns."

"It'll come to you."

She chuckled good-naturedly. "The raid has to be the flashpoint. I hate to admit this, but Denise Branson is good. She's got me completely rope-a-doped."

Will had worked these kinds of cases before. He saved Faith the explanation. "Internal Affairs won't release any paperwork on the shooting-gallery raid until they reach a decision. They can't legally discuss the details because the reputation of an officer or officers is at stake, or because there's possibly going to be a lawsuit. There's a gag order on everyone involved, and even without that, no one will talk to you because you're the bad lady from the state who's sticking her nose where it doesn't belong."

"In a nutshell," Faith confirmed. "I have a teenage son, so I know I should be used to being hated, but this is a whole new level."

Will wanted to tell her it got better, but he couldn't lie.

Faith tucked her phone back into her pocket. "I went in there expecting them to turn on Lena, but she's worshipped around that place. They talk about her like she's the best detective on the squad. I don't get it. And when I ask them why she's so great, they just look at me like it's so obvious, I must be some kind of idiot for not seeing it."

Will couldn't explain why Lena engendered such loyalty. He'd witnessed it in Grant County, too. For someone who continually screwed up, she seemed to have more than her fair share of supporters.

He asked, "What about Denise Branson? Did you get a temperature on her?"

"They're a bit cold on her, but that's to be expected. She's higher up the food chain. She's self-confident. She's a woman. Three strikes." Faith asked, "What else did you get out of Tony Dell?"

"Big Whitey this, Big Whitey that."

"That makes me nervous."

Will didn't address her concern. They'd had many conversations about how dangerous it felt for Tony Dell to keep throwing the name around. "I convinced him Big Whitey's probably going to kill us. Loose ends."

"Makes sense." Faith stared at the interstate. Will could guess her thoughts, which more than likely mirrored his own: It was time to make a move on Big Whitey. Will would have to get in deeper with Tony Dell, possibly through Cayla the pharmacy nurse.

He said, "Tony thinks we should try to arrange a sit-down. Let Big Whitey know we're not a threat. See if we can do business with him."

Faith nodded, but she still didn't look at Will. "Give me the details as soon as you have them."

"Maybe you could tape a gun to the back of the toilet tank for me." She didn't respond. "Like in the—"

"I've seen *The Godfather*."

Will followed her gaze to the line of cars. I-475 was backing up with lunchtime traffic. Every big-box store and fast-food restaurant imaginable was crammed along the exit.

He asked, "You think of a pun yet? For the entrepreneur on the toilet?"

"It doesn't seem so funny anymore."

Will stared back at the cars. A truck swerved into the wrong lane to pass a van. Horns blared. Faith lifted her hat and brushed her hair back up underneath it.

He asked, "Is she okay?"

Faith shook her head. "I haven't heard a word come out of her mouth. It's like talking to a brick wall. She won't respond to anything. Won't look at me. I was thinking about holding a mirror under her nose to make sure she's still alive."

Will waited for Faith to realize that wasn't the question.

She said, "Sara's all right. Tired. She didn't say, but I can tell it's hard for her to be here."

Will nodded.

She finally looked up at him. "You need to tell her, Will. This is getting too close to the bone."

He rubbed his jaw. He felt a knot coming up where Vickery had punched him. "Lena didn't say anything?"

Faith stared at him for a second longer, then shook her head again. "I tried to go in there like she was just another witness. Then I tried to talk to her like a cop. But the whole time, I've got sweat dripping down my back because all I can think is am I going to be the next cop she gets killed." Faith shrugged her shoulders when she added, "Or you."

Will wasn't sure what to say. He shrugged his shoulders, too.

They both turned when they heard a cackling laugh. A group of doctors had made their way up to the roof. Will walked gingerly around the shed. He kept his back to the metal wall. The pea gravel crunched as the group walked toward the edge of the building.

He checked that the coast was clear, then slipped through the door.

Will looked over the railing before heading down the stairs. His toolbox was still outside the ICU. He grabbed the handle and pushed open the door. And then his heart stopped because he hadn't checked the window first. Luckily, no one was there but the cop and the nurse.

The man's hand went to his gun.

Will held up his ID. "Maintenance. I got a report that a pipe's leaking?"

The cop gave Will a hard look. His hand stayed on his gun.

"Officer Raleigh, it's okay." The nurse stood up from her desk. "Lordy, Bud, it took you long enough." She apologized quickly. "I'm sorry, that's probably not your fault."

"I'm sorry anyway," Will told her. "Got hung up on the last job."

"It's Ruth." She smiled, motioning for him to follow her.

Will hefted the toolbox into his other hand as he walked down the hall. He had been in the ICU once before to check a hissing air conditioner. The basic layout was a horseshoe that squared off around the nurses' station. The rooms were small. The only windows looked into the hallway. Will guessed patients in the ICU didn't really care about sunlight, but the whole floor made him feel claustrophobic.

Officer Raleigh blocked the doorway to Jared's room. He grabbed the ID hanging around Will's neck. He scrutinized Bill Black's photo. Will was close enough to see the fine down on the young officer's cheek.

"What's the deal here?" Ruth seemed perplexed. "This is Buddy. He's been up here before."

Will studied the woman. She was older with dark hair that showed a little gray at the part. He wasn't sure why she kept covering for him. Will was pretty good at remembering faces and he was certain he'd never met this particular nurse before.

"All right." Raleigh finally moved out of Will's way.

Will tried to keep his expression neutral as he walked into the room, but Lena, who was folded into a chair in the corner, wasn't as careful. Her mouth opened in surprise.

Ruth misunderstood her reaction. She told Lena, "I'm sorry, sweetheart. We need to get this leak checked out. Only take a minute."

Will couldn't help it. He looked everywhere in the room but at Jared.

"It's there." Ruth pointed at a brown spot in the ceiling.

Will was tall enough to reach up and touch it. The tile was wet and smelled like apples. He looked at the food tray beside Jared's bed. The apple juice container was empty.

Will lowered his hand. Ruth was watching him in a way that made him uncomfortable.

She winked at him, then said in a breathy whisper, "I'm a friend of Cayla's."

Will was trying to summon up one of Bill Black's grunts when Faith finally appeared.

"What the hell's going on?" She directed her anger at the cop. "I know Chief Gray taught you better than this. Did you check this guy out?"

Raleigh hesitated. He clearly had a healthy fear of his chief. "The guy's got an ID."

"You can get those at Kinko's." Faith nodded toward the doors. "Go downstairs and check with HR."

"Yes, ma'am." Had Raleigh been a few years older, he would've told Faith where to stick her order, but he was new enough to jump when she snapped her fingers.

Ruth looked up at the ceiling, all business as she asked Will, "What do you think, Bud?"

Will looked up, too. "I think something's leaking."

Faith suggested, "Maybe we can move Mr. Long to a different room?"

Ruth shook her head. "It's just me up here for the next hour and I can't move him by myself."

Faith offered, "I can help."

"We're not really allowed to—"

Will interrupted, "I'll need the room cleared anyway." He pushed up the ceiling tile and used the flashlight on his belt to look inside the drop ceiling. Will had been looking into ceilings in the hospital almost every day of the last ten. He knew that his chances of finding at least one suspicious-looking pipe were good, but the nest of lines crisscrossing the ICU still surprised him.

He pushed the tile aside so everyone could see as he tried to sound authoritative. "That'll be oxygen, the condense line for the AC, PVC pipe, some old polybute. I'm gonna need a schematic so—"

"I get it," Ruth stopped him. "Let me call my supervisor and see if I can get her up here."

She left, Faith on her heels. Will kept his flashlight pointed toward the ceiling, but his eyes were on Jared Long.

The young man's face had blown up like a balloon. There were tubes sticking out of everything. His eyes were taped shut. Dried blood was caked around his nostrils. The flesh on his hands was a waxy, yellow color. No cop wanted to see another cop in a hospital bed. Will wasn't normally superstitious, but he had to suppress the shiver working its way up his spine.

Then again, Jared Long wasn't the only cautionary tale in the room.

Slowly, like she didn't want to break anything, Lena uncurled herself from the chair.

Will asked, "You holding up?"

"No." She stood on the other side of the bed with her arms wrapped around her waist. "Sara doesn't know you're doing this, does she?"

Lena had always been an astute observer, but Will wasn't going to talk to her about Sara. He glanced over his shoulder, checking Ruth. The nurse was talking on the phone. Faith was practically glued to her side.

Lena said, "I won't tell her. I haven't told anybody." She rubbed her lips together. They were cracked and dry. "You'll find out eventually. I'm good at keeping my mouth shut. I've learned to do the right thing."

Will asked, "What happened last night?"

"They shot him." Lena stopped the story there, dismissing her involvement in a wholly predictable way. Still, Will could tell she was reeling from the aftershock. Her eyes were bloodshot. The bruise under her eye mottled the skin. She couldn't seem to keep her balance. Her pupils were wide open, though he didn't know if that was from the dark room or some kind of medication.

He said, "Tell me what brought this on."

Her head moved slowly side to side.

"Was it the raid last week?" He paused. "Two cops were hurt. Were you part of that? Were you on the team?"

She paused before answering, "I'm not allowed to talk about the raid."

"You and I both know you don't play by the rules."

"Ask Branson."

"I'm asking you."

Her head started shaking again. She looked down at Jared. Her voice was barely a whisper when she told her husband, "I'm sorry, baby. I'm so sorry."

Will said, "Lena, something happened to set this off."

She didn't respond.

He tried to be diplomatic. "Did Jared pull somebody over who might want to hurt him?"

She gave Will a confused look, as if it never occurred to her that a motorcycle cop working part of a drug corridor that ran up the Eastern Seaboard might find himself in a dangerous situation.

She asked, "You think he got in the way of some traffickers?"

"I don't know. You tell me."

She seemed to think about it. "They would've shot him then and there."

Will knew she was right, but he still asked, "Jared didn't mention anything?"

"We weren't really talking."

Will let her words settle. He wasn't surprised there was marital discord. The first thing he'd seen when he walked through the front door of their house was a pillow and sheet on the couch.

Will asked, "What about you?"

"What about me?"

Will checked on Ruth again. Faith made a motion with her hand, indicating that there wasn't much time.

He tried to keep his patience as he told Lena, "Whatever brought this on—I know you didn't mean to do it. You're not a bad person. But you did something, and it got us here, and you need to tell me what that thing is so I can stop whoever did this."

There was still a small shake to Lena's head. Her hand was resting on the guardrail. She flexed open her fingers, letting the tips graze the sheet covering Jared's body.

Will said, "You know you can trust me. There's a reason I'm here."

She didn't acknowledge his plea. "Your partner. You work with her long?"

"Faith." Will tasted blood on his tongue. Without thinking, he'd chewed at the cut in his cheek. "A while."

"She any good?"

"Yes." Will tried another tack. "Who's Big Whitey?"

That snapped her out of it. He saw a flash of anger as the old Lena started to surface. "What did Branson say?"

"Who is he?"

"No one." She seemed genuinely afraid now. "He doesn't exist. He's a lie."

"Lena—"

"Stop." Her voice took on a pleading tone. "Listen to me, Will. If you love Sara, you'll stay away from this." She gripped the bed rail, desperate. "I mean it. Stay away."

Will looked back at the nurse again. She was obviously finishing up her phone call.

He told Lena, "Talk to me. Let me help you."

Lena shook her head. Tears started to flow. "We're supposed to protect people. We're supposed to keep them safe."

"The best way to keep Jared safe is—"

"How do you decide?" She swallowed hard. The sound was louder than the hum of the machines. "How do you decide whose life is more important?" Her hand went to her stomach. The palm was flat, fingers splayed. "He would want this," she whispered. "This is what Jared would want me to do."

Faith cleared her throat loud enough to announce her return.

Ruth was behind her. She asked Will, "How bad is the leak? I mean, are we talking the whole ceiling's gonna come down?"

Will took his time, clicking off the flashlight, dropping it back into the loop on his belt. Finally, he shook his head and shrugged at the same time. "I won't know until I get up there."

Ruth sighed. "It's gonna be an hour before my boss can help move him. Can you come back?"

Bill Black took over. "You're gonna have to put in another request."

Ruth sighed again, but she was obviously used to dealing with the hospital bureaucracy. "All right, Buddy. Thanks for coming, anyway." She went to Jared and started checking the machines. Lena watched her like a hawk. It was unnerving the way she just stood there. Except for stretching her fingers, she didn't reach out to him. She barely looked at his face.

Ruth must've felt it, too. She told Lena, "It's okay to touch him, hon. He's not gonna break." As if to prove this, she put her hand to Jared's cheek. And then she kept it there. Her brow furrowed.

Something was wrong.

Ruth's hand went to Jared's forehead. Then his neck. Then his wrist. She looked at her watch, checking his pulse against the flashing number on the monitor. Will could see the thumping heart was beating faster than usual. The blood pressure was low.

"What is it?" Faith asked.

"He's just a little clammy." Ruth grabbed the control and raised the foot of the bed. The floor vibrated beneath Will's feet. The nurse put some false cheer in her tone. "I'm sure it's nothing, but let me get the doctor, all right?" She left the room at a brisk pace. Faith followed her, though Will doubted Lena would tell him anything else.

He picked up his toolbox. He tried one last time. "Lena, I know you think you've got all of this under control, but you don't."

She didn't look up as she said, "I've never been able to control anything in my life."

Will waited, giving her another chance to come clean. She ignored him. She just stood there staring down at Jared. Her hand was still pressed flat to her stomach. Her mouth moved soundlessly, as if in prayer.

All Will could do was leave the room. Ruth was on the phone by her desk. She barely registered his presence, which Will took as a bad sign. Jared's condition was obviously a more serious matter than she'd let on.

He walked down the hallway toward Faith. She was reading her emails. Or pretending to. Will could see the screen was dark.

He stopped a few feet away from her and opened his toolbox.

Faith kept her voice low. "Well?"

Will found his clipboard and pen. He looked at Ruth again. She had her back to him, the phone pressed to her ear.

Still, he kept his voice down. "She's protecting someone."

"She's protecting herself."

Will wasn't so sure about that. He checked some boxes on his form. "I think she was at the raid on the shooting gallery. She told me she wasn't allowed to talk about it."

"Of course she was at the raid. I wouldn't be surprised if she was leading it."

"She warned me off Big Whitey."

Faith looked up from her BlackBerry.

Will kept checking boxes. He was giving himself time to decide whether or not to tell Faith the rest. In the end, he knew he didn't have a choice. "She told me if I love Sara, I'll drop the case."

Faith looked back at her phone. Her thumb scrolled across the black screen. She seldom registered any emotion beyond irritation, but Will could tell Lena's words had hit home.

She asked, "Why do I get the feeling that, five years ago, she told Jeffrey Tolliver the same thing?"

7.

THE DAY BEFORE THE RAID

Lena sat at her desk staring at her computer monitor. Fireworks filled the screen. She knew if she tapped one of the keys, the desktop would appear. She also knew what the files would be—open cases, closed cases, court documents, witness statements, suspect statements—endless bytes of data that summed up the lives of thousands of people.

There was only one life on the computer that she cared about.

Not that there was life anymore.

Lena closed her eyes. Let the grief have its way.

She had been electrocuted once. Not electrocuted like on death row, but shocked by an electric current. Lena was fifteen when it happened. She'd been helping Sibyl with her hair. They were both standing in front of the mirror. The glass was steamed over from a recent shower. The smell of mold was in the air.

The house they grew up in had been wired by their uncle Hank, so they were used to smoking outlets and popping lightbulbs. He'd also built the bookcases that had no shelves, and removed a load-bearing wall, which resulted in the roof settling into a camel-back sway. Just walking through the front door, you knew you were taking your life into your own hands.

Which is why Lena should've known better than to plug in the hair dryer without first unplugging the box fan. The shock had streaked up her arm, down her spine, then legs, and into the tips of her toes, which happened to be touching standing water from the shower. There was some sort of delay. Lena didn't feel the brunt of the electrocution until she saw the water. She thought, *This is dangerous.* The lights zapped out. Her body seized. Then, the next thing she knew, she was lying on the bathroom floor and Sibyl was screaming for Hank to call an ambulance.

That's what Lena felt like now—shocked. Almost electrocuted. Laid flat on her back. Her body tensed. Her nerves on fire. Only this time, there was no one around to help her. This time, she was completely alone.

Lena watched the colorful bursts of light explode across the computer screen. She rested her hand on the mouse. She gently pressed down. The desktop came up. She moved the arrow to the file that contained the ultrasound. Lena had torn up the photo, but the video remained. Her hand froze on the mouse. She didn't need to open the file. She didn't need to see the picture. The image was forever seared into her retinas. She felt weak as rain every time she saw it.

Little black bubble. White folds and ridges. The tiny flutter of a beating heart that was no bigger than a drop of rain.

How could she love something so much when she couldn't even see it with her naked eye? How could she feel that heart beat inside of her when it took a machine just to let her know it was there?

How could she have lost it so easily?

How could one horrible moment erase weeks of happiness, destroy a prospective lifetime that had made Lena's heart feel weightless with anticipation?

The arrow hovered over the file. There was a slight shake to the image.

Her cell phone rang. Lena moved her hand off the mouse and picked up the phone. "Detective Adams."

"Oh." The woman seemed surprised that Lena had answered.

"Yes?" Lena asked. She touched her hand to the mouse. She didn't need to see the file again. She should get rid of it. Throw it in the computer's trash.

"Ma'am?" the woman said. "Hello?"

"Yes." Lena turned away from the computer. She made herself listen to the call.

The woman was saying, ". . . from Dr. Benedict's office? You saw me yesterday?"

Lena couldn't stand people who raised their voices at the end of every sentence. "Are you calling about the bill? We haven't gotten it yet."

"Oh, no, of course not." She sounded offended. "I just wanted to check on you? Your husband said you were back at work?"

Lena rubbed her eyes with her fingers. Jared had slept on the couch last night. He was gone this morning when Lena woke up. She'd checked the duty roster when she got in. He'd changed shifts so he didn't have to see her.

"Ma'am?"

Lena dropped her hand. "Is there something you wanted?"

"Dr. Benedict asked me to check on you, see if the cramping's subsided?"

Lena put her hand to her stomach. "It's better," she said, not knowing whether or not this was the truth. Every time she thought about it, she could feel it happening all over again. The excruciating pain that woke her from a deep sleep. The panic as she tried to dress herself. The fear as they raced to the hospital. The agony as they heard the doctor's words. The screaming argument she'd gotten into with Jared when they got home.

He wouldn't let Lena throw away the bloody sheets. He said she was trying to pretend it hadn't happened. That she was unfeeling. Incapable of grieving. That throwing away the sheets was her way of getting rid of the evidence.

As if Lena needed a visual reminder to understand what she had lost.

They had lost.

"Ma'am?"

Lena shook her head, trying to get rid of the thoughts. "Yes?"

"I asked, no excessive bleeding?"

Lena didn't know what "excessive" meant. She had no point of reference.

"Mrs. Long?" The woman's voice filled with a warmth that was ten times worse than her stupid interrogatory tone. "I can have Dr. Benedict write you a note for work. You shouldn't be back so soon. Most women take a few weeks, sometimes a month or even two if they can get off that long."

"Well, I can't do that," Lena said. Yesterday was bad enough. They'd gotten home from the hospital around ten in the morning. Lena had slept away the afternoon, then stayed up arguing with Jared well into the night. The thought of being trapped at home again with nothing to do but wait for Jared to walk through the door was unbearable. Besides, no one at work even knew she was pregnant.

Had been pregnant.

Lena told the woman, "I have work to do."

"I'm sure you do, Mrs. Long, but people will understand. What you lost—"

"I'm fine," Lena interrupted. She wanted to correct her, to tell the woman that her last name was Adams, that Jared had told her to keep it because Lena Long sounded like something you'd buy off an infomercial.

Instead, Lena said, "I don't need a note. Thank you."

"Oh, darlin', please don't hang up." She was obviously concerned. "You should go home. Be with your husband. Trust me, he might not be showing it, but he's hurting just as much as you."

Lena pressed her fingers into her eyes again. Jared was showing it. Lena was the problem. According to her husband, she was some kind of machine. She wasn't the woman he'd married. He wasn't sure she was the woman he wanted to stay married to.

Lena looked at the clock. She had a briefing in five minutes. Her team was waiting for her. She should end the call. She should shut up. But the words came out of her mouth before she could stop them. "I wondered—"

Instead of pushing Lena, or making an inane statement with her voice raised at the end, the woman was silent. The trick was a good one. Lena used it in interrogations. People naturally wanted to fill silences, especially when they felt guilty about something.

Lena said, "I had an abortion."

Still the woman was silent.

"Six years ago." Lena put her hand to her face. Her skin felt hot to the touch. "I wondered—"

"No. That has nothing to do with what happened the other night." The answer had a certain finality to it. "If that were the case, I wouldn't have my two little ones."

Lena felt some of the tension leave her chest. She opened her mouth for air. For just a moment, she could breathe again.

The woman said, "Give yourself time to grieve. You and your husband can try again. Trust me, what you're going through now—it gets easier. It doesn't ever go away, but it gets different."

Lena pulled a box of tissues out of her desk. She had to get her shit together. She was at work. She had to stop dwelling on this. There was no way she could lead her team if they saw her sobbing at her desk. She wiped her eyes, blew her nose.

"Okay," Lena told the woman. "Thank you. I need to get back to work."

"Mrs. Long. Lena. You really should go home. Don't do this to yourself. Nobody gets a medal for being tough."

"Okay." Lena made her voice stronger. "Thank you for calling. I have to go."

"But—"

Lena hung up the phone. She blew her nose again. She wiped her eyes until they felt raw. Maybe it was different at a doctor's office, but at the police station, they gave out medals all the time for being tough.

Lena turned to her computer. She clicked on the ultrasound file and dragged it into the trashcan. She clicked on the Finder menu, then scrolled down to Empty Trash. Her finger stayed pressed down on the mouse. Her heart thumped in her chest.

"Lee?" Paul Vickery banged on the door as he walked into her office. He stopped. "What's wrong? Somebody yank your nose hair?"

"I've gotta stupid cold." Lena scrolled back up the menu, went to Edit, then selected Undo Move to Trash. She didn't look up at Paul until she saw the file safely back on her desktop. "What is it?"

"You make a decision yet, boss?"

The decision. They'd planned the raid for next week, but their snitch had told them a big shipment was coming in tonight. Even before she lost the baby, Lena wasn't comfortable moving up the schedule. She wanted more time to prepare. Apparently, no one else felt this way. She was feeling pressure from all sides to go in. More money, more guns, more dope, more jail time.

She told Paul, "Yeah, everybody else knows but you."

"Just checking, Kemosabe. No need to get your panties in a wad."

She heard a familiar chug from her computer. Paul wasn't the only one who was getting antsy. Denise Branson had sent another email. Lena scanned the first line, which dove straight into the fact that after last night's overtime, Lena's investigation had crossed the one-million-dollar mark.

"Damn, girl." Paul read over her shoulder. "You pissed her off something righteous. What're you gonna do?"

"She'll be fine once she gets her picture in the paper."

"Vanhorn and Gresham," Paul read from the email. "Sid Waller's lawyer's from that firm, right?"

Lena clicked the email closed as she stood up. "We're gonna

draw straws to see who goes down into the basement first. I'm gonna hold them. One person gets to pick from each team."

Paul grinned like a possum. "Good thing I'm feeling lucky, partner."

"Did y'all finish taping off the diagram?"

"Yeah. Had to keep DeShawn from using his protractor."

"Good. We're going to rehearse this thing until we know it in our sleep." Lena grabbed her jacket on the way out.

Paul said, "It's eighty degrees in the shop."

"Thanks for the weather update." Lena pulled on the jacket as she walked down the hallway. Her hormones were still out of whack. She was cold all the time, except when she was burning up. That's what she should've asked that stupid woman from Dr. Benedict's office about, not something that had happened six years ago.

Paul said, "You're going to—"

"Shit." The zip was caught in her shirt.

"Here." Paul stood in front of her. He started working on the zipper like she was three. Paul wasn't the only one who'd been treating her more delicately lately. Lena guessed she was putting out some pregnant woman pheromones. Or at least she had been.

Paul said, "I think we're gonna have a problem with Eric. He's acting weird."

"How?"

"He's being too quiet." He added, "That thing in the van the other day was funny, but he's hiding something."

"Hiding what?"

"Exactly."

Lena watched Paul's fingers as he tried to free her shirt from the zipper. She thought about the little blue jacket she'd ordered online. Jared's family loved Auburn football to the point of making it a religion. Lena had yelled at him for painting the nursery, but she couldn't resist going online last week and ordering a baby-sized Auburn hoodie from Tiger Rags.

The jacket was on back order. She wondered when it would be delivered. What day in the near future would she go home and find a tiny jacket waiting for little arms that would never exist?

"Lee?" Paul asked. "Where'd you go?"

She shook her head. "It's too late to switch out Eric. He's just gonna have to man up."

He finally freed the zipper. "You're the boss."

The word grated; it had started taking on mocking undertones. "Lucky me," she muttered. Technically, their lieutenant was supposed to be the boss, but a particularly aggressive form of leukemia had taken him out of the equation and Denise Branson had yet to find a suitable replacement. At first, Lena had been happy to fill the role, but now she was seeing the downside of her new responsibilities.

Paul said, "Shit, look smart." He puffed out his chest and pressed his back to the wall as he stood at attention.

Lena didn't have to ask why. Lonnie Gray was talking on his cell phone as he walked down the hallway. He ended the call when he saw Paul and Lena. There was no preamble. He asked, "Status?"

Lena provided, "We're doing run-throughs. No mistakes this time. We're gonna nail Waller."

Gray's voice was stern. "That's exactly what needs to happen, Detective."

"Yes, sir," she said, knowing he wasn't kidding around. Lena had seen more than one detective leave the Macon PD before he was planning to because he'd disappointed the chief. "You have my word that the entire team is at one hundred percent."

Paul added, "You can count on us, sir," sounding like a third-grader bringing an apple to his teacher.

"Good." Gray headed back down the hallway, but not before giving Paul a curt nod. Lena could practically hear Vickery's ball sac quiver. She felt the same respect toward Gray, but she hoped she didn't look like she was creaming her pants every time the chief was around.

As soon as Gray was gone, Paul clapped his hands together. "You heard the chief. Let's rock this bad boy."

He preceded Lena down the hall toward the shop. Paul was obviously pumped, and not just because of the chief. He walked on the balls of his feet in that weird way that made him look a little effeminate. Lena knew Paul had served two tours in Afghanistan before a piece of shrapnel got lodged in his arm. Physical therapy had brought him back to one hundred percent, but being home had made him lose his taste for war.

Paul still relished a good fight, though—one of the many characteristics they both shared. At first, Lena thought their matched temperaments made for a good partnership, but she was beginning to see that maybe a differing opinion would offer a better balance.

Part of the reason Lena had respected Jeffrey Tolliver so much was that he'd always told Lena when he thought she was wrong.

Paul kicked open the door to the shop. The sound of metal hitting metal reverberated through the hangar-like building. The shop was where they brought seized automobiles and boats so they could take them apart and look for drugs or contraband. They also used it to do routine maintenance on the squad cars, which was why three cruisers were hanging on lifts.

The mechanics had cleared out a large space for Lena's team to work. The footprint of the shooting-gallery house was thirty-five by sixty, and even in the large building, space was at a premium. They were using the log sergeant's duty desk as their workspace, which had infuriated the sergeant, but orders were orders. Lena was surprised Denise Branson hadn't taken the space away from them. She was pissed enough at Lena to strike out, and Branson didn't get to the rank of major without knowing how to punish people.

DeShawn Franklin, Mitch Cabello, and Keith McVale stood around the duty desk. Lena took the lead ahead of Paul. She lengthened her stride so that he wouldn't pass her. Back in Grant

County, Lena had been the only female detective on an all-male force. She knew the rules when she signed up. Every second of the day, she had to fight to keep her place in the pecking order.

"Hey, boss." Mitch looked up from the diagram they had gotten from the tax assessor's office. "You gotta cold?"

Lena knew what she probably looked like: red-rimmed eyes, bloodshot from crying. She wiped under her nose with the back of her hand. "Yeah. Jared gave it to me."

"I bet he gave it to you." DeShawn made a grunting sound that invited a chorus of porn music from the team.

"Shut up, assholes. I just ran into Chief Gray in the hall. He made it clear we'd better come back here with Waller or keep on driving out of town." She gave DeShawn a pointed look. "That means you, too, golden boy."

Mitch made a "rut-roh" sound straight out of a Scooby-Doo cartoon, though they all knew DeShawn was one of Gray's favorites.

Lena looked around the shop. The mechanics had gone to lunch and the duty sergeant was probably sulking in his car. The B-Team had worked surveillance last night. Lena told them they could come in late. During the raid, they were assigned to guarding the perimeter, so they didn't need to run the inside drills like the rest of them.

Still, someone was missing.

She asked, "Where's Eric?"

DeShawn provided, "Shitting out lunch from the sound of it."

Lena glanced at Paul, whose face tended to show every single thought that crossed his mind. He was still worried about Eric. Maybe he had a right to be. To mangle the old saying, Eric's stomach was the window to his soul.

DeShawn asked, "Something wrong, boss?"

Lena tried to summon up her old self. "Yeah, I gotta bunch of little girls on my team."

They greeted this with the expected howls and finger pointing. Lena ignored them. She looked down at the concrete floor where they had taped off the house. The diagram was to exact scale. Den, two bedrooms, bathroom, dining room, kitchen. They could pace off the steps here so that it came as second nature when they were doing the raid in real time.

The only unknown was the basement.

Thumb latch. Deadbolt. Slide lock. There was no telling how the door would be secured, though they had wasted plenty of time considering the options.

The biggest issue was the four guys, maybe five, who were usually in the house. Sometimes a couple of junkies stayed the night, but that tended to be after a weekend of partying. Traffic started flowing around seven-thirty in the morning—either kids on their way to school or adults on their way to work. Two or three hours later, the moms came in their SUVs, seeking a bump to get them through their daily chores. Lunchtime traffic was unreliable, but rush hour started at four-thirty and didn't slow down until after three in the morning.

This was when Sid Waller showed up. Like clockwork, he took the northbound exit onto Allman Road, hung a left onto Redding Street, then slowly drove his Corvette down the rutted gravel driveway to the shooting gallery.

Waller usually stayed at the house for three hours. No one knew what he did while he was there. It was too dangerous to send in the snitches at that time of day. They were usually passed out by then, anyway. Paul thought Waller was sampling the product. DeShawn thought he was banging some girls. Denise Branson thought he was counting all the money.

Lena prayed to God he was doing all three, and that by the time they made their way into that dark, dank basement, Sid Waller was too stoned, too fucked, and too scared to do anything but watch helplessly as Lena ratcheted the cuffs around his wrists.

She looked up. They were all waiting on her. DeShawn was staring at his hands like he was trying to decide whether or not he needed a manicure. Mitch and Keith were mumbling to each other because the two of them couldn't shut up if you held a gun to their heads. Paul's face said it all. He was like a puppy, bouncing around on his feet, about to wet himself with anticipation.

The door creaked open. Eric Haigh gave a sheepish smile as he walked into the shop. Paul was right. There was something off about the man. He seemed too hesitant, which became enormously clear as he joined the rest of the team around the desk. They were all ready to go. Eric looked like the only place he wanted to go was back out the door he'd just walked in.

Well, they all had shit going on in their lives.

"All right, ladies." Lena clapped her hands together. "Decision's been made. We're hitting this place at oh-dark-thirty tomorrow morning."

8.

THURSDAY

Sara sat in the passenger's seat of Nell's truck watching the Macon landscape scroll by. Atlanta was a city filled with beautiful gardens and trees, but there was something about being surrounded by a forest that made Sara feel at home. Like Macon, Grant County was a college town, located in a part of the state that still moved at a slower speed. Just seeing the trees made Sara feel like her lungs were working again. The vulture on her shoulder had temporarily left its perch. She felt more like herself.

Maybe it wasn't entirely the scenery that had brought her this sense of calm. While Nell was shopping for cleaning supplies, Sara had frantically poured her heart out in a long email to her sister. Tessa's response had been just as long, but instead of filling the message with clichés about soldiering on or enjoying sweet revenge, she'd made lists: Ten things she loved about Will Trent. Three of the stupidest jokes their father had ever told. Eight new words that Tessa had said around Izzie, Sara's niece, that would probably end up sending Tessa to hell. Six reasons no one would ever be able to make biscuits as good as their grandmother's. Five things that their mother did that they both swore they would never, ever do, but that they were now doing almost every single day of their lives.

The only direct acknowledgment to Sara's situation came in the postscript:

Please don't start listening to Dolly Parton again.

Nell said, "I do that all the time."

Sara was pulled from her thoughts. "What's that?"

"Remember something about Jeffrey and smile." Nell smiled, too. "He loved being in the woods. Used to go hiking all the time when he was in high school."

Sara opened her mouth to correct her, then thought better of it.

"It's all right," Nell said. "You save whatever story you just thought of for Jared when he wakes up. We'll all smile about it then."

Sara nodded. This was a familiar refrain that Nell had started the minute they'd left the hospital. She needed to get some clean pajamas for when Jared woke up. She needed to make sure the house was clean for when Jared woke up. Sara didn't begrudge Nell the goal. She could tell it was the only thing keeping her going.

Nell's cell phone beeped. She was using the GPS to find Lena and Jared's house. "I guess it's down here," she murmured, taking a lazy, right-hand turn.

Sara pressed her lips together. Nell drove like an old woman, never exceeding the speed limit, slowing to let over every car that even looked as if it might want to merge. Occasionally, she would stop the truck in order to read a sign or remark on a pedestrian. She was still stuck in small-town time, where rushing was considered rude and you didn't beep your horn unless a dog was in the road.

Nell took in the houses lining the street. "Not too bad," she commented, which was the most positive thing she'd said about Macon since they got into the truck. "I guess they got all the plans from the same magazine."

Sara followed her gaze. There was a uniformity to the subdivision, but the houses weren't overbuilt for the lots or stuffed with extra bedrooms that no one would ever use. People kept their lawns tended. There were minivans in the driveways. American flags hung from porch posts. The street looked exactly like the kind where you'd expect to find two police officers living.

Nell didn't need her GPS anymore. She parked near a white GBI crime scene van. Charlie Reed stood at the open back doors. A younger man handed him plastic crates that Charlie packed carefully into the cargo area. Sara recognized the sealed evidence bags from her medical examiner days. The past started to creep up again, especially when she noticed the two cops standing around a cruiser parked at the end of the street.

"Well," Nell said. She was looking up at the house with some trepidation.

Sara guessed the woman had been expecting something closer to a witch's cottage, not the quaint, single-story clapboard house at the top of a steep hill. The structure was shotgun style, deeper than it was wide, with the front door planted squarely in the middle. Instead of an American flag on the front porch, there was an orange and blue banner with the logo of Auburn University.

Nell seemed to approve of the flag. She said, "At least he's still standing where he's from."

Sara made some mumbling noises that might be interpreted as encouragement. Maybe it wasn't Nell, but Sara who was having a hard time thinking about Lena living in this house. The lawn was a dark carpet of green. There were some leggy petunias planted around the mailbox. Monkey grass splashed over the front walk. The front door was painted red. More petunias spilled from wooden planters on the porch. Sara couldn't imagine Lena tending flowers, let alone sitting down and taking notes from a book on feng shui.

"You coming?" Nell asked.

Sara pushed open the door. The air felt chilly compared to the stuffy cab of the truck. The police officers at the end of the street stared with open curiosity. Sara waved. She got two nods in return.

Nell told Sara, "I'm'll call Possum and see if he checked in with the nurse yet." She flipped open her phone and dialed the number. Her hand went to her hip. She looked up at the house as she waited for Possum to answer.

Sara hoped Nell was reconsidering her plans. The first thirty minutes of their drive had been spent discussing the realities of what cleaning the crime scene would entail. Sara hadn't held back toward the end. She'd been fairly brutal, which only seemed to galvanize Nell's resolve.

Nell spoke into the phone, "How is he?"

Sara walked away from the truck to give her privacy. A breeze stirred the air as she headed toward the crime scene van. Sara rubbed her arms, wishing she'd thought to bring a jacket.

"Dr. Linton." Charlie Reed smiled at Sara. He was a nice-looking man except for a well-groomed handlebar mustache, which gave him the appearance of a lounge singer. "Please tell me Amanda finally managed to snag us your services?"

"Lord no." The last thing on earth Sara would ever want to do is work for Amanda Wagner. "I'm here with a friend." She indicated Nell. "Her son's Jared Long."

"Oh." Charlie's smiled dropped. "Surely, she doesn't want to see . . . ?"

"Worse than that. She wants to clean it up."

Charlie indicated for Sara to follow him to the front of the van. He glanced at Nell, probably to make sure she couldn't hear them. "It's pretty bad in there. I mean, not as bad as most, but they used a shotgun and there was quite a struggle. The volume of blood—"

Sara held up her hands. "I would gladly leave right now if I thought I could get her to go with me."

Charlie looked at Nell again. Her determination must've been apparent. "Well, it's good that she has you here to walk her through it."

"I'm still trying to change her mind."

"She doesn't look like the type who does that," he noted. "I can give you a quick rundown if you like?"

Sara nodded, ashamed that she was so eager to hear the details.

Charlie's voice took on a practiced tone. "The man we're calling Assailant Two entered through the front window." He indicated the window in question. Black fingerprint powder smeared the white trim. "He more than likely used a pocketknife. Slid it between the frames, pushed open the thumb latch."

Sara nodded. The entry method was typical for burglaries.

He continued, "We can assume from fingerprints that Assailant Two then opened the front door, letting the man we're calling Assailant One enter the house. From the gunpowder residue on the floor and walls, we can conclude the first assailant was standing in the front room at the mouth of the hall when he initially fired the shotgun. Sawn-off Remington 870, twenty-eight gauge."

Sara knew from past cases that a shotgun blast from that distance could rip apart a half-inch piece of plywood. The sawed-off barrel had spread the pellets, which was probably the only reason Jared hadn't dropped dead on the spot.

Charlie said, "I've read the hospital admitting report. My preliminary field investigation supports the shotgun pellets mostly clustered in a twenty-centimeter circle in the victim's thoracic region, roughly T-2 through T-7, with some penetrating the skull. At the scene, a few pellets were found lodged into the wood around the doorframe. We can assume that the majority of the pellets went into the victim."

Sara had gotten out of the practice of listening to people talk as if they were giving testimony. "Jared was standing in the doorway?"

"Yes. The victim's body was almost exactly centered in the

doorway. He likely had his arms crossed or in front of him. According to the hospital report, he had no wounds on the back of his arms or hands. He was wearing a toolbelt, which we can surmise is where Detective Adams got the hammer."

Sara had been wondering about that detail. She didn't imagine Lena kept a hammer in the bedroom, though who knew what the hell she got up to.

Charlie continued, "Adams used the hammer to take out the first assailant, the shooter, at the doorway to the bedroom." He pointed just below his eye socket. "Claw went in here. Got lodged in the orbita, went straight through the vitreous. The shotgun went off a second time, blasting a hole approximately thirty-two centimeters into the far wall. At some point, the assailant fell to the floor, whereupon the hammer was yanked out of his face. We found splatter and bone on the walls approximately ten to sixteen inches from the floor, so he was likely supine when it was removed. Some spatter arced onto the ceiling as it was wrenched away." Charlie shuddered. "Sorry, hammers freak me out."

"You're not alone."

"Nonetheless." He shuddered again. "At some point, Assailant Number Two tried to come to the rescue. Residue puts him at approximately six feet outside the bedroom when he fired three shots from a Smith and Wesson five-shot revolver. He ended up shooting his buddy instead. I'm not certain how that happened, but Assailant One was standing with his back to the door when he was shot. Obviously, he fell to the floor shortly after. Then somehow the second assailant fell, and Adams went at him."

"The second assailant fell before she hit him?"

"Fell to his knees," Charlie clarified. "Sorry. We found knee and hand prints in the blood where he fell to the floor. This was when Detective Adams likely hit him in the head with the butt of the shotgun. We've got blood and hair on the gun, and the spatter on the wall and bed, which is approximately thirty-two inches from the floor, backs up a baseball swing. We took the dislodged

teeth for evidence, so at least the mother won't have to see them."
He glanced at Nell again. She was off the phone now, digging
around in the back of the truck for her bags of cleaning supplies.

Sara asked, "What happened after the second shooter was
taken out?"

"The neighbors arrived." Charlie nodded up the road. "There
are two officers on the block as well as a paramedic and a fireman.
Sorry, firewoman. They got Jared's heart pumping again. Fortunately for me, the on-duty officers who responded to the 911 call
stayed out of the bedroom. The scene was fairly pristine when I
arrived."

Sara asked, "You said Jared's heart stopped?" That would explain why they'd taken him to the closest hospital instead of the
trauma center.

"Correct," Charlie answered. "As I understand it, the neighbors worked on the victim for quite a while before the ambulance
arrived. I'm surprised he made it, if you want to know the truth.
He lost a significant amount of blood. My estimate—and don't
quote me on this until I do the math—is maybe two liters."

Sara let the information settle. If Charlie was right, Jared had
suffered a Class III hemorrhage, losing thirty to forty percent of
his blood volume. The cascade of respiratory distress and organ
failure were second and third only to severe tachycardia. If not for
his neighbors physically pumping Jared's heart, Sara would've
met Nell at the funeral home this morning instead of the hospital.

And that didn't even take into account the severity of the
wounds that had caused the bleeding in the first place.

"Hello," Nell said. Plastic shopping bag handles cut into her
hands, but she shook her head when Sara offered to take some.
She told Charlie, "I'm Darnell Long, Jared's mama."

"Charlie Reed," he answered. "I work for the state. I'm so sorry
about your son, Mrs. Long. I know he's in capable hands."

"The Lord never puts more on us than we can bear."

Charlie clasped his hands together. " 'He who follows Me shall never walk in darkness.' "

Nell seemed surprised to hear the man quoting from the Bible. Sara felt the same. Charlie had never struck her as a churchgoer. Then again, he was born in the South, where babies drank Scripture with their mother's milk.

"I should get back to work." Charlie's smile said he was pleased with their reactions. "If you'll excuse me, ladies." He headed back to his van.

"Well," Nell said, watching Charlie leave. Sara was beginning to understand that there was a certain amount of judgment in the word, which Nell had first uttered when she'd seen the packed parking lot of the strip club beside the dollar store.

She asked Sara, "What's with that mustache?"

"Charlie's one of the top forensics experts in the state. And very nice. He cares about what he does."

"Well." Nell didn't say anything else. She headed up the driveway. The bags were heavy. Sara could see the crisscross of the handles cutting off the circulation to her fingers.

She asked, "Are you sure you don't want me to help with those?"

"I've got it, thank you." Still, Nell grunted as she made her way up the last part of the driveway.

Jared's police bike was parked in front of the garage. The floodlight above the door was still on. Sara looked back at the street. There was no mistaking that a police officer lived here. Even in the dark of night, the light would've put the bike on display.

Nell asked, "What do we do about this?" Police tape was draped across the door, but Charlie had yet to seal the house.

"They've got more," Sara told her, pulling the tape down. She didn't open the door yet. "Nell, I need to tell you again that this is a bad idea. It's going to be so much worse than you're thinking.

There was a violent fight. Jared lost a lot of blood. It'll be on the floor, on the walls, on every surface. It's a biohazard. Medical waste has to be properly disposed of. You really need to leave this to the professionals."

Nell hefted the bags. "I think I know how to clean up a mess."

"I can let you borrow the money. Or give it to you. I don't care which—"

"No," Nell said, her tone making it clear that she was finished discussing the matter. "Thank you."

She stood waiting. Finally, Sara turned the knob, pushed open the door.

There was a distinctive odor that could be found at all crime scenes—not the metallic scent of blood that came from the oxidation of iron, but the stench of fear. Sara had always been a firm believer in intuition. There was a baser part of the human brain that cued every living being to danger. That part became fully engaged the minute Sara walked through the front door of Lena and Jared's home.

A man had died here. Two men had almost been killed. A woman had fought for her life. The threat of violence lingered in the stale air.

Sara watched Nell take it all in. Her posture changed. She nearly dropped some of the bags. Sara suggested, "Why don't you sit down?"

"I'm all right."

"Let's sit down."

Nell shook her head. She looked around the front room of the house. The floor plan was open, with a combined family room and kitchen. Sunlight streamed in through the windows. The ceiling fan over the couch gave a soft whine as the blades moved. Nothing bad had happened in this space. The furniture was not overturned. The walls were a muted light gray. The only area in disarray was the kitchen, which was obviously being remodeled. Flat packs of unassembled cabinets were stacked in a neat pile.

The kitchen sink was a bucket resting on an old washstand. The dishwasher was in the corner, the cord and drain hose wrapped around it like a bow. The stove was pulled away from the wall, but Sara could see the gas line was still attached.

Without thinking, she said, "He's just as bad as Jeffrey."

Jeffrey always had to have some sort of project going. Restoring an old car. Adding a second sink in the bathroom. Redoing his kitchen. Fixing things gave him a sense of accomplishment, if not completion. When he was dating Sara, a thick plastic sheet served as the outside wall to his kitchen. The refrigerator was in the dining room. A garden hose ran through the front window and attached through various valves to the ice maker.

Nell said, "Jeffrey always liked working with his hands." She set the bags down on the countertop, which was a piece of plywood on some two-by-fours. She ran her finger along the wood. Her eyes traveled to the sink bucket, the bare but cleanly swept floor. "I guess I can't fault her housekeeping. There's no way Jared cleaned up like this."

Sara didn't answer. Lena had always been neat. Her desk at the station looked like something out of an office supply catalogue.

"I'll get his daddy in here to finish this up." Nell nodded toward the stacked boxes. "Possum'll get those assembled in a day. I'll help him hang the top cabinets. He can do the bottom on his own. I don't guess they have a countertop, but we'll pick something out that—" She stopped talking. Sara followed her gaze to the couch. There was a pillow with a sheet neatly folded on the top. On the coffee table beside the remote were a pair of glasses, a glass of water, and a plastic case for a retainer.

"Hello?" Faith Mitchell walked through the open front door. She'd already met Nell and Possum at the hospital. Sara had made the introductions.

Faith asked, "You just get here?"

"Yes, ma'am." Nell wouldn't take her eyes off the couch. Faith seemed to note the arrangement, but made no comment. She

smiled at Sara in a way that let her know there was enough dis-
comfort to go around.

Sara said, "We saw Charlie."

"He's still packing up the van."

Nell noisily started unpacking the bags, banging the bottle of
bleach and box of gloves down on the plywood counter.

Faith walked around the front room, picking up items, obviously trying to get a feel for the place. Will's partner was one year
his junior, but she'd come up through the Atlanta police force before joining the GBI and was equal parts pragmatic and cynical.
Sara could not have wished for a better agent to back up Will.
Faith was clever and competent. She hated taking risks. In other
words, she was the complete opposite of Lena Adams.

She was also nosy as hell. She walked around the room with a
judgmental air, taking in the curtains and furnishings with the
same sharp eye as Nell.

Sara felt slow on the uptake. Nell wasn't just here to clean.
Lena was pushing her out of Jared's hospital room, so Nell was
invading Lena's home.

Nell had finished unpacking the bags. She braced her hands on
the wooden counter. "I should probably look at it first."

There was no use arguing with her. Nell was obviously determined to keep moving forward. Sara and Faith silently followed
her toward the hallway.

Nell didn't get far. She stopped just outside the guest bathroom. The shower curtain was pulled back. A dirty sliver of soap
was beside a bottle of Axe shampoo. The seat was up on the toilet. The counter was cluttered with men's toiletries—deodorant, a
razor and shaving cream, a toothbrush that needed replacing and
a half-empty tube of toothpaste. Little hairs filled the sink where
Jared had shaved and failed to wash out the bowl.

Nell continued down the hall, mumbling, "I guess she kicked
him out of the bathroom, too."

Faith mumbled in an equally low voice, "You couldn't pay me to share my bathroom with a man."

"Amen," Sara answered as she trailed Nell down the hallway. She stepped over a white chalk outline on the floor where Charlie had taken some DNA. Sara guessed from the look of it that someone had spat in the hall, probably to make a point.

Which further supported the idea that the shooters hadn't randomly chosen their victims.

There was a spare bedroom on either side of the hall. The first one was being used as an office. The second appeared to be another unfinished project. The walls were a cheery yellow. The closet door was propped up on two sawhorses. Nell shook her head as she passed by, probably adding it to the list of Possum's chores. She stopped a few feet from the master bedroom.

Sara heard Nell draw in a sharp breath. The woman's hands shook as she grabbed the doorframe.

Charlie's estimate may have been too conservative. Despite the passage of time, the pool of blood where Jared had fallen was still congealing. Light glimmered on the wet surface. The edges had curdled into a dark rust that seeped into the hardwood floor.

The rest of the blood had dried hours ago, leaving burgundy stains that told the story of violent altercation. The ceiling and walls weren't the worst of it. Large boot prints mixed with Lena's bare footprints back and forth across the floor. Splatter. Spatter. Spray. Drops. Knee prints. Handprints. Smears where an area rug must've gotten bunched up beneath Jared's body. Tracks that showed where someone had crawled toward the bed. Still more shoe prints indicated where the neighbors and first responders rushed in to work on Jared. They must have all been covered in blood by the time they left. Long trails of red even managed to seep into the grout lines in the bathroom floor.

But the area around the door to the bedroom told the real story. This was where Jared had been shot. This was where Lena had first taken on the intruders. The dried blood splattering and spattering the walls and ceiling could fill a forensic textbook. They varied in size and shape, in coverage and scope, and would help map out every second of what had obviously been an extremely violent struggle. Even with the pieces of tooth and bone gone, the hammer and weapons taken into evidence, the shadow of death lurked in every corner.

Nell's voice caught. "I can't . . . I don't know what . . ."

Sara didn't say anything.

Nell sniffed, but no tears came. "Do you think a wet-vac would . . ." Her voice trailed off again. Her grip tightened on the splintered wood around the door.

Sara looked at Faith, who just shook her head.

"All right." Nell thrust herself into the room. She picked her way toward the dresser. Though she was careful, there was no way to avoid the carnage. Her sneakers walked across dried footprints. Boot prints. Shoe prints. Handprints.

Her voice came out at a higher pitch. "Jared's always been more comfortable in his pajamas." She started opening drawers, which had presumably been photographed and inventoried by Charlie's team. "No self-respecting man sits around in a hospital gown. I know he'll want to put on something normal as soon as possible."

Sara stood outside the door with Faith. They both silently watched the woman riffle Lena and Jared's private things. The top three drawers obviously belonged to Lena. Her underthings were mostly utilitarian, though Nell managed to make a huffing sound when she found something that crossed the line. The bottom drawers belonged to Jared. They were filled with basketball shorts, T-shirts, and boxers. He wore a uniform eighty percent of his day. He probably had one suit in the closet for weddings and funerals and a couple of polos and khakis for less formal occasions.

Nell stopped her search. She rested her hands on her hips as she looked around the room. "I know he hasn't stopped wearing pajamas."

Sara kept her mouth shut right up until Nell made her way to the bedside table. "Nell."

She looked up, but kept her hand on the drawer pull.

"That's probably Lena's." Sara indicated the flattened book, which was clearly a romance novel, beside the hand lotion and tube of lip balm.

When Nell didn't move, Faith said, "You probably don't want to know what your son's wife keeps in her bedside table." She added, "Or your son, for that matter."

"What on earth does that—"

She was cut off by the sound of motorcycle engines. Sara turned around. The front door was wide open. She saw at least six motormen in the street. If Sara knew cops, they'd come here to look after Jared's mother. And just in time, too.

Faith seized on the opportunity, suggesting to Nell, "Why don't you go talk to Jared's friends? I'm sure they want to know how he's doing."

"I don't have time to be everybody's mama," Nell grumbled, but she stomped out of the room anyway.

"Man." Faith waited until Nell was out of earshot. "That woman has a razor for a mouth."

Sara kept her own counsel. "Did you talk to Charlie?"

"He briefed me earlier." Faith looked back at the bedroom. "Nell's gonna get a call in a few minutes from the hospital. Jared's fever is up."

"He has an infection?"

"That's what the nurse said."

Nurses were seldom wrong about these things. Sara thought of Nell's steely determination, all the plans she'd made in the last few hours for when Jared finally woke up. "I don't think she'll make it if he dies."

"It's always the strong ones who break the hardest."

Sara tucked her chin to her chest.

Faith entered the room, walking across the dried blood with a cop's impunity. "I guess I should look for those pajamas. Maybe that'll make her feel like she's helping him."

"Maybe." Sara leaned against the doorjamb as Faith searched the closet. She stared at the footprints scattered across the floor. The blood was so dry that it had skeletonized, but Charlie had been careful. Sara could still track the progress. It helped that Lena had such small feet. Sara always forgot how petite she was, barely five-four and probably one-ten on a heavy day.

Charlie Reed had said that four initial responders came from the neighborhood. Judging by the bloody prints on the floor, they had each waited by the bathroom door as the others took turns working on Jared. That left the two sets of boot prints to the assailants. They had both sported the cowboy variety, with flat plastic soles that left distinct exclamation points in the blood. One had a skull and crossbones carved into each heel. The other pair was an off brand with a generic set of furrows. Both of the attackers pronated, probably from riding motorcycles.

But that didn't account for all of the prints.

Sara walked over to the bed. She knelt down, asking Faith, "Two attackers, right?"

Faith's voice was muffled as she dug around the closet shelves. "That's right."

"Four responders?"

"Uhhh . . ." She drew out the word. "Yep. Two cops, an off-duty paramedic, and a chick with the fire department."

"What about this?"

Faith turned around.

Sara pointed to a shoe print right up against Jared's bedside table. This one was also from a boot, but it was larger than the other two and the heel had the distinctive logo of a Cat's Paw no-slip rubber sole.

Faith turned back to the closet. She didn't seem interested. "I'm sure Charlie got it."

"But look at the prints. Lena was barefooted. The attackers wore cowboy boots." She pointed to the other prints. "Two of the neighbors wore sneakers, the third one probably had on bedroom slippers, and the fourth one was wearing socks."

Faith pulled a couple of pairs of sweatpants off the shelf. She added a T-shirt from the dirty-clothes basket. "These can pass for pajamas, right?"

Slowly, Sara stood up. "Aren't you concerned that a third assailant might've been here last night?"

"Are you saying that I'm not doing my job?"

"No." Sara felt properly chastened. "No, of course not."

"You're forgetting the EMTs." Faith counted it off on her fingers. "Three crews, right? Jared was taken out first. The second shooter was next, the first was taken to the morgue, so that's six more guys at least, which is twelve more possibilities for prints. And God only knows who traipsed in here from Macon PD."

"Charlie told me the cops from the 911 call stayed out of the bedroom."

"Really?" Faith didn't sound happy, but Sara kept talking.

"He also said that the first ambulance took a while to get here. The extraneous blood would've been dry in five, ten minutes tops. So unless an EMT purposely stepped in the pool of blood around Jared, then walked over here, there's no way that any of them could've made this third print." Sara put a finer point on it. "Whoever left this boot print was here when the crime occurred."

"That's where the second assailant fell," Faith said, her voice straining to sound reasonable. "I'm sure one of the first EMTs checked on him. Right? They wouldn't just rush in, see one body, and leave the other two without checking on them."

"The EMTs were most likely in 5.11 Tacticals." Sara was familiar with the boots, which were specifically designed for paramedics and firefighters. "And even without that, the blood was obviously dry by the time they got here. You don't see any other prints from the EMTs, do you? Not even around Jared."

Faith gave a heavy sigh. "There was a lot going on in this room last night. There's no telling where that print came from. All right?"

Sara nodded, but only to keep the peace. It was absolutely possible, even probable, that one of the EMTs had checked on the second assailant before leaving the house. But there was no way in hell he'd stood over the body and leaned down to do it. The EMT would be on his knees as he ran vitals. Unless he was a contortionist, there was no reason for him to wedge his foot against the bedside table.

"Look." Faith closed the closet door. "I know you're good at this, Sara, but this is Charlie's scene. He's been here practically from the minute Jared was carried out. Maybe it's Charlie's shoe that made the print, or one of his guys. Or maybe he's tracked it back to an EMT who tripped or stepped where he should'nt've or whatever. Charlie will do all the rule-outs and trace it back to someone. You know the process. No stone unturned."

"You're right," Sara agreed, but she had seen Faith lie enough to know what it looked like. Obviously, something else was going on.

Faith said, "Come on. Let's see if my plan worked." She left the room.

Sara assumed she was supposed to follow. She took one last look at the boot print before heading back up the hallway. Her medical examiner's mind wouldn't shut off just because she hadn't done the job in years. The Cat's Paw logo said a lot about the owner of the boot. He was frugal, the type of person who would resole a shoe rather than throw it out. Going by the size, he was at least six feet tall or more. He worked in a job that required a nonconducting, nonslip sole—probably a mechanic or electrician or builder. Analysis would show if there was any oil or residue trans-

ferred from the porous rubber sole. Known associates of the assailants could be narrowed down from there. Barring that, a
simple phone call to the shoe repair stores in the area could easily
generate a list of customers who'd purchased Cat's Paw soles.

Which was probably what someone on Charlie's team was
doing right now.

Faith was right. Charlie was very good at his job. So was Faith,
for that matter. If they were hiding something, it was probably for
a good reason. As much as Sara felt otherwise, she had to keep
reminding herself that she was firmly on the outside looking in.

Faith stood at the open front door. In the street, the motormen
had surrounded Nell in a protective huddle. They all seemed relaxed and talkative. Sara was sure they were telling Nell stories of
Jared's many exploits. Whether or not they were true didn't matter. There was no better liar than a cop spinning a yarn.

"I'm shocked they listened to me," Faith admitted. "I told them
to take up donations for the cleaning service. I figured even old
Razor Mouth wouldn't be rude enough to say no."

Sara laughed despite herself. "That's pretty smart."

"One of Amanda's tricks—but don't tell her I'm using it. People think they're gonna be judged if they hire someone else to
clean up their mess. I think it's a southern thing." She walked back
to the kitchen. "I'll see if I can get them to pitch in and finish the
kitchen, too. Jesus, I woulda killed him myself if I had to wash
dishes out of a bucket."

"It's not as bad as it looks," Sara pointed out. The bucket had
a hole in the bottom that led to the drain. A garden hose was
threaded to the faucet to extend the reach. It was exactly the kind
of thing that Jeffrey would've done—completely rigged yet un-
questionably functional.

By contrast, Will would've been horrified by the contraption.
He shared a lot of qualities with Jeffrey, but he would not rest
until a project was not just finished, but finished right. Or at least
the way he felt was right. It drove Will crazy that the builder who'd

worked on Sara's apartment hadn't painted the top edges of all the doors.

"Do me a favor?" Faith was rummaging through the stack of mail on the kitchen table. "Check to see if Nell's still outside."

Sara stood on the tips of her toes to see down the hill. Nell was still talking to the cops. "Yes. Why?"

Faith ripped open one of the envelopes.

"Isn't that illegal?"

"Only if I get caught." Her eyes skimmed what looked like an invoice. "Jared opened it, right? Only he can't remember because of his head injury."

"That's inviting some bad karma."

"And it wasn't even worth it." Faith folded the invoice. "You'll be pleased to know that Lena's Pap smear was normal." She tucked the paper back into the envelope. "I should go tell Nell about Jared. The doctor should've called by now."

"Wait." Sara said, "I know it's not likely to come up, but Nell doesn't know about Will. I mean, me and Will. Together." She felt her heart start to jump, like she was telling a fib to her mother. "I'd like to keep it that way."

If Faith was surprised, she didn't show it. "Okay. I won't say anything."

Sara felt compelled to give an explanation. "It's just that Will's still legally married and . . ." She let her voice trail off. There was no reason to lie. "They just loved Jeffrey so much. They wouldn't understand how I was able to move on." Sara paused. "Sometimes, I wonder how I did it myself."

"I'm glad you did." Faith leaned against the table. "Will loves you, you know? I mean, crazy love. He was never this way with Angie. From the day he met you, his feet stopped touching the ground."

Sara smiled, though the last thing she wanted to think about right now was Will's elusive wife.

Faith said, "Seriously, I've never seen him like this before. You've changed him. You've made him—" She shrugged, as if she couldn't quite believe it. "Happy."

Unreasonably, Sara felt tears well into her eyes. "He's made me happy, too."

"Then that's all that matters." Faith wriggled her eyebrows. " 'This, too, shall pass.' "

Sara wiped her eyes. "There's been an alarming number of people quoting Bible verses at me today."

"My mother got my name from the Bible. I'm supposed to be the substance of things hoped for. Talk about wishful thinking." Faith pushed away from the table. "I really should get Nell. How bad is an infection at this stage?"

"They'll probably bring in somebody from the CDC." The Centers for Disease Control had a dedicated team serving the Atlanta area. "It's good that we're close."

"That doesn't sound cheerful."

"No," Sara admitted. "Infections are unpredictable. People respond differently to treatment. No two patients have the same outcome. If the infection is somewhere like his heart or his brain, then the odds are low he'll survive, and even then, it's a tough recovery." She felt the need to add, "But he's young and otherwise healthy. That counts for a lot."

"Shit, here she comes." Faith waited for Nell to make her way up the porch steps. She had a FedEx padded mailer in one hand and a small envelope in the other.

"I guess you'll get your wish." Nell tucked the envelope into her back pocket. "They say they take up a collection when stuff like this happens. I didn't want to be rude, but it's not like I'm an invalid." Her words were hard, but Sara could see the relief on Nell's face. The deep lines had smoothed from her forehead. Some of the tension was gone from her jaw. "They're nice boys. I shouldn't complain."

Faith said, "They feel as helpless as you do, Mrs. Long. Doing something for you, even something that you're capable of doing on your own, makes them feel better."

"I suppose," Nell admitted. She held up the FedEx mailer. The word PERSONAL was written across the back in red marker. "The delivery guy dropped this off while we were in the street. It's addressed to Lena. Says it's personal. I didn't know if I should open it or not."

"Is there a return address?" Faith sounded disinterested, though Sara knew better.

Nell squinted at the label. "It's all smeared. Should I open it?"

Faith's shrug was almost believable. "If you want. It might be something Lena needs."

Nell guffawed. "They say the same thing here as in Alabama—you can piss on my face, but don't tell me it's raining?"

Faith's smile showed her teeth.

"That's what I thought." Nell went to the kitchen and retrieved her purse from the counter. Sara wasn't surprised when she pulled out a large utility knife, but Faith obviously was. Her eyebrows shot straight up.

"Let's see what personal thing we got here." Nell sliced open the top of the padded mailer. She peered inside the envelope, her eyes narrowed as if she wasn't quite sure what she was seeing.

Sara asked, "What is it?"

Nell reached into the package. "I don't—"

The mailer dropped to the floor.

Nell held up a tiny jacket, the sort of thing you'd buy for a baby. It was dark blue with orange piping down the sleeves and an Auburn University logo across the back.

Her lips parted in surprise. She looked at Sara, then Faith, then down at the little jacket again. She cupped the hoodie sewn into the back of the collar.

Wordlessly, Nell ran into the hallway, her shoulder catching the corner. Sara was close on her heels as Nell entered the spare bedroom.

"He didn't—" Nell's voice caught. She stood in the middle of the room, the jacket gripped tightly in her hands. "How could he not—" A strangled cry came out of her mouth. She buried her face in the small jacket. "Oh, God."

Faith came up behind Sara. Her mouth was set. Guilt virtually radiated off her skin.

"This is a nursery," Nell whispered, clutching the jacket to her chest. "He was working on a nursery." Her fingers traced the back of the closet door. The outline of several balloons had been drawn with a pencil. Cans of brightly colored paint were on the floor. There were art brushes and sponges and trays to hold the paint.

Nell stared at Faith. Her tone was deadly sharp. "You knew."

Faith didn't bother to lie this time.

A phone started ringing. Nell checked her pocket for her cell phone. Her voice shook as she answered, "Possum, what is it? I'm busy now." She listened, nodding a few times before she closed the phone and put it back in her pocket. "Jared's got an infection." Her tone was matter-of-fact. "They say I need to get back up there."

"I'll drive you," Sara offered.

"No." Nell held the baby's jacket against her chest. "I need some time alone, all right? Can you drive her back?" She was talking to Faith. "I just need some time, okay?"

Nell didn't wait for an answer. She left the room. All the air seemed to go with her.

Faith let out a long sigh. "That was awful."

Sara said nothing.

Faith studied her carefully. "Sara?"

Sara shook her head as she took in the nursery, the way the light from the windows fell across the floor. The yellow walls were cheery and warm. She could imagine sheers hanging in the windows, a summer breeze rustling the edges. Balloons would be painted around the walls to match the closet door. The jacket would hang on a tiny plastic hanger—something colorful to match the décor. The hoodie wasn't sized for a newborn, but at three to six months, Lena's baby would be big enough to wear it.

Faith said, "I'm sorry I didn't tell you."

Sara could only keep shaking her head. She didn't trust herself to speak.

One of the last things that Sara and Jeffrey had planned together was adopting a baby. Sara couldn't have children of her own. It had taken years for her and Jeffrey to be in the same place about adoption, to decide that they were ready to raise a child together.

Then Jeffrey had died, and Sara had come completely undone. The adoption agency returned their application. At the time, Sara barely registered the rejection. She'd been incapable of taking care of herself, let alone a baby.

"Sara?" Faith asked. "Will you please say something?"

Acid filled Sara's mouth.

It wasn't fair.

That's what Sara wanted to say. To scream at the top of her lungs.

It just wasn't fair.

Lena wasn't strong. She would bend, not break. She would recover from this tragedy the same easy way she recovered from every other tragedy before.

Even if she lost Jared, Lena would always know what it felt like to have his child growing inside of her. She could always hold her baby's hand and think of holding Jared's. She could see her child laugh and learn and grow and play sports and do school projects and graduate from college and Lena would always, always remember her husband. She would see Jared in her grandchildren and great-grandchildren. On her deathbed, she would find peace

in the knowledge that they had made something beautiful together. That even in death, they would both go on living.

"Sara," Faith said. "What's happening here?"

Sara wiped her eyes, angry that she was back in the same dark
place she'd started at this morning. "Why does everything come
so damn easy to her?" She struggled to speak. Her throat clenched
around every word that wanted to come out of her mouth. "Everything just opens up, and she always walks through unscathed
and—" Sara had to stop for breath. "It's just so easy for her. She
always has it so goddamn easy."

Faith indicated the door. "Come on."

Sara couldn't move.

"Let's go." Faith took Sara by the arm and led her out of the
room. Sara thought they were leaving the house, but Faith stopped
at the kitchen table. She held up the envelope she'd opened before.

Sara didn't take it. "I don't care about her Pap smear."

"Look who it's from."

Sara scanned the return address. Macon Medical Center.
Driscoll Benedict, OB-GYN. "So?"

Faith opened the envelope, unfolded the doctor's invoice. She
held it up for Sara to see. The treatment date was ten days ago.
The amount was zeroed out with the advisory that the hospital
would bill Lena separately for her emergency room visit.

Across the bottom, someone had written, "God bless you both.
You are in our prayers."

Sara took the invoice from Faith. Her knees felt weak. She sat
down at the table. Even without the note of condolence, she recognized the medical billing code.

Lena had lost the baby.

9.

Will rode his motorcycle down a neglected state highway, his head rotating like a gun turret. While there was the occasional eighteen-wheeler on the back roads, it was the deer he was most worried about. Less than ten minutes ago, Will had seen a buck dart right out in front of him. The creature was magnificent. There was no other word for it. Muscles rippled along his chest and back. His spindly legs were like a ballerina's. His antlers were branched like a tree. The animal hadn't even bothered to look Will's way, which was good because Will would've been humiliated if any living creature had seen the look of sheer terror on his face. He did not need a mathematician to calculate the odds of survival when a speeding motorcycle slammed into a speeding deer. The coroner would've spent the rest of his days picking pieces of Will out of the buck's rib cage.

He supposed there were all sorts of wild animals living close to Atlanta, but the possibility seemed remote when you stood amidst the skyscrapers, watching buses and cars and trains zoom by.

One of the most startling things Will had found in Macon was not the wildlife, but the divide between rich and poor. In Atlanta, Will's modest house was only a few blocks from Sara's penthouse apartment, which in turn was not far from a methadone clinic.

Macon didn't really have a literal wrong side of the tracks, but a meandering avenue skirting the city limits seemed to be the point at which the carpet ran out. Old mansions gave way to cottages, which gave onto clapboard houses and derelict trailer parks and, eventually, unpainted shacks. Working cases around the state, Will had seen his share of poverty, but there was something particularly depressing about fresh laundry hanging outside a structure that looked as if it didn't even have running water.

Will slowed the bike. He squinted up the road, checking for loose deer. Closer proximity revealed a yellow Volkswagen Bug—not the new kind that looked like something George Jetson would drive, but the older model that emitted a sound like a child blowing a raspberry. There were bumper stickers all over the back. The blinkers were flashing in lieu of brake lights. Will downshifted another gear. The Bug swung into the oncoming traffic lane, doing a sharp U-turn toward a row of mailboxes on a strip of dirt. A hand went out, a mailbox was checked, then the Bug swung another heavy U-turn that would've provided a nice ramp for Will's bike if he hadn't been paying attention.

He shifted the gear down another notch and pulled over opposite the mailboxes. He checked the time on his cell phone. Will had given himself almost an hour to make what was supposed to be a twenty-minute journey. He wasn't good with directions, and a phone that told you to go left or right was not exactly helpful to the average dyslexic. Also, he felt mired in a quicksand of guilt. Sara wasn't happy with him being undercover. She sure as hell wouldn't be happy with the prospect of Will going on a date. Not that he was technically dating Cayla Martin, but the fact that the nurse seemed to think so gave the exercise an air of uncomfortable legitimacy.

After talking with Faith, Will had decided that it was time to confront the Big Whitey of it all. He'd spent nearly an hour looking for Tony Dell. Cayla Martin seemed like a good fallback plan. The nurse was much easier—in more ways than one. Will was eating his lunch in the cafeteria when a furtive hand slid a note under his tray. The move was practiced. No one seemed to notice. Will wanted to believe he rose to the occasion, discreetly tucking the note into his pocket like Aldrich Ames. Though Will was pretty sure the master spy hadn't read his missives while hiding in a toilet stall.

7 p.m.—Left off exit 12, right on dirt road. Only house with lights on. Don't be late!!

Cayla had put a smiley face under the exclamation points, which served to heighten Will's guilt. He left smiley faces for Sara sometimes. He texted them to her. She texted them back. Once, when they were fooling around, she kissed them all over his stomach.

Will let out a long, pained sigh as he got off the bike.

He pulled up the telephone keypad on his iPhone. He dialed in the twelve-digit code to access the secret apps. The screen flashed up quickly, so he had his finger ready to select the number-cloaking program. The app opened. He dialed in a ten-digit number.

The edge of the phone bumped his helmet. Will undid the strap and hooked it on the handlebars. Four unusually long rings passed before Sara answered. In the background, Will heard a piano playing and the soft murmur of conversation.

Instead of saying hello, Sara asked, "Brunswick?"

Will guessed the cloaking app had done its job. "Not exactly." He tried to identify the background noise, which sounded more like a bar than a hospital. "Where are you?"

"Where am I?" Her drawl was more pronounced, which tended to happen when she got away from the city. "I am drinking a glass of scotch at the hotel bar of the Macon Days Inn."

Will immediately thought of all the scumbugs who were probably trying to hit on her. He worked to keep his cool. "Yeah?"

"Yep." She hit the *p* hard at the end. Will thought about the shape of her mouth. The bowtie of her lips. And then he imagined some idiot in a gold necklace sidling up to her and asking if she wanted a refill.

He said, "That's not like you to be in a bar."

"No," Sara agreed. "But I'm doing a lot of things today that aren't like me."

Will couldn't decipher her tone. She didn't sound drunk, which was a relief. He'd never known Sara to be a drinker.

He offered, "I could probably get there around midnight, one at the latest."

"No, sweetheart. I don't want you anywhere near here."

Will felt a jolt of fear. Sara usually called him sweetheart when he was being dense. Had she figured out he was in Macon? Will ran through the possibilities, trying to find an area of weakness. Faith wouldn't tell—at least not without giving Will a warning. Denise Branson knew better, and even if she didn't, she had no idea who Sara was. Lena had promised to keep quiet, but what kind of idiot trusted a woman who killed a man with a hammer, then lied about what came next?

"Will?"

He swallowed back his paranoia. One thing he knew about Sara was that she didn't play games. If his cover was blown, she'd be demanding an explanation, not listening to piano music in a bar.

He asked, "How's Jared doing?"

"Not good." She paused to take a drink. Will heard the glass hit the bar when she finished. "One of his surgical incisions turned septic. He went into shock. They've got a guy from the CDC running the case. He knows what he's doing, but—" She stopped. "Lena was pregnant. She lost the baby ten days ago."

He still couldn't decipher the edge in her tone. Sara couldn't have children, but that didn't have anything to do with Lena. Will asked, "Does Faith know?"

"She was there. I basically lost my shit in front of her."

Will looked at his bike. He should turn around right now and go see her. The Days Inn was just off the interstate, less than half an hour away.

Sara said, "Faith was very nice about it. I guess if you're going to lose your shit, she's a good person to do it around."

"Yeah." Will heard a semi barreling down the road, the lights slicing through the dusk. The noise of the engine vibrated the air, cut out whatever Sara was saying.

He asked, "What?"

"Doesn't matter." He heard the tinkle of ice cubes, her throat work as she swallowed. "Are you sitting on the side of the road?"

"I wanted to check on you. You were pretty upset this morning."

"Well, I'm pretty upset tonight," she quipped. "You know, my daddy told me a long time ago that wanting revenge is like sipping poison and waiting for the other person to die."

"Is that what you're doing?"

"I don't know." She paused again. "I feel like I've trespassed. Like I've stolen something from Lena. Something private that didn't belong to me." She gave a harsh laugh. "My pound of flesh isn't nearly as filling as I thought it'd be."

Will stared at the mailboxes. Numbers had been spray-painted on the doors in various colors by different hands. Someone had drawn a daisy on one box. Another had the Georgia Bulldogs logo.

Sara said, "I miss you."

Will had seen her less than twelve hours ago, but hearing the words made him realize that he ached for her. He tried to think of a way out of this mess. He should tell her that he was sorry for keeping secrets. That he was sorry he wasn't there right now. That he was a coward and a liar and he didn't deserve Sara but he was pretty sure he would fade away to nothing without her.

"Anyway." Abruptly, her tone changed. "Since one scotch is clearly my limit, I should go back to the hospital and sit with Nell.

I told her that Lena lost the baby. She already knew. I guess Lena told her. I don't know. She's not talking much. Of course, neither am I—at least not to Nell." Sara gave a stilted laugh. "I'm sorry I'm rambling. I'm just tired. I've been up since this time yesterday. I tried to sleep, but I couldn't."

"Are you going home tonight?" Will started to make plans. He'd finish with Cayla, then jump on his bike and head straight to Atlanta.

Sara quashed the idea. "I already booked a room for the night. The dogs will be fine, and I shouldn't be driving long distances right now."

"I could come get you." He tried not to beg. "Let me come get you."

"No." There was no equivocation in her voice. "I don't want you here, Will. I want you separate from this."

He felt trapped by his own lies. "I'm so sorry."

"I don't want you to be sorry." She paused again as if she needed to catch her breath. "I want you to keep doing whatever you're doing, wherever you're doing it, and then when it's over I want you to come back home to me and for us to have dinner and talk and laugh and then I want you to take me into the bedroom and—"

Another truck roared by, but Will heard every single pornographic detail she whispered into the phone.

Sara asked, "Can you do that?"

Will's tongue felt too thick for his mouth. He cleared his throat. "I can do all of that."

"Good, because that's what I need, Will. I need you to make me feel like I'm firmly planted in my life again. The life I have with you."

The piano music had stopped. Ice hit a glass. Someone laughed.

She said, "What we have is good, right?"

"Yes." At least on that point, he could give her a straight answer. "It's really good."

"That's what I think, too."

"Sara—" Will heard the desperation in his voice, but he couldn't think of anything to say but her name.

"I need to go."

"You don't have to."

"Just think about later, all right? Us at home, and what you want to eat for dinner, or maybe we'll go to a movie, or walk the dogs. Just live our lives. That's what I'm thinking about right now. That's what's getting me through this."

"We'll do it. We'll do all of it." He waited for her to say something else, but she ended the call.

Will stared down at the phone as if he could make Sara get back on the line. Not that he had any words of great comfort. If anything, Will had been too quiet on the call. He realized that now. He'd forced Sara to do most of the talking when it was obvious that she was waiting for Will to say something—anything—that would somehow bring her some peace.

He mumbled, "Idiot."

Will dialed the twelve-digit code again to access the app. He wasn't fast enough when the screen popped up. Will dialed the code again, but he stopped shy of the last two numbers.

He didn't know what to say to her. He wanted to go to her. He could be there in ten minutes if he blew through all the red lights. He would do everything she wanted him to and more.

And then she would ask him how he'd gotten there so fast.

Will had ten minutes to figure out how to tell her. Fifteen if traffic near the Days Inn was bad. He unhooked his helmet from the handlebars. A chunk of paint had been scraped off. He strapped the shorty on his head. Once he was on the bike, he turned the front wheel back the way he'd come.

He didn't have a choice anymore. The only thing to do after that call was go straight to the hotel, or the hospital, and sit down with Sara and tell her exactly what was going on. Faith was right— this was too close to the bone. What had started out as a small lie of omission had built up into a giant deceit that could take out their entire relationship.

Will wasn't going to have Sara drinking poison for him one day.

He gunned the bike as he headed back toward the interstate. He looked up at the darkening sky. The hotel was near an airport, so he could use the planes to make sure he was heading in the right direction. At least Will assumed that was the Days Inn Sara was talking about. The chain was big. There was probably more than one location in Macon.

He just happened to glance back down in time to notice a black pickup truck parked in the middle of the road. The oncoming lane was blocked by a white Honda. Will slowed the bike, wishing he had a horn. There was no way to pass on either side of the road—at least not without risking a slide down an embankment. Will let his boots scrape the ground as he stopped the bike.

"Hey!" Will shouted. "Get out of the way!"

"Hold your horses!" The pickup driver craned half his body out of the cab. Will recognized Tony's voice before he saw his face. "Damn, Bud, what're you doin' comin' from that way? Cayla's is down there."

He was pointing to a dirt road shooting off at a steep angle. Tall trees obscured the entrance. There was no sign, no marker to indicate that this was anything but a dirt track. Will would've never been able to find it, and Cayla had played this game well enough to know she was better off giving a man an address he had to locate rather than a phone number he could use to cancel.

"Come on." Tony waved for Will to follow him.

Will revved the bike, pretending he wasn't checking out the driver in the white Honda. He saw the top of a head, dark wavy hair and a high forehead, as the window snicked up.

Tony turned onto the dirt road. His radio was loud enough for the melody to make its way back to Will. Lynyrd Skynyrd. "Free Bird." Not much of a surprise.

Will hung back from the truck, which kicked up enough red

dust to suffocate an elephant. There was no way to get out of this now. Will would spend two hours at Cayla's, tops, then find Sara and do what he should've done in the first place.

She was probably on her way to the hospital. Will couldn't very well ambush her in front of her friends, and besides, what he needed to say to her should be said when they were alone. He would tell her at the hotel. They'd never been in a real fight before. He couldn't guess what Sara would do. Maybe she would throw things or cuss him like a dog. Then again, he'd never seen her throw anything out of anger and she seldom cursed, a by-product of working around children all day.

Maybe she would get really quiet, which she did when she was worried. Will hated when she got quiet. Though that might be better than the alternative. All he knew for certain was that he'd pretty much lie down in front of a speeding train to keep her from leaving him.

The back wheels of Tony's truck spun as he dipped into a rut. Will steered the bike away from the pothole, which was filled with muddy water. The dirt road thinned to a single lane. Will tried to take in his surroundings, but he could only see the outlines of a few houses. Day was completely giving over to night. Tony was too far ahead for his headlights to do Will any good. The man drove with his foot on the brake. The taillights turned the red road an icy black.

Will wondered if Tony was leading him to the middle of no-where to kill him. The man didn't seem capable of murder, but Will had been surprised before. Death generally didn't announce itself. He'd bet the forty-three-year-old entrepreneur who died on the toi-let last week wasn't planning on being found with his pants down.

A small lighted sign announced the entrance to a trailer park. Palm trees surrounded the flowing script announcing the com-pound's name. The place was well tended, obviously catering to families. Children's bicycles were stacked neatly in front of porches. All the trashcans had been collected from the road. Cars were parked evenly in their spaces. He could see the soft glow of televisions behind drawn curtains.

The road doubled up again as the trailer park disappeared in Will's side mirror. He squinted up ahead. Tony's hand was raised in the air. He was snapping his fingers to the music. George Michael's "I Want Your Sex." A song like that could get a man killed this far from civilization, but Will guessed Tony didn't care.

Suddenly, the dirt road gave onto a paved street. The bike kicked up. Luckily, Will wasn't going fast, otherwise he would've taken a vault over the handlebars.

Streetlights illuminated every inch of the paved surface. Foundations had been poured for hundreds of houses, but the builder had either run out of money or run out of town. Probably both. Plumbing pipes and drains stuck up from the poured slabs like toothpicks. Incongruously, some of the driveways had mailboxes but no houses. Others had weeds breaking through the white concrete sidewalks.

Cayla Martin's was one of four completed houses at the end of a cul-de-sac. Macon wasn't the only city in America that had its share of abandoned subdivisions, but Cayla's had a particular sadness about it. The lawn was overgrown with weeds. The one sad tree by the front door was bent and dying. No one had cared about this house from the very beginning. The trim paint was peeling where the wood had not been primed. Some of the windows had been installed crookedly. Even the front door had a strange tilt like no one had bothered to plumb it in. Will wondered if the builder was related to the lazy jackass who'd worked on Sara's apartment.

Tony Dell pulled into a short driveway, parking the truck behind a black Toyota. The door opened. Tony practically fell out of the truck. The F-250 was too big for him, like a kid clomping around in his daddy's shoes. Tony had the same jaunty gait as he approached Will in the semidarkness. "Damn, Bud, ain't your balls freezin' on that thing?"

Will shrugged, though the man was right about the cold. He nodded toward the truck. "Where'd you get that?"

"Borrowed it from a friend."

"Nice friend," Will noted. The truck was a considerable step up from Tony's impounded Kia.

"Hope you weren't plannin' nothin' romantic tonight." Tony tucked his hands into his pockets as he walked toward the house. "I kinda invited myself over. Cayla's gotta faucet been leakin' for a while, so I said I'd come by and fix it."

"She knows you're going to be here?"

"Sure," Tony said, but his voice went up a bit higher than honesty would dictate. "You get off work early?"

"Little bit." His boss was six months from retirement and had a lady on the side. Will was about to say something derogatory about Salemi's work habits, but then Tony Dell stood under the porch light and Will was rendered speechless.

The man had gotten the shit kicked out of him. There was no better description. His nose was sideways. Both eyes were bruised. A long, open gash on his cheek had been sewn shut with thick black stitches.

Tony smiled, despite the pain it must've caused. "Cop caught up with me."

"Vickery?" Will guessed. He'd joked about it with Faith before, but now that he saw Paul Vickery's handiwork, it wasn't funny. "What the hell happened?"

"We're cool, Bud." Tony held up his hands in defense. "I didn't tell him a damn thing. I think that ol' boy just needed to give somebody a beat-down. Coulda been you. Ended up bein' me."

Will couldn't believe the man's cavalier attitude. "You gonna file a report on him?"

He practically guffawed. "Shit, that's funny, Bud. Like they work for us or somethin'." He raised his hand to knock on the door. "Act like you invited me, all right?"

"Like—"

Cayla had a huge grin on her face when she opened the door. And then she saw Tony Dell and looked like she wanted to murder him. "What're you doin' here?"

"Bud invited me." He patted Will on the back. "Didn't you, Bud?"

Will mumbled, "Yeah."

Cayla didn't seem concerned that Tony had been beaten. She sneered at him, saying, "You sneaky little prick."

"Aw, don't be like that." Tony pushed himself into the house. He had to slither under Cayla's arm to do it.

For the first time since he'd met Tony Dell, Will was glad to have the little freak around. Cayla had obviously prepared for their date. Her makeup was so heavy that it clumped in the corners of her eyes. Her jeans cut her into two separate parts and her white lace blouse clearly showed the dark purple bra underneath. Even from the porch, Will could smell her perfume. He didn't know enough about these things to guess whether the scent was cheap or not, but going by how much she used, Will hoped she got a volume discount.

Tony made a show of sniffing the air. "Damn, girl, you smell pretty."

"Shut up, Tony. I told you not to talk to me that way." She gave Will a tightly coiled smile as she motioned him inside. "He's my brother."

"Stepbrother," Tony corrected. He winked at Will. "Not by blood."

Cayla groaned as she shut the door. "His daddy married my mama when we were in junior high. Ever since then, he's been a sticky turd I can't scrape off my shoe."

Tony's laugh said he took this as a compliment.

Will grunted, not out of any Bill Black response but because he was at a complete loss for words.

"You look nice," Cayla said, though Will had specifically dressed down for the occasion. His jeans were torn at the hem.

Van Buren Public Library
115 S. First Street Box 405
Van Buren, In. 46991

His blue Oxford shirt had been nice two years ago, but the collar was frayed. The black T-shirt he wore underneath had holes in the armpits.

"You wanna beer?" Cayla asked.

"I'm good." Will didn't drink or smoke, which presented a serious handicap as far as his con cred was concerned. "Maybe later."

Tony said, "I could do with a cold one."

"Then get your scrawny ass back in that truck and go get you one," Cayla suggested. Tony grumbled a response. They certainly talked to each other like brother and sister.

Will looked around the room as he waited out the argument. The house was clean if not tidy. Cayla liked her figurines. Large dolls in fancy dresses were on almost every available surface. Some were under glass like wheels of cheese. Others were on stands that helped them hold up umbrellas or push baby carriages. Cayla had decorated everything in pastels, mostly pinks and blues. A large flat-screen television took pride of place across from a baby blue sectional sofa.

The fight was over. Or at least Tony seemed to think so. He hurdled the back of the sofa and plopped down in front of the set. "We gonna eat out here? I think the game's coming on."

"You can eat out here by your damn self." Cayla motioned for Will to follow her, telling him, "Just so you know next time, I prefer it's just me and you."

Will grunted as he trailed her into the kitchen. The house was choppy, which was strange for a new build. The wall bisecting the kitchen and family room looked taped into place. The saloon doors in the middle weren't even on the same plane. At least an inch separated the top edges, like blocks in a game of Tetris.

"We can eat in here." Cayla held open one of the saloon doors.

Will glanced around the kitchen, which was small and crowded but smelled so good he felt his stomach start to weep. Even the stench of a cigarette burning in the ashtray couldn't hide the delicious aroma of fried chicken, biscuits, and some kind of sweet cobbler.

"You hungry?"

Will nodded. His mouth was too filled with drool to answer. Sara could do a lot of things, but she could not cook to save her life.

"I told you I gotta good scald on some chicken." Cayla took down a plate from the cabinet. There were pots warming on the stove. She picked up a spoon and started to fill the plate.

Will sat down at the table.

She asked, "You hear that cop's not doing good?"

Will didn't answer.

"Got an infection or something. Went into septic shock."

Will tried to keep her talking. "What's that mean?"

"Means he's got blood poisoning." She took her cigarette from the ashtray as she placed the heaping plate of food in front of Will. Fried chicken, green beans, black-eyed peas, mashed potatoes and gravy, and two biscuits perilously balanced on top.

She put the cigarette to her lips and inhaled deeply. "Sepsis happens a lot with surgeries. They got all those tubes going in and out of them. Bacteria gets into the bloodstream. The heart can't take it. Poison floods through the body, shuts it all down."

He noticed her grammar had suddenly improved. Cayla Martin seemed to have an accent for every occasion. "Sounds bad."

She took another long drag before stubbing out the cigarette. "Yeah, it can be. You want that beer now?"

Will nodded. "Is he going to make it?"

"The cop?" She was at the refrigerator. She looked back over her shoulder. Underneath all the makeup, Cayla Martin wasn't unattractive. She seemed to have that weird quality that made otherwise smart men do stupid things. "He might make it. He's young. Pretty strong. Why do you care?"

Will shrugged as he picked up his fork. "I don't."

The saloon doors opened. Tony eyed them suspiciously. His jealousy was like a lighthouse beacon scanning the room.

Cayla gave him a nasty look. "I thought you were watching the game."

"I bet you did." Tony walked into the kitchen with his hands clenched. He told Will, "I heard you were up there today. In the ICU."

Will took a big bite of peas. The bacon grease and salt caressed his taste buds.

Tony asked, "She recognize you?"

Will glanced at Cayla.

"It's all right." She popped open the beer and put the can in front of Will. "He tells me everything whether I wanna hear it or not."

"The cop," Tony pushed. He was just as changeable as his stepsister. Suddenly, he was sounding less like a nuisance and more like a criminal.

Will let some time pass before answering. "What about the cop?"

"She recognize you?"

"No." Will shoveled another mound of peas into his mouth. And because there was some space left in his cheeks, he crammed in half a biscuit to help soak up the grease.

Tony pulled back a chair from the table. He sat down a few feet away, arms crossed, legs spread. His injuries were more pronounced in the harsh kitchen light. The gash on his face would leave a bad scar.

Tony said, "That was smart thinking, Bud. Make sure she don't recognize you. Make sure we don't gotta problem."

Will struggled to swallow. "I don't know about you, but I don't have a problem."

Cayla laughed. Just as quickly, her expression turned dark. "What are you doing down here?"

Will turned around. There was a little boy standing in the

doorway. His hair was a mess. His pajamas were too big for his spindly body. He clutched a picture book to his chest. The material seemed a little young for him, but Will was hardly an expert.

"Shit," Cayla cursed. "What did I tell you about staying upstairs?"

The boy opened his mouth to speak, but she didn't let him answer.

"I told you you'd get hungry." She got up from the table to fix another plate. She introduced the kid to Will: "This'n's Benji, my sister's kid. Benji, this is Mr. Black."

"Her *real* sister," Tony amended. He pushed his chair back until it touched the counter. Benji wouldn't go near him. He took the long way around, sitting opposite Will with the book in his lap.

"Here." Cayla plopped down a plate that was considerably less generous than the portions she gave Will. She asked Tony, "I guess I gotta feed you, too?"

"Gimme one a them breasts." He grabbed at her, giggling like it was a game.

Cayla slapped away his hands. "Jesus, Tony." She turned back to the stove, muttering to herself.

Will looked at Benji, who was staring down at his lap. Will tried not to be too obvious as he studied the boy. He had a familiar look about him, like he expected at any moment that something bad was going to happen. His shoulders were rolled inward. He kept his head bowed. His ears practically rotated as he listened for a change in tone, an indication of danger. Will recognized the survival tactic. When adults got mad, kids usually ended up being collateral damage.

Will asked Benji, "Are you from Macon?"

Rather than answering, the kid looked at his aunt.

Cayla supplied, "Baton Rouge. At least that's where they were this last time. His mama's on the pipe. Can't break the habit. The po-po found 'em livin' in her car." She rested her hand on Benji's bony shoulder. Will would've missed the flinch if he hadn't been watching.

Cayla said, "I couldn't let 'em put Benji in a home again. Last time, he near about got killed. And I mean real killed, not just pushed around."

Will guessed Benji knew all of this, but he didn't like that the kid was hearing it again. He asked Benji, "How old are you?"

This time, he answered himself, showing Will nine fingers.

"What's that book you're reading?"

Benji held up the book. Will couldn't read the cursive letters, but the C at the beginning and the smiling monkey told him he was looking at Curious George. The book had obviously been read a lot. The pages were dog-eared. The cover was worn. Will wondered if something was wrong with the boy. "Which school do you go to?"

Benji returned the book to his lap. He stared down at his hands.

Cayla blew out a put-upon sigh. "What's gotten into you, child? Tell him where you go to school."

Benji's voice was squeaky. "I'm in Miss Ward's fourth-grade class at Barden Elementary School on Anderson Drive."

Will gave a low whistle, as if he was impressed. "That sounds like a nice school. Do you like it there?"

The boy's slender shoulders went up in a shrug.

"What's your favorite subject?"

He glanced at Cayla, but before she could answer for him, Benji said, "Math."

"I like math, too," Will said, which was actually true. Numbers had offered a respite, some sort of weird proof that despite Will's inability to read like the other kids, there was at least one thing he could do right.

"Fractions," Benji whispered. "My mom does them with me." He looked up at Will, his eyes moist with tears. The fluorescent bulbs made the corners glow. He looked so desperate that Will couldn't meet his gaze.

"Eat up, hon." Cayla pushed Benji's plate closer. She'd given him a spoonful of peas, a biscuit, and a chicken leg. The meal didn't seem like enough, but Benji didn't complain. He didn't start eating, either. He seemed to be waiting for permission.

Will picked up the large piece of fried chicken Cayla had smothered in gravy. She was right about her scalding skills. The crispy skin practically melted in his mouth. Too bad he wasn't hungry anymore.

Will had seen a lot of shell-shocked kids passing through the Atlanta Children's Home, but Benji was the loneliest child he'd ever shared a table with. He resonated at a different frequency. His movements were stilted. His expression was a mask of neutrality, but his eyes—there wasn't a nine-year-old on the planet who had yet mastered concealing the kind of pain Will read in Benji's eyes.

He missed his mother. She had obviously neglected him, likely abused him, but he still needed his mom. She'd helped him with his fractions. Maybe she'd worked on the rest of his homework, too. She'd undoubtedly moved him around a lot, staying one step ahead of child welfare services because even crack whores didn't want to admit that they were bad mothers.

Benji's lack of accent was the big giveaway. He'd probably never stayed one place long enough to pick one up. He sounded better educated than the three adults in the house. He had better table manners, too. He used his fork and knife to peel away the skin on the chicken leg.

Tony snorted. "Where'd you learn them airs, boy?"

"Leave him be," Cayla shot back. She moderated her tone as she asked Will, "You like working at the hospital?"

Will nodded and talked with his mouth full. "How long have you been there?"

"About five years," she answered, which was a lie. Cayla's tax records had her working part-time for several different doctors before landing the pharmacy job six months ago. Even then, she still rotated in and out of the offices on her off days, probably to help pay her DUI fine. And pay for a house with a mortgage that was so far underwater she could see China from her front porch.

She said, "The hospital's all right. I like the pharmacy hours. With Benji here, I've gotta be home when school's out."

Benji stiffened, as if he was surprised to hear the news.

"How long has he been living with you?" Will asked.

"This time?" She shrugged. "I guess a couple of weeks or so. Ain't that right, Benji?"

"A month," Benji told Will. He probably had a calendar in his head where he marked each day. His voice was quieter when he said, "They took me away a month ago."

Tony offered, "I been at the hospital a year. Can't say I like it. Cleaning up shit and puke all day. People treatin' me like I'm the help."

Cayla's face creased with an angry frown. "Then why don't you go back to Beaufort, with the rest of the Geechees?"

Will ignored her sharp tone, concentrating on her words. "Beaufort? That's where the Sea Islands are, right? Over in Carolina?"

Tony narrowed his eyes at Will. "Why you askin'?"

Will shrugged his shoulders. "I rode my bike through there a while back. Hit Charleston, Hilton Head. Made my way down to Savannah. Pretty coastline."

Cayla's lighter snapped as she lit another cigarette. "Yeah, well, Tony ain't from the pretty parts. He spent his summers livin' with his mama on the wrong side of Broad."

While Will wasn't surprised to learn that Tony was on the wrong side of anything, he was very curious about this new piece of information. The GBI had run an extensive background check on Anthony Dell. He was born just outside of Macon. His records had him living in the area all of his life, but there would be no mention in the files of where Tony spent his school vacations.

Will asked Tony, "You ever been to Hilton Head?"

Instead of answering, Tony just stared at Will. Suspicion oozed out of every pore.

Will stared back, wondering how far he should push it. Big Whitey had been tracked through both Hilton Head and Savannah. Tony had probably been hearing about the man for years. It suddenly made sense why he was so desperate to be part of the action. Little guys always wanted to run with the big dogs.

Cayla supplied, "Tony spent a coupla three summers on Hilton Head." She arched an eyebrow at Tony. "His mama was a waitress when she wasn't spreadin' her legs for rent money."

Tony's face soured, but he didn't contradict her.

Cayla continued, "She hopped around all the dive bars, worked until they got tired of her or realized she was stealing too much." She took another hit from the cigarette. "Tony lived with her every summer since he was, what, Benji's age? Weren't you eight or nine when they got divorced?"

Tony gave a sulky one-shoulder shrug, but at least Will knew why this bit of history hadn't come up on the background check. Unless a kid got arrested or ended up in juvie, there were very few public records until they turned old enough to buy a car, rent an apartment, or start paying taxes.

Will said, "I like it up there."

"You mean over there," Tony countered. His eyes went beady. "It's over, not up."

Cayla cut in, "It's over *and* up, you idiot."

"I know what a map looks like."

Will let them argue. Geography had never been his strong suit, but he knew that South Carolina's Lowcountry dangled into Georgia's coast. He waited for a lull in the sibling spat, then said, "Better beaches on the coast than Florida's got, anyway."

"Whatta you know about Florida?" Tony demanded. He seemed angrier than the conversation warranted, which led Will to believe he was on the right track.

Will said, "It's a state."

"Don't fuck me around, son."

"Jesus, Tony." Cayla huffed a stream of smoke. "What crawled up your ass?"

Tony leaned forward, his fists pressing into the table. He asked Will, "When you ever been to Florida?"

"He's from Georgia," Cayla said. "Where else is he gonna go on vacation?"

Tony wasn't mollified. His anger filled the room. Benji went into lockdown mode. He slid down in his chair. His neck all but disappeared into his shoulders. He stared at his book like he'd never read it before.

Will took a bite of chicken. He chewed slowly, drawing out the time. Tony fidgeted. He was not a patient man. Will finally swallowed. "I was at MacDill."

Cayla asked, "You were in the Army?"

"Air Force." Will stared at Tony as he took another bite of chicken. The man had damn good reason to be suspicious. The coincidences were stacking up. MacDill Air Force Base was in South Tampa, not far from Sarasota, where Big Whitey had reportedly killed his first cop off the Tamiami Trail.

Cayla asked, "Were you an officer or anything?"

"I was target practice." Will used a biscuit to soak up some grease on the plate. He popped it into his mouth, still keeping his eyes on Tony.

Cayla asked, "They kick you out?"

"We agreed to go our separate ways."

She laughed, like he'd made a joke. "I woulda liked to've seen you in your uniform. You got any pictures?"

Will pretended he didn't hear the question. Tony seemed incapable of doing the same.

"Why do you want a picture of him?" Tony yelled. "You ain't never asked for no damn picture of me."

Cayla rolled her eyes. She asked Will, "You ever been to Miami?"

Will shook his head. "Didn't seem worth the trip." Because Tony had a racist streak, he added, "A little too dark down there for my taste."

Tony nodded, but he was still on edge. He obviously thought he had a shot at Cayla, which was equal parts alarming and disgusting. Will guessed it was better for Tony to be jealous than suspicious. Either way, he kept his eye on the man. It was always the little ones who fought dirty.

"Hey, Tony." Cayla tried to break the tension. "You remember I went up the Tamiami a few years ago. Hit Naples, Venice, Sarasota. Me and Chuck took his Harley up the trail."

"That fuckin' tool," Tony grumbled, the name obviously grating.

Will feigned disinterest. He peeled off the last piece of chicken and tossed it into his mouth. There was a toughness to Tony's posture that he hadn't seen before. Faith had a working theory that Tony Dell was more dangerous than they suspected. Will had shot her down because the guy came across as an irritant, more like a gnat. Looking at Tony now, Will wondered if Faith was right.

"You gonna drink that?" Tony asked.

He meant the beer. Will shrugged. "Help yourself."

Tony pounded back the beer. His Adam's apple bobbed as he drank too fast. Beer slid from the corners of his mouth. The requisite burp was followed by a bang as he slammed the can on the table.

Cayla ignored the display. She twisted the tip of her cigarette in the ashtray, shaping the end. She asked Will, "What were you in for?"

She meant jail. Will shrugged.

Cayla eyed him. "I bet you gotta strong temper on you." She said it as a compliment. "That what got you into trouble?"

Will shrugged in a way that let her know she was right.

"Think I'll have another." Tony walked around the table, pressing his hand on the top of Benji's head as he went to the fridge. Bottles rattled as he opened the door. Cayla had enough beer for the zombie apocalypse. There was hardly any food.

Tony asked Will, "Why'd you bail on the Air Force?"

Will gnawed at the chicken bones, sucking the marrow.

Again, Cayla tried to intervene. "I love those Gulf beaches with their white sand. Don't you think, Tony? The Atlantic's too cold."

Tony beamed. All it took was a little positive attention. The tough guy was gone. The gnat was back. He joked, "Shit, girl. You don't know what you're talking about."

"I know what beach I like."

"You don't know nothin'."

Will let Tony and Cayla debate the finer points of sands and tourist bars while he watched Benji. The boy moved like a bird, his arms held close to his sides like he was afraid of knocking something over. At the children's home, they had all eaten like ravenous animals, shoveling down food, wrapping their arms around their plates to keep thieves at bay. This kid had obviously been trained to be seen in public. He kept a napkin in his lap. He wiped his hands and mouth. He made sure that he chewed each bite before swallowing.

Will was a teenager before he realized that the reason he kept choking every time he ate was because he wasn't chewing enough.

Benji gave Will a furtive glance. He knew he was being watched. Will winked at him. Benji quickly looked back down. He was probably thinking about his mother—wondering where she was, if she was thinking of him, what he'd done wrong to make her go away in the first place.

Will had seen that look before, too.

"Hey." Tony snapped his fingers in Will's face.

Will was with Bill Black on this one. He slapped away Tony's hand.

"Damn, son." Tony held his hand to his chest. He nodded toward the faucet. "I was just asking could you help me with that?"

Will realized he'd been hearing the leak since he walked into the kitchen. "Probably needs a new washer."

Cayla's voice got high-pitched, the way some women's did whenever they asked a man to help them. "You wouldn't mind fixing it for me, would you, Bud? I'm not good with tools."

Will hesitated. Fixing things was what he did for Sara, like replacing a blown lightbulb or painting the tops of her doors. "Don't have the right tools."

"I got some in the truck," Tony offered.

Before he could stop himself, Will said, "I thought you told me you borrowed the truck."

Tony grinned. "Borrowed everything on it, son."

"You got a washer?" Will asked. "That's probably what it is. Might be ceramic. That's not a cheap faucet."

Cayla seemed pleased to hear this. "I got it at the Home Depot. Figured I could treat myself for once."

"Store's still open." Tony started playing with the faucet. "Why don't you and me go fetch a washer, fix this sink right up?"

Will sat back in his chair. He felt trapped between his job and Sara. He hadn't forgotten about their conversation on the phone. His girlfriend needed him. At least she would until Will told her the truth. Then again, Tony seemed relaxed and chatty. He might be more forthcoming about his past without Cayla around.

Tony turned off the faucet. "Shit, Bud, come on. It ain't like I'm askin' you on a date."

"Speaking of which," Cayla inserted. "Bud, why don't you follow Tony on your bike? That way you can drive yourself back here."

"Hey, now," Tony said. "That ain't nice."

"Ya think?" she countered. "Come on, Bud. That sink's been driving me crazy for weeks."

Will looked at Benji. The kid stared back. Will asked him, "What do you think?"

Benji chewed his lip. The skin was chapped. His eyelids were heavy. Will could see dark circles underneath. Maybe he stayed up nights looking out the window, waiting for his mother. Or maybe he couldn't sleep because the guilt of losing her was too much.

Will stood from the table. Being around this kid was screwing with his head. "All right," he told Tony. "Let's go."

Will rode alongside Tony in the truck. His bike was in the back, strapped down with some bungee cords Cayla had in her garage. Every turn, Will could hear the bike groan in protest, but the night had turned cold and rainy and Will was grateful to be in the warm, dry cab.

Tony was supposed to drop him off at the home improvement store. Will still couldn't decide whether or not he was going back to Cayla's. She'd seemed certain Will would return. She'd kept touching him—rubbing his back, grabbing his arm. She'd even kissed his cheek before he left. Will had tolerated the contact, but he couldn't stomach the thought of returning to that cramped house with its stuffed dolls and air of desperation.

Besides, Tony was looking like the better way into Macon's ever-changing drug scene. He'd loosened up on the drive. He talked a bit about Hilton Head, his boyhood summers spent sleeping on the beach and stealing wallets from stupid tourists who left their stuff out in the open while they swam in the ocean.

As with the previous night when they'd driven to Lena's house, Tony was fidgety—playing with the radio, tapping his fingers on the dashboard, keeping one hand barely on the wheel. His music selection was surprising. The Madonna CD in the player was from the eighties. He hit the replay button on "Like a Virgin."

"I saw her at the Atlanta Omni back in '87." Tony took a sip of beer. He'd already washed down a couple of pills from a Baggie in the glove compartment. "She's a tiny little thing. Got them weird bras make her tits look like bullets."

Will stared out the window.

"Sorry about before," Tony said. "When I got mad about Florida."

Will shrugged.

"I had some bad shit go down in Sarasota when I was sixteen."

Instead of asking for more, Will shrugged again. "No problem."

"Got arrested down there. Near 'bout got my ass throwed in jail." He gave a wet-sounding belch. "Gave the cops my brother's name. Half brother. He's a stupid little shit. Got hisself thrown in for twenty years off a bank holdup." Tony laughed. "Dumbass hit a bank. Can you believe that?"

Will shook his head. As crimes go, robbing a bank offered the lowest payout with the highest risk. "Not too bright."

"You damn right. They tracked him straight back to his old lady's door." Tony finished the beer. He rolled down the window and threw out the can. "Don't tell Cayla what I said about giving his name to the cops."

"She won't hear it from me."

"Good deal." He popped open another can of beer. "Cayla's all hung up on us being related, but my daddy was with her mama less than two years. That ain't nothin'. And even if it was, I don't care."

Will held back a response.

"I seen you lookin' at her, Bud. I don't mind that. I know she's pretty. Lots of men like to look at her." He pointed his finger Will's way. "Just don't touch her."

There was a threat in his voice, but Will was so far removed from being interested in Cayla Martin that he couldn't take it seriously.

"Her mama's got four other kids. They put me in the basement with the boys. She used to come down there when she was drunk and show me a good time."

Will's shock must have been apparent.

Tony snorted beer up his nose. He coughed it out of his mouth. "No, man, not the mama. I'm talking about Cayla. She'd come down them stairs wearing her panties and a tight shirt and pretty soon the sheet I'm under's lookin' like a pup tent." He chuckled at the memory. "I can't even tell you the shit we got up to down there. Liked to burn down the house."

Will fervently hoped he would not. "How long have you known her?"

Tony didn't have to think about it. "Been in love with her since we was fifteen."

"That's a long time."

"Damn right it is."

Will looked out the window as Tony chugged his beer. There were three cans left in the six-pack. Will guessed from the shape and color of the pills in the Baggie that Tony had taken some Oxy.

Will said, "Slow down."

Tony's foot was already on the brake. He pressed the pedal, but the speed barely changed. "I know Cayla gives me shit sometimes, but I'm the one she always calls when she needs something." He glanced at Will. "That's when you know how a woman feels about you. The shit hits the fan, who does she call?"

Will tried not to think about Sara.

"You hear what I'm sayin'?"

Will nodded.

"I mean it, Bud. I love her. She's the only damn reason I get up some mornings." He wiped under his eyes with the back of his hand. "She's all I got."

Will didn't have many male friends, but he gathered sitting around talking about love while listening to Madonna was not high on the list of manly pursuits. "You're gonna grow a vagina if you keep talking like that."

Tony barked a laugh. "Hell, Bud, that's just what she does to me. Ain't you never been in love?"

Will was so in love that he couldn't see straight.

"What was it like at MacDill?"

Will took his time answering—not because he had to recall the details, but because Bill Black wasn't the type to volunteer information. "Why do you want to know?"

"I dunno, man. Just curious. I knew a couple pilots from there. Sold 'em amp to keep 'em awake on long flights."

So, that's what Tony Dell was doing in Sarasota.

Tony pressed, "What was it like?"

"Hot."

"That's Florida all right."

Will stared out the window. They were on the highway now. Several cars were out, stragglers with a long commute. "What's the story with your nephew?"

"Benji." Tony put a nasty spin on the name that Will didn't like. He probably thought the kid was in his way. "His mama's a whore. Cops caught her smoking crack in front of him."

"That's too bad."

"He's a little shit. Keeps mouthing off at school. Cayla had to leave work to pick him up. He was suspended for two days."

Will couldn't imagine Benji mouthing off to a kitten. "He's a skinny kid."

"Yeah, well, that's what happens when you're too busy hittin' the pipe to stop and feed 'em." Tony turned the radio back on. He scrolled through the song selections and settled on Cyndi Lauper.

"Seriously?" Will asked.

"I like strong women." Tony hit the blinker as he slowed for a turn.

"Where are we going?" Will asked. Home Depot was by the hospital. They were heading in the wrong direction.

Tony held up the beer can. "Thought we'd get a real drink."

"I'm not thirsty."

"You're not driving." Tony took the turn. His voice had changed. The tough demeanor was back. "You serve overseas?"

"Why?"

"Just wondering." Tony drank some more beer. "You been in Macon, what, two weeks?"

"Almost."

"You lived in Atlanta before that?"

Will didn't answer.

"How'd you get the job at the hospital?"

Will tried to turn the situation back on itself. "You're asking questions like a cop."

"Shit." Tony laughed. "You think I'm a cop?"

"Are you?"

He looked at Will over his beer can. "Are you?"

"Hell no, I'm not a cop." Contrary to urban legend, law enforcement officers were free to lie with impunity. "Otherwise, I would've busted your ass ten days ago when I saw you taking pills off that cart."

Tony laughed at the memory. "Near about shit my pants when I saw you looking."

Will doubted that. Tony had clearly been testing him.

The window rolled down again. Tony tossed the can out. "Cayla used to sell 'em for me on Craigslist."

"That's dangerous for a woman."

"I always did the drops." Tony opened another beer. "College kids, mostly. We ain't sellin' the cheap stuff."

Will didn't press for details, but he was looking at Tony Dell in a new light. Faith would need to make some calls to Hilton Head and Sarasota. Tony struck Will as exactly the type of criminal who would flip on his own mother if it saved him jail time.

"Anyway," Tony said. "We ain't doin' that Craigslist shit anymore. Big Whitey kicked my game up a notch. I got more cash than I know what to do with."

"Craigslist is safer."

"Nickel and dime, bro."

"Big bills, big problems."

"The bills get big enough, you can buy your way outta the problems." Tony turned the wheel hard into a packed parking lot.

Will recognized the building. They were at Tipsie's. The neon sign on the roof showed a woman sliding up and down a pole. "You sure you wanna be back here?"

"It's cool." Tony parked the truck. "I was by here before I went to Cayla's."

Will felt the hair on the back of his neck go up. "Why'd you do that?"

"Same as you checking out that cop in the ICU, seein' did somebody recognize me."

Will didn't believe him. "And?"

"And . . . we're cool." The affable Tony was suddenly back. He pulled the keys out of the ignition, shouldered open the door. "Come on, Bud. I'm still thirsty."

Will got out of the truck, though every atom of his being told him something bad was about to happen. He didn't really have a choice. Jared Long was in the hospital. Lena Adams had almost been killed. There was a drug dealer out there who seemed to enjoy hurting people. If Will didn't do his job right, a lot more people would wind up at the hospital. Or in the ground.

"Come on, Bud." Tony walked like a bantam rooster. He was obviously hiding something. And he was very pleased with himself about it.

Will slowed his pace, trying to figure out what he was walking into. Not for the first time, he found himself wondering if Tony Dell was, in fact, Big Whitey.

Faith had brought up the possibility almost from the start. She was generally good at seeing around corners, but Will had disagreed with her. He'd met Tony Dell. He'd spent time with the man. He didn't come across as a master strategist.

Maybe that was the point.

Everything about Tony screamed petty criminal. He worked a shitty job. He drove a shitty car. He lived in an apartment that was three doors down from a strip mall. As for his police record, he'd been arrested twice under the open bottle law, both misdemeanors. There was one charge for possession that had rolled off after a successful stint in rehab. Another charge for dealing had disappeared from the court docket on a technicality. Loitering. Jaywalking. He was a nuisance criminal, not a heavy hitter.

If Tony Dell was really Big Whitey, then the man was a genius.

Will's iPhone was in the front pocket of his jeans. He wondered if the tracking chip would work through the club's metal roof. Sara had GPS in her car. The system cut out the minute she drove into an underground parking lot. Will guessed it was all the steel and concrete messing with the signal. Probably the same thing would happen to his phone inside Tipsie's.

They were ten yards from the door, but the music pounded so hard that Will felt it traveling up from the asphalt. His eardrums turned the noise into one long rumble.

Tony glanced back at Will before pushing open the door. He wasn't smiling, which should've been Will's first warning. The second warning was more obvious. The minute the door closed behind Will's back, a hand gripped his shoulder.

Will turned around. He was used to being the tallest guy in the room, but the man behind him was approximately the size of a refrigerator. Not a standard one, either—more like a Sub-Zero with the motor on the top.

There was no use asking questions.

The Refrigerator nodded toward the back. Will got the message. The man's hand stayed clamped to Will's shoulder, acting as a rudder as he pushed Will through the crowded bar.

Tony led the way. He didn't appear to be surprised by this latest development. He certainly wasn't worried. There was a nasty grin on his face, which Will saw every time the man glanced over his shoulder to make sure Will was following. The strobe lights and mirror ball picked out the cuts and bruises on his face, making them look like badly applied makeup. Tony must've been hurting, but his expression was one of pure glee.

There was no denying that he'd set this up beautifully. Tony had wormed his way into Cayla's house. He'd tricked Will into leaving with him. It was Tony's idea to fix the sink. It was Tony's idea to strap Will's bike into the truck. He'd obviously anticipated the problem. There just happened to be a winch in the back of the truck along with a couple of four-by-four posts to use as a ramp. When this was all done, he would probably use them to roll the bike into the river.

Will took the deepest breath he could manage. The sour smells of alcohol and sweat filled his lungs. He reached his hand into his pocket. His thumb found the power button on the phone. He pressed it three times to engage the recording device. Either Amanda would listen to Will talking to some bad guys or she would listen to some bad guys murdering Will.

The Refrigerator jerked Will to the side, avoiding a crowd of boisterous drunks. The route to the back of the club was circuitous. The stage snaked through the room. Every pole had a woman doing something obscene to it. The men crowded in, pushing against the stage until a bouncer shoved them back, then pushing forward again on the off chance that it'd work the third or fourth or hundredth time.

Tony stood at a closed door with a sign on it. The shit-eating grin was still on his face. He waited for Will and the Refrigerator to catch up. The grin got wider as Tony pushed open the door. The room was dark. The hand on Will's shoulder shoved him forward. Will saw that the room wasn't a room, but a long hallway. What little light they had came from the open door. The last thing Will saw was the Refrigerator closing it.

Tony's mouth went to Will's ear. "Move." He pushed Will down the hallway.

Will considered his options. He could easily take Tony Dell. He'd pushed him around like a rag doll before. But that had been the old Tony, not the Possibly Big Whitey Tony. Sometimes, the physical size of a man didn't matter nearly as much as the size of the fight in the man.

And Tony had help.

He had a lot of help.

Will pressed his hand to the cement-block wall as he walked down the hallway. He became painfully aware of his full bladder. Sweat dripped down his back. He imagined his Glock, the way the grip felt in his hand, the fact that the safety was a hair trigger built into the main trigger that only engaged when your finger pulled back. Not that any of this mattered. The gun was locked in a safe in his closet back in Atlanta.

There must've been soundproofing in the back of the club, because the music wasn't so unbearable anymore. Will felt something in front of him. He panicked, then realized he was touching a curtain. Will pushed the material apart. There was more light in this part of the hall, courtesy of a green Exit sign over the door. Will would've run full out toward it if not for the second Refrigerator blocking the way. He made the first Refrigerator look more like a mini-fridge. His arms bulged at the sleeves. His shoulders were almost as wide as the doorway. He had a Bluetooth device stuck in his ear. As Will approached, he tapped the earpiece and mumbled something incoherent.

Refrigerator Two pulled back a curtain on the wall. There was another door with a sign. Will could recognize words he'd seen a million times before. This one said OFFICE. The second Refrigerator opened the door. His hand was so big that the knob completely disappeared.

Will shaded his eyes against the sudden bright light. The back room of the club was remarkably similar to the type he was used to seeing in mob movies: Black ceiling, dark red walls. Liquor posters with naked women. A white shag rug. A large metal and glass desk. A black leather couch with three fat rednecks sprawled across it.

They were eating pizza from a box on the glass coffee table in front of them. The odor of cheese and sausage turned Will's stomach. He tasted bile, felt some black-eyed peas roil up into his mouth.

The rednecks examined Will and Tony with idle curiosity. In a mobster movie, they would've been well-dressed Italians. Macon's version was considerably more down-market. They wore T-shirts that stretched across their bellies. Their jeans were low on their hips, but only because they didn't want to go up six sizes to accommodate their expanded waistlines.

Refrigerator Two closed the door. Will saw that he'd missed something across the room from the couch.

There was a man tied to a chair. Rope cut into the bare flesh of his arms and chest. His head hung down. The scalp was ripped at the crown. The head wound wasn't the only source of blood. His hands and feet had been sliced open. There were dozens of X's cut into his chest and abdomen. The wounds weren't deep enough to kill, but deep enough to cause excruciating pain.

The man had been tortured.

"Damn," Tony said, not with shock but with admiration. "Didn't know y'all had company."

"Shut up," one of the rednecks said. He used a folding knife to clean underneath his fingernails. "You do what I tell you to do?"

"Don't I always?" Tony answered.

"Watch your tone with me, boy."

"Yessir," Tony demurred.

So much for Tony being Big Whitey. Will gathered the redneck was in charge. He had the air of a man burdened with responsibility. His two henchmen ate their pizza like they were waiting for their turn at the bowling alley. One of them had a bottle of beer to wash it down. The other had a Diet Coke.

The redneck kept cleaning his nails. No one seemed interested in rushing him.

Will just stood there. This wasn't the first time tonight that he'd wondered whether or not Tony Dell was leading him to his death, but it was the first time he actually saw how it might happen. The man in the chair was still alive. Blood didn't run like that if the heart had stopped beating. His breaths were shallow. His muscles twitched involuntarily—first the arm, then the calf. A low humming noise came from his throat. He was probably praying for his death. They had cut him. They had beaten him. And then they had taken a dinner break because they were in no rush to end his suffering.

Tony wasn't as patient. Or maybe he was just stupid. He took a Baggie of pills out of his pocket and tossed them onto the desk. "Where's the big man? You said we were gonna talk."

"Shut up," the redneck repeated. He finished cleaning his nails. The knife blade was about four inches—not long, but sharp, with a wicked curved tip. He slowly folded the blade back into the handle, his eyes on Will the entire time. "You gotta problem?"

Will shook his head.

"We gonna have a problem?"

Will shook his head again.

The redneck stood up, groaning from the effort. He was a big guy, not muscular like the matching refrigerators but fat around the middle.

He walked over to the desk. His gait was slow, cumbersome. He picked up a file folder from the desk. "William Joseph Black."

Will waited.

The redneck picked up a pair of reading glasses. He didn't put them on. Instead, he used them like a magnifying glass on the file.

He read, "Born in Milledgeville, Georgia. Sealed juvie record. Joined up at twenty-two. Got kicked out at twenty-five. Couple of assaults on some women. Beat down a mall cop. Served time in the Atlanta jail. Pissed off some feds in Kentucky. Wanted for questioning on a stickup and a couple break-ins." The redneck waited. "That about sum it up?"

Will didn't answer.

He tossed the file back on the desk. "You're renting a room at the Star-Gazer Motel off the interstate. Number fifteen. You park your midnight-blue Triumph motorcycle in the space two doors down. You eat at the RaceTrac. You work at the hospital. You come here to get your dick hard. Your mother died while you were serving in Iraq. Your father is unknown. You have no siblings and no family to speak of."

Will let his lips open a slit to take in some air. The only reason he'd chosen to ride a bike was to make sure no one followed him to Atlanta. To Sara. Will's heart thumped as he waited for the redneck to tell him her address.

Instead, the redneck asked, "Zeb-deeks?"

This time, Will didn't respond because he didn't know what the hell the man was talking about.

"Zeb-deeks?" the redneck repeated. "You know him?"

It was a name. A man.

The redneck waited. His patience seemed in endless supply.

Will stumbled through Bill Black's life. There was no high school or college, just Air Force and jail. The name sounded foreign, but his military file wouldn't have those kinds of details. Zeb-deeks was probably a nickname, which normally wouldn't help Will except that there was only one guy in Bill Black's life whose name started with a Z.

Zebulon Deacon had been knifed at the Atlanta jail for ratting out his crew. Bill Black had been in the same cell block. He would know of the guy. He would certainly know the nickname.

More importantly, Black would also know you didn't rat out anybody without a fight.

Instead of answering the redneck, Will shrugged.

"You don't know him?"

Again, Will shrugged.

The redneck said, "Junior?"

One of the henchmen lumbered up from the couch. Junior was as big as his boss, but younger. Undoubtedly stronger.

There was no preamble. Junior punched Will so hard in the face that he saw flashes of light. His head snapped back. His neck cracked. The bridge of his nose felt like a hatchet had struck bone.

"Zeb Deeks," the redneck said.

Will shook his head—not to disagree, but to get his senses back. He'd been punched in the nose more times than he could count. The worst part came when you sniffed and the chunk of blood sitting in the back rolled down your throat. Will struggled not to vomit as he swallowed it down.

For the fourth time, the redneck said the name. "Zeb Deeks?"

Junior pulled back his fist.

"All right," Will said. "Yeah, I know him. Snitch got what he deserved."

"Where'd he get it?"

"Quad."

"Where'd he get it?"

"In the junk," Will said. "They stabbed him with a broken toothbrush. He bled out in the yard."

Tony chuckled. "Bet that hurt."

The redneck's chest rose and fell. He studied Will for a moment, then nodded toward the last henchman on the couch. The third man stood up just as slowly as the others, his knees popping, his gut bulging. Contrary to physics, he and Junior worked fast. Before Will knew what was happening, his arms were pinned behind his back.

The redneck walked over to Will. He smelled of pizza and alcohol. He was a smoker. He breathed like a steam engine. He was big and he was white, but Tony had made it clear the redneck wasn't Big Whitey. Will doubted he would ever meet the man who was in charge of this gang of violent hillbillies. He doubted he would see anything other than the moldy back room of this club for what little time he had left in his life.

The redneck held up his hands so Will could watch what he was doing. The handle on his folding knife was pearl with gold accents. The light caught on the blade as he opened it. There was blood on the hinge, caked into the rivets, probably from carving X's into the man tied to the chair. The redneck was a natural with the knife. He held the handle with a light grip, almost like another thumb or finger.

Will flinched as he felt the sharp stainless-steel blade trace across his neck. Then up the side of his face. Then underneath his eye. The redneck pressed a little harder and the skin opened. Will was so terrified that it didn't even hurt. He wouldn't have even known he was cut but for the bead of blood that rolled down his cheek.

Will closed his eyes. He wasn't here. He wasn't in this room. Maybe talking to Cayla and Tony about the beach set him off. He could smell the salt in the air, feel the warm, gentle breeze rolling in off the ocean.

Three months ago, Sara had taught Will how to fly a kite. They were on the beach in Florida. The kite was yellow and blue and had a long white tail. Will had never taken a beach vacation before. All his knowledge about Florida came courtesy of Wikipedia and *Miami Vice*. Sara was a good teacher. Patient, kind. Sexy as hell in her bathing suit. Her father had taught her how to fly a kite when she was little. He'd been worried that Sara would feel pushed aside by her new baby sister, so he'd taken her on little day trips to make her feel special.

Will's eyes shot open. The knife was in his ear—not the soft fleshy part, but the bit right at the inside where a thin layer of cartilage lay against the skull.

The redneck was smiling, enjoying the effect. The man had perfect white teeth. His gums looked almost blue against them.

Will didn't move. The knife was needle sharp. The tip broke

through his skin, sliced open the cartilage. A drop of blood slid inside his ear. With excruciating slowness, it traveled down the canal. Will felt a shudder coming on. It started slow, like the rumble of an oncoming train. A slight tremble, then a shaking that built and built until the earth started to move and his teeth were rattling and the ground felt ripped out from under him.

The redneck jerked out the knife just in time.

"Fuck!" Will shook his head violently. The grip on his arms got tighter. He shook his head again. The blood was still moving inside his ear.

The redneck laughed as he folded the blade back into the handle. "Take off your clothes."

Junior and number three released him. Will jammed his pinkie in his ear and moved it like a clapper in a bell.

"Take off your clothes," the redneck repeated.

Will glared at him. "Go fuck yourself." He headed toward the door, but Junior stopped him.

The redneck offered, "We can do this the hard way."

Junior pushed Will into his partner, who in turn slammed Will into the wall.

The redneck asked, "Hard way, easy way?"

Will couldn't think about the beach anymore. He couldn't think about Sara or anything else but staying alive.

Bill Black could handle this. He had been in his share of back rooms. He had dealt with lowlifes and bad guys all of his life. According to his records, he'd *been* a lowlife and bad guy all of his life.

Will didn't know what boot camp was like other than what he'd seen in the movies, but he was very familiar with the intake process at the Atlanta jail. Bill Black would've been one of at least a hundred new inmates the guards checked in that day. They'd stripped him, searched him, shaved him, deloused him, then thrown him into a five-by-nine cell with another man and an open sewage pit for a toilet. There were communal showers. There were occasional cavity searches. There was nowhere to hide.

Undressing for a bunch of violent hicks was not something that would faze a guy like Bill Black.

Will ripped open his shirt. Some of the buttons popped loose. His T-shirt came next, then his jeans. Will used the toe of one boot to brace the heel of the other as he stepped out of the shoes. He kicked off the jeans.

The room went silent but for the muffled beats of club music.

They stared at him like an exhibit at the zoo.

Will didn't look at his body much. As grateful as he was to Sara, he didn't know how she could stand it. There wasn't a part of him that didn't tell some story of abuse—the cigarette burns around his ribs, the electrical burns that had seared a scattershot of black powder into his skin. The scars on his back where he'd been clawed by a woman who got high from huffing spray paint all morning and thought Will had bugs crawling underneath his flesh.

And that didn't include the wounds that were self-inflicted.

Tony broke the silence. "Shit, Bud. What the hell happened to you?"

Will said nothing.

For once, the redneck seemed to view Will as a human being rather than a problem to be dealt with. He asked, "Iraq?"

Will considered his options. His scars were not part of his cover. The redneck had obviously managed to get his hands on Bill Black's police record. He'd made some inquiries up the criminal food chain. Did the man have enough juice to get a military file? The GBI was good, but the United States government had offered only cursory support for Bill Black's stint in the armed forces.

The redneck pressed, "One a them ragheads get hold of you?"

Instead of answering the question, Will turned his head and looked at the wall. He figured Bill Black would feel the same way Will did. Someone had hurt him really badly, and he wasn't proud of it.

"Never mind." The redneck seemed resigned to never know-ing, but he wasn't finished with his search. "Take off the shorts, too."

Will gave him a hard look.

The redneck seemed almost apologetic. "I knew a guy got caught by a cop with a wire taped to his balls."

Will knew he didn't have a choice. Either he'd undress himself or the two henchmen would. He pushed down his underwear.

The redneck glanced down, then took another look before say-ing, "Okay, then."

Tony raised his eyebrows. "Damn, hoss."

Will pulled his underwear back up. He reached for his jeans, but they were snatched out of his hand.

Junior searched the pockets. Bill Black's wallet and phone were found. The wad of cash he'd taken off Tony this morning was tossed onto the desk.

"Let's see what we got," the redneck held out his hand. He started with the wallet. The Velcro ripped open. Cayla's hand-written address was in the photo sleeve. He flipped past it, check-ing the pockets. He found four twenties, two credit cards, and the speeding ticket that passed for Bill Black's license. "Fifty in a school zone." The redneck tsked his tongue against his teeth.

Junior handed him the phone. Will grabbed his jeans.

The redneck asked, "What's the password?"

Will said, "Four-three-two-one." He yanked up his jeans as the man dialed in the code.

The redneck was more proficient than Will as he scrolled through the various screens. His lips moved when he read. "Who's the woman in Tennessee?"

Will pulled on his T-shirt. The hole in the arm had torn, rip-ping out the side seam.

Tony provided, "He's gotta baby by her." He felt the need to ask Will, "She the one into topiary?"

Will put on his Oxford shirt. There were three buttons left on the placket. He concentrated on closing them, though his fingers didn't want to work.

The redneck seemed to be scrolling through every screen. Will had tested the phone himself when he first got it, trying to see if there was a way to accidentally reveal the cloaked apps. Each time, he was foiled, but every system had a flaw. Will had never tested the phone with the recorder turned on. Maybe there was a software glitch that would pop up the apps and make the redneck pull out his knife again.

"Where's this?" He showed Will a photograph, one of the shots he'd taken from the highway.

"Off 16," Will said. "Thought it looked nice."

The man countered, "Geotag says it's off 475."

Will shrugged, but he felt his mouth go bone-dry. He'd forgotten about the geotags. They were part of the iPhone's location service and showed the longitude and latitude of where the pictures were taken. He had no idea whether or not the GBI program cloaked them.

"You get these off the Internet?" He showed Will the naked women.

Will's brief feeling of safety evaporated. He'd downloaded the photos from his computer in Atlanta. He didn't know what the geotag would record—where Will was when he downloaded the photos or where they had originally been taken.

Will waited, watching the man's finger swipe across the screen.

"Don't like Asians myself." The redneck kept scrolling.

Will buttoned the cuffs of his shirt, pretending like he hadn't almost pissed himself. One of the buttons was dangling by a thread. It came off in his hands. Will didn't know what to do with it. He put it in his pocket.

If he died, he wondered who would find the button in his pocket. Probably the medical examiner. Pete Hanson had retired a few months ago, but Amanda had brought in a new guy who was young and cocky and believed everything that came out of his mouth. Will wondered what he would make of the button. He wondered if Sara would hear about it. Would she think about Will every time she put on a shirt?

He took the button out of his pocket and tossed it onto the floor.

Tony made a clicking sound with his tongue. Will looked at him. Tony winked, like they were in this together. Like he hadn't delivered Will to these men for slaughter.

What had turned Tony against him? It had to be the dinner. The only way that Tony could know about the date was if Cayla told him. She must've known Tony would show up. Will could see she liked playing them off each other. Stepbrother or not, she'd obviously been stringing Tony along for years.

Or maybe it was something more dangerous. Maybe Tony still thought Will was a cop. Running into Lena's house last night hadn't been Will's smartest move. No con in his right mind ran toward gunfire, even if he had a hundred pregnant girlfriends threatening to sue him.

"All right," the redneck finally said. He handed Will the phone.

Will didn't know what to do but take it. The case was warm. His hands were so sweaty that he nearly dropped it before he could get it back into his pocket.

The redneck leaned across the desk and pressed a button on the phone. There was a buzz, then he pressed the button again. It was some kind of signal. They all waited. And waited. Will counted off the seconds in his head, but then he lost track and had to start all over again.

A cell phone rang. The redneck took his time. The Droid was buried under a stack of papers on the desk. He answered on the sixth ring. He listened, nodding occasionally. His eyes slid Will's way. He said, "Yeah, I think you're right," then ended the call.

"That Big Whitey?" Tony asked. He was as eager as a kid. "He tell you we're cool?" He slapped Will on the back. "I told you I'd make this right, man."

The redneck took a stack of hundreds out of his pocket. He glanced at the Baggie of pills Tony had thrown on the desk and counted out ten bills. He held out the cash to Tony. "That's more than you deserve, bringing this ass-wipe into our business. Get rid of him."

Will felt panic rise, but then he realized the redneck meant the man tied to the chair. Will looked at the guy. He'd forgotten all about him. At some level, Will realized he already thought of him as dead.

The redneck said, "Leave him somewhere he'll be found."

"No problem." Tony walked over to the chair. He slapped the man's head. "Let's go, dude."

The man groaned. Spit slid out of his open mouth.

"Come on." Tony slapped him harder. "Stand up, cocksucker. Time to go."

The man struggled against the rope. Even if he wanted to, there was no way to get up.

"You believe this asshole?" Tony's eyes looked as if they were on fire. He obviously enjoyed hurting people. He kicked the chair again. There was none of the gnat about him now, just a wiry tough guy who had no problem punching above his weight.

The redneck had had enough. "Stop fucking around and get him out of here."

Tony pulled a knife out of his boot. This wasn't a folding knife, but a ten-inch hunting knife with a nasty-looking serrated edge. He cut the rope around the chair. The man pitched forward, moaning from the release. Tony caught him before he hit the floor. He flipped the knife in the air and pointed the handle toward Will. "Get his feet."

Will sawed through the rope that tied the man's legs to the chair. He glanced up as he sliced through the last few strands. The man's eyes were swollen slits in his face, but Will could see the bloody whites at the edges. Blood had trickled down his forehead, clotted in his eyelashes. His front teeth were broken. The bridge of his nose was smashed. Still, he looked familiar, but Will didn't have time to figure out why.

"Wake up, asshole." This time, Tony's fist came from below. The man's head arced back. Blood went flying. "I ain't playin', dude. Stand the fuck up."

The man tried to obey. His bare feet stuck to the rug. His legs shook. His knees wouldn't straighten.

Will stepped in. He couldn't watch this. He shouldered the man to standing, practically carrying all of his weight.

"Please . . . ," the man begged, his voice barely audible.

Will glanced around the room, but no one seemed moved by the plea. If anything, they were annoyed.

"Get him outta here," the redneck ordered. He went back to the couch, sat down in front of the open pizza box.

Will tried to drag the man to the door. If he could leave this room, if he could manage to get out of this club, then there might be a way to save him.

The redneck picked up a slice of pizza. "I'll be in touch, Bud. We have a job that Mr. Whitey thinks will suit your special skills."

Will grunted, but only from the effort of carrying the man. There was no helping him walk. Will lifted his full weight onto his back. Five feet to the door. Maybe three feet to the exit. Around the building, then to the parking lot. Will would take Tony's truck. He'd sucker punch him from behind, take away his keys. He would drive the man to the hospital. He would get Faith to put him into protective custody. And then Will would find Sara and fall down at her feet and pray for her to make everything better.

Will told Tony, "Get the door."

"What about the rug?" Junior asked. "Ain't no way that can be steamed out."

"Shit," Tony complained. "I ain't no damn rug cleaner."

"Take it and burn it." The redneck finished his slice of pizza. "Dump the body on his front lawn. That oughta be public enough."

Tony made it clear he thought he was doing them a favor. He hitched up his pants. He got down on his knees. He started rolling the edge of the rug. Will turned because there was nothing to do but watch him and wait.

This was when the man decided to make his move.

Without warning, he pushed away from Will.

The man grabbed at the doorknob. His coordination was shot. His hands were slick with blood. Instead of opening the door, he fell against it. He started screaming, pounding at the door like there might be help on the other side.

Will's instincts took over. Of all the guys in the room, he was the least lethal. He grabbed the man around the waist. He tried to cover his mouth. The man kicked him, bit him, punched him, until Will couldn't hold on anymore.

There was nowhere to go—no windows, no doors but the one they'd come through. The man was so crazed with terror he was practically spinning in circles. The rug bunched up under his feet. He careened off the coffee table, the desk. Tony tackled him from behind, throwing him face-down on the floor.

Tony straddled him. The hunting knife was in his hands. He pounded the blade into the man's back, his shoulders, his neck. Again and again the knife went up and down like a piston. The blade made a pop-slap noise as it pierced skin. Spaghetti strings of blood flew around him like he was inside some kind of horror-house snowglobe.

Junior jammed a gun into Will's chest, making it clear he should stay out of it. The muzzle felt like it was touching bare bone. Junior was eerily calm as Tony wailed away with the knife. He caught the redneck's eye, gave him a single shake of the head as if to ask, *What got into that guy?* His counterpart sat passively on the couch, watching the murder unfold the way he might watch a card game.

The stabbing continued long after the man was dead. Tony only stopped when he ran out of steam. He sat back on his heels.

He was panting. Sweating. He wiped his face with the sleeve of his shirt. Forehead, mouth, cheeks. Blood smeared everywhere.

Junior put the gun back into the holster on his belt. Will could move now, but he didn't have anywhere to go. Twice in as many nights, he'd watched one human being attack another.

At least Lena had been responding to a threat. Tony Dell was like a jackal destroying its prey. He'd enjoyed each and every second of the kill. He'd grunted and screamed as the knife went in. The spray of blood that washed up into his face had only made him hungry for more.

And now he was laughing.

Blood smeared his teeth like lipstick. He asked Will, "How 'bout that, Buddy? You seen this nut job runnin' around? That was some crazy shit."

The redneck was not pleased. "You see the mess you made?"

"You was gonna throw away the carpet anyway."

"You didn't just get it on the carpet, did you?"

Tony looked around with awe at what he'd wrought. He shook his head, then wiped the hunting knife on his pants before trying to jam it back into his boot. The blade was bent, probably from striking the thick bone of the skull. Tony had to torque the handle to sheath the knife. And then he saw the open wound across the palm of his hand. "Shit, musta slipped over the hilt." He asked Will, "You mind takin' me to the hospital, Bud? This is the kind of shit gets infected."

The redneck sounded more put out than disgusted. "Junior, go get some of the girls to clean this up." He told Tony, "Get the body outta here. Drop him in his front yard, like I said."

Tony asked, "You sure 'bout that?"

"Came straight from Big Whitey. Put him somewhere he'll be found. The only way to send a message is make sure everybody's got a chance to read it." The redneck directed his next order to Will. "Keep an eye on him. Make sure he doesn't fuck it up."

"I ain't gonna fuck it up," Tony yelled. "You tell Big Whitey I'm the one what took care of this for him."

"You really want credit?" the redneck asked. He shook his head at Junior, who returned the gesture.

Will said, "We'll take care of it," because he thought that would get them out of here faster. He knelt down on the floor. "Roll the body onto the rug."

"Take a cue from your pal there, Tony. Good soldiers follow orders." The redneck sat back on the couch. He took out his knife again to clean his nails. "Like I said, Mr. Black. We'll be in touch."

Will wasn't going to wait around for more. He motioned for Tony to move. "Hurry up. Roll him onto the rug."

Tony pushed the body, but the physics were against him. The man was dead weight. Tony's boots skidded against the concrete floor. His face twisted into a mask of sheer determination. Finally, the man flopped onto his back. His arm was over his eyes like he didn't want to see anymore.

Tony picked up the hands and crossed them over the chest. He started toward the other side of the rug.

"No," Will said. "We have to roll the body." He took the shoulders because that was the heavier end and he couldn't watch Tony pushing around the corpse anymore.

Tony asked, "Ready?"

Will looked down at the man's face. He recognized him now, though even in death, the pain still twisted his features. Faith had shown Will his picture on her phone just a few hours ago.

The man in the chair was Detective Eric Haigh.

10.

FRIDAY

It was just past midnight, and Sara was once again sitting on the couch in the ICU waiting room. She flipped through a magazine, trying to tune out the conversations around her. More patients had been admitted that afternoon. Family members filled the small room. The new people were a communal bunch. They wanted to swap stories. They wanted to compare tragedies. Nell had not been pleased. She couldn't take the prying, the crowded space. She'd easily let Sara talk her into going back to the hotel room to get some sleep.

There was no reason for her to be at the hospital right now anyway. Jared's condition remained unchanged despite the antibiotics they were pumping into him. Sara had dealt with surgical infections before. They were as relentless as they were indiscriminate. There were very few antibiotics left that could successfully treat them.

So, as Sara had many times throughout the day, she found herself back at the same point she'd started at this morning. The twenty-four-hour clock had been reset. Jared had survived the surgery. Only time would tell if he survived the infection.

Sara put the magazine back on the table. She'd read the same celebrity gossip story three times and still couldn't follow the details. She was in some sort of weird fugue state. Yet again, she regretted the large scotch she'd had earlier that evening. Self-medication was never a good idea, but stress, alcohol, and thirty hours straight without sleep were a lethal combination. Sara had all of the hangover and none of the buzz. Her head ached. She was jittery. The fact that Sara knew when she was drinking the scotch that she was making a huge mistake only added to her misery. Her only consolation was that she hadn't ordered another one after talking on the phone with Will.

There was a conversation she wished she'd never had. Either Sara was a very cheap drunk or their relationship wasn't heading in the direction she'd thought it was. Her desperate sexual enticement had gone over like an IRS audit. Thank God she hadn't told him that she was in love with him. She could only imagine how embarrassing it would've been to have her pronouncement met with complete silence. Will was obviously pulling away. Sara had either done something or said something wrong. He was probably relieved she hadn't asked him to make the drive down. Or up. Or over. Sara still had no idea where he was.

She was just glad that he wasn't here.

And she fervently wished that she wasn't, either.

Sara couldn't sit anymore. She stood up and stretched her back. The vertebrae felt fused together. Polite smiles greeted her around the room. She walked into the hall for some privacy.

The lights were dimmed in deference to the late hour. Possum was exactly where she'd seen him thirty minutes ago. His back was to Sara. He stood at the closed doors to the ICU, looking through the window. He couldn't see into Jared's room from that angle. The cop was in his line of sight. Sara could tell the vigilance was grating on the young man. He kept glancing at Possum, then looking back at the nurses' station as if the poor woman could help him.

Possum could barely speak to Sara—not out of rudeness, but

because every time he saw her, his eyes filled with tears. She didn't know whether he was crying over the loss of Jeffrey, the threat to Jared, or the unbearable combination of both.

Sara just knew she was sick of being here.

She went to the elevator, then decided the stairs would at least give her some exercise. She needed some air, to be in a room that wasn't stale with fear and tragedy. And she should probably have a conversation with herself about Will. Maybe she'd been blind to the deeper truth behind his silences. Sara had never told Will that she loved him, but then Will had never told Sara the words, either.

In her experience, the simplest explanation was usually the crappiest one.

Sara went down two flights before she saw a pink and blue sign. The maternity ward. She gladly took the detour. Whenever she was having a particularly horrendous day at Grady, she would go look at the babies. There was something so reassuring about watching brand-new eyes blink open, toothless mouths pucker into a smile. Newborns were proof that life could not only continue, but thrive.

Sara guessed not many people would be there at this time of the morning, and she was right. Visiting hours were well over. There was no nurse to send stragglers away. No one had bothered to lower the shade over the large windows so the babies could sleep in peace.

The dimmed hallway lights cast a warm glow on the rows of bassinets. The newborns were all wearing pink or blue knit hats. They were swaddled tightly in matching blankets. Their little faces were like raisins, some of them so new that their heads moved gently side to side, as if they were still floating in the womb.

Sara pressed her forehead to the window. The glass was cold. One of the babies was awake. His squinty eyes scanned the ceiling. Colorful cartoons were painted overhead—rainbows and fluffy clouds and plump rabbits. This was more for the parents than the babies. Newborns were extremely nearsighted. The basic eye structures were there, but months would pass before they learned how to use them. For now, the ceiling art was a pleasant blob.

The door behind Sara opened. She turned, expecting to find a nurse coming out of the bathroom.

Instead, it was Lena Adams.

She had a tissue in her hand. Sara could see the dismay when their eyes met, then something like resignation.

Lena headed toward the elevator.

"Wait," Sara said.

Lena stopped, but didn't turn around.

Sara instantly regretted the word. She didn't know what to say. Was she sorry? Certainly, she felt bad that Lena had lost the baby. But that didn't change what had come before.

All Sara could manage was, "You don't have to leave."

Slowly, Lena turned. She didn't acknowledge Sara. Instead, she walked over to the viewing window. Her fingers rested on the edge of the sill. She leaned her forehead against the glass, the same as Sara had. She seemed to wall off everything else around her. There was something so tragic about the way she looked at the newborns. Her longing seemed to pierce the glass.

The familiar sense of trespass took hold. Sara opened her mouth to take her leave, but Lena didn't give her a chance to speak.

"Is he the same?"

"Jared?" Sara asked. "Yes."

Lena just nodded, her eyes still trained straight ahead. She moved her hand to her stomach, pressed the palm flat.

Again, Sara struggled against the instinct to offer comfort, to spin the situation in a more positive light. In the end, she couldn't summon the energy. Somewhere in the pit of her chest, there was the capacity to feel compassion for this woman. Sara felt it stir occasionally, like a car engine trying to start on a cold day. It would rev and rev, but eventually, it always sputtered out and died.

Again, Sara tried to leave. "I should—"

"I never realized they were so small." Lena's features softened as she watched the newborn in front of her. "It must be scary to know how fragile they are." Her breath fogged the glass. She seemed to be waiting for a response.

"You learn what to do." Sara had grown up around babies. She couldn't imagine a life without them.

Lena said, "I've never held a baby before."

"You don't have cousins?"

"No. And I never babysat or anything." She gave a low laugh. "I wasn't the kind of teenager people trusted with their kids."

Sara could imagine.

Lena stuttered out a long sigh. "I didn't think it was possible to love something that needed me so much."

"I'm sorry," Sara said. "For what it's worth."

"For what it's worth," Lena repeated. "Nell doesn't hate me so much anymore."

Sara had felt the change, too, but she wasn't sure it would last.

Lena said, "It was better when she hated me. I knew how to deal with that. We both did." She turned her head to look at Sara. "It's like she thinks losing the baby makes me a better person."

Sara weighed the words, trying to decipher her motivations. Lena wanted something. She always wanted something.

"Thank you, Sara." Lena turned back to the window. "I knew I could depend on you to not feel sorry for me."

Sara needed to leave. She couldn't muster her old hatred right now, but she knew she could be persuaded. "I should check on Possum."

"It kills him every time he sees you."

Sara couldn't argue with that. "Still—"

"Did you get my letter?"

The letter.

Four years ago, Sara had opened her mailbox to find a hand-written letter from Lena. Sara had shoved the sealed envelope into her purse. She was late for work. She didn't want to read it. Neither, apparently, did she want to throw it away. For almost a year, the letter had traveled around with Sara. To work, to the store, to dinner, back home. She moved it when she switched purses. She saw it every time she pulled out her wallet or searched for her keys.

Lena was studying her. "You read it."

Sara didn't want to admit it, but she said, "Eventually."

"I was wrong."

"Really?" Sara asked. The letter was three pages from a legal pad. Three tedious, tearstained pages filled with excuses and lies and blame shifting. "Which part were you wrong about?"

"All of it." She leaned her shoulder against the glass. "I knew Jeffrey would come save me. And I knew that I was putting his life in danger."

Sara felt her face start to flush. Her heart was a bird trapped in a cage. She had waited so long to hear this admission, this validation, and now all she could think was that Lena was working an angle.

Lena said, "You can't light a match, then act surprised when your house burns down."

Sara worked to keep her tone even. "You tried to warn him." At least Lena had said as much in the letter. She'd devoted four lengthy paragraphs to her regret that Jeffrey simply would not take her sound advice. "You said you told him to stay away."

"I knew he wouldn't." Lena stared openly at Sara. "I should be dead now, not him."

Sara didn't buy the sudden conversion. She tried to trick Lena, quoting the words Jared had told Nell. "He knew the risks when he put on the badge."

"You think Will feels the same way when he goes to work?"

From nowhere, Sara was seized by the impulse to slap Will's name out of her mouth. He'd investigated Lena almost two years ago when she'd let a suspect die in custody and stood by as another cop was stabbed nearly to death. Sara had been more disappointed than Will that he couldn't make the case stick.

She told Lena, "The only thing you know about Will Trent is that he almost sent you to prison."

"Almost." Lena's lips teased into a smile. The mask was starting to fall. "You know what I remember about my time with Agent Trent?" There was a strange lilt to her voice. "Seeing that he was already lost in you. And you're in love with him, too, right? I can see it in your face. You were always so good at being in love."

Sara shook her head. Now she could see where this was going. "It doesn't make up for it."

"You've obviously moved on," Lena told her. "Both of us have moved on."

"I didn't have a choice, Lena. I had to move on because my husband was murdered." Sara bit back the venom in her mouth. "I didn't have a choice."

"No matter what you think, I'm not a bad person. I let myself believe that for a long time. I let you convince me I wasn't good enough. Wasn't worthy enough."

"Well, I'm so sorry," Sara quipped. "Please tell me how I can make it up to you."

"You're going to find out eventually that I've changed."

"You haven't changed. Neither one of us would be here if you had." Sara struggled to keep the bitterness out of her tone. "Everything is always a game to you. What we're doing right now is a game. You never walk away. You never let anybody get the upper hand. You think you're a good cop, but you don't care about the job or anyone else who's doing it. You just want to make sure that you win no matter what it costs."

Lena smirked. "Whatever you say, Doc."

"I'm not doing this." Sara started to walk away.

"I can't believe I used to be jealous of you."

Sara turned, mouth open in disbelief.

"Your family. Your life. Your marriage. Everybody in town respected you. Worshipped you." Lena shrugged. "And then I realized one day that I didn't want to be like you. Couldn't be like you if I tried. No one can. You're too perfect. Too demanding. Nobody can meet your high standards. Jeffrey couldn't." She shook her head, as if she genuinely felt sorry. "Will doesn't stand a chance."

For a moment, Sara was too stunned to speak—not because of what Lena had said, but because she'd so masterfully turned the conversation.

Sara said, "You want me to feel guilty for moving on with my life?"

The smirk on Lena's face said it all. She echoed Sara's words from before. "Now you know how it feels."

Sara asked, "Are we going to do this now? Are we really going to do it?"

"Aren't you scared I'm going to win?"

Sara crossed her arms, waiting.

"All those years I wasted thinking you were better than me. Poor Sara, the tragic widow. And then I find out you jumped right back into the saddle with the first cop you could find."

Guilt flooded Sara's senses. Lena had always been a shark who could smell even the tiniest drop of blood in the water. "That's not how it happened."

"That's exactly how it happened," Lena shot back. "You're just a fancy piece of trim. You know that?"

Sara laughed, relieved that was the worst of it. *Trim* was slang for women who slept with cops. "And?"

"You know what you loved about Jeffrey? That he took risks. That he went out there and beat down anybody who got in his way."

"Is that all you have?"

Lena stepped closer. "You never would've given him the time of day if he was just some pussy who let everybody else fight his battles."

"You mean like you?"

Lena pursed her lips, the only indication that she'd heard the words. "I saw the way you used to look at him—your hero. Your big, tough cop. I bet it's the same way with Will. Funny how you just slotted in one cop for the other. Wonder how Jeffrey would've felt about that?"

Sara shook her head, as if the blows weren't landing. "Is this going somewhere?"

"You wanted Jeffrey out there fighting the good fight. You loved it when he swung his dick around, kicked ass, and took names. Lemme tell you something, Sara, he took risks because you wanted him to. You got some kind of cheap thrill out of pushing him to the edge. I gave him a place to go, but you—*you*—were the one who rewarded him for it."

"Shut up," Sara snapped. The cut was too deep. "Just shut up."

"Doesn't feel so good, does it? Being blamed for something you couldn't control."

"This conversation is over." Sara tried to walk away, but Lena grabbed her arm. "Get your hand off me."

"I thought we were doing this."

Sara jerked her arm out of Lena's grasp.

Lena said, "You always think you're so damn smart, but you can't even see what's right in front of you." She gave a surprised laugh that echoed down the empty hallway. "Hey, I guess you make mistakes after all."

"You think I don't make mistakes?" Sara's voice shook with rage. She could barely restrain herself. "I was the one who told Jeffrey to hire you. I was the one who told him to promote you. I was the one who thought you could do your goddamn job and keep him safe."

Lena was backed against the window. Sara loomed over her. She couldn't remember moving, couldn't understand how her finger had jammed into Lena's chest or how her hand had clenched into a fist.

Slowly, Lena turned her head, offering her cheek. "Go on," she said, her voice smooth as silk. "Take your best shot."

There was a weird tickle in Sara's feet. She felt as if she was standing at the edge of a bottomless pit. She forced herself to look over Lena's shoulder at the rows of newborns swaddled in blankets. The cheerful rainbows and clouds painted on the ceiling above them.

Sara couldn't let Lena win. Not this time. Not like this. She stepped back from the edge. She dropped her hand. She straightened her spine. Sara held up her head as she walked down the long hallway.

Lena asked, "That's it?"

She just needed to make it downstairs. Once Sara was outside, once she had fresh, cold air in her lungs, she would find a way to put this behind her. The last five minutes were not going to erase the last five years. Lena had no idea what Sara had been through. How she'd struggled. How she'd carved out a new life for herself. She didn't know Jeffrey and she sure as hell didn't know Will.

The sound of slow clapping echoed down the hall. Sara forced herself not to flinch. Each clap sounded like a gunshot.

"Good for you, Doc." Lena clapped louder. "Ride your high horse right on out of here."

Sara didn't turn around. She couldn't turn around. She'd end up giving Lena the catfight she'd been spoiling for.

She pushed open the door to the stairs. Her hands would not unclench. Sara rounded the landing at a jog. Each step she took only served to ramp up her anger.

Of course Sara had loved Jeffrey because he was tough. There wasn't a woman alive who didn't want a strong man in her life. That didn't make Sara responsible for his murder. She had begged him not to trust Lena, to just once let her hang herself with her own rope. And the idea that Sara could just slot in Will for Jeffrey was preposterous. The two men had nothing in common, except that both of them would've kicked Lena to the curb if they'd heard her talking to Sara the way she just had.

Sara almost wept with relief when she reached the main floor landing. She found herself in another dimly lit hallway. There were no stragglers or visitors at this time of night. Sara followed the green line on the floor, knowing it would take her to the elevators, to the exit.

Too demanding.

Too perfect.

If only.

Sara couldn't stop herself from making mistakes. She was overwhelmed with mistakes. Little ones. Big ones. Life-altering, earth-shattering fuckups had followed her for the last five years of her life, culminating in her drive down to this godforsaken hospital.

Her cell phone rang. Sara didn't answer. She passed the closed gift shop. Mylar balloons were pressed against the ceiling. The cooler was chained shut. Sara's phone stopped ringing. Almost immediately, it started back up again. She let it ring out, go to voicemail. There were a few seconds of silence, then the ringing started up again.

Sara checked the caller ID.

JASPER, GA.

Will.

A few hours ago, his phone said he was on the coast. Now, it said he was in the mountains.

Sara answered the call. She fought to keep her tone even. "I can't talk right now."

"Where are you?"

"I'm at the hospital."

"Upstairs?"

"No." She wiped away tears. The main entrance was up ahead. The lights from the parking lot gave the lobby an ethereal luminescence. "I'm leaving."

"To go to the hotel?"

"To go home." Sara didn't realize until she'd said the words that they were true. Her purse was locked in the back of her car. The keyfob was in her pocket. The rest of her stuff was at the hotel. She'd brought a change of clothes and some toiletries she kept in her locker at Grady. None of it was worth postponing her escape. The hotel cleaning staff could throw it out or keep it. Sara didn't care. She would call the front desk on her way out of town.

"Sara?" Will asked.

"I can't talk." Her hand was clenching and unclenching. Her teeth ached from grinding them together. "I'll call you later."

"Don't hang up."

She shook her head. "I can't do this now."

"I need you to just stop. Right now."

"Will, I—"

"Sara, stop walking."

Sara stopped.

"I need to talk to you."

Sara looked down at the phone. Then she looked up. How had Will known she was walking? She scanned the empty lobby. "Where are you?"

"I need to tell you what happened." He sounded desperate. "Not just before, but tonight. Last night."

She saw him then. He was standing outside the glass entrance doors. He was wearing dark pants and a gray shirt. Sara had seen the uniform before. The hospital maintenance staff wore it.

His hand went up to the glass.

She gave him an out. Insanely, she gave him an out. "You're working with Faith."

Will didn't answer, and Sara finally understood. The rolling phone calls. The undercover assignment he wouldn't talk about. The guilty look on his face this morning. His refusal to tell her what he was hiding. There was only one reason he would lie to her.

Sara said, "You're investigating Lena again."

"No, but she knows I'm here." Will said, "I'm sorry, baby. I'm so sorry."

Sara's eyes burned with tears. Lena didn't just know that Will was here. She knew that he'd left Sara completely in the dark.

You always think you're so damn smart, but you can't even see what's right in front of you.

"You asshole," Sara hissed into the phone. She could still hear Lena's laughter ringing in her ears. "You let her make a fool of me."

"I'm sorry." Will's hand went up again. He pressed his palm to the glass door. "I didn't think that far ahead. I didn't—" He stopped. "I need you to go easy on me, Sara. Please."

"You lied to me." Her voice was shaking again. Everything was shaking. She'd blamed herself for pushing him away when all the time Will was the one keeping her at arm's length. "You looked me right in the face and you lied to me."

"I didn't tell you because I thought you would leave me."

She felt something snap inside of her. "You were right."

"Sara—"

The pain was too much. She clutched the phone in her hand, wishing she could break it into pieces. And then she realized she could. Sara smashed the phone against the wall. Chunks of plastic and glass popped back into her face. She picked up the pieces and threw them back at the wall.

"Sara!" Will shouted. He was still outside, pulling on the closed glass doors. "Sara!"

What an idiot she'd been. She'd opened her heart to this man. She'd shared her bed with him. She'd told him things she'd never even told her husband.

And he'd given Lena Adams a knife to stab into Sara's back.

"Sara!" The locks rattled on the closed doors.

She turned away from him, heading back toward the stairs.

"Wait!"

Sara kept walking. She wasn't going to wait on him. She would never wait on him again. She had to get out of this building. Out of this town. Away from Lena. Away from Will and his lies. There was nothing else Sara could do but run away. She'd been stupid and blind. He'd betrayed her. She had given him everything, and Will had betrayed her.

"Sara!" Will's voice was louder. He was inside the building.

She quickened her pace. Will's footsteps pounded through the empty lobby, echoed down the hall. He was coming after her.

Sara started running. She couldn't bear the thought of seeing his face again. She pumped her arms, lifted her knees. Will's footsteps grew louder. The door smacked against the wall as she ran into the stairwell. Instead of going up, she went down. The staff locker room would be in the basement. Maintenance. Storage. The morgue. There would be a loading dock or an exit she could use to get the hell out of here.

"Sara!"

She was on the landing when the door banged open above her. Will yelled, "Wait!"

She tripped, grabbing the handrail as she slid down the last few stairs. Sara pulled open the door. Another hallway. The bright lights were like needles in her eyes.

"Stop!"

Will was already on the landing. He was faster than Sara. She would never make it to the exit without him catching her. Her shoes skidded on the floor as she darted into an open doorway.

"Let me explain! Sara!"

She slammed the door shut, furiously checked for a way to lock it.

The door pushed open. She fell backward. Will grabbed her arm. He jerked her toward him. Sara slapped at him as hard as she could. He caught one of her hands. She punched him with the other one. She hated him. She wanted to scratch out his eyes. To tear his heart out of his chest the way he had torn out hers.

"Sara, please—"

She punched him again. She couldn't stop. Hitting him felt too good. She slapped his face. Her fingernails drew blood. He caught both of her hands in one of his own. Sara couldn't break free. He pushed her back against the wall. Her head banged against the cinder block. She brought up her knee, but Will was too close for her to do any damage.

He kissed her. Their teeth clashed. His fingers gripped open her jaw. His tongue filled her mouth. Sara slammed her fist into his chest. He ripped open her jeans. Sara didn't stop him. She helped him. She felt numb. Every emotion had drained away but one. She was sick of taking care of people. She was sick of being the good friend, of doing the right thing, of letting things go.

Will spit in his hand. It wasn't enough. Sara gasped as he pushed inside of her. He went deep. Too deep. It took her breath away. Still, she gripped his shoulders, holding tight, meeting each thrust until her body took over and she felt herself give.

Sara's mouth found his. She sucked his tongue. Bit his lip. Her heels dug into the backs of his legs. Will flinched when her hands slipped underneath his shirt. She didn't care. She scratched the scarred flesh on his back. Words came out of her mouth—filthy words that told him exactly what to do. Again and again she met each thrust until she had to clench her teeth to keep from screaming.

There was no slow build, just an uncontrollable rush that flowered deep inside her. The ecstasy was unbearable. Sara bit down on Will's shoulder. She tasted the salt of his sweat. Every molecule in her body pulsated from the intensity. She cried out his name. She couldn't help herself, couldn't stop the exquisite torrent of release.

Will collapsed against her. Neither one of them could stand. They slid to the floor, both breathless, both shocked by what they had done.

"Sara—"

She covered her face with her hands. She couldn't look at him. Couldn't acknowledge what had just happened.

"Sara—" Will's mouth was close to her ear. The brush of his lips brought an involuntary shiver. "Oh, God," he whispered. "Sara, please—"

She pushed him away. She could still feel him throbbing between her legs. She felt craven. Deviant.

"Sara . . ."

She shook her head, wishing she could disappear. "Go," she begged. "Please, just go."

"Sara—"

"Go!" she screamed.

Will struggled to stand. She heard him zip up his pants, tuck in his shirt. There was a loud click as the door opened, then again as it closed.

Sara looked up.

He was gone.

11.

Lena sat in the cramped surveillance van with her hands thrust into her jacket pockets. There were three monitors in front of her. The computers under the desk were blowing out heat. DeShawn and Paul were wearing short-sleeved shirts. They were both sweating, but Lena was so cold she could've been sitting in an igloo. She was only six weeks pregnant and already her body was out of whack. This was why pregnant women were always so cranky. Their thermometers bounced up and down like Ping-Pong balls.

DeShawn scrolled through the security cameras, asking, "Where are you, Mr. Snitch?"

"Mr. Snitch," Paul echoed, giving the name a showman's flourish.

All confidential informants had code names. Protecting a CI's identity was part of the devil's bargain. You used the name on all your paperwork. You used it in the field, where the slip of a word could mean the death of an informant. "Mr. Snitch" wasn't the most creative name, but it suited the junkie they'd turned a few days ago. There was something about the man that was slithery, like a snake. Lena thought maybe it was his scaly skin and beady little eyes.

"Come on, Snitchy." DeShawn tapped the keyboard, toggling

back and forth through the cameras outside the Chick-fil-A. "Here, Snitchy-Snitchy."

Paul reminded him, "We padded in an extra hour for a reason."

Lena watched the monitors change as DeShawn scrolled through the different angles. She'd always hated junkies— probably because her uncle was one. Hank was clean now, but that didn't change his basic, junkie personality. Everything about him asked, *What's in it for me?*

"Here we go." Paul pointed at one of the monitors. A white car pulled into a parking space near the door. The emergency brake was pulled. The windows rolled shut.

Lena asked, "Does he have his mic on?"

DeShawn twisted the dial on the tuner that picked up Snitch's transmitter. They heard his car radio playing an ad for a pizza place. The sound cut. Keys jangled. The car door opened.

Snitch was short and wiry and needed a shave. His ballcap was pulled low on his head. Dark sunglasses wrapped around his face. He was dressed in black jeans and a black T-shirt. He kept checking over his shoulder, looking left and right, as he walked toward the restaurant.

"Moron," Paul groaned. "He couldn't just get a neon sign?"

Snitch kept looking around as he entered the restaurant. He stood in line at the counter. A woman steered clear of him as she headed toward the side exit. Lena had scheduled the meet for just after the lunch rush, but a few stragglers were waiting around for refills. She heard soft conversation under the rustle of clothes. Snitch moved up in line. He ordered an iced tea. He kept scratching himself, shifting from one foot to the other.

"Junkie needs his pills," DeShawn noted.

Lena said, "Junkie needs to do what he's supposed to do before I pull his immunity."

Mr. Snitch waited at the counter. He kept twitching. Lena wanted to reach through the monitor and make him stop.

Their entire operation depended on this junkie scumbag. For almost two weeks, Lena's team had been surveilling a shooting gallery off an anonymous tip. They didn't want to just shut it down. They wanted to decimate Sid Waller's operation. The job had quickly become an exercise in futility. Normally, there was always some lowlife who was willing to flip for cash and prizes. This time was different. No one would turn on Sid Waller. No one would wear a wire while they made a buy. No one would go on the record about the drugs and guns.

No one, that was, until Mr. Snitch.

Paul seemed to read her mind. He asked, "You still think Snitch is working both sides?"

"I don't know," Lena admitted. Mr. Snitch had asked for her by name. She'd been leaving the doctor's office when the call came through. Her celebratory dinner with Jared had turned into take-out at the station. "It's weird that he showed up right when our case was falling apart."

Paul asked, "How would he know it was falling apart?"

Lena shrugged. "Snitch was locked up for less than two hours when he told the guard to get me. How did he even know my name?"

Paul and DeShawn guffawed. Lena liked to break balls. Every junkie in town knew her name.

"All right, all right," she allowed. "Still, we've all been at this long enough to know that nobody does you any favors."

"I dunno," Paul said. "Scrawny guy like that, his first time behind bars—two hours sounds like the right amount of time for him to freak the fuck out."

DeShawn added, "Oxy's hard to come by in the pokey."

"Not if you suck enough dick." Paul held up his hand for a high-five. DeShawn readily obliged.

"Where'd he go?" Lena leaned forward, scanning the monitors.

DeShawn worked the cameras again, toggling through the different views. "There he is."

Lena saw the top of a door closing. Snitch had gone to the playground. Brightly colored plastic slides and swings circled around a sandpit. Two kids were playing on the rope climb, a boy and a girl. There were more cameras on the playground than inside the restaurant. Every corner was on display.

Snitch sat down on a bench. The sun was on his face. He stretched his arms out along the back like he had all the time in the world. They heard him humming through the microphone taped to his chest.

"They're gonna kick him out," Paul said. "Grown man ain't allowed on the playground without a kid."

"I think he'll be okay." Lena could see the staff moving lethargically behind the counter. They had all downshifted for the post-lunch lull. One of the kids tossed a cup in his hand. The others watched him with a mixture of boredom and exhaustion.

"Looks like Mom's not gonna be a problem." DeShawn pointed to a lone woman sitting in a booth. She was typing on her iPad while simultaneously talking on her cell phone. Papers were spread out on the table. She was obviously working.

Paul said, "I bet she tells her husband she's spending time with the kids."

Lena held back a response. Now that she was going to be a mother, she found herself far less judgmental. "We've got forty-five minutes, right?"

"Give or take," DeShawn said. "Waller has a reputation for being late."

Paul always had to contradict. "He might show up early, case the joint."

"Call me on my cell if he does." Lena pushed open the door. "I'll be right back."

She kept her head down as she walked across the parking lot. There was little chance of her being seen. They had set up in front of a Target, fifty yards from the Chick-fil-A. Tapping into the restaurant's wireless security system was less than legal, but the manager should've better encrypted his wireless hotspot. They weren't going to use the video anyway. DeShawn wasn't recording. They were keeping a tight leash on Mr. Snitch. At least Lena was. She didn't trust just the audio. She wanted to see him with her own eyes.

There was something wrong with the guy. She'd only met him a few days ago, but in her gut, Lena knew there was something off about him. She had felt it when she first sat across from him at the jail. She had especially felt it when he'd told her he could hand her Sid Waller.

Sidney Michael Waller.

Lena was more than familiar with the name. Everyone at the station was. Waller wasn't just a drug dealer. He wasn't just a pimp and a gunrunner. Last year, they'd all worked around the clock to make a case against Waller for raping his niece and murdering his sister. And then the niece had recanted. Witnesses disappeared. People changed their stories. The case had fallen apart three days before the trial started and everyone, especially Lena, had walked away with a bad taste in their mouths.

But then Mr. Snitch had showed up with a golden ticket. She couldn't have written a better script for the man. He'd confirmed details about the shooting gallery off the interstate. The guns. The whores. The vast amount of drugs moving through the city while Sid Waller sat back and counted the dough. The case practically made itself. Waller would spend years behind bars. He'd get far more time for the guns than he would have off the rape.

But only if Lena ignored her gut. She had to keep tamping down the little voice inside her head that said this was too easy. She'd been gunning for Waller for a year and suddenly he fell into her lap? What was Mr. Snitch getting out of this? The immunity deal was good, but was skipping eight months in prison really worth risking his life?

Lena couldn't let herself dwell on the questions too long. She couldn't let this operation fall apart.

The truth was that Sid Waller had gotten under her skin. Lena was determined to return the favor. She brought him in for questioning every time she found a plausible excuse. She couldn't put him behind bars—yet—but she could certainly run up his legal bills. Just last week, Waller had called her a cunt during an interview. Two weeks before that, he'd told her all the different ways he could fuck her. That all of this had been recorded for prosperity didn't seem to bother him. Waller had a good attorney, the kind of attorney who knew the law better than most cops.

Maybe that's why the judge was being so difficult. Lena had tried to get a warrant for the shooting gallery based on the suspicious traffic at all hours of the night. The judge had said no. Denise Branson presented evidence that Mr. Snitch, a confidential informant, had given up the location. The judge had said no. It was only through blind persistence that they had talked the man into letting them record today's meeting. And even then, he'd only authorized audio.

This was their last chance. Lena knew there was no way the judge could say no if they got it on tape. All Mr. Snitch had to do was get Waller to talk about the house, to say something about the guns or the drugs or the money, then they could go in and bust some bad guys.

At least that's what Lena was praying for. Sid Waller was the last big case she was going to work for a while. She was looking at months of her life being consumed by her pregnancy, then a couple of weeks, maybe another month, home with the baby before she returned to work.

Just the thought of being away from the job that long made her feel antsy. Lena had always been a cop. She couldn't lose that part of her identity. Lately, it seemed like she wasn't going to have a choice. She was too tired to sleep, too sleepy to concentrate. She had to pee all the time. She was cold. She was hot. She was cold again. If this was what pregnancy was like, Lena wasn't sure she could handle it. And the nausea was unrelenting. Why did they call it morning sickness when it was more like all-day sickness?

Lena sat on a bench in front of the Target. She had to unzip her jacket because she'd started sweating at some point during the easy walk across the parking lot. She found a tissue in the pocket and blew her nose. She wasn't sure why her nose ran all the time now. Jared said she was making snot for two.

Lena checked the time on her phone. Sid Waller wasn't due for another forty minutes. She'd rest for a little while, then go back to the van. That is, if she didn't fall asleep first. Her eyelids felt heavy as she looked around the parking lot.

Lena found herself wondering if the world had always been filled with so many kids or if she was just seeing them now because she was pregnant. A toddler screamed as his mother pulled him toward the store. A child ran screeching around a minivan as his harried mom chased after him. Just outside the entrance to the store, another poor woman was bouncing a wailing baby on her hip.

Topping off this happy tableau was an extremely pregnant woman who was loading bags into the trunk of her car. Her belly was the size of a beachball. Sweat glued her hair to her head. She was parked in one of those expectant-mother parking spaces that Lena had always resented but now completely understood. The woman deserved to be closer to the door. She looked miserable. She dug her fist into her back as she unloaded the last bag from the cart. Her dress was way too tight. Even from a distance, Lena could see the thong sticking like dental floss between her ass cheeks.

"Jesus," Lena whispered. She felt like a cow glimpsing behind the counter at the butcher's shop.

Lena shivered. Her hands were cold. That's how it usually started. The change in temperature worked its way from the edges. She stuck her hands into her jacket pockets. Her fingers curled around the photo. Lena guessed the ultrasound could be called a photograph. At the very least, it was a snapshot of what was going on inside of her.

Over the years, Lena had looked at her share of X-rays and medical reports. She'd seen ultrasound pictures taped on refrigerators, shown on TV screens, and even presented as evidence in court cases where the mother had been murdered.

Lena had never been particularly moved by the images. To her, they were just black and white blobs. She assumed that the ability to ooh and ahh over the tiny splotches and weird folds was lost on her. Also, there was something disturbing about looking at a person's interior workings. Maybe Lena was a prude, but she couldn't be the only one thinking that showing an ultrasound was tantamount to showing the world irrefutable proof that you'd had sex.

But that was before Lena had seen an ultrasound of her own baby. Everything had changed two days ago. She couldn't understand it. How had that tiny, pulsing little bean opened up such a large space in her heart?

And how had it made Lena love Jared so much? She couldn't explain the shift. Loving Jared was nothing new, but the sudden depth of her feeling was terrifying. Lena had never felt this way about a man before. She was completely out of control, incapable of hiding her vulnerabilities. At night, she clung to him. During the day, she couldn't stop touching him. At first, Jared had been mildly annoyed. He generally wasn't up for touching unless it led to something, but he'd become more receptive over the last few weeks. There had to be some hormone Lena was giving off. Even the guys at work were looking at her differently.

Work.

Lena couldn't think about what would happen when she started to show. Not that she wasn't already. They probably just thought she was getting fat—which she was. Her pants cut into her waist. She spilled out of her bra. Jared was ecstatic about this particular development. All Lena could think was that there was no way she could chase after some thug with her breasts flopping around. In a few months, she'd probably end up stuck behind a desk. She'd be doing paperwork and following up on witness statements while everyone else had all the fun.

Was it worth it?

Lena looked down at the ultrasound. She touched the tiny little bean resting in white crescent arms.

Of course it was worth it.

Her phone vibrated in her jacket pocket. Denise Branson. She was probably pacing the station house waiting for news.

Lena said, "What's up, D?"

"Any news?"

Lena looked at the time. She should head back to the van. "He's got another thirty minutes, but he's always late."

"I'm already pushing back a meeting," Denise said. "You know it's both our asses on the line now."

"I know." Lena reluctantly pushed herself up from the bench. "I appreciate it."

"Listen." Denise seemed eager to move on. "I got another piece of the Big Whitey puzzle."

"Denise—"

"Just hear me out like I do with you, okay?"

Lena owed her that much. "Okay."

"I found an article in the *Savannah Tribune*. Eighteen months ago, two white girls showed up dead behind a church. Runaways from good homes. Heroin overdoses, both of them. From honor students to stone-cold junkies in less than a month. The needles were still in their arms. That sound familiar?"

"Honor students OD on heroin all the time," Lena told her. "I could find a hundred other cases on the same day. Maybe thousands."

"It's just like what happened here."

There was no use arguing. "Denise, I'm saying this as a friend. You're obsessed with this. You're too close."

"So what if I am?"

Lena shook her head as she made her way back across the parking lot. Only in law enforcement was obsession considered an asset.

Denise said, "You're obsessed with Sid Waller."

"And I'm about to bust him," Lena countered. "I've got a case. I've got a witness. I've got leads, photos, timelines. All you've got is a ghost."

"You start out with all of that or did you put it together?"

Lena didn't want to admit she had a point. Before Mr. Snitch magically appeared, Denise could've been asking Lena the same questions about Waller. But she hadn't. She'd given Lena the support and time to do what she needed to do. "Did you track down that law firm?"

"I'm working on it. There's some kind of connection there."

"If you're right, then maybe we can help each other out. Sid Waller's the big man on campus. Once we take him down, he can give us Big Whitey."

Denise huffed a laugh. "You think Sid Waller's gonna turn? He's got just as much juice inside the joint as he does out."

She was right. The gangs ran the prisons and Waller would be a top dog. Still, she said, "It could happen."

"I'm not giving Waller any deals. He can rot away his sick ass in jail. I can get Big Whitey on my own."

Lena realized her fist was stuck in her back, just like the other pregnant woman. She dropped her hand. "All right. If you think you can put together a case, then you should get help. This is too big for one person. Two, if you count me, because you know I'm there for you."

Denise snorted. "You know I'm off-book. How am I gonna go to Lonnie for help when he told me to shut this down months ago? He's not gonna spend one dime of department money on Big Whitey. At least not until it's too late."

She was right again. By budgetary necessity, police forces were more reactive than preventative these days.

Lena had an idea. "I know somebody with the state who can give us a hand."

"I can't jump over Lonnie's head."

"I know that," Lena said. Gray was relatively new to Macon, but he'd spent the past fifteen years heading up forces all around the state. They both respected him too much to stab him in the back. Not to mention that when push came to shove, Gray could twist that knife right back in theirs. "You could reach out informally. I know an agent who's discreet." She didn't mention that the man had investigated her almost two years ago. "He's a cop, but he doesn't act like one. He'll give you the support you need. At the very least, he can help you put together some of these pieces."

"You think I'm gonna let the GBI come stomping onto my turf and taking credit?" She gave a harsh laugh. "You know how many hours I've put into this? How many miles on my car? How many sleepless nights? I've got blood in this fight, Lee. I'm not going to let go of it now."

Lena recognized the righteous indignation in her tone. Five years ago, Lena would've been saying the same thing, sounding the same way. She'd been so sure of herself before Jeffrey died. She was the one who was always right. She didn't need help. She didn't need some asshole trying to grab credit. Lena had taken on the world single-handedly every day—right up until the world knocked her flat on her ass.

Denise said, "If you'd talked to that girl, listened to her mama, then you'd feel the same way as me."

"I know," Lena said. She was glad she hadn't spoken with either of them, otherwise she probably would've been sucked in right along with Denise. "You work the case. You don't let the case work you."

"What does that mean?" Denise shot back.

"This ghost you're chasing—it's affecting your life."

"In what way?"

Lena didn't answer. Denise wanted some bowling pins she

could knock down. Lena knew from experience that the job wasn't kind to lonely women. It could make you too driven. Too hard. It could scare people away from you.

Having Jared in her life had changed that for Lena. He'd shouldered some of the burden. He'd made her feel like it was okay to let go.

And then there was the baby. Lena put her hand to her stomach. Her face felt hot. An idiotic grin spread across her mouth. It was the hormones. She was glad she wasn't in the van with Paul and DeShawn. She was probably fucking glowing.

"Come on, Adams," Branson prompted. "Give it to me straight."

Lena shrugged off the challenge. "Did you hear DeShawn's getting divorced again?"

"And you think 'cause he's black and I'm black that we're a match made in heaven?"

"Please, he should be so lucky." As hypocritical as it sounded, Lena told her, "I'm just saying that you can't do both—be married to the job and married to a wife. What are you working for if you don't have someone to come home to?"

Denise's words were pointed. "You mean husband."

The phone line was deadly silent. Denise Branson went to church every Sunday. She made the appropriate noises when a good-looking man walked by. But so had Lena's sister, and Sibyl had been as gay as a three-dollar bill.

Denise was all business again. "Call me as soon as the meet's over. If you can't get Waller on tape, Lonnie's gonna give us a come-to-Jesus talk. And I'm not gonna argue with him, because he'll be right."

"Denise, give me a break."

"Don't talk about break, girl, talk about broke. Do you know how much this is costing the department? Twenty-four-hour surveillance going on ten days. Overtime for everybody and their mother. We passed the half-million mark last weekend. I can't even do the math on where we are now. I've been waiting for this meet to pan out so when I take it to Lonnie, he doesn't kick my ass out the door."

"I know you're taking heat for me."

"Shit," Denise muttered. "I wish it was heat. I'm standing in a damn ring of fire."

Lena was almost to the van. She glanced around, making sure she wasn't being watched. "I'll get Waller. I promise."

"You don't, then get a newspaper. We're gonna both need to start looking for new jobs." She let the phone slam down in Lena's ear.

Lena slipped her hand back into her pocket. She traced the edge of the ultrasound as she walked toward the white van with the AT&T logo on the side. As far as she knew, no one had bothered to get clearance from the phone company. Lena figured they should shut up and take the free advertising.

"Hey, boss." DeShawn came around the side of the van. He was so big he cast her completely in shadow.

Lena's hand went to her throat. "You sure move light for a Mack truck."

"That's what the ladies say." He winked at her. "You doing all right?"

Lena felt her defenses go up. "Why?"

He shrugged and shook his head. "No reason."

"You take yourself off the monitors and stand out here waiting for me for no reason?"

He had the grace to admit he'd been caught. "I know this whole Waller thing's been weighing hard on you."

"Why? Has Lonnie said something?" Lena knew that DeShawn was Gray's eyes and ears, but she'd never thought of him as a tattletale. "What did he say?"

"Nothing, and I didn't say anything to him." DeShawn looked at her like she was paranoid for no reason. "Come on, gal. You know I'm on your team."

"What's going on?" Lena asked. Now that she was looking at him, he seemed on edge, like something else was going on. "Why are you acting weird?"

DeShawn gave a heavy sigh. "I just noticed you've been tired lately."

"So? We're all tired. We've been butts to nuts for weeks."

He gave the sigh again. "I just wanted you to know that it's okay by me if you decide to take a back seat on—"

"Fuck your back seat," Lena snapped. "I've never taken a back seat on anything in my life."

"All right." He held up his hands. "Just worried about you, is all."

"Worried about me why?"

His mouth twisted to the side, like he was debating whether or not to tell her something. Lena knew DeShawn's sister had two girls. Maybe he'd figured out that Lena was pregnant. In which case, she had to shut this down fast.

She said, "Get your panties out of your cooch, Shawn. I appreciate your concern, but the best thing for both of us right now is for you to do your job and me to do mine. All right?"

He held up his hands in surrender again. "You're the boss."

She knocked on the side of the van. "It's me."

Eric Haigh cracked open the door. The whole gang was here. He told Lena, "We got a call from Waller's tail. He's about five minutes out."

Paul couldn't help but add, "I was right. He's probably coming early to case the restaurant."

Lena wasn't interested in giving credit. She started to hold out her hand for help, then decided it would be better to show DeShawn she was capable of moving her own weight. Still, she groaned as she pulled herself up.

DeShawn vaulted in without assistance, probably to prove a point. He slammed the door shut behind him.

"Jesus Christ." Lena clapped her hands over her face. The smell was disgusting. "What've you guys been doing in here?"

"Sorry," Eric said. "I had Mexican for lunch."

"Thanks a lot, dickslit." Paul punched him in the arm. Eric rewarded him with the wettest-sounding fart Lena had ever heard.

"Oh, God." She pinched her nose closed and breathed through her mouth. "Please tell me Snitch is still there."

Paul provided, "Mr. Snitchy is on the bench looking at the kiddies."

"Looking at them how?" Lena checked the monitor to see for herself. Snitch still had on his sunglasses. His arms were sprawled across the back of the bench. "Are you sure he's not asleep?"

"Look at his foot."

He was right. Snitch's heel was hopping up and down so fast the camera barely registered the movement. Lena asked, "Where's Mom?"

DeShawn was back in his chair. He pulled up the appropriate camera. The mother was still on the phone, stretched out in the booth as if she planned to stay there for a while.

"Good thing he's not a pedophile," Lena said. She motioned for Eric to get out of her chair.

Eric said, "The seat might be a little warm."

Paul laughed again, and she slapped him on the back of the head. "Why is everyone in this van an asshole except for me?"

Paul asked, "You okay, boss?"

Lena scowled at him. "Since when am I the boss?"

"You're in charge, right?" Paul indicated his empty chair. "What's going on with you? Your face is all red."

She put her hand to her cheek. The skin was hot. "It's probably gas poisoning."

"You sure about that?" He cocked an eyebrow at her, but he didn't push it.

"All right, ladies and Lena." DeShawn rubbed his hands together. "Mr. Waller has arrived."

A red Corvette idled in the parking lot. The windows were down. Sid Waller circled the lot twice before parking in a space by the road. He'd brought weight with him. Diego Nuñez was in the passenger seat. He had his arm resting on the door. A cigarette dangled from his fingers.

Eric squinted at the monitor. "Is that a joint?"

DeShawn checked it out. "Looks like it."

"Damn," Paul said. "Chick-fil-A don't like queers. What're they gonna do with a spic toking a doobie?"

"Shut up," Lena said. She tried to tune out their voices as she watched Sid Waller get out of the car. The metal chain on his wallet swung as he strutted across the parking lot. His long, skanky hair was pulled back in a ponytail. He wore ragged jeans and a flannel shirt with the sleeves ripped off. Tattoos covered both arms. Like Paul, he was incapable of just opening a door. He flung it open to announce his presence.

All four of them swiveled their heads in unison, watching the monitor that showed the lobby camera. Waller raised some eyebrows inside the restaurant, but this was Macon and it was hard to tell a harmless long-haired redneck from a violent one. The girls behind the counter figured it out quickly. Lena had always believed that women were better than men at spotting danger. It was why her gut wouldn't let go of the bad feeling she had about Mr. Snitch.

The junkie in question had noticed Waller's arrival. He sat up straight on the bench. His hand shot up in a wave. And then he kept waving, because Waller wouldn't look his way. Finally, Snitch stood up and went to the door. Instead of going inside, he motioned for Waller to join him on the playground.

Lena checked on the woman in the booth. The mother's jaw dropped when she saw Sid Waller.

DeShawn said, "Come on, Mama. Time to check on the kid-dies."

Waller jerked open the door. Lena startled when his voice blared from the speaker in the van. "What the fuck, dumbass?"

Snitch nervously looked at the kids.

Thankfully, their mother had scrambled to the door on the other side of the playground. They heard her strident tone on Snitch's concealed mic. "Britney. Randall. Now."

The children didn't have to be told twice. Sid Waller had a way of clearing a room.

"Move over," Waller said, and Snitch slid down the bench. "What're you doing here? I thought they didn't let faggots in this place."

Snitch chuckled like he was in on the joke.

"Shut up, pencil dick." Waller took a pack of cigarettes from his pocket. He shook one out, fumbled for his lighter.

Snitch looked around, checking all the corners.

"You worried about something?" Waller asked. He held the open flame of the lighter a few inches from his cigarette.

Snitch shook his head.

"Take off those fucking glasses."

Snitch took off his sunglasses.

Waller lit the cigarette. He inhaled half of it down before blowing out a long stream of smoke. "What are we doing here?"

"I got some more pills." Snitch reached for his pocket.

Waller stopped him with a look. "I look like a drug dealer to you?"

Snitch froze, his hand halfway in his pocket. They'd told him to pass the pills so at the very least, they'd have Waller on taking stolen narcotics.

Inside the van, they all tensed.

Eric said, "Look at him. He's freaking out."

He was right. Snitch was panicking.

Waller stood up to leave.

"Come on," Snitch said. "Don't be that way."

Instead of opening the door, Waller leaned against it. His arms crossed over his broad chest. The cigarette dangled from his mouth.

Lena held her breath. She watched the two men. They were having some kind of staring contest.

Unbelievably, Snitch won. Waller looked down as he tapped the ash off his cigarette.

Snitch said, "I wanna move up."

Waller put the cigarette back in his mouth.

"I can get more product."

"What makes you think I need it?"

Snitch stood up. He took off his ballcap and ran his fingers through his hair.

Lena asked, "Was that a signal?"

"I think he's just sweating," Paul said. "Look at the way he keeps pulling his pants away from his sac."

He was right. Snitch couldn't keep his hands off his crotch.

"Well?" Waller prompted. "You gonna make your case?"

Remarkably, Snitch remembered his lines. "I've gotta source at the hospital. I can get the good stuff. Name brand. Not that shit from China."

Smoke wafted up into Waller's eyes. He was thinking about it. Lena knew that he was thinking about it.

"Come on," she begged. Everyone in the van edged closer to the monitors. This was the make-or-break moment—maybe their only chance to get him.

Waller turned around and opened the door.

"Fuck." DeShawn banged his fist against the table. The monitors shook. "I can't believe he blew it."

Snitch seemed to be thinking the same thing. He took off his hat again. "You're a dumbass."

Waller stopped.

Eric whispered, "Holy shit."

"Shut up," Lena ordered.

Waller was turning around. He didn't speak until the door had closed.

"What'd you just call me?"

"I said you're a dumbass."

Lena felt her heart stop beating. Waller was coiled like a snake. They would have to peel him off Snitch before he killed him.

"You think I'm a dumbass?" Waller asked, like he wanted to be absolutely clear.

Instead of backing down, Snitch said, "I offer to double my deliveries, to give you top-notch product, and you walk away from me?" He took a step toward Waller, seemingly blind to the fact that he was taking his own life into his hands. "I want to move up, Sid. I been a good soldier, but I want to be a general one day."

Waller seemed amused. "That so?"

"Yeah, that's so." Snitch jammed his hat back on his head. "I think I've earned some respect."

Waller took out his cigarette pack again. He lit a fresh one off the old one. "What do I get out of this?"

"You know I'm an earner," Snitch said. "You know I can do the dirty work."

"Seems to me you like the dirty work."

"You wanna get me wet?"

Waller didn't answer, but Lena shook her head. Snitch was pushing it too far. He was asking if Waller wanted him to murder someone.

Waller flicked the old cigarette into the sandpit. "Let's stick with what you know how to do. Double the order. Bring it to the house off Redding. We got junkies clawing at the door."

DeShawn offered silent high fives all around. The shooting gallery was the house off Redding. They had their probable cause.

Snitch wouldn't leave well enough alone. "When do you want it?"

"Soon as you can. Shipment's late this week." Sid puffed his cigarette. "We had a truck rolled in Miami. Cubans took two hundred K worth of Oxy."

Snitch's inner junkie took over. "I get payment on delivery. That's the deal."

Waller laughed. "Look at the big man giving orders." He patted Snitch on the back so hard that Snitch almost fell into the swing set. "I go by the house at three every morning. Don't be stupid and don't be late."

"Holy motherfucker." Lena laughed incredulously as Sid Waller took his leave from the playground. "Ho-lee shit."

Paul was laughing, too. "Grab your ankles, Waller. Get ready for the big pokey."

Eric cut a bugle of a fart, which made the men laugh harder.

Lena groaned as she crawled past them to the front of the van. "You're all disgusting."

They were laughing too hard to hear her.

She plopped into the driver's seat. She rolled down the window and filled her lungs with clean, fresh air. She prayed to God she wasn't carrying a boy. Or worse, two boys. Twins ran in families. Dr. Benedict had told her they'd know for sure when he did the next ultrasound.

Lena took out her phone and pulled up Denise Branson's number. She could see the Chick-fil-A building through the windshield. The distance was too great for detail, but she could tell that Snitch was still on the playground. He had returned to the bench, arms and legs spread wide. The sunglasses were back on. Lena couldn't see his expression, but she gathered he was feeling pretty pleased with himself. He knew he was safe now. The minute he'd gotten Waller to talk about the house, Snitch's immunity deal was set in stone.

Lena heard Denise Branson's voicemail. She ended the call. Denise was probably in a meeting. Lena pulled up the text messaging and typed out a quick note: *Baldy will have package within the hour.*

Baldy was their nickname for the judge who kept telling them no. Lena was probably being paranoid, but she didn't want to take the chance that her phone was hacked.

She checked over her shoulder. The men were still celebrating, trying to one-up one another with crass jokes about prison rape.

Lena rolled her eyes as she turned back around. Mr. Snitch was still on the playground bench. The sun was in his face. Kids were playing on the swings in front of him. He didn't have a care in the world.

She hated this part of the job. The junkie had been caught selling pills to kids, and he would go back to selling them pills because the police had let him go. There was no way for her to sit on him, wait for the inevitable fuckup. No criminal would ever deal with Lena again if they knew she couldn't be trusted. She would have to sit back and wait for Mr. Snitch to screw up on his own.

Or maybe she wouldn't.

Lena pulled up email on her phone. She selected the Google account that she used for ordering off the Internet. The email address could probably be traced back to her, but she didn't really care. She was going to take the advice she had just given Denise Branson. No cop should go it alone. There was no shame in asking for help. Besides, Mr. Snitch's immunity deal was with Macon, not the state of Georgia.

Lena couldn't touch Anthony Dell, but Will Trent could.

12.

FRIDAY

Will stumbled out of the hospital. Even outside, he could still hear Sara crying. Could feel the marks she'd left on his skin. Could smell her. Taste her.

He passed his bike, crossed the parking lot. His foot hit the curb. He stepped up, walking into the woods behind the building. Will didn't get far. He fell to his knees. He opened his mouth, tried to bring up the acid eating him inside.

What had he done?

He pressed his forehead to the cold ground. His mind kept flipping through the last twenty-four hours. All the violence. All the pain. What Will had seen. What he had wrought. Lena with the hammer. Tony with his knife. And then there was Sara.

What had he done to Sara?

He had lost her. In that one brutal moment, he had lost her forever.

"Hey, asshole!"

Will looked up. Paul Vickery was barreling toward him. Before Will could react, the man kicked him in the head.

Will slammed to the ground. Stars burst in front of his eyes. The air was knocked out of his chest.

Vickery jumped on him. He rained down punches like a wind-mill. Will bucked, trying to heave him off. Vickery grabbed Will's neck. The man put all of his weight into it, crushing Will's wind-pipe. Will tried to pry away his fingers. His mouth gaped open. Vickery pressed harder, strangling him. Will's tongue swelled. His eyes burned. He started to black out. Was this how it was going to happen? After all he had survived, was this how he was going to die?

Suddenly, the pressure stopped. Will gagged on the sudden rush of air.

Paul Vickery flew off him. He landed hard on the asphalt. His head thumped against the curb.

Will coughed so hard his feet kicked out.

"Are you okay?" Faith was there. She had a twenty-inch-long steel police baton in her hand. She asked Will again, "Are you okay?" She kept looking at Vickery, then back at Will. "Can you see me?"

Will saw two of her, then three.

Vickery tried to push himself up.

Faith slammed the baton into Vickery's kidneys. Two brutal blows, one after the other.

"Bitch!" he screamed, writhing on the ground. "Jesus!"

Faith jammed the baton in Vickery's face. "Stay down."

"He murdered a cop!"

The baton stayed in Vickery's face. She drew her Glock on Will. "Get up."

Will blinked at the gun. Her finger was on the trigger guard. He wasn't sure he could move. He hurt so bad. Everything hurt so bad.

"Black," Faith said. "I told you to get the fuck up."

Black.

Will didn't understand what she was saying. Was it some kind of a code?

"Up," Faith repeated. She was using her cop voice, the one that said she had drawn down on a suspect before and was ready to do it again. "I said get the fuck up."

Finally, Will's brain managed to make contact with his arms, his legs. He pushed himself to sitting. The effort almost wasted him.

"Stay there," Faith ordered, as if Will had a choice. "Bill Black, I'm placing you under arrest for parole violation."

"Parole?" Vickery shouted. "He killed a fucking cop!"

"You got proof?" When Vickery didn't offer an answer, she told Will, "You have the right to remain silent."

Vickery muttered, "Stupid cunt."

Faith talked over him. "Anything you say or do may be used against you in a court of law."

Will leaned over and threw up. Peas. Something white. Green beans. He couldn't remember eating any of it.

"You have a right to consult with an attorney."

Will sniffed. The sensation almost made him vomit again.

"If you cannot afford an attorney, one will be appointed for you by the courts."

"Okay." Will held up his hand for silence. The sound of her voice was an ice pick in his brain. "I waive my rights."

Faith holstered her Glock, but kept the baton at the ready. She tossed Will her handcuffs. "Put those on."

Vickery saw an opportunity. He tried to stand.

Faith flicked the baton, cracking it against Vickery's ankle. The sound was like a twig snapping.

"Bitch!" Vickery screamed in agony. "You fucking bitch!"

"Stand up." Faith grabbed Will's arm. She couldn't move him. "Come on." She leaned down to help. Her whisper in his ear felt like she was talking underwater. "Please."

From somewhere deep inside, Will summoned the strength to stand. He staggered like a colt taking its first steps. Faith wrapped her hand around his arm, pulled him toward the parking lot. He tripped over the curb again. Faith labored to keep him upright.

She coached, "Keep walking. Just keep walking."

Will tried to do as he was told. His feet were floppy, like the tendons had come undone. The ground looked strange. Everything was too large or too small. He was walking through a funhouse mirror. If not for Faith propping him up, he would've fallen flat on his face.

Paul Vickery wouldn't give up. "I got a witness puts him in the back room at Tipsie's tonight." He limped after them, keeping his distance. "Same place as the shooters who went after Lena."

Faith didn't answer. She pulled Will, urging him to go faster.

"Ask him where he went afterward," Vickery said. "Ask him where he was when my fucking team was being attacked."

Faith raised the baton in warning.

Vickery hung back. "I'll get him at the station."

"He's not going to the station." Faith leaned Will against a black Suburban. "I'm taking him to the field office. He's in state custody."

"You won't be able to hold him there."

Faith opened the back door. She kept her body turned toward Vickery as she tried to help Will into the seat. He was too heavy for her to manage. In the end, all Will could do was fall in.

"You'll have to process him," Vickery warned. "You send him to county, you send him to Fulton, I'll get at him somehow."

Will's wrists were still cuffed. He clenched his stomach muscles so he could straighten up in the seat. The pain was excruciating. He opened his mouth. He was going to be sick again.

"Stay back, Vickery. I mean it." Faith closed the door. She used the remote to lock it. The baton stayed out as she walked around the front of the Suburban.

"You're dead, Black!" Vickery punched the door. He banged his fists against the glass. "You hear me? I will fuck you up!"

Will closed his eyes. Everything was spinning. The car kept shaking. Vickery was putting his shoulder into it, like he thought he could roll a five-thousand-pound vehicle.

"Back the fuck up!" Faith yelled. She was at the front of the car. She said something else, but Will's hearing was going in and out. He heard Vickery call her every name a man could use against a woman. Faith cussed him right back, giving as good as she got.

The driver's-side door opened.

Faith yelled, "Bet on it, cocksucker." She slammed the door shut. The sound was like a cannon. The engine turned over. The car jerked as she put it in gear. The wheels squealed against pavement.

Will leaned forward. He rested his head on his knees. His hands were clasped together, trapped between his chest and legs. Spit and blood dripped from his open mouth. He waited for Faith to say something. To yell at him. To ask him what the hell he'd been doing.

She rolled down the windows a few inches. Will felt the cold night air swirl around him. He closed his eyes. Breathed through his mouth. The light grew softer. The tires hummed against the road.

Faith kept driving. She didn't say a word. Didn't even turn around.

Will's breathing started to even out. Eventually, the nausea passed. Unfortunately, so did the numbness. His body came alive with pain. His nose felt broken. His eyelids throbbed. His lip was split. His neck felt as if it had been scraped with a razor, and his head pounded along with the beating of his heart.

Faith accelerated. They were on the highway. Will could tell from the steady, low grind of the engine. He didn't know how much time passed before she finally slowed for a turn. The sound inside the Suburban changed from a gentle hum to a fragmented crunch. The brakes squeaked as Faith slowed to a stop. She put the gear in park. The emergency brake clicked when she pushed down the pedal.

Faith opened the door. Will heard her walk around the car.

He pushed himself up. He had to move slowly. He winced at

the pain in his head. His throat felt raw. He couldn't get the taste of blood out of his mouth.

The back door opened. Faith still didn't speak. She turned on the dome light. Will blinked, squinting. The handcuffs came off. Will rubbed his wrists, trying to get the circulation to come back. Faith opened the first aid kit from under the seat. She pulled out a roll of cotton squares, various packets, antibiotic ointment, Band-Aids. Will heard cars on either side of them. Faith had parked in a restricted area that cut across the highway median. Trees surrounded them. Broken beer bottles and used condoms littered the ground.

She said, "Look at me."

Will turned his head toward her. He closed his eyes. Packets were ripped open. Alcohol wipes. Disinfectant. He kept his eyes shut as Faith tended his scrapes and cuts. She was efficient if not gentle. Will was grateful. Sara had doctored him before. She always touched him so softly. She caressed him, kissed the places she said needed extra help to heal.

Faith wiped underneath his eyes with a tissue.

Will parted his lips to help get more air in his lungs. He wanted to thank her, to acknowledge how much her silence meant to him. Faith had always been a bull in the china shop of his life. Will was too broken now to tell her what had happened with Sara tonight.

Faith scrubbed at the blood around his nose. She said, "Eric Haigh is dead."

"I know." Will could barely speak. He tried to clear what felt like a wad of cotton trapped in his esophagus.

Faith said, "We found the body an hour ago."

"His front yard," Will whispered. "I helped Tony Dell put him there."

Faith's hand stopped.

Will opened his eyes. "I watched him kill him. Tony Dell kill Eric." Will coughed. The cotton had turned into razors. "It was at Tipsie's. Hunting knife. Dell wears it in his boot. Wore it." Will tried to swallow, but his throat refused. "We threw the knife in the river. I don't know which one. Concrete bridge. No houses around."

"We'll find it."

"You need to find Tony."

"He's gone. His house is empty. His car's still in the impound lot." Faith tore open a packet of antibiotic. "He used his ATM card to clean out his bank account." She squeezed some ointment onto a Q-tip. "We've got a BOLO on him."

Will still couldn't swallow. There was only an empty clicking noise. "Three men were there. Rednecks. Big guys. Fat." Will couldn't remember whether or not he'd told her where this had happened. "At Tipsie's. That's where Tony killed Eric Haigh."

She dabbed the Q-tip to his forehead. "I'll put somebody on the club."

"They were in the back room. Dell took me there to meet them. I didn't know until we were inside that that's what he wanted."

Faith squirted more ointment onto the Q-tip.

"They knew my Bill Black cover. All of it. They were watching me. Not when I went back to Atlanta—they couldn't follow me on my bike—but they knew about the hotel, my habits." Will felt in his pocket for his phone. He looked down at the shattered glass.

Sara had thrown her phone against the wall. Will had watched it break into pieces. He had never seen her throw anything like that before.

Faith asked, "Will?"

His phone was in his hand. The glass was shattered. Will slid it back into his pocket. "One of them was called Junior." He finally managed to swallow. The pain nearly made him pass out. "He had a gun to my chest. Pearl-handle Smith and Wesson. The knife had a pearl handle. The redneck's, not Tony's. We threw that off a bridge."

Faith ringed the Q-tip underneath Will's eye. He remembered the redneck cutting him; the first cut of the night.

He said, "My clothes are in a trash bag in my locker. I had to change, take a shower. Tony was in the ER. He cut his hand when he stabbed Haigh. They had to stitch it up." He felt the need to add, "I don't know how many stitches."

Faith said, "His wife found him."

"Tony has a wife?"

"Eric Haigh. His wife found his body outside the house. There was a lot of confusion at first. She didn't recognize him."

Will remembered, "They told us to put him on the front lawn. The order came from Big Whitey." He saw the question in her eyes. "On the phone. I didn't meet him. The redneck took the call, then he told Dell where to dump the body, that the order came straight from Big Whitey."

"We'll see if we can trace the call to the club."

"It was a cell, probably a burner."

"We'll check it anyway." Faith tossed the Q-tip into the first aid box. The cotton was soaked red. She told Will, "Haigh'd been missing for two days. His wife didn't say because he'd been acting weird since the raid. She knew Internal Affairs was involved. She didn't want to get him into trouble."

"The raid," Will repeated. Faith had talked about it earlier, but Will couldn't recall the conversation. "They tortured him."

"I know."

"The redneck told Dell . . ." He lost his train of thought. "What did I say?"

"The redneck told Dell?" She tried, "We were talking about Eric Haigh."

The prompt didn't help. "He said he'd be in touch with me. That he had a job for me."

"What time were you at the club?"

"Time?" The question didn't make sense.

"What time?"

Will took his phone out of his pocket. The glass was shattered. Still, the screen came on when he pressed the button. He told Faith, "It's 1:31 a.m."

Faith tilted his head back up so she could look at him. "Should I take you to the hospital? A different hospital, I mean."

Will shook his head. He wasn't going to any hospital.

"I think you have a concussion."

"Why?"

"Paul Vickery kicked you in the head."

"When?" Will asked, but that wasn't the right question. He knew Vickery had kicked him. "I mean, why was Paul at the hospital?"

"Someone took a shot at him." Faith made herself more clear. "Paul Vickery was at the hospital because someone tried to kill him tonight."

"I'm sorry I keep forgetting things."

"It's all right." Faith spoke more slowly than necessary. "Vickery was at home. A gunshot was fired through a front window at his house. That's why he had the bandage on his arm."

Will couldn't remember seeing a bandage. "Is he okay?"

"Okay enough to attack you." She frowned. "He fights like a woman. You've got scratches on your neck." Faith turned his head. "Did he bite you?"

Will looked away. Paul Vickery hadn't made those marks. Sara had scratched him. She'd kicked him and bitten him and Will hadn't stopped because everything she did only made him want to fuck her harder.

Faith gave up on the Q-tip. She smeared antibiotic onto her finger and rubbed it on Will's face. "They went after DeShawn Franklin, too. He was jumped outside a movie theater tonight. His girlfriend started screaming. She called 911."

"They took him to the hospital?"

"Will, look at me." She made sure she had his attention. "Someone went after Franklin and Vickery on the same night that Eric Haigh's body was dumped on his front lawn."

Will already knew these details, but the way she put them together so succinctly finally made them click. "It was coordinated."

"Right. Someone was sending a message." She peeled open a Band-Aid.

"That's what the redneck said—there's no use sending a message unless everybody can read it."

"Well, if you ever see him again, tell him the message was received loud and clear. Turn that way."

Will turned his head. Faith stuck the Band-Aid on his neck to cover the scratches.

He asked, "Is that why you were at the hospital? Because they were all attacked?"

"I was looking for you."

"Because of DeShawn Franklin." Will shook his head. That was wrong. "You went to the hospital because of Eric Haigh. You saw him and you thought they had done the same thing to me."

"I thought he *was* you," Faith said. "His own wife didn't recognize him. I went to the hospital thinking I was going to have to identify your body."

"I'm sorry."

"Thank God Sara wasn't answering her phone." She indicated for him to look up again. The scratches were too wide for just one Band-Aid. "It was a real party after that. Paul Vickery and De-Shawn Franklin were wheeled in right as I was coming up from the morgue. I was talking on the phone to Amanda."

"Did you have to tell them Haigh was dead?"

"Yes," Faith answered, her voice straining. "But then they saw Tony Dell getting his hand sewn up and decided to take it out on him." She didn't make Will ask. "It took six cops to get them off the guy."

"Why'd they go after him?"

"I guess because Dell's car was parked outside Lena's house the night they were attacked. I'm sure whoever Vickery's witness is who saw you at the club also saw Tony. It's not a leap to think you both had something to do with Haigh's murder."

It wasn't a leap because it was right. "What's Tony saying?"

"Who knows?" Faith sounded exasperated. "I told you five seconds ago that it took six cops to peel DeShawn and Vickery off Tony Dell. By the time anybody thought to look, Dell was gone. We turned the hospital upside down, but he managed to get away."

"He probably had ten escape routes already planned." Will remembered something. He took out his wallet. Cayla Martin's handwritten note was still in the photo sleeve. "This is Tony's stepsister. Check her house."

Faith took the note with some skepticism. "Dell didn't have any siblings on his background check."

"It was only a few years," Will said. "He's in love with her."

Her look said she was considering the hospital again.

"I know it sounds weird, but it's true. She's a nurse at the hospital."

"I'll send a car."

Will coughed. He looked at his palm, expecting to find blood. "Vickery called me a cop killer."

Faith shook her head like she didn't understand it, either. "Maybe he saw you leaving Eric Haigh's house?" She answered herself. "No, if he saw you leaving Haigh's, he would've killed you in the street. Do you remember seeing Vickery tonight? Or any of them?"

Will considered the question. He could feel it roll around in his brain like a marble that wouldn't settle.

Faith said, "I'm going to call Sara."

"Don't."

"She has a right to—"

"No." Will grabbed her arm. He let go just as quickly. "She knows everything."

Faith examined his face. He wondered what she saw. The bruises wouldn't show for a few hours. The side of Will's head probably had a print from Paul Vickery's shoe. The bridge of his nose would be red. His split lip would show blood. The scratch mark. The bite mark. What would she make of those?

She said, "We need to get to the field office."

Will wanted to go back to Atlanta. He had to get his dog from Sara's apartment. His toothbrush, the clothes he'd left in the drawers she'd cleared out for him. She shouldn't have to see any reminders of Will. It was the least he could do.

"It's over," he told Faith. "With Sara. It's over."

"Are you sure?"

"Yes." Will had never been so sure of anything in his life.

Faith closed the first aid kit. She clicked the plastic lock. "Well, that's her loss."

"She has good reason."

"No, she doesn't," Faith insisted. "No matter what you did, Sara's not the woman I thought she was if she can't forgive you."

Will held his tongue. She would find out the truth soon enough.

Faith said, "Get in the front seat. We're going to be late."

"For what?"

"Branson." Faith's tone made Will think maybe she'd said this before. "I saw her at the hospital. She's ready to talk."

"Why now?"

"Somebody tried to take out two of her detectives—three if you count Lena. Eric Haigh was tortured and stabbed to death. Jared Long was almost murdered. Hell yes, she's going to talk to us. She's getting her files. We're supposed to meet at the field office." Faith looked at her watch. "Ten minutes ago."

"What files?"

"The ones from the shooting gallery." Faith motioned for Will to move. "Denise Branson has been lying to us all along. She's finally going to show us her files from the raid."

Will stared into the bathroom mirror at the GBI field office, assessing his damaged face. Life had left him a wound expert. He knew the difference between a cut that scarred into a thin white line and a cut that left nothing but a faint memory. By his estimation, the only lasting reminder of the night would come from the redneck's knife. The tiny slice below Will's eye probably should've had at least one stitch. But that had to be done at a hospital, and Will was never going to another hospital ever again.

At least the nausea had passed. His head was aching at a lower frequency. The trembling had stopped, which he took as a good sign that he wasn't having a stroke or a seizure. Swallowing was still an issue. He found this out the hard way when Faith made him drink two bottles of Coke. Then she'd stood over him while he choked down a pack of cheese crackers. Will had gotten irritated at her for bossing him around, which probably meant that whatever she was doing was working.

He looked at his neck, lightly touching the reddish bruises that were starting to come up. If Will had one talent, it was surviving. He'd made it through the night. The redneck hadn't done too much damage. Tony Dell hadn't killed him, though he was obviously capable. Paul Vickery had gotten in many, many good blows, but Faith had probably cracked his ankle, which was a nasty enough payback.

So, Will had survived. He had a right to feel good about that.

But then there was Sara.

When Will was a kid, he'd imagined all the slings and arrows thrown his way were easily portable. He didn't have to keep them inside. He could shove them all into boxes. After a while, there were a lot of boxes. There was nowhere to put them. They floated over his bed at the children's home. They followed him to school. They chased after him like bullies when he ran down the street.

As Will got older, storage became an issue. Or maybe the metaphor evolved alongside him. The floating boxes turned into pieces of paper. The papers went into files. The files were put in filing cabinets. The cabinets were locked so that he never had to see them again.

When Sara came into his life, Will forgot about the file room. He forgot about the endless pieces of paper. The rusted cabinet locks that wouldn't turn sometimes.

That was over now.

Standing in the bathroom, Will put Sara Linton into a file and closed the drawer.

"Will?" Faith knocked lightly at the door. "Are you okay?"

He turned on the faucet to let her know he was alive. The water was icy cold. He wanted to splash some onto his face, but the liquid would probably roll right off. Faith had used so much antibiotic ointment that his skin glistened.

Will opened the door. Faith was standing there with a bottle of water in each hand.

His voice sounded like an old man's. "Scared I'd die on the toilet?"

"That's not funny."

"It can happen," he croaked. "I read about it in the paper."

She handed him the water. "You weren't sick again?"

"No." He regretted the loss of her previous silence, but he wasn't cruel enough to tell her. "I'm fine. Thank you."

"Drink all of that water." She led him down the hall. "I sent a cruiser for a knock-check on Cayla Martin's house. Took them forever to find the place. It's not on MapQuest, Google, anything."

Will nodded. He would've never found the road without Tony's help.

"Anyway, the point is they eventually found it. Martin was home. She said Tony Dell could go to hell for all she cared. And then she asked if there was a reward for helping to find him."

Will nodded again. That sounded like Cayla Martin.

"The cruiser's gonna swing by a few more times before they go off shift to make sure Dell doesn't show up. Meanwhile, I caught up Amanda on everything that happened tonight. We're trying to

Skype her into the conference room, but there are some technical difficulties."

Will assumed the problems weren't on this end.

"Lonnie Gray is here. The Macon chief of police."

"Amanda called him?"

"Denise Branson did. My hat's off to her for manning up to the boss. They're outside talking while we try to get the feed up. And by talking, I mean Denise is mostly listening to him screaming. Gray's so far up her ass he's probably in her gallbladder by now."

Will took a sip of water. "She lose her job?"

"If she's lucky, that's all she'll lose. Gray had no idea Branson was lying to us. She could be looking at obstruction charges or worse." Faith glanced over her shoulder. "I haven't told Gray what Vickery did to you yet."

Will shook his head. "Don't. I'll settle it with Vickery."

"You'll have to beat Amanda to it. She's ready to scalp him."

Will kept shaking his head. "I wish you hadn't told her."

"Yeah, well, I wish I hadn't lost my virginity during a midnight screening of *Die Hard*. Get over it." Faith pushed open the door.

The conference room was eerily similar to just about every other conference room at every other GBI field office in the state. Fake oak paneling covered the walls. A long table split the center of the room. Worn pleather office chairs were crammed so tight that two large men couldn't comfortably sit by each other. A small plasma television was on top of a rolling metal cart. Wires hung down to the various electronics on the shelf below. The screen showed what was obviously Amanda's personal Skype photo. The image had to be from the 1980s. She was dressed for tennis. A wooden racket rested on her shoulder. A Jane Fonda headband poofed out her hair. She was smiling, which was probably the most disconcerting part.

Amanda's voice squawked from the speaker on the table. "Can you see me waving my hand?"

"No, ma'am." Agent Nick Shelton, head of the field station, didn't touch the laptop in front of him. Instead, he jammed his fingers into his eyes as he shook his head. "I'm trying everything I can. Are you sure it's not on your end?"

"Yes, I'm sure," Amanda snapped. "I can't see anything but the GBI logo. There's no video at all."

Nick shook his head at Faith. He held out his hand to Will. "Agent Trent."

"Is Will there?" Amanda asked. "I can't see a thing."

Will tried to make his voice as strong as he could. "Yes, ma'am."

"Why are you whispering?"

Faith said, "Because he was nearly strangled to death."

Amanda showed her usual concern. "Sit close to the speaker, then. I don't want to have to ask you to repeat yourself every two minutes."

"Yes, ma'am."

"I'm going to have a word with that idiot who set up my computer," Amanda complained. "He's been out here three times, and it stops working the minute he leaves."

Faith couldn't help herself. "You know you can catch more flies with honey."

"Yes, Faith, thank you. That's exactly what I need is more flies."

Will slumped into a chair as the two women exchanged more helpful suggestions. The table was set up for a formal meeting. Five bottles of water were in front of five chairs. Notepads and pens were laid out beside them. Will had been at a lot of briefings where a lot of cops lost their jobs, but he felt sorry about this one. Denise Branson had made a career-ending mistake, but she'd probably done it for reasons she felt were right.

It was just a matter of time before Lena Adams did the same.

Will looked at the digital clock on the wall: 3:01 in the morning. He should be exhausted. Maybe the caffeine in the Cokes had sparked him up. Or maybe his body had finally accepted the fact that he was going to live.

He stared at the water bottles Faith had shoved into his hands. One was about a quarter empty. Will's mouth was bone-dry, but just thinking about taking another drink made his throat hurt. He felt like he was drowning in the ocean.

The door opened. Nick stood up. "Ma'am, Chief Gray and Major Branson have entered the room."

Denise Branson was no longer in her shiny uniform. She wore jeans and a loose-fitting blouse. Her previously erect posture was gone. There was something beaten down about her. The leather briefcase was the only indication that she was the same woman they'd talked with in Atlanta yesterday morning.

For his part, Lonnie Gray was decked out in full regalia. His gold epaulets glimmered in the overhead light. He carried his hat under his arm. He was older, but had the look of a guy who started his day with a hundred push-ups before the sun came up. He also looked furious as hell. His mouth was a barely visible white line under his mustache. His forehead was furrowed like a plowed field.

They all shook hands. Will stayed in his chair, hoping they would understand.

"Chief Gray," Amanda said. "I'm sorry for the technical difficulties. I'm doing the Skype program from my home."

Will didn't know which was worse, the photo of Amanda playing tennis or the thought of her talking to them in her nightgown.

"That's fine." Lonnie Gray sat across from Will. He did a double take. So did Denise Branson. She slowly sank into the chair beside her chief, lips parted in surprise.

Will guessed he was going to have to get used to people staring at him for a while.

Nick said, "Ma'am, we're all seated."

"Thank you," Amanda said. "Lonnie, my condolences on your son. I hadn't heard that he passed away."

"Thank you." Gray obviously didn't want to talk about his personal life. He quickly got down to business. "Mandy, I want to apologize to you, your agents, and your agency for the actions of one rogue officer. Rest assured, my house will be put in order." He shot Branson a look. "Starting now."

"I appreciate that, Lonnie." Amanda didn't sound like she appreciated it at all. "Major Branson, I need to inform you that because you are officially under investigation, this conversation is being recorded. Anything you say may be used against you. You're entitled to an attorney—"

"I don't need an attorney," Branson said, though they all knew she did. "Give me the form."

Nick was prepared. He pushed a sheet of paper over to Branson so she could officially acknowledge that she'd been Mirandized.

Branson didn't read the form. She'd probably seen it thousands of times. She clicked the pen and signed her name on the line before pushing the paper back toward Nick.

Lonnie Gray gave her a nod to begin.

Branson didn't start immediately—not because she was playing games again, but because she probably knew this was the last briefing she would ever give.

Finally, she took a deep breath and jumped in. "Approximately three and a half weeks ago, Detective Adams came to me about a suspected shooting gallery off Redding Street. I authorized her to investigate. She monitored the house for a few days and determined the intelligence was good." Branson paused. She started playing with the ballpoint pen, balancing it between two fingers. "During the course of surveillance, Detective Adams realized that the shooting gallery was being run by a man named Sidney Waller."

Gray took over. "Waller's an extremely violent, high-level drug runner. When I came in two years ago, my number one priority was capturing and prosecuting him. Even with the full force of the department behind it, we were never able to make any charges stick."

Will thought it was pretty decent of the man to acknowledge his failure.

Branson seemed to appreciate it, too. She nodded at him before continuing. "We knew we could shut down the shooting gallery pretty quickly, but with Sid Waller involved, we saw an opportunity. I spoke with Detective Adams and decided that we should expand the operation with the goal of capturing and convicting Waller."

Gray provided, "This was where I came in. We got the DA on our side, formed an intra-agency task force. There were a lot of moving pieces. Denise and I had to coordinate together."

Will saw Branson flinch when he used her first name rather than her rank. Still, she said, "We were ten days into the operation when we realized that catching Waller was unlikely. We couldn't turn anyone. People were terrified of him. The junkies went to ground. No one would wear a wire. It was looking like we would have to go into the house and settle on rounding up whomever we could find. We could time it so Waller was there, but that wasn't much of a consolation."

Amanda said, "Because you couldn't prove that Waller was in charge, he'd bond out with the rest of the junkies." She sounded impatient. "But obviously, something changed?"

Branson said, "Detective Adams was contacted by a confidential informant. He was in lockup for selling pills to Mercer students. Not on campus, but at one of the coffee shops."

The distinction was important. Sale or distribution of illegal substances inside a school zone jacked up the prison time exponentially.

Amanda asked, "This was one of Adams's usual CIs?"

"No, she'd never met him before. He was locked up less than two hours, and he asked for her by name." Branson added, "Adams has a reputation with the junkies around town. This wasn't necessarily a red flag."

Amanda's brain was working faster than Will's. "The snitch was Tony Dell?"

Branson hesitated. "Yes, ma'am. He told her that he would trade Sid Waller for immunity off the drug deal."

Will glanced at Faith. At least now they knew why Lena had sent Will the email. She didn't want Dell to skate.

Amanda told Branson, "You got Waller on tape, which gave you probable cause for an arrest warrant?"

"Yes," Branson confirmed. "We commenced the raid four days later. The snitch said a big shipment was coming in. Detective Adams and her team breached the house. They found this." She nodded to Nick.

He tapped some keys on the laptop and Amanda's tennis shot was replaced by a crime scene photo.

Will stared at the screen. Two dead men. Hispanic. Shirtless. They were sitting on a tattered old couch. Their throats were slit open.

Nick asked Amanda, "Can you see it, ma'am?"

"Yes."

Branson said, "The one on the right is Elian Ramirez, an Oxy freak who was at the wrong place at the wrong time. The guy on the left is Diego Nuñez. He was Waller's right-hand man. Professional thug. He spent his twenties inside for manslaughter coupled with time-plus for bad behavior."

Branson nodded for the next photo, and Nick slid over the laptop so she could do it herself.

Branson narrated the next picture, which showed a man with the top of his skull chopped off. "Thomas Holland. He's new to the scene, got hooked on crack his senior year. We don't know why he was there except to get high. He was taken out with an ax." A picture of Holland's scalp flashed up, then his face from another angle. He was young, probably seventeen. Blond hair, piercing blue eyes. Except for the missing part of his head, he could've been on a poster for a Disney movie.

Branson flashed through some more innocuous photos, showing stills of the bedrooms, the bathroom, the dining room. Will had been inside shooting galleries before. The scene was familiar: crack pipes and needles scattered on the floor, mattresses in every room. He never understood where the mattresses came from, or why someone who was shooting poison into their veins required a comfortable place to pass out.

"Here." Branson stopped on a photo. It showed an open basement door. There were metal braces on each side. A two-by-four was on the floor.

She said, "The basement. This is where Sid Waller was hiding."

Will wondered if his head was still messed up. If someone locked you in a basement, you weren't hiding. You were trapped.

Branson said, "Two detectives breached the basement. Mitch Cabello and Keith McVale."

Faith stiffened. They both recognized the detectives' names. McVale had taken leave from his job and Cabello had been admitted to the hospital the day of the raid.

Branson said, "Detectives Adams and Vickery stayed in the kitchen. Cabello and McVale called the all-clear on the basement. They relayed to Detective Adams that they'd found a large amount of money. We believe it was shortly after this that Sid Waller came out from his hiding place."

She pulled up the next photo, which showed a hanging piece of wall paneling with a dark, wet hole behind it that someone had dug into the earth. The photo was not great, but Will could tell the hole was deep enough to hide a grown man.

"Waller knocked out Cabello with a strike to the head. He then took McVale hostage—quietly. Shortly after, Detective Adams went downstairs to help secure the money. She walked into the hostage situation. She drew on Sid Waller, who had a gun to McVale's head. There was a standoff. Rather than being taken in by Detective Adams, Waller shot himself in the head."

Will silently replayed her words, which were wholly unexpected. He managed, "Sid Waller shot himself?"

"All three detectives told exactly the same story." She held up her hands, stopping the obvious question. "The crime scene techs support every word of their statements. The autopsy confirmed the wound was self-inflicted. The tox screen showed there were enough pills in Waller to make a Buddhist monk go postal. At no point do the facts diverge. Everything says Waller took his own life."

Amanda wanted a second opinion. "Lonnie?"

Gray stirred in his chair. "Our snitch recorded Waller referring to a breakdown in supply. One of his trucks was rolled by some Cubans down in Miami. I made a call to some contacts I still have down in Florida. Waller was on the verge of a war with the Cuban cartel."

Branson said, "Sid knew he wouldn't last more than a day in prison. Better to eat a bullet than take a shiv from some Cuban in the yard."

Amanda moved them along. "Where does Big Whitey fit into all of this?"

Gray looked at Branson. He seemed sad, like one of his children had disappointed him.

She told them, "I was working the case off-book. Chief Gray told me not to pursue it, even on my own time, but I was obsessed with tracking Big Whitey down."

Amanda asked, "This is connected to Waller?"

"Tangentially," Branson conceded.

"Is there a reason you're not taking us down that tangent?"

Branson reached into her briefcase again. She took out a file that was several inches thick. Then she took out another one. Then another one. She stacked them on the table.

Faith wasn't shy. She grabbed the whole pile and slid it toward her.

Branson said, "Big Whitey came onto my radar eighteen months ago. I like statistics. I like to run the numbers, track the crimes, see where we need to move people around to stop the bad guys." She paused. Will could tell she had just realized she wasn't going to get to do this anymore.

"Anyway," Branson said, "it's what you said yesterday, the same thing that happened in Savannah and Hilton Head. It felt like there was a larger, organizing factor. Our usual lowlifes were stepping up. There's a law firm here they all use, ambulance chasers, sloppy and cheap. Suddenly, they merged with a white-shoe firm out of Florida."

"Vanhorn and Gresham." Faith looked up from the report she was reading. "The shooter who went after Jared Long is represented by the firm."

"Correct," Branson said. "We started seeing low-level cons like Fred Zachary walking on solid charges because of these guys. I started talking to folks, meeting with my detectives, and figured out there was a new player in town."

Faith said, "Big Whitey."

"Correct," Branson repeated. "Whitey started out banking legit through a series of pain management clinics. It's the usual deal. They were using junkies to cash the scripts. Rednecks, mostly. They control the meth trade, so it was natural for Whitey to tap into an existing market."

Gray felt the need to explain himself. "I wasn't persuaded Big Whitey existed. There were some sketchy details from Florida, but no name, no description, no affiliation. He was a ghost." Gray shrugged. "And we had a lot going on at the time. There was a rash of heroin overdoses at one of our private schools. Young women from good homes. Not the type we were used to seeing in that situation."

"Rich white girls," Faith supplied, skipping the political correctness. "They die or just end up at the hospital?"

Branson said, "Three died. Six went to the ER, then got carted off to white-girl prison." She meant rehab. "They were from some of our better-known families. There was a lot of heat to make arrests. Like I said, Whitey was running pills through rednecks.

Most of our non-pharmaceutical dealers were black and Hispanic. It's easy to spot who's working for whom."

Faith put it more succinctly. "So, the white people freaked out and demanded justice. You arrested a bunch of blacks and Hispanics." She used sarcasm to make her point. "I'm sure that went over well."

Gray was obviously uncomfortable with Faith's directness, or maybe he was more conscious that the conversation was being recorded. "We arrested the dealers who were known to sell heroin. My department is not in the business of racial profiling and never will be."

Will assumed from Gray's tone that he'd faced these accusations before. Atlanta had enough political scandals of its own to fill the local news, but Will had a vague recollection of seeing some reports about the mayhem down in Macon. Lonnie Gray must've gone to work every day wondering if he was going to keep his job.

Branson spoke reluctantly. "Because of the clampdown, we crippled Whitey's competition in the streets. We created a racial firestorm that split apart the city and made all the politicians start screaming for blood."

Gray admitted, "That's when I shut down Denise's investigation. We had too much going on to waste resources on a man we weren't even sure existed."

"This—" Will tried to clear the squeak from his voice. "This was Big Whitey's endgame? To take over the heroin trade?"

Branson answered, "He took over everything. Remember, chess, not checkers. He comes into town and makes friends, pays up the food chain to guys like Sid Waller so that everybody stays happy. Whitey has operating capital. He opens up some pain clinics, gets his regulars, puts the junkies on his payroll so they start dealing. Then he spreads out his business to the malls, into the suburbs. He gets the kids with money hooked, then when they want something more, he moves them on to heroin." She shook her head, though he could tell part of her was impressed. "Once his business model's up and running, he starts taking out the competition."

Amanda asked, "You know this is a pattern how?"

"Because I drove to Savannah and talked to some retired detectives who were too scared to tell me this over the phone."

Gray's clenched fists indicated he was just hearing this. He shot Branson a withering look.

Will couldn't let go of something. He asked, "Chief Gray, you didn't think Whitey existed?"

Gray reluctantly turned his attention away from Branson. "We're not used to this level of sophistication in our criminal underworld. Mandy, you know I've worked all over the state, but this is more like something you'd see out of Miami or New York."

There was a big fish/little pond logic to Whitey taking on the smaller cities. He'd also managed to pick two areas in Georgia where the population was predominantly African American. It was as if he was franchising his business model.

Will asked Branson, "Major, why were you so sure Whitey existed?"

"May I?" Branson was talking to Faith. She wanted one of her file folders back.

"Help yourself." Faith pushed the stack back across the table.

Branson flipped through one of the files until she found a photograph. She put it on the table. The young girl in the picture was pretty and blonde, posing for the camera in that seductive way that teenage girls don't know is dangerous.

Branson said, "Marie Sorensen. Sixteen years old. She worked at a cheese shop in River Crossing, one of our upscale malls. Lots of bored suburban kids hang out there. Sorensen's by far the prettiest. She managed to catch Big Whitey's eye."

Nick told Amanda, "I'll scan it in for you."

"Don't bother." Amanda guessed, "Big Whitey got Sorensen hooked on heroin?"

"He got her into his car." Branson took out another photo, this one showing Sorensen looking ten years older and twenty pounds lighter. Both eyes were bruised. There were open sores on her face. Patches of hair were missing from her head.

Branson said, "Another one of Big Whitey's patterns, but this one he does himself because he enjoys it." She put the pictures side by side on the table. "He tells them that he works for a modeling agency. They buy it because they've been told they're beautiful all their lives. He gets them to the car, forces them into the trunk, then drives them to a hotel on the coast—Tybee, Fort King George, Jekyll. He rapes them. His friends rape them. He shoots them up with heroin. He tricks them out."

Branson paused. She looked away from the photos.

"Sorensen was defiant at first. He put her in a dog crate to teach her a lesson. Took about a week to break her, then he put her up for sale on the Internet. One-sixty for the lunchtime special, two-fifty for an hour. Four hundred for two hours. She does ten, fifteen clients a day. Her habit runs a couple hundred dollars. Not a bad business model. Do the math."

Faith stared straight ahead. She couldn't look at the photos, either. Will wondered if she was thinking about her daughter.

Will asked, "What happened to her?"

Branson said, "Sorensen got old real quick. That's the problem with these young girls. They don't stay young for long. After two months, she was moved to the next stop on the circuit. That's what these guys do—they move them around, never let them get settled in one place."

She paused again. The pain was obviously still fresh. "Eventually, the girls get sent out to California, where they're tricked out on the streets. Sorensen ended up in LA. She managed to call her mom a few times, tell her what happened. Mom hired a private detective to try to find her."

Faith asked, "She didn't file a report in Macon? The girl was sixteen years old."

Branson's face told the story. This was the ball she had dropped. This was why she was so obsessed with the case. "We filed a missing persons report when she disappeared. When the mom told me about the phone calls, I reached out to LA. They told me it was a lost cause. They've got so many girls streaming into the city that they had to close the Hollywood bus station."

Faith smoothed her lips together like she was putting on lipstick.

Branson slid out another photo. Will recognized the tiny ruler beside Marie Sorensen's head as the kind that medical examiners used during autopsies.

She said, "The private dick in LA tracked down an address. The police searched the apartment three times before they found her. She was crammed into a suitcase underneath the bed. Still alive." Branson let out a slow breath. "Still alive."

She looked down at the autopsy photo. No one pushed her to go on.

Branson took another deep breath.

"Mom got the first plane out to California. Marie's in the hospital for three weeks. They patch her back together, get some weight on her, take her down off the heroin, only they can't heal her brain. Two weeks after mom gets her home, she sneaks out and kills herself. Heroin. Cops found her behind the church. She was six months to the day from walking out of that mall with Big Whitey."

They were all silent after that. Will looked at the three photographs. Branson hadn't exaggerated. Sorensen was beautiful. He could imagine the girl would believe a modeling agency was interested. The autopsy photo was a sharp contrast, a dark reminder that the only person who would want her now was her grieving mother.

Finally, Amanda asked, "You talked to Sorensen when she returned to Macon?"

"Yes." Branson looked down at her hands. "He never gave her

a name. She was told from the start to call him Big Whitey. She didn't know his real identity, couldn't give us any actionable intelligence. She was blindfolded most of the time, and when she wasn't being sold, she was locked in a closet or a suitcase. The description she gave was spotty—dark hair, dark eyes. No distinguishing features."

Faith asked, "Do you think she was lying?"

"Yes," Branson admitted. "She was terrified of him. Couldn't sleep in her own bed. She stayed in the closet the whole time she was home, back to the wall, waiting for him to come get her."

"She was abducted at the mall," Faith said. "What about CCTV?"

"The cameras were out. We don't know if he had someone from security on the payroll or if he was just lucky." Branson added, "He's always been lucky."

Faith asked, "No one saw anything at the mall or in the parking lot? No customers or friends?"

"No. And there was nothing on her cell phone or email, so he obviously made her keep it on the down low." Branson added, "That's what he's good at, not being seen."

Amanda finally spoke, and Will realized she hadn't been silent out of respect. She was livid. "I'm curious, Ms. Branson, as to why you've got a sex-trafficking case in your town and the Georgia Bureau of Investigation doesn't know anything about it."

Branson's cheeks darkened with a blush. "You're right. This is all on me. I was ashamed that I couldn't do anything to save her, and I was angry that I was told not to pursue Big Whitey." She turned to Chief Gray. "I should've told you, Lonnie. I was hell-bent on proving you wrong. Instead of running around behind your back, I should've gone to you for help."

Gray wasn't kind. "You're goddamn right about that."

"I'm sorry."

"That's enough," Gray said. "Tell them what you found in the house."

"You mean the shooting gallery?" Faith sounded surprised. She'd obviously thought that part was over.

Will had a sinking feeling that he knew the answer, but he asked, "What was behind the panel?"

Branson turned back to the laptop computer. She tapped the screen awake, then advanced the next image.

The photo of a young boy appeared on screen. The picture was grainy, obviously taken with a cell phone. The boy's eyes were blackened slits. Like Marie Sorensen's, his face was emaciated. His lips were dry. Sores caked his skin. It was his eyes that made Will finally turn away. He could not stand to see the hollow look in the boy's eyes.

Amanda broke the silence, asking, "Cause of death was dehydration? Malnourishment?"

Branson seemed surprised. "No, he's alive."

Will felt truly shocked for the first time since the meeting had started.

Branson said, "We have no idea who he is. He can talk, but he won't."

Faith looked as if she wanted to grab Branson across the table. "He hasn't said anything for a week?"

Branson didn't answer. She'd been keeping this all to herself for so long that she'd lost perspective. Talking it out had obviously revealed her catastrophic errors.

Faith said, "I haven't seen anything about him on the news."

"I entered it into the FBI databases, but I kept Macon out of it." Branson glanced at Chief Gray. The man's hands were gripped so tightly together he looked as if he was trying to break the bones. "If the local stations picked up on the story, then Whitey would know the boy was still alive. The only thing we know for sure about this guy is he murders anybody who gets in his way. He'd kill that boy just as sure as I'm sitting here."

Faith asked, "Which hospital is he in?"

"He's been under close medical supervision." Branson didn't

offer any further explanation. She told her chief, "Chances are he was abducted in another state. Wherever he's from, the local police force got the notice. For what it's worth."

Will knew that everyone in the room had gotten the notice. There was no way to read them all. Nearly 800,000 children were reported missing each year, which translated into more than two thousand notices a day.

Branson said, "The boy doesn't have any identifying marks. We don't know what region he's from. We don't know when he was taken. We've been combing through all the stranger abduction reports, but—" Branson seemed to realize how thin her excuses sounded. Her voice was weak when she said, "He's the only living witness who can identify Big Whitey."

Faith demanded, "How do you know that if he's not talking?"

"Because of his reaction when I said Big Whitey's name. Because he has . . . distinguishing marks . . . on his body that are the same as Marie Sorensen's."

"Wait a minute," Faith said. "Back up. Who else knows about this?"

"No more than I can count on my hand." Branson listed them. "Detective Adams stayed downstairs while I cleared everyone from the scene. Only two paramedics were allowed in the basement— girls I've known since high school. Both of them have been taking turns watching the boy around the clock. We couldn't take him to the hospital. He's being kept at an undisclosed location. Dr. Thomas is treating him. I've known Dean since I was a child. There's one other officer who guards him when I can't. Only the people I trust with my life know where that kid is."

Will looked at Lonnie Gray, easily judging from the man's expression that he'd learned about this cabal just a few moments before the rest of them. His face was bright red. His mustache looked like a piece of chalk over his mouth.

Gray demanded, "And who exactly is this other officer who's watching the boy now?"

"She's with the sheriff's department. She's a good friend." Branson wouldn't look at Gray. Her cheeks darkened again. Will guessed the deputy was more than a friend. "I trust her."

"More than you trust me, apparently."

"I'm sorry, sir. I knew if you found out, you'd have an obligation to report this to the state. Other people in the department would find out. We wouldn't be able to keep him safe. Big Whitey has too much reach. The boy would be dead in a matter of hours."

"That again." Gray addressed the speaker on the table, telling Amanda, "Denise theorizes that Big Whitey has a mole on my force."

Will thought about the file on the redneck's desk. They had Bill Black's police record. They had his military details. It wasn't so much of a stretch to think Whitey had a cop or two working for his side. If the pattern held, he had more than a few.

Faith analyzed the situation differently. She told Branson, "You think someone tipped off Big Whitey about the raid."

She shrugged, but said, "The raid team breaches the house and finds three dead guys. Sid Waller's locked in the basement with an abducted boy. It practically had a bow tied on it."

Gray turned on Branson, demanding, "Who do you think is the mole? Vickery and Franklin were nearly killed tonight. Adams was attacked. Eric Haigh was tortured before he was murdered." He added, "Why do you think that is, Denise? Why do you think they tortured him?" He answered his own question. "They're looking for the boy. If they had someone on the inside, they wouldn't have to torture cops for information."

Branson looked down at the table. The room went silent.

Will thought about Lena Adams in the ICU. She had told Will that he would eventually find out she was doing the right thing. She had said the words as if they would redeem all the ills that came before. Had she thought that saving the boy would make up for losing her baby? Or was it simply a matter of Lena's eternal conviction that everything she did was for the greater good?

Will asked, "Does Lena know where the boy is?"

"I sure as hell don't," Gray interrupted.

Will tried again, asking, "Does she?"

Branson shook her head. "Lena has no idea. I let her believe the state was already involved, that we had to be quiet about what happened to keep him safe. I doubt she even told Jared."

Gray realized, "She lied to Internal Affairs. None of this was mentioned during any of her interviews." He sounded disgusted. "Jesus Christ, Denise. You forced her to lie on record."

Branson defended, "Lena was protecting the boy. She knew what Big Whitey would do if he found out there was a witness."

"And I assume you let her believe I was okay with this?" Gray waved away any response Branson might come up with. "For the love of God. I can't believe I trusted you."

Faith said, "Obviously someone figured out the boy was alive. Why else attack Lena in the middle of the night? Why else go after the rest of the team that was there during the raid?" She told Branson, "Thanks for wasting my fucking time and nearly getting my partner killed."

Amanda took over. "Where is this boy now?"

Gray turned to his former confidant, making a show of waiting for an answer.

Branson equivocated. She told Amanda, "I'd rather not say on an open line, but I'll take your people to him as soon as this is over."

Surprisingly, Amanda didn't argue. "Denise, tell your paramedics to get ready for transport. We'll keep it quiet, but we have to move that boy to Atlanta."

Branson's inner cop took over. "Logistics might take a while. We'll need to get an ambulance. My paramedics are working alternating shifts. Dr. Thomas will need to get him ready."

Amanda moved a split second ahead of Will. "Sara Linton's still down there, right?"

Faith looked at Will. She answered, "Right."

Amanda said, "Will, do whatever it takes to get Sara in that ambulance to Atlanta. If there really is a leak down there, we need to use our own people as much as we can."

His mouth went dry. He couldn't swallow again.

Amanda took his silence for agreement. "We still have an active manhunt for Tony Dell. Even if the boy won't talk, we might be able to flip Dell. Again. Will, what time does your shift start?"

Will had forgotten about Bill Black's hospital job. "Eight."

"Don't go in early. Maintain your cover. You're a con. Dell is on the move. There's a heavy police presence. It would make sense for you to start asking questions."

He said, "There's a nurse I've been working. Dell's stepsister. She knows I was sent up for assault. I think if I work it right, I can scare her into talking."

"Terrorize her if that's what it takes." Amanda seemed ready to get started. "Lonnie, I'll be in touch."

"Thank you," Gray said. "I appreciate your—"

"Sir." Nick was apologetic. "She already terminated the connection."

Chief Gray didn't bother with formalities. He turned on Branson like a raging lion. "You have some nerve, lady. Make me come here in the middle of the night like I'm some goddamn schoolboy being called to the principal's office. Make me look like a fool in front of one of the most respected peace officers in the state. And I gather you'll still refuse to tell me the boy's location?" He waited for her to answer. When it was clear she wouldn't, he mumbled, "You worthless piece of shit. It sickens me to think you ever wore the uniform."

Tears came into Branson's eyes as she tried, "Sir, with all due respect—"

"You don't know the meaning of the word." Gray snatched his hat off the table. "Human Resources will be in touch. Don't try to reach out to me or any of my officers. Don't try to plead your case. Don't even say my name. As far as I'm concerned, your involvement with me and my department is over." He stormed out of the room.

Branson's throat worked. She looked down, pressing her palms flat to the table like she needed a moment to collect herself.

Faith didn't give her the time. "You're gay?"

Will was surprised by the bluntness of the question. Branson seemed ashamed. She looked away, her head turned to the wall.

Faith said, "Jared Long got a call from you on his cell phone a few minutes before he was attacked."

Branson seemed to understand. She wiped the tears from her eyes. "You thought I was two-timing with him."

"Why else would you be calling Lena's husband in the middle of the night?"

"I was worried about her. Something wasn't right."

"Because of the raid?"

"No, before that. She was just—" Branson tried to find the right words. "We're friends. That's *all* we are. But something's been wrong with Lena for a while. She was happy, pumped about taking down Waller, and then when it all came together, she just got sad. She wouldn't talk to me about it. I thought maybe Jared could tell me what was going on."

Will guessed that Lena hadn't told Denise Branson about the baby.

Faith quickly moved on. "Where are you keeping the boy?"

Branson took a deep breath. She held it for a while. Will could see the turmoil in her face. Every second of her life for the last eight days had been devoted to keeping the boy safe. She'd risked alienating her friends, losing her job, pissing off her chief. No cop ever wanted to hand over a case, especially one that ripped at their heart.

"Okay," Branson finally said. "We're keeping him at my girl-friend's farm."

"The sheriff's deputy?"

"Yes. She works two counties over. We've been together about a year. Nobody knows about us."

"Good," Faith said. "How far away is the farm?"

"Not far, but it's gonna take some time to put this together. We don't make phone calls. As you clearly know, all calls can be traced, even blocked ones. I didn't want any of their numbers showing up on my line. We check in on a message board for gay first responders." Branson looked at her watch. "Dr. Thomas comes in at six before he goes to work. My ex is already there—one of the paramedics. Her girlfriend will come at six to relieve her. My deputy is spelling me. I was supposed to take the night shift, but then the shit hit the fan."

Faith checked her own watch. "So, everyone will be there in a little over two hours?"

"Unless they read the message boards at four in the morning." She asked Nick, "Can I use your laptop?"

Nick offered, "The computer in my office is more private." He scooped up the Big Whitey files, telling Faith, "I'll get started on these."

Branson followed him to the door, but she didn't leave. "I'm sorry for wasting y'alls time. I always try to be tough as I need to be, never tougher than I have to be."

Will nodded, but Faith wouldn't give an inch. She waited for Branson to leave, then blew out a puff of air.

Will said, "What do you think?"

"I think Tony Dell's closer to Big Whitey than we thought."

He nodded, though they both knew that's not what he was asking about.

"Whoever this Big Whitey is, he's a freaking genius." Faith couldn't keep the admiration out of her voice. "He played them like a fiddle."

"The two men in the house." Will coughed a few times before he could continue. "I could see Tony slitting their throats, then going after the third guy with an ax. He's a killer. He likes using his hands. He takes out the three of them, puts the brace on the basement door so Sid Waller's trapped, then he walks away."

"He was feeding Lena intel. He knew when the raid was going to happen." Faith waited out another coughing fit. "You still think Tony's not Big Whitey?"

Will gagged down some water. "I don't know what to think anymore. He's more like the point at the edge of somebody else's sword." Will coughed again. "And I know he's got that weird thing with his sister. Stepsister. But I can't see him with little boys. He couldn't stand to be in the same room with his own nephew."

"You never know what people get up to," Faith said. "Do you think the stepsister knows anything?"

Will shrugged to save his voice. He'd have to find a way to get Cayla Martin to talk. There was no other option.

Faith stared at the grainy cell phone photo on the screen. "Poor little lamb. He can't be more than seven."

Will didn't want to look at the screen, but once he did, he couldn't take his eyes off the boy. It didn't seem possible he was still alive. How had he survived living in that dank, dark hole? And what had been done to him while he was there?

"I'll call Sara." Faith took out her cell phone and dialed the number.

Will opened his mouth to tell her there was no point. Nothing came out. He couldn't speak, but not because of his sore throat. It occurred to him that the boy was not talking because he had nothing to say.

His expression in the photo told the story. The boy would never be the same again. He would never sleep as deeply or play with the same abandon. Chasing a ball, flying a kite, helping his mother set the table—none of this would ever be done without constantly checking for danger. The boy did not want to go back to his parents. They wouldn't recognize him. They would take one look and ask who was this damaged creature and what had he done with their real son. It was all captured in the grainy photo on the screen—the fear, the loneliness, the overwhelming shame.

Marie Sorensen had the same look. She had been stolen. She had been abused. She had been thrown away. Even when she got home, she never felt safe. She had made the only choice that was truly her own.

Will couldn't blame her.

There wasn't a box in the world that was big enough to contain those horrors. Everything she'd survived had made her want to die. Who could fault the boy for thinking the same thing?

"Sara's not answering." Faith ended the call. "Do you think she's at the hospital?"

He didn't answer.

Sara was finished with Will. That much was obvious. But somehow, for the brief time they were together, she had managed to change him. She had tamed his beasts. She had made him feel safe. She had made him feel whole. Sara hadn't completely shuttered the file room, but she had made it seem further away—like someone else's memory, someone else's life.

Will had to tell her this, had to explain why she was so desperately needed.

"I'll find her," he told Faith.

If anyone could coax the boy into talking, it was Sara Linton.

13.

"Sara?"

Sara turned over in bed, trying to get away from the noise. She hadn't fallen asleep last night so much as collapsed from exhaustion.

"Sara?" Nell said. "Sara?"

Sara woke slowly, rousing from a deep, dreamless sleep. She put her hand over her eyes. "What time is it?"

"Just after four-thirty."

Sara dropped her hand. She looked up at Nell. They were in the hotel room. After what happened with Will last night, Sara didn't have it in her to drive back to Atlanta. "Is Jared okay?"

Nell gave an odd smile. "Possum just called. He says they're going to wake him up. I was about to leave for the hospital."

Sara forced herself to sit up. She hurt in all the wrong places. "I'll go with you."

"You need to get the door. There's a man who wants to talk to you."

Sara finally managed to put together the conversation. There was only one man in Macon right now who would want to talk to her. She wasn't sure she wanted to talk to him. Still, she brushed her fingers through her hair as she went to the door.

And then her jaw dropped when she saw Will.

For just a moment, Sara found herself thinking that she was responsible for the damage to his face.

Then she realized that he'd been beaten.

"What happened?" She reached up to him, but there was nowhere Sara could touch Will that wasn't injured. Even the blood vessels in his eyes were broken. "Did someone choke you?"

He swallowed. The pain made him cringe. His voice was hoarse. "Amanda sent me."

Sara could hardly understand him. "Come in."

Will didn't move. She grabbed his arm, pulling him into the room.

"Nell, this is a friend of mine." Sara let herself believe she was holding back details because Will was undercover. "He lives in Atlanta."

"Nice to meet you." Nell dug her hand into her purse, but her eyes were on Sara's hand, which was still wrapped around Will's arm.

Sara let go.

Nell said, "It's good, Sara. I'm happy for you." She held up her keycard. "I'll be at the hospital."

She nodded at Will before she left. The door closed automatically, slamming hard against the metal jamb.

Sara knew it would be pointless to go after her. She asked Will, "What happened?"

He put his fingers to his larynx as if he could force up the volume. "We've got about an hour."

She stared, disbelieving. "What?"

"I know you don't want me here." He coughed, the effort from talking obviously too much. "Amanda asked me to—" He coughed again. And again. His face started turning red.

"Sit down." Sara was still angry, but she couldn't let him pass out in front of her. She found a tiny bottle of Tennessee whiskey in the minibar. "Drink half of this."

Will sat down, but he wouldn't take the bottle. He hated alcohol.

"You won't get drunk," Sara told him. He still wouldn't take it.

She stuck the bottle in his face. "Think of it as medicine. It'll numb your throat."

Will reluctantly took the whiskey. He opened the cap. Instead of drinking the alcohol, he sniffed it. He scowled at the smell. He looked at the label even though Sara knew he couldn't read the cursive script.

"Will, drink the goddamn whiskey."

Her tone was sharper than she intended, but it worked.

He managed to swallow a mouthful before he gagged.

"Christ!" He heaved a cough from deep inside his chest. His eyes watered. He shook his head like a dog.

Sara crossed her arms to stop herself from soothing him. She'd been too worn out last night to think beyond closing her eyes, but now it all came rushing back. Every ounce of concern she felt kept getting overwhelmed by anger.

Will coughed a few more times. He screwed the cap back on the bottle and threw it into the trashcan.

Sara asked, "Are we going to talk about what happened?"

He blinked to clear his eyes. "Amanda—"

"Sweetheart, if you say her name one more time, one of us is going to have to leave. And it won't be me."

His jaw set.

Sara wasn't going to give in. "I mean it, Will. You come in here with your face all banged up. That cut should be stitched. You've got blood in your ear. You probably need an MRI. And I'm just supposed to pretend none of this exists, the same way I pretend you didn't have a childhood and you don't have scars all over your body and—" She couldn't go on. The list was endless. "Talk to me, Will. I can handle the strong, but I can't take the silent anymore."

Predictably, he did the exact opposite. He crossed his ankle over his leg. She saw the bottom of his boot. The Cat's Paw logo was on the heel.

Sara had to close her eyes for a moment so she didn't lose control. She counted to ten, then twenty, before she could look at him again. "Will, your not talking to me about things is what got us into this mess in the first place."

He swallowed. The alcohol had worked. He didn't flinch this time. "I'm sorry."

Sara felt like a schoolmarm, but she couldn't stop herself from asking, "Sorry for what?"

He picked at the stitching on his boot. "When I chased you. When I—" He stopped. "What I did when I caught you."

Sara blushed at the memory.

He said, "I was out of control."

She couldn't let him take all the blame. "We were both out of control."

"I hurt you."

"I'm not Amish, Will. I've had rough sex before."

His startled look told her he thought it was something else.

"I didn't tell you to stop." Sara couldn't understand how he could be so wrong about something so obvious. "I was never afraid of you. I was furious. I wanted to hurt you. But I wasn't afraid."

His eyes glistened. She couldn't tell if it was from the whiskey anymore.

"Will, I was mad at you—I'm still mad—because you lied to me. Not just once, but repeatedly. Obviously, something happened to you last night, too. We took it out on each other. It's what adults do sometimes. But you need to know that you can't just fuck me silly and make everything better."

He was still upset. His voice was filled with self-recrimination. "I never wanted to be that way with you."

"Baby—" The word came out of her mouth so naturally. Sara could see the effect it had on him, and she understood that as bad as things were for her last night, they'd gotten so much worse for Will after he left.

Sara sat down on the edge of the bed. "Please, just talk to me."

He didn't look at her. He leaned forward, elbows on his knees.

She could see his jaw clenching and unclenching. A dark red mark crisscrossed the side of his forehead. There was a waffle print to the pattern, as if someone had kicked him.

He said, "I came here for somebody else."

"Who?"

Will gripped his hands together. He stared at the floor. When he finally spoke, his voice was so soft that she could barely hear him. "I feel like I'm disappearing."

Of all the things he could've said, this was the least expected. Sara didn't know how to respond.

Will obviously didn't expect her to. His jaw worked again. She could tell every fiber of his being wanted to stop. Still, he said, "All my life, I've been invisible. At school. At the home. At work. I do my job. I go home. I get up the next morning and I do it all over again." He gripped his hands tighter. Seconds passed before he managed to continue. "You changed that. You made me want to get up in the morning. You made me want to come home to you." He finally met her gaze. "You're the first person in my life who's ever really seen me."

Sara still couldn't speak, but this time it was because she was too overwhelmed. The sound of his desolation broke her in two.

"I can't go back to that." His voice was gruff. "I can't."

Sara couldn't let him. Her anger slipped away like sand through her fingers. She gently cradled her hand to his face. She knew this man. She knew his heart. Will hadn't hurt her on purpose. He'd been stupid and stubborn, but not malicious. And Sara couldn't be the woman Lena Adams thought she was. She couldn't demand perfection. She couldn't set her standards so high that no one could meet them.

She had already lost the first love of her life. She couldn't lose the second one.

"Okay." She rested her hand on the nape of his neck. "We'll be okay."

His eyes scanned her face, looking for any sign of equivocation. "Do you mean that?"

She nodded.

He nodded, too, as if he still needed to convince himself. "I'm sorry I hurt you. I was wrong."

"Please, don't do it again." Sara closed the distance between them. She wrapped her arms around his shoulders. "I'm your girlfriend. This isn't just about keeping things from me. It's about trusting me. I may not understand, or agree, but you have to trust me enough to tell me the truth."

"You're right." He held her close to his chest. His fingers stroked through her hair. She felt his lips press against the top of her head. "I need you to promise me something."

She pulled back so that she could see him. "Okay."

"Promise me we're never going to break up again."

She started to laugh, but there was a sincerity to his tone that stopped her.

Will said, "Actually, I'll promise. I'll never leave you." He sounded more certain than she had ever heard him. "You can tell me to go, but I won't. I'll sleep in my car outside your house. I'll follow you to work. To the gym. If you go out to dinner, I'll be at the next table. If you go to a movie, I'll be in the row behind you."

Sara felt her brow furrow. "You're going to stalk me?"

He shrugged his shoulder, as if this was all a done deal. "I love you."

She finally laughed. "Well, that's a really shitty way to say it."

"I love you."

Her response came as naturally as taking a breath before jumping into the deep end of the water. "I love you, too."

He leaned in but didn't kiss her. Despite his forceful words, he waited for permission. Sara touched her lips to his as softly as she could. The kiss was chaste, but it was enough.

He said, "We're okay."

She nodded. "We're okay."

He held her hand in both of his. He kissed her fingers. Then he turned her wrist and looked at her watch. "We need to go."

"Where?"

He stood abruptly. "I'll tell you about it on the way. Lena found something."

Sara guessed, "A winning lottery ticket?"

"No." He helped her up from the bed. "She found a little boy."

Sara pulled her BMW into an open garage bay. There were two other cars inside the metal structure, which was several yards from a sprawling, single-story house. They were on a horse farm. She could see a few mares and a colt out by a red barn. The sun was just cracking the horizon. The horses silently chewed some grass as they watched the garage door close.

Sara recognized the black Suburban parked beside them as a G-ride, or a government-issued SUV. She assumed either Faith or Amanda was here. The sheriff's cruiser in the far bay probably belonged to the owner of the farm. Keeping horses was as costly as it was risky. Normally, amateur farmers had to seek out more steady employment. Sara had been thrown from a horse twice in her life. She imagined owning a horse farm was only marginally less dangerous than being a sheriff's deputy.

Will got out of the car. He opened the back door and retrieved her medical bag from the back seat. He didn't hand Sara the bag. He carried it for her.

"This way," Will said, heading toward a side door.

Sara followed him as he picked his way past various small machinery taking up the last bay in the four-bay garage. She took Will's hand to steady herself as she stepped over a tractor attachment that looked like a gigantic yard rake. He held on longer than necessary. She stroked his fingers with her thumb, wishing she could erase the past twenty-four hours and start all over again. Or maybe not. In so many strange ways, she felt closer to Will than ever before.

Faith opened the door before Will could. She avoided looking at Sara. "Find it okay?"

Sara said, "The GPS led us straight here."

"Good." She reached into her purse and pulled out a handful of Jolly Ranchers candy. "The boy's still asleep. We didn't want to wake him until we had to. Denise and her girlfriend are in the house with one of the paramedics. The doctor read the message board, so he knows not to come."

"Sounds good." Will took the candy and shoved it into his pocket. "I've got around two hours before I'm due at the hospital. What's the plan?"

Sara felt her stomach lurch at the thought of him going back undercover, but she kept her thoughts to herself.

Faith said, "The other paramedic is on her way with the bus. I was about to head over to dispatch. I want to be sitting on the supervisor so no one panics when they go off-radio. We don't know how far this thing reaches. I'll stay there until I get the word that the boy's in Atlanta."

Will asked, "Who's going to follow the ambulance? Sara's not going without backup."

"Denise will be behind them the whole way. She'll have her piece and her shotgun. Amanda thinks a larger escort team would alert Big Whitey."

Will held out his phone to Sara. "Use this to check in with Faith every half hour."

Sara tried not to bristle at being ordered around. "I've got my hospital BlackBerry."

"The 689 number?" She nodded, and he pocketed his phone. "I'm serious. These people don't mind collateral damage. You need to call Faith every half hour until you're safe at the hospital."

Sara wasn't sure this was necessary, but Will didn't give her a chance to disagree. He headed toward the house. She saw him take one of the candies out of his pocket. Instead of peeling away the wrapper, he bit it off with his teeth.

Again, Sara followed Will. He was back in top form—back in charge. Even in that awful maintenance uniform, he seemed like his old self. She watched him walk, the easy, athletic gait, the muscular line of his broad shoulders. Her big, tough cop. If Sara was trim, at least she was the kind of trim who didn't settle.

Faith walked beside Sara. She was silent as they trudged across the yard. The tension crackled between them like static electricity.

Sara said, "You are a fantastic liar."

Faith grinned. "I really am."

Sara couldn't stop herself from smiling back.

Faith asked, "Did Will fill you in?"

"He told me everything."

Faith raised an eyebrow.

"Everything that's happened in Macon," Sara amended. Will had started talking the minute they'd left the hotel room. She'd never heard him speak for such an extended period of time. He'd told her about Lena's emailed tip, the rednecks, the boy found in the basement and Denise Branson's part in protecting him. The only detail Sara could've done without was the fact that Will had been riding a motorcycle, but even her shocked gasp did not stop him from talking. She'd actually slowed the car at one point, relishing his sudden candor, wishing he would extend it to the rest of his life. His childhood. His family. His bad marriage.

There weren't enough miles in the road.

Faith said, "Remember when you told me a while ago that you had to be on Will's side?"

Sara remembered the conversation well. Faith had asked her for details about Will's background. Sara hadn't felt right about sharing what little she knew. "I get it. You need to be on his side, too."

Faith smiled, obviously relieved.

Sara asked, "Did the doctor give you any treatment information?"

"The first few days, he gave the boy fluids, a round of antibiotics, but that was it. He's mostly been dropping by to give him a sense of routine and make sure nothing new pops up."

"That probably helped more than anything else. Kids always need structure."

"He's still in survival mode. Denise thinks his food might've been drugged while they held him. He won't drink Coke, but he'll drink bottled water. He tears everything apart like he's looking for a pill. He'll eat a bite, then wait to see if it makes him sick or sleepy, then he'll eat another bite. They've tried feeding him stuff that isn't easily tampered with, like fruit roll-ups and deli meats. He still breaks it apart before he eats it."

Sara nodded because there was nothing to say. She felt overwhelmed by the knowledge of the terrible things that happened to children. Faith must've been feeling the same. She was quiet until they reached the house.

The door opened and a petite African American woman came out. She was dressed in jeans and a T-shirt, but she had a gun on her hip and looked capable of using it. Her toned arms indicated she was no stranger to farm work. She spoke in a surprisingly soft voice. "Are you the doctor?"

"Yes," Sara told her.

The woman rested her hand on the butt of her gun as she stepped aside, letting them enter the house.

The kitchen was warm and cheerful. Obviously, the owner wasn't into decorating, but she'd managed to create a welcoming space with lots of soft wood tones. Sara guessed Denise Branson was the woman sitting at the table. She had the look of someone who'd lost everything that mattered. She slumped at the table. A mug of tea was in front of her. Rather than drink it, she aimlessly stirred the tea bag around by the string.

Faith said, "Denise?"

Denise looked up, managing a strained smile. "Dr. Linton?"

"Sara." She offered her hand to the woman. "I hear you've been taking good care of my patient."

Denise gave a wary look, as if she wondered whether or not Sara was making a cruel joke.

Faith covered the awkward moment. She opened the kitchen door. "I'm going to head over to dispatch. Just call me when you're ready. Will, keep your phone on you at all times."

He nodded before she left. Sara didn't like the look that passed between them.

The deputy locked the deadbolt with a key that she put in her pocket. "I'm Lila, by the way. Jasmine's in the back with the boy. You're Will?"

"Yes," Will answered. He put Sara's medical bag on the counter and shook Lila's hand.

The deputy had to crane her neck to look up at him. "I already said this to your partner, but thank you for doing this. We've been going it alone for a while."

"You're not alone anymore," Will told her. And then his eyes lit up when he noticed the box of Pop-Tarts by the stove. "Do you mind?"

She retrieved the box for him. "Help yourself."

Will swallowed the candy in his mouth. He coughed several times, but that didn't stop him from ripping open the packet.

Lila told Sara, "The boy's still asleep. I haven't fed him yet. I was going to make crepes. He wouldn't eat the pancakes yesterday. I think they were too thick."

Sara asked, "Do you eat with him, or just serve him?"

Lila was at the open refrigerator. She seemed disappointed in herself. "Damn. If he sees us eating the food, he knows it's safe." She shook her head as she took out a carton of eggs and a jug of milk. "I just served him a tray the same as his captors probably did."

Sara tried to take away some of the guilt. "You guys have been here all along. It's easy for me to come in with a fresh eye."

Lila said, "He won't leave the room. I put a television in there for him. He keeps the sound off, reads the captions. Denise got him some books, but he won't touch them. They can read at that age, right?"

"Yes," Sara answered. "He's probably used to having to read aloud, though."

"He read to his mom," Denise said, more to herself.

Will had finished one packet of Pop-Tarts. He opened another. "Did you try video games?"

Lila's face fell again. "Video games." She asked Denise, "Why didn't we think of that?" She scraped a pat of butter into the frying pan. "I should've taken my brother's Xbox. He's too old to play it, anyway."

Denise said, "We should've left him to the experts all along."

"You kept him safe," Sara said. "That's all that matters."

Denise stared down at her tea again. Lila started cracking eggs into a bowl.

Sara wondered what would become of these women. Denise Branson was looking at disciplinary actions, possibly criminal charges, but her fate rested with Lonnie Gray. From what Sara knew about the man, he was fair, but he also believed in swift justice. She hoped that Lila was safe. Unless someone told the sheriff, the deputy's part in this enterprise would remain anonymous.

"He's awake." Sara guessed from the paramedic's uniform that the woman in the doorway was Jasmine. Like her friends, she was petite, but there was something about her that indicated she wasn't going to be messed with. Faith had the same bearing. Sara guessed that knowing you could take down a two-hundred-pound ex-marine like Paul Vickery with a steel baton engendered a certain amount of confidence.

Sara said, "I'd like to go ahead and see him now."

Lila moved the skillet off the burner. "We'll go with you."

"Maybe not all of you." Sara chose her words carefully. "You've been so good to him. You've taken care of him. Denise, you literally rescued him." She paused. "He might feel that you won't like him anymore if he tells you what happened."

Again, Lila was quick to find fault with her own actions. "We've been reinforcing his silence by walking on eggshells."

Sara corrected, "You provided a safe environment for him to heal."

Lila turned back to her cooking. She didn't seem mollified.

Sara told Will, "You come, too."

They all seemed to recoil at the idea.

Sara said, "I know it seems counterintuitive, but sometimes victims feel safer with men around. They think that brute strength can protect them."

Lila acknowledged, "I've had rape victims ask for a male detective. Sometimes, not always."

Will seemed more hesitant than any of them. "Are you sure?"

Sara advised, "Just sit down when you get in the room. Let him get used to you first. Seven-year-olds are highly adaptable. They're also extremely inquisitive. He'll want to know details about what's going on, what's happening next."

"We didn't tell him anything," Lila said. "We just kept saying he was safe."

Jasmine offered, "That's what he needed, Lila. You heard the doctor. He needed to feel safe and we made him safe." She looked at Will. "I don't know about you, though. I'm sorry, but he's just a little boy, and the people who hurt him looked a hell of a lot like you."

Sara didn't want to force it, but she said, "I'd really like him in the room. I think it would help."

The tension seemed to ramp up. Lila was the first one to break the silence. "She's been right about the other stuff. I say we give it a shot. If the boy freaks out, then Will can always leave, right?"

Will readily agreed. "Right."

Denise and Jasmine exchanged a look. Sara could tell they were used to acting by consensus.

Lila said, "Dee, if something ain't working, then you stop doing it and try something else."

Denise said, "The boy's already broken."

Lila pointed at her with the spatula. "Maybe it's time we let the professionals help put him back together."

Denise cupped her hands around her mug. She looked at the dark tea. Finally, she said, "All right. But the minute he even starts to look upset, you have to promise to leave."

"I promise," Will said, though he still seemed to be the most reluctant person in the room.

Denise stood up from the table. "I'll be right outside the door so he knows I'm there."

"Thank you." Sara retrieved her medical bag from the counter.

Denise preceded them down the hallway. Sara could tell the woman wanted to stop this, to push both Will and Sara out of the house and do what she'd been doing from the moment she'd rescued the boy from that dark basement. They had been protecting the child for more than a week. They had tended him, fed him, looked over him like guardian angels. Letting a six-foot-three man waltz into the room seemed like the last thing the boy needed.

At first, it looked as if the boy agreed. His eyes went wide when he saw Will. He shot up in bed, his back pressed against the headboard.

Denise gently soothed, "It's okay, baby. These people are friends of ours. They're here to help you."

The boy pulled up the sheet around his chest. They had dressed him in Spider-Man pajamas and put matching linens on the bed. There were toys on every available surface—Matchbox cars, a giant Transformer, enough Legos to build a small town. Picture books were stacked on the dresser. Nothing looked as if it had been touched. Someone had obviously gone to the local children's store and asked the clerk exactly what to buy for a seven-year-old boy, but this particular seven-year-old wasn't interested.

"Good morning." Sara entered the room, keeping her tone as even as possible. She'd always made it a practice to never talk down to children. "I'm Dr. Linton. This is Agent Trent. He's a police officer, but he works for the state, which is why they call him an agent instead of a detective." She indicated for Will to enter the room. "Dr. Thomas isn't going to be here this morning. He told me to say hello to you. I'm going to look after you if that's okay."

The boy didn't move, but he didn't protest, either.

Sara did a quick visual exam. Dr. Thomas had done a good job. For all intents and purposes, the boy looked like any healthy seven-year-old. His color was good. His weight appeared to be on the low-normal side. There were no indications of dehydration or neglect. The wounds on his face were healing well. Except for his fearful, cowering demeanor, she would never have guessed that the boy had been abducted.

Sara motioned Will toward the chair in the corner. "Agent Trent's been in a fight with some very bad men. That's why his face is bruised. You can see the red marks on his neck. They're going to heal in a few weeks. Have you ever been bruised before?"

The boy stared at Will. He gripped the sheets up around his neck.

Sara continued, "In about two days, Agent Trent's bruises will look dark purple or maybe even black." She opened her medical bag. "Around ten days from now, they'll start to turn green, then they'll turn brown, then after about two and a half weeks, they'll just disappear." She asked the boy, "You've been bruised before, right?"

He still didn't answer, but he looked at Sara now instead of Will.

"I'm going to put my fingers on your wrist, okay?" The boy didn't flinch when Sara took his pulse. By seven years, he'd probably been to a doctor's office dozens of times. He was used to the routine of examination.

Sara asked, "Do you know what causes a bruise?"

The boy didn't respond, but she could tell he was listening.

"It's blood trapped underneath the skin. That's kind of gross, isn't it?"

He stared at Sara.

"Well, I think it's gross, and I'm a doctor."

The boy's gaze went back to Will, but he was studying him now rather than staring.

Sara pulled out her stethoscope. It was an old one she kept as a spare. Her parents had bought it for her when she first entered medical school. Sara held the chestpiece to her mouth and warmed it with her breath. The boy didn't need to be told what to do. He leaned forward in the bed so Sara could listen to his lungs.

She pulled up the back of his shirt. There were burns on his skin. Sara pretended to ignore them.

"Deep breath," she said, then listened longer than necessary. Dr. Thomas had treated the burns, but left them uncovered to prevent infection. There would be scars—scars similar to the ones Sara had seen on Will.

"Wow," she finally said. "Your lungs are very strong." The boy leaned back so she could listen to his heart. He gripped the sheets at his waist now, but his head kept turning in a triangle pattern. He looked at Denise, who stood in the doorway, then back at Will, then up at Sara. He was constantly checking his surroundings. His fingers worked the hem of the sheets as if he wanted to be ready at any minute to hide under the covers.

Sara told the boy, "You know you're in the state of Georgia, right? That's right above Florida."

The boy didn't answer, though there was something in his expression that told Sara that she was telling him things he already knew.

Sara said, "In a few minutes, we're going to ride in an ambulance like you did before. Only this time, we're taking you to Atlanta." She paused. He was paying close attention now. "The trip will take about an hour and a half. When we get there, you'll be at a hospital. I'll be with you the entire time."

The boy looked at Denise.

She told him, "Jasmine and Vivica will drive you. I'll be in the car behind the ambulance. Lila will come up later to check on you." She smiled as if they both shared a secret. "I told you we're not going anywhere."

Sara guessed Vivica was the other paramedic. She told the boy, "We won't have the siren on because this isn't an emergency. You're not sick. You're probably just tired and very scared. And you're not talking, so I need to look inside your mouth and make sure nothing's stopping you. Okay?"

The boy's eyes snapped back to Sara. He knew she wouldn't find a medical explanation for his silence.

"Just give me one second." Sara dug around in her bag the same way Nell did when she wanted to look busy. "I don't have a tongue depressor," she lied. She turned to Denise. "Do you have any Popsicles?"

Denise obviously didn't understand. "Popsicles?"

"I can use the wooden stick for a tongue depressor. Maybe there's some in the freezer?" She stared her meaning into Denise. "Could you go look?"

Denise obviously didn't want to. Still, she told the boy, "I'll be in the kitchen. Okay?"

The boy didn't nod, but there was some sort of unspoken language between him and Denise. She understood that his permission to leave was granted.

Sara rummaged around in her bag again. She said, "I like Denise a lot. Don't you, Agent Trent?"

Will had to clear his throat before he could answer. "Yes. They're all very good people."

She told the boy, "Agent Trent sounds funny because his throat is sore."

The boy looked at Will again, probably taking in the bruises ringing his neck.

She said, "Agent Trent doesn't like to brag, but he knows some good jokes. Don't you?"

Will looked stunned, then slightly panicked.

She tried not to use the same tone as she had with the boy. "Why don't you tell him a joke?"

Will seemed at a loss for words. He was always telling her silly jokes. She had no idea why he couldn't think of any now.

Sara prompted. "How about SpongeBob? Didn't he get into some trouble lately?"

Will took a candy out of his pocket. He fumbled with the wrapper. Sara was about to let him off the hook when he said, "Butterflies taste with their feet."

The boy just stared at him. Sara did, too. She had no idea what he was talking about.

Will popped the candy into his mouth. "Butterflies don't have mouths that can chew or bite, but they've got these straw things that they use to suck nectar. That's how they eat." He cleared his throat. "But how do they know what to eat? They land on leaves and things with their feet, and that's how they taste whether or not it's good. Their taste buds are in their feet."

The boy's eyes narrowed. He was skeptical, but intrigued.

Will could obviously tell this, too. He pulled his chair a few inches closer to the bed. "Did you know that most turtles can breathe through their butts?"

The boy shot an excited look at Sara, probably because Will had said "butt."

"It's true." Will pulled his chair closer. "They've got these little air sacs in their butts. So they keep their heads down under water and just stick up their butts when they need to breathe."

The boy had stopped gripping the sheet around him. He stared at Will with open curiosity.

Will said, "Actually, I just heard there was some kind of battle going on in the forest." He cleared his throat again. She hoped he didn't get cut off by another coughing fit. He said, "Insects versus the animals. Did you hear about this?"

The boy still would not answer, but he was leaning slightly forward.

Sara said, "I think I read about it in the newspaper."

"I'm sure you did. It's been all over the news." Will asked the boy, "Did you see it on television?"

There was an almost imperceptible movement from the boy as he shook his head.

Will told him, "They finally decided to have it out. The animals and the insects. They scheduled a football game. The winner gets to be the king of the forest forever and a day. And I mean forever, plus an extra full day." Will leaned his elbows on his knees. He asked the boy, "Are you sure you didn't hear about this game? It was huge."

This time, the headshake was more apparent.

"It was an epic game," Will said. "I mean, unforgettable. For years, the insects and the animals will be telling their kids about it."

The boy leaned forward even more, waiting.

"The first two quarters, it was no contest. The animals were pounding the insects. I mean, obviously, they've got physical superiority." Will feigned throwing a football. "One after the other, touchdown, touchdown, touchdown. The animals dominated the field. The insects couldn't do anything to stop them. Then halftime comes." Will held up his hands as if to stop everything. "The insects were crying like babies in the locker room. They were going to lose this thing. They knew it. They could feel it in their exoskeletons. Humiliation for the rest of their lives. But they still go back out onto the field. They can't just walk away, right? Not after all these years. They may be invertebrates, but they're not quitters. Am I right?"

The boy nodded. He was hanging on Will's every word.

"So, they start the third quarter, and suddenly, the caterpillar walks onto the field. He's strutting his stuff. He takes up the wide receiver position—and I mean really wide. You can imagine the turning radius on this thing. So, the cricket snaps the ball, and suddenly, *whoosh*"—Will swooped his hands through the air—"the caterpillar takes off. He's hogging the ball, running up and down the field like crazy. Touchdown after touchdown. I mean, the caterpillar is on fire. He doesn't just win the game. He runs up the score. At the end, it's animals 34, insects 212."

The boy's lips parted at the very thought.

"The insects are ecstatic," Will continued. "They all run out onto the field. They lift the caterpillar up in the air. They're carrying him around. They can't believe it. They're king of the forest forever and a day. And then somebody says to the caterpillar, 'We could've won this thing before halftime, man. Where were you all that time?' " Will paused for effect. "And the caterpillar says, 'Puttin' on my shoes!' "

The boy sucked in a shocked breath, then exploded with laughter. His mouth opened. He doubled over. His tiny fists were clenched from the effort. He looked at Sara, as if to ask, *Can you believe that?* Sara didn't have to pretend to laugh along with him. The boy's unrestrained joy was the sweetest thing she'd heard in a long while.

He fell over onto his side. The sheets were a forgotten memory. For a brief moment, he was just a kid again.

Then, like a curtain being drawn, the laughter died out and the memories came crushing in. Slowly, the boy pushed himself back up against the headboard. He tucked the sheets tightly around his waist.

Will pulled a handful of Jolly Ranchers out of his pocket. "You want one?"

The boy chose a watermelon-flavored candy. With careful dexterity, he peeled away the wrapper. Sara held out her hand for the trash. The boy's lips puckered as he sucked on the candy. Something was different. She knew that his guard was still up, but there was daylight between the cracks now.

"You know," Will began, "the man who did this to my face will be in a lot of trouble when they catch him." He crossed his ankle over his knee, casual. "He'll end up in prison for the rest of his life. Maybe Denise or Lila will arrest him. Or maybe somebody else. There are a lot of cops out there who are good people. They make sure that the bad guys get locked up so they can't hurt anybody else."

The boy rolled the candy around in his mouth. Sara could hear it click against his teeth.

Will said, "People who do bad things always get caught. Did you know that?"

The boy seemed to consider the question. Finally, he shook his head.

"You don't know it or you don't think it's true?" Will asked.

The boy shook his head again, then stopped. Instead of talking, he held up two fingers.

Will said, "You don't think that's true?"

The boy nodded.

Will told him, "I know you're a smart little boy, but you're wrong about that. This is what I do for a job. I chase down bad people and I lock them up."

The boy looked down at the sheet. He picked at the stitching again.

"I arrested some really bad guys a few months ago. They told this little boy that his mommy and daddy would get hurt if he talked to the police."

The boy looked up, shocked.

"The bad guys were lying," Will said. "They were just trying to scare the little boy. His mommy and daddy were safe all the time. And when he told me what happened, I arrested the bad guys and brought the little boy home." Will leaned forward again. "Do you understand what I'm saying?"

The boy seemed to understand, but he didn't acknowledge it.

Will said, "The sooner you tell me what happened, the sooner I can get you back to your family. And trust me, they want you back so badly. You are all they can think about. No matter what the bad men did to you, they just want you back so they can take care of you and make sure you're safe."

The boy looked down at the sheet again. Tears slid down his cheeks.

Will said, "It's okay to talk to me, buddy. Whatever happened to you, it wasn't your fault. You're just a kid. And your mommy and daddy love you so much. They want you back home. That's all they care about. No matter what the bad men did to you, they will always, always love you."

The boy kept his head down. His mouth moved. He had to think about how to turn sounds into words again. "What about Benjamin?"

Will glanced up at Sara.

She asked, "Is that your brother?"

The boy nodded.

Will said, "I'm sure he wants you back, too. Even if you fought with him or didn't get along, none of that matters. Benjamin wants you back home with him."

The boy finally looked up at Will. "He's not home," he whispered. "He was in the basement, too."

Sara felt her heart stop. She was too paralyzed to speak. Another boy, a brother, still out there suffering horrible cruelties. Or, worse, not still out there, but lying somewhere in a shallow grave.

Will was obviously considering the same possibilities. He visibly struggled to keep his calm. "Benjamin was in the basement with you?"

The boy nodded his head. "The bad man took him away."

Will's cool started to slip. His voice cracked. "Can you tell me your name?"

The boy didn't answer.

Will said, "I met a little boy last night, and he knew the name of his school. Do you know the name of yours?"

The boy still did not answer. He was getting scared again, worried that he'd said too much. He slid down the bed, pulled the sheets up over his head.

Will opened his mouth to say more, but nothing came out. He didn't want to give up, but he didn't know how to keep going, either.

Sara rested her hand on the boy's arm. He was shaking. They could hear his cries through the bedcovers. She told him, "It's okay, sweetheart. You don't have to say anything else for now. You were very brave to tell Agent Trent what you did. And you're still safe. Nothing bad is going to happen to you."

Denise Branson cleared her throat. She was standing in the doorway.

Sara told the boy, "We're going to leave you alone for now, but we're all here if you need us." Sara stood up. She motioned for Will to follow her. "I'll be in the kitchen, okay? You don't have to talk anymore until you're ready."

Sara left the room, though she felt like part of her heart stayed with the boy. His brother had been taken, too. Why hadn't they found him at the house? Where had he been taken?

Sara told Will, "I'll try again in a few minutes."

Will pulled out his phone. The glass was shattered, but the phone seemed to be working. Sara assumed he was calling Faith, but then he said, "This is Agent William Trent. I need a national alert issued immediately on the authority of Deputy Director Amanda Wagner. Two missing brothers, both disappeared on the same day, possibly more than a week ago. No name on the first kid, but he's around seven years old, has dark hair and brown eyes. The second kid is called Benjamin."

Sara told him, "Or Ben. Or Benji."

Will's expression showed absolute shock. He almost dropped the phone. "What did you just say?"

She knew that he wasn't good with nicknames. "Benjamin is sometimes shortened to Ben or Benji."

"Benji?" Will braced his hand against the wall. He seemed stunned.

She asked, "What is it?"

"Give me your keys."

14.

Will pushed the needle on the BMW's speedometer past one hundred as he sped away from Lila's farm. She lived only a few miles from the interstate. He barely slowed for the turn. The tires skipped across the road, but the BMW stayed upright. Will cut off a lane of cars as he merged onto the interstate. He was going fast, but it didn't feel fast enough. He shot past the exit for Macon General. The engine screamed as he gunned it harder.

He was coming up on the exit that led to Cayla Martin's house when his phone finally rang. Will drove one-handed as he answered, "Did they get him?"

Faith said, "They can't find Cayla Martin's street."

Will cursed under his breath. "What about the cops who knocked on her door last night?"

"They're both off-duty. Neither is answering their phones. They're probably asleep."

"Send somebody to wake them up."

"Don't you think I did?"

Will tried to tamp down his frustration. "They have to find the house, Faith. Tell them to send out a helicopter."

"The state highway is thirty miles through that zip code, Will. We've called the road crews. We've called the park service and waste management and the post office and the middle school. We've got three cruisers out there already. They're trying."

"It's a dirt road. There's a trailer park and—"

"We'll find it."

"Tell them to look for me. I just passed Macon General. I'm taking exit twelve now."

The phone was muffled as Faith relayed the information. She came back on the line. "Cayla Martin was seen at the hospital half an hour ago. She was picking up her paycheck. Her car is still in the parking lot, but we can't find her."

"Did they check the employee entrance? She goes out there to smoke."

"Hold on." Again, Faith put her hand over the phone to talk to the dispatcher. "They're checking now."

"Did you find an Amber Alert on two missing brothers?"

"We've got nothing."

"That's impossible," Will argued. "Two brothers went missing on the same day. Why didn't we hear about it?"

"Maybe the police thought it was a parent abduction?" Faith pointed out the obvious: "Something like that wouldn't make it on the news cycle unless there were bodies." She asked Will, "Are you sure the boy wasn't making it up? Kids that age lie about everything. Maybe the other kid was a cousin or friend, or—"

"He wasn't lying," Will said. "And you don't believe in coincidences. Benjamin's not a common name around here."

"You're right," Faith admitted. "Amanda's talking to the Mounties." The Canadian federal police. "Their news doesn't trickle down much unless you're in a border state. She thought maybe the boys came from up there."

"What about the French-speaking parts?" Will asked. "The Mounties don't serve those areas."

"Did either of the boys sound French?"

"Maybe they're bilingual. I don't know, Faith. Just tell her to call everybody."

Faith said, "I'm sending her a text right now."

Will was silent, waiting for her to type it out. His head was spinning. He didn't know how this had happened. Benjamin had been right there in front of him. He'd practically begged Will to help him. He'd said he'd been taken a month ago. Will had thought the kid meant taken away from his mother by the police, not abducted by a sadist.

Big Whitey.

Will knew what had happened to Marie Sorensen. He'd seen the cigarette burns on the boy's back this morning. Denise Branson had rescued him from the basement. What happened to the boys who weren't rescued? What despicable things were being done to Benjamin right now?

"Okay," Faith said. "I sent Amanda the text. We got a no on Cayla in front of the employee entrance to the hospital. She's not on the roof or in the stairwells, either. How far are you from the house?"

Will slammed on the brakes. The car shook. He jerked the gear back into reverse. He'd almost missed the turnoff. "The road's at a steep angle from the main highway, roughly ten miles from the interstate." He silently berated himself for not resetting the odometer when he got off the interstate. "There are a lot of overhanging trees. There's a yard sign where the turn is." He recognized the logo. "It's for the trailer park. It's got palm trees on it."

"I'll let the cruiser know."

Will laid on the gas as he sped down the dirt road. Red dust curled up behind him. The screen on Sara's dashboard flashed black. There was no map in the GPS system for the dirt road. Will muttered another curse at his own stupidity. The screen had been in front of him the whole time.

He told Faith, "Track my phone. Maybe the roads will show up on the military GPS."

"I'm on it," Faith said. "Call me when you get there."

Will ended the call and tossed his phone onto the seat. Then he thought better of it and jammed the phone into his back pocket. As long as the trip to Cayla's had felt the night before, the trip this morning seemed unending. The road spread out ahead of him. It felt like half an hour passed before he saw the trailer park. Kids were out playing in the yard. Will slowed, looking at their faces, checking for Benjamin. They all stared back. Some of them headed home. They'd probably been taught to run if a strange man ever looked at them twice.

The steering wheel jerked as the BMW hit a large pothole. Will fought the turn, overcorrecting. He straightened the tires just in time for another loud bump as the wheels finally hit solid pavement. He was in the subdivision now. The empty lots and unfinished building sites were even more desolate in the light of day. Fortunately, Will could easily see the cluster of completed houses. He skidded to a stop in front of Cayla's driveway. There was no car there. He jumped out of the BMW. He checked the windows to the garage. Empty.

Will dialed Faith's number as he ran up the front walk. He said, "I'm here. There's no car. The house looks empty."

"The cops from last night are on their way. They've got two more cruisers with them. I know you don't have your gun. Wait for backup."

"I'm not waiting." Will ended the call. He stepped back from the front door, then kicked it open. "Benjamin?" he called. His voice echoed through the house. "Benjamin?"

Will opened the coat closet. He checked the back wall to make sure there wasn't a hidden panel. Next, he went into the garage. The space was unfinished, just the structural studs. There were no hiding places.

The kitchen looked the same as the night before. Will's cleaned plate was still on the table. The pots and pans were still on the stove. Tony Dell's beer cans were stacked on the counter.

"Benjamin?" Will called. He took the stairs two at a time. He stopped outside the bathroom, but didn't go in. There was a surface bolt on one of the bedroom doors. A heavy-duty combination lock held it closed.

"Benjamin?" Will banged on the door. "It's Mr. Black from last night. I'm a police officer. I'm here to help you." The lock was secured with bolts, not screws. There was no way for Will to pry it loose. "Benjamin, I need you to stand back. I'm going to break open the door."

Will waited a few seconds, then raised his foot and kicked the door. The lock rattled against the wood. He kicked again. The wood around the jamb started to splinter. He raised his foot and kicked it again. Then again. Finally, by sheer repetition, he was able to break apart the wood. The door popped back on its hinges. The knob stuck in the sheetrock.

Benjamin was chained to the floor. He was sitting in the corner, his back to the wall. He was obviously terrified.

"It's okay," Will told him. "I'm a police officer. I'm here to help you."

Benjamin didn't respond. Will quickly took in the situation. A pair of handcuffs linked the boy's ankle to the chain. The end was attached to an eyehook screwed into the floor. Someone had doused it with Liquid Nails to keep the boy from backing out the screw. Probably Tony. It seemed like the kind of half-ass job he'd do. Tony should've thought about the fact that Benjamin wouldn't have anywhere to use the toilet. The wood had softened from urine. Will easily wrenched the hook out of the floor.

Then he heard a car door slam shut.

Will ran to the front window. Paul Vickery got out of a white Honda. He had a gun in his hand.

"Shit," Will muttered. He should've known Vickery was involved in this.

Will took out his iPhone. He asked Benjamin, "Do you know how to send a text message?"

Benjamin nodded, his eyes still wide with terror.

"You're going to send a text to my partner." Will swiped the screen. He selected the right app, then dialed Faith's number before handing the phone to Benjamin. "Type in your name. Tell her that you're hiding in Cayla's house. Tell her to hurry." Will scooped up Benjamin in his arms as he left the room. There was an attic hatch in the hall. Will had seen it when he stood at the top of the stairs. He held Benjamin up. The boy didn't have to be told what to do. He pushed open the hatch and climbed into the attic.

Will told him, "Don't make any noise. If they find you, don't go anywhere without that phone. Do you understand? It's got a tracker in it. We can find you if you keep the phone. Put it in your pocket. Don't lose it."

Benjamin pulled up the chain around his ankle. The hatch fell into place just as the front door slammed open.

Will barreled down the stairs at a full run. Paul Vickery had attacked him two times before, but each time, the man had surprise on his side. This time, Will had the upper hand. He also knew that crooked as Vickery was, he was a trained police officer. He'd do exactly what Will had done. Check the closet. Check the garage. Check the kitchen.

Vickery was coming out of the kitchen when Will launched himself off the stairs. Vickery's mouth opened. He didn't have time to scream. Will tackled him to the floor like a pile driver. Vickery's gun skittered out of his hand. Will slammed his fist straight into the man's face. As awful as the situation was, Will couldn't help but feel the sweet victory of payback as Vickery's nose exploded like a blown tire.

Will reared back for another go, but Vickery didn't move. Like most bullies, he had a glass jaw. One hit and he was unconscious. Will sat back on his heels feeling supremely disappointed.

"Damn, Bud," Cayla Martin said. She was standing at the busted-open front door. She had a Taser gun pointed at Will's chest.

The M26-C carried a compressed-nitrogen air cartridge that shot two tiny barbed probes up to fifteen feet away. The probes were attached to insulated conducting wires. The wires were attached to eight double-A batteries that delivered up to fifty thousand volts of electricity. Enough juice to cause complete neuromuscular incapacitation.

Will lunged for Vickery's gun, but he wasn't fast enough to outrun the nitrogen charge. The probes dug into the back of his neck.

He was unconscious before he hit the floor.

15.

FIVE DAYS BEFORE THE RAID

Lena laid back on the table at Dr. Benedict's office. Her head was elevated, but her legs dangled uncomfortably over the end. She tried to keep the paper gown from riding up. It was no use. She was quickly learning that you had to choose between being pregnant and being modest. This was the first of many compromises Lena saw in her future. She already had the sensation of her body being taken over. She was peeing more. Sleeping more. Hell, she was even breathing more. The weird part was that instead of feeling invaded, Lena felt happier than she'd ever been in her life.

"You decent?" Jared peered around the door. He saw Lena and gave a low whistle as he walked over to the table. "Babe, I'm seeing some bedroom opportunities here."

She rolled her eyes, even though she felt a strange thrill when he talked like this. And he was talking like this a lot lately.

She asked, "What'd you say to get out of work?"

"Told them I needed some personal time. They think I'm having an affair."

She slapped his arm. "That's not funny."

He laughed good-naturedly as he looked around the room. "What is all this crap?"

"Got me," Lena said, though she recognized the ultrasound machine. Just looking at it made her nervous. She didn't know what she would do if something was wrong. No heartbeat. The baby's brain growing outside of its head. Horror stories were all over the Internet. She'd turned off the computer last night and thrown up in the hall bathroom.

Jared pulled out one of the stirrups. "You think they sell these tables at Costco?"

"Can you not be disgusting?" She slid the stirrup back in with her heel. "It's bad enough I'm gonna be poked and prodded for the next eight months."

"Seven and a half." He picked up the plastic model of a uterus. The pieces fell apart in his hands. "Shit, the baby went under the table."

Lena watched him get down on his hands and knees to retrieve the plastic fetus. His ass was in the air. His uniform pants stretched in a not unpleasant way. They worked out at the gym together almost every morning. Sometimes, Lena watched him doing squats while she ran on the treadmill.

"Found it." Jared stood up, holding the fetus like a toothpick between his thumb and forefinger. "You okay? Your face is red."

Lena put her hand to her cheek. She changed the subject. "I saw this pregnant woman at the store yesterday. The checkout lady patted her stomach like she was a dog. Then she said, 'Good job, Mom,' like it takes a special skill to get knocked up."

Jared grinned. "You think people are gonna pat my crotch and tell me good job?"

"Not unless they want my Glock up their ass."

He laughed, putting the plastic baby in the uterus, snapping the pieces back together. "You know my mom's gonna wanna be here when it happens."

Lena didn't want to talk about that. Today was supposed to be happy.

"I'm just warning you," Jared said. "And telling you that I want her here."

"Do I have a choice?"

"Your skeevy uncle will probably come, too."

"At least Hank will have the decency to stay in a motel and leave the next day."

Jared couldn't argue with that. Hank had visited a few times since they got married. He was very mindful of outstaying his welcome.

She said, "It's bad luck to talk about any of this now." Lena couldn't help adding, "Like painting the nursery. And looking at cribs. We need to wait another couple of weeks."

He put the uterus back on the counter with a thud.

She tried, "Besides, if you're going to work around the house, you should finish the kitchen."

"It'll be finished before the baby comes."

"It'd better be." Lena felt a fight brewing. She pulled back, not wanting the day ruined. All week, Jared had been talking about seeing the baby for the first time. She couldn't mess this up for him.

Lena asked, "You're never late. What kept you?"

"They put in the marker for Lonnie's son this morning. Some of us rode by to pay our respects."

"That's nice." Lena felt a swell of sympathy for the chief. His son had died after a long illness. Lonnie wouldn't let him go, even when it was clear that nothing could be done to save him. In the end, they'd hooked him up to every machine in the ICU.

Jared said, "Something bad like that happens to me, promise me you'll pull the plug."

"I'll pull it right now."

"I mean it," he said. "Don't let me hang around like that. Peeing in a bag. People touching me like I'm a baby." He asked Lena, "What's the point of touching somebody who's in a coma? What if they don't want you to? They can't stop you. They're just trapped there. That's some creepy shit." He shuddered. "And don't let my mama dress me up in pajamas. You know she'd get crazy like that."

Lena felt her lip start to tremble.

He stared at her, confused. "Are you crying?"

"Yes, I'm crying, you dipshit." She wiped her eyes with the back of her hand. "Why would you talk about dying in the hospital when I'm carrying your fucking baby?"

"Jesus," he muttered. He pulled a tissue out of the box on the counter. There was only one left. He handed it to Lena. "Don't be crying like that when the doctor comes in. He's gonna think I hit you or something."

Lena blew her nose. "Talk about something else."

He easily found a different subject. "How's the raid going?"

Jared had tipped her off about a shooting gallery on Redding Street. He was following the case like a gambler who'd placed a large bet.

She told him, "It's going to shit, is how it's going." She used the dirty tissue to wipe her eyes. "I need more Kleenex."

He opened the door and called, "Nurse? Can we get some more Kleenex?" He waited in the open doorway, asking Lena, "You get anybody to flip on Sid?"

"What do you think?" She wiped her nose again. "Denise is about to have a stroke. She's convinced this is our way into Big Whitey."

Jared rolled his eyes. He liked Denise, but girls like Marie Sorensen ran off all the time. Using Big Whitey as the bogeyman took some of the blame off her shoulders.

Lena felt the need to take up for her friend. "He could exist. Denise found his name on a wire out of Florida."

Jared shook his head with the sort of disregard that made her want to smack him. "I'm with Lonnie on this one. It's a dead end."

"Sid Waller is the key," Lena insisted, though she had come to accept lately that Waller was still going to be walking around free when her kid graduated from high school. "Once he's locked up, he'll start singing."

"Mean ol' Big Whitey will kill Waller before he lets that happen. Right?"

Lena narrowed her eyes at Jared. He was giving her shit again.

He said, "Trust me, as soon as Sid Waller's dead, Chief Gray is gonna get out of the Big Whitey business. It's just too dangerous for him right now. And we both know he lost his edge when his son died."

"Right," Lena said, her tone matching his. "Lonnie Gray is going to back down for the first time in his life."

The nurse handed Jared a fresh box of tissues. He told her, "Thank you," then pivoted back to Lena. "Maybe Lonnie is really Big Whitey. Did you ever think about that?" The door clicked shut. He grinned at Lena. "How crazy would that be? Chief Gray is secretly a dope-swingin' kiddie pimp."

"Stop talking out of your ass." Lena grabbed some tissues and blew her nose as loudly as she could. She hated that his stupid idea actually made a weird kind of sense. Gray had started out in Florida. Over the years, he'd either worked or consulted in several towns up and down the coast, including Savannah. All the mayhem they were seeing in Macon had coincided with Gray coming on board. If Denise was right and there was a mole in the department, then it had to be a mole who knew everything. What better cover was there than being the chief of police?

And what bigger idiot was there than a woman who believed every harebrain theory that came out of her husband's mouth? Less than five minutes ago, Jared was saying Big Whitey didn't even exist. Last week he claimed he'd heard from a guy that Fort Knox had been robbed of all the country's gold. Why on earth was she listening to him now?

Lena shook her head, hoping to God she was suffering from pregnancy hormones and not losing her mind.

He asked, "Why are you shaking your head?"

She didn't answer, knowing there was no point. "I'm stressed about the raid crapping out. Denise and I are both putting our asses on the line over this, and you know Lonnie doesn't forgive or forget."

Jared moderated his tone. "Lookit, something will come up." He waited for her to blow her nose again. "Something always comes up. You're a good cop, babe. You're smart and driven and you never give up. You'll make it happen."

Lena couldn't help it. There was something about the way he looked at her that made her want to cry again. She slipped her hand into his. Jared's arm tensed, but he didn't pull away. He wasn't used to affection. His mother was a cold fish. Lena had never once seen Nell touch any of them. Of course, Lena wasn't the clingy type, either. She couldn't explain why touching Jared was the only thing that soothed her nerves lately. This wasn't the kind of thing she could ask Dr. Benedict about. She'd tried to look it up on the Internet, but most of the pregnant women online seemed to hate their husbands. And there were only a limited number of phrases you could Google on pregnancy before you were inundated with some seriously disgusting porn.

Jared asked, "You okay?"

She chewed her lip, silently willing herself not to start crying again.

He turned sheepish. "You know I love you, right?"

"Yeah," she managed. "Tell me that when I look like I should be swimming in a tank at SeaWorld."

"Babe, as long as you keep getting big in other places, I'm fine."

Lena rolled her eyes. Then she jerked her hand away when the door opened.

Dr. Benedict walked over to the sink to wash his hands. He told Lena, "I'm sorry I kept you waiting."

Jared winked at Lena. This was the first thing the man said every time he entered the room. They joked that his wife probably heard the same thing when they were in bed.

"Lie back for me." Benedict pulled out the extension on the table.

Lena laid her head on the pillow and straightened her legs. She looked up at Jared. He put his hand on her forehead. The move was clumsy—more like he was checking her for a fever—but she didn't complain.

Benedict turned on the ultrasound machine. Unceremoniously, he lifted the paper gown. Lena saw what she'd been denying all week. Her underwear was tight. Pretty soon, it would be rolling under her stomach like a rubber band. She looked up at Jared, expecting a joke. He wasn't laughing. He was watching the monitor, even though nothing was on the screen yet.

Benedict shook the bottle of gel over Lena's stomach. "A little cold," he said, sounding just as practiced as usual. He squeezed the bottle. Nothing came out. He told Lena, "Just a moment," then rolled his chair over to the door. He called into the hallway, "Could you bring me some more gel?"

He rolled his chair back to the table. His cold hands touched Lena's stomach as he felt around for things he didn't bother to articulate. She wondered again if she should've gone to a female doctor. Then again, her regular doctor was a woman and she had the bedside manner of a dingo.

The door opened again. Lena was glad her feet weren't up in the stirrups. The hall was filled with people.

"Here you go." The nurse was the same one who'd brought the tissues. She handed the doctor a new bottle of gel. "I got this off the warmer?"

Lena didn't know which was more annoying—the way the woman raised her voice at the end of the sentence or the fact that no one had warmed the first bottle.

Benedict didn't seem to notice the difference. He shook the bottle and repeated, "A little cold."

Lena looked up at Jared as the warm fluid hit her skin. He winked at her again. She felt the ultrasound probe press against her belly. The fat rolled around in a way she wasn't ready to acknowledge. Instead, Lena watched the monitor, the shifting white and black folds.

This was really the stupidest thing she'd ever done. Lena understood why the doctor had to see the image, but there was no reason for Jared to watch her insides get pushed around. There was a pregnant secretary at the station who framed every ultrasound photo she got. Lena couldn't walk through the office without tracking the progress of the weird little alien blob. It seemed like nothing was private anymore.

Benedict's eyebrows were furrowed. He stared at the screen as he pressed the probe harder.

Lena asked the words she'd been dreading. "Is something wrong?"

Benedict didn't answer, which made it ten times worse.

The nurse said, "Listen." She turned one of the dials on the machine. A slow *wah-wah* sound came out of the speakers, like something you'd hear in a submarine movie.

Lena thought she'd missed whatever she was supposed to listen for, then the rapid thump-thump-thump of a heartbeat filled the room.

Jared gasped. "Is that the—" He looked down at Lena. "It's the heartbeat." He pressed his hand to her chest, felt for her heart. "It's different."

He was right. Lena's heart was beating its usual slow rhythm, while the baby's heart sounded like the wings of a hummingbird fluttering against a windowpane.

The nurse said, "See your baby?"

Lena looked at the monitor. Nestled inside the folds was a little black dot. Dr. Benedict moved his hand around, and the dot turned into a bean. Lena could see the heart flashing.

"Holy shit," Jared whispered. "Holy shit."

Lena heard herself thinking the same words in her head. How had they done this? How had they created something so perfect?

She couldn't take her eyes off the little bean. The round edges, the curve in the center that was going to be a stomach. Soon, the bean would sprout real arms and legs, and a head with sweet little eyes and a crescent-shaped mouth.

But for now, he was just a tiny, fluttering little bean.

Her bean.

Lena had never seen anything so beautiful in her life.

Dr. Benedict said, "Everything looks good. You're six weeks along. Come back next week around this same time." He tapped some buttons on the ultrasound machine. A printer whirred to life. Benedict stood up. He went to the sink to wash his hands. "I'll make sure you get a disc with the ultrasound. The picture should be ready in a few minutes."

Jared leaned down, looking Lena in the eyes. "This is it, babe. You and me and the beginning of everything."

Lena's brain told her the words were melodramatic, but her heart—her heart took in the tears in his eyes, the silly grin on his face, the touch of his hand as his fingers laced through hers, and started to crumble.

He told her, "Nothing's ever gonna be the same again. One day, we're gonna both be sitting in our diapers at the old folks' home and talking about how this is the moment that changed everything."

Lena put her hand to his cheek. Her thumb traced his lips before she gently pushed him away. She wasn't going to start crying again in front of strangers.

Jared understood. He winked at her, joking with Benedict, "Thanks, Doc. Good job."

"You're welcome." Benedict obviously wasn't fond of getting off routine. He studied the nurse as he dried his hands. "You're filling in for Margery, right?"

"Yes, Doctor." The woman smiled warmly as she started wiping the gel off Lena's belly. "I've worked in your office before? I'm Cayla Martin?"

16.

FRIDAY

Will's brain burned in his skull. His muscles were still vibrating from the Taser. At least his body wasn't tensed up like a fist anymore. His hands and feet were no longer clenched into balls. His knees and elbows could straighten. Despite all that progress, sitting up felt like an impossible task. He lay with his back on the floor. Overhead, he heard Cayla Martin walking back and forth across one of the bedrooms. At least he assumed it was Cayla. Paul Vickery was bound and gagged beside him. Whoever was upstairs was walking in high heels.

Detective work.

The throbbing pain in his head had to be from something more than the Taser. Will had been Tasered before. Amanda had said it was an accident, but the way she cackled made him think otherwise. Will tentatively moved his head. There was a tender spot at the back. He blinked, wondering how many times his vision had gone wonky over the last twenty-four hours. He couldn't dwell on that. Actually, he couldn't dwell on anything because his mind yet again could not hold on to one thought.

Benjamin.

That was the one word that would not slip away. Benjamin was in the attic. He still had the chain around his ankle. Will had told the boy to text Faith. Where the hell was she? She'd told Will the cruisers were on the way.

Will had to get out of here. He had to find the police before Cayla disappeared. Paul Vickery was out cold, and not just because Will had hit him. There was a deep gash on the side of the man's scalp. He needed medical attention. Obviously, despite Will's assumptions, Vickery wasn't working with the bad guys after all. Whether this was a recent development or not was less clear.

Will tried to sit up. The muscles would not respond. He could only flop over onto his side. That was when he saw his wrists. They were tied together with twine. The knots were tight. The twine cut into his skin. Will tried to move his legs. His ankles were tied together, too. At least now he knew why he couldn't feel his toes.

Will struggled to sit up. His feet slipped. His hands couldn't find purchase. Finally, he angled himself up to sitting. He only had to close his eyes a few seconds before the nausea passed. Then he opened his eyes and felt sick all over again.

There was a man sitting on the couch. He had a Glock pointed at Will's head.

Will had never met Detective DeShawn Franklin in person, but he recognized the man from the photograph on Faith's cell phone. He was built like a linebacker, with broad shoulders and legs the size of fallen trees. He took up two cushion spaces on Cayla's sofa. The gun in his hand looked like a toy, though Will knew the police-issued Glock was a man-stopper.

Will checked on Paul Vickery again. He was still tied up. Hogtied, really. Which didn't explain why DeShawn Franklin was pointing his gun at Will.

Franklin lowered the Glock, resting the weapon on his knee. "Paul was coming here to save you."

Will didn't give him the satisfaction of hearing the string of curses that came into his mouth. He asked, "My partner sent him?"

"Your partner sent anybody who was listening on the scanner." DeShawn smiled. "Thanks for taking Paul out before I got here. Beat-downs aside, he's not a dirty cop. Woulda been hard explaining to him why I had to tie y'all up."

Will didn't acknowledge the comment. He had to assume the GPS tracker on his phone wasn't working. Faith knew he was at Cayla's house. She would send the cruisers. It was only a matter of time before twenty cops busted down the door.

Franklin seemed to read Will's mind. He took away his options one by one. "I told the cops me and Paul would secure the house. Last we saw, you were headed toward the woods on foot. They're setting up a perimeter on the other side of the highway." He told Will, "The whole damn force is out there looking for you, son."

Will rubbed his face with his hands. His fingers felt cold, probably because the twine around his wrists was cutting off the circulation. "You're working with Cayla?"

"I'm doing a favor for an old friend."

Will got the feeling he wasn't happy about it. "Where's the boy?"

"You tell me. He's not in the house. He's not in your BMW." He smiled again, showing his teeth. "That's a nice ride. State must pay a hell of a lot more than Macon PD."

Will asked, "You're Big Whitey?"

He laughed, genuinely amused. "I'm Big Blackie, motherfucker. You colorblind?"

Will didn't know what he was supposed to say. "Who's Big Whitey?"

Franklin didn't answer immediately. He looked down at the Glock, twisting it back and forth against his knee. "I was friends with his son. Chuck and me grew up together. We both graduated from the academy at the same time. Both moved around together.

He got his lieutenant bars before me, but that's how it goes sometimes."

Will shook his head, trying to break a memory loose.

"Eight, maybe nine months ago, we were out running. Chuck's
leg snaps like a twig. No reason, just snaps."

Will had heard about this kind of thing before. He guessed,
"Leukemia?"

"Now you're putting it together."

"Not really," Will admitted.

"Chuck was supposed to take over the family business. With
him gone, who knows?"

"Chuck," Will echoed. The name was so familiar.

"I thought you state boys were smarter than this."

Will said, "I've had a bad couple of days."

"I hear you, brother. Doesn't look like it's gonna get much better."

Will heard something heavy drop on the floor upstairs. It was
similar to the sound of a clue dropping into his lap. He told Franklin, "Cayla Martin told me she drove up the Tamiami Trail with a
guy named Chuck."

Franklin smiled. "Maybe you're not so stupid after all."

Will realized there was a wall behind him. He slid over so he
could lean back against it. The rest did him good. He said, "Chief
Gray's son died recently." Will remembered something Faith had
told him yesterday morning. "You were handpicked by Gray to
follow him to Macon when he took over the force."

Franklin waited.

Will made a calculated guess. "Chief Gray is Big Whitey."

Franklin didn't acknowledge the revelation, but he told Will,
"Lonnie was working in Jacksonville, but he lived in Folkston.
Me, my baby sister, and my mama were up by the Funnel. Not
many black kids around there, but Lonnie didn't bat an eye when
he found me sitting at his dinner table."

"You should be glad he didn't kidnap and rape you."

The gun went up. Franklin pointed the muzzle at Will's head again.

Will said, "You didn't know Lonnie was into kids, did you?"

Franklin glared at him for a beat. Finally, he lowered the gun back to his knee. "He raised me more than my own daddy ever did." Disgust showed on his face. "Never heard Lonnie say anything about kids. Never saw him looking at them, talking to them, nothing. I guess as good as Lonnie was at fooling strangers about one thing, he was really good at fooling his friends about the other."

Will asked, "How'd it feel when you found out?"

Franklin let his silence answer the question.

Will said, "Being a badass drug dealer and a murderer is one thing. Raping kids is a whole other category." He could tell Franklin agreed with him. "It crosses the line, doesn't it? You put a cap in a junkie's ass, that's pretty much what he signed up for, but children are innocent. They didn't sign up for anything."

"I told you I didn't know."

"Denise Branson knew."

"You think anybody listens to that stupid dyke?"

Will didn't point out that the stupid dyke had been right all along.

"Lonnie was a God to me. To all of us. I had no idea he was . . ." Franklin couldn't even say the words. "I'm glad Chuck didn't live to find out. It would've killed him all over again."

"How did you find out?"

"The house," Franklin said. He meant the shooting gallery. "I sent my guy in before the raid to take out Waller and his crew."

Will guessed Franklin's guy was Tony Dell. There wasn't another player in this thing who was so adept at killing.

Will asked, "What did your guy find?"

"What we expected. Three of them were in the front room watching TV. No problem, my guy takes them out quiet. He goes down into the basement looking for Waller and finds these two little kids instead." Franklin shook his head, and Will could see his turmoil was real. "One of the boys was already dead. Just laid there, my guy said."

Will thought of the boy back at Lila's farm. Playing dead had saved him from countless more miseries.

Franklin continued, "The second kid was barely breathing. My guy brought him here for Cayla to look after."

Will wondered if he knew how Cayla had looked after him. "The kid identified Big Whitey?" Franklin nodded, and Will tried not to think about Benjamin feeling safe because Franklin had a badge. "Your guy said Waller wasn't in the basement?"

"Right. Only, he's leaving out the back with the kid when he hears Waller bust in through the front." Franklin shrugged. "Waller runs down into the basement to check on his stash. My guy braces the door, traps him down there, and walks away."

"Why did you want to take out Waller's team before the raid?"

Franklin was obviously reluctant, but he answered, "I was worried about Lena getting hurt."

Will must've looked as dubious as he felt.

"I'm not an animal, man. I got two nieces. I helped raise up my sister after my daddy died." Franklin said, "I knew Lee was pregnant. Cayla fills in at a lot of the doctors' offices. She heard Jared telling Lena that he thought Lonnie was Big Whitey."

Will replayed the words in his head, making sure he understood them. "Was Cayla eavesdropping?"

"Nope. Jared was standing in the open doorway. Half of the office heard him call out Lonnie."

"And Cayla thought he was being serious, just tossing off that theory at the doctor's office in front of everybody?"

"That's what Cayla said."

"What did you think?"

"That he was bullshitting." Franklin shrugged. "Jared's a talker. All those bike boys are. They think they can run with the big dogs, but they don't know jack."

Will had to take another moment to process the information. If what DeShawn said was true, then Lena was right. She hadn't been the one to bring all of this down on them. Jared Long had. "Did Lena believe Jared?"

"I don't think so. At least Lee never said anything to me or the guys," DeShawn admitted. "But she's smart when she latches onto something. Jared puts a thought into her head, maybe she starts paying attention to things she didn't notice before. I had to keep her busy. She was all over the Waller thing. I knew she'd jump at the chance to take him out."

Will felt everything finally coming together. "So, Cayla tells you about the conversation at the doctor's office. You reach out to a pill pusher named Tony Dell. Tony gets arrested. He flips on Waller two hours later and gives Lena the evidence she needs to go into the shooting gallery."

"I know you think I'm stone cold, but I was trying to protect her." Franklin explained, "Lena busts Waller, she's covered up in paperwork for the next six months. I figured that'd run out the clock while she's pregnant, then maybe once she has the kid, she decides she wants to be a mommy and doesn't come back to the job."

Will wondered if there was a single man in Lena Adams's life who'd ever avoided taking risks for her. "Lena lost the baby."

"I know." Franklin seemed regretful. "Cayla called her, tried to get her to take some time off. She wouldn't listen. That girl never listens to nobody."

Will couldn't argue with that. "What about Jared?"

"What about him? He's writing tickets and sweeping broken windshield glass off the road. He can't start an investigation."

"Lonnie Gray wouldn't leave that loose end," Will guessed. He'd seen with his own eyes what a hard-ass the man could be. "You didn't tell him about the conversation at the doctor's office, right? Cayla did. And Gray was a lot more convinced than you were."

Franklin didn't answer, but they both knew that Cayla was that malicious. Franklin put a nicer spin on it, saying, "Cay dated Chuck for six years. Stuck by him when he was dying. She got close to Lonnie at the end. She cares about him."

Will bet she did. Cayla gravitated toward drama the way the tides gravitated toward the moon. "That's why you're here, as a favor to an old friend."

"I can't let her get locked up. I owe it to Chuck."

Will knew there was a code, even among criminals, but he had a hard time thinking Cayla Martin was worthy. He said, "Lonnie sent the rednecks after Lena and Jared."

Franklin nodded.

"He had them torture Eric Haigh to death."

Franklin's expression darkened. "Threw him out like a piece of trash."

"Lonnie's trying to clean house," Will said. "You were attacked outside the theater last night. Somebody took a shot at Vickery. Tony Dell's still out there. Big Whitey's not going to stop until you're all dead."

"Lonnie's not gonna touch me. He was looking for the little boys. He knew somebody found them in the basement. Both kids saw his face, knew who he was. I ain't saying it's right, just that it's something that could come back on him."

"Would that be a bad thing, letting all this come back on Lonnie? Stopping him from hurting more kids?"

Franklin shrugged, but he was obviously talking for a reason.

Will said, "You didn't know about the kids until the raid."

"And?"

"And you put the hit on Sid Waller and his team before you knew about the kids." Will guessed the Big Whitey business model was being franchised after all.

Franklin said, "Things changed after Chuck died. Me and Lonnie weren't so close. I thought it was the grief at first, but then I figured it was something else."

"Waller and Lonnie were both pedophiles. They weren't doing it for money. The only time Lonnie ever took a risk was when he was grooming a new kid."

"You're right," Franklin said. "Only, I found out after Waller was dead that they were doing it together."

"Stalking kids together?"

"Doing everything together." DeShawn looked like he wanted to spit the bad taste out of his mouth. "Lonnie said it was the most fun he ever had."

Will gathered the two men had had several lengthy conversations, none of which had been good for DeShawn Franklin. He said, "It started to fall apart before the raid. You knew something was wrong. You saw that Lonnie and Waller were getting close. You were worried Lonnie would pass on the business to Waller."

Franklin snorted a laugh. "I wasn't worried about it happening. I already knew it was going down. Lonnie told me before the raid. Before Cayla heard Jared. Before any of that shit started, he sat me down and told me it looked like Waller had a better handle on things. Wanted me to be a second to that redneck bastard. Pitched it like he was doing me a favor." Franklin gave a bitter laugh. "I guess he didn't love me like a son after all."

Cayla Martin asked, "Who loved you?" She tromped down the stairs carrying a large suitcase. She'd packed it too full. She couldn't hold on. The case bumped down the stairs and didn't stop until it hit the front door.

Cayla didn't seem to mind. She walked down the rest of the stairs, picking her way carefully on high heels. She was dressed up, or at least it seemed that way to Will. Her tight leather miniskirt looked brand-new and the matching silk blouse was cut so low that it showed the pink bow on her bra.

Franklin told her, "Wait in the car."

"Nuh-uh." She took a pack of cigarettes out of her purse. "I gotta say, Bud, you really fucked me over lettin' Benji go like that."

Will looked at Franklin, but the man didn't offer an opinion.

She said, "I had a family in Germany ready to pay thirty grand for him."

"Family?" Will didn't know if she was deluded or naïve.

"Good thing I got that goddamn plane ticket now." She put a cigarette in her mouth but didn't light it. "Except for Shawn picking me up at the hospital, my happy ass would probably be in jail. Ain't that right, hon?"

Franklin didn't answer. He just sat on the sofa looking like he didn't think he'd ever manage to get up. Part of him still had to be a cop. He'd tried to protect Lena. Paul Vickery had been tied up, not murdered. Franklin had done his best to keep Tony Dell's name out of the story. And then there was the immutable fact that Will was still breathing.

DeShawn Franklin was finished with all of this. Maybe it was the kids. Maybe it was Lonnie Gray's betrayal. Either way, he was done.

"Shit, Shawn." Cayla seemed to sense his faltering resolve. She walked over to Franklin, teetering on her high heels. "You know you gotta do this."

Franklin reached into his pocket. He pulled out his car keys. "Just leave it in the lot."

"Oh, hell no." Cayla's head started shaking back and forth. "No, sir."

Franklin said, "You're leaving town. Whatever I end up doing is on me. It's got nothing to do with you. I owe it to Chuck to make sure your name stays out of it."

"She-it, you can't do anything, Shawn, and I ain't eatin' Wiener schnitzel for the resta my damn life." Cayla flicked the lighter and touched the flame to her cigarette. "Come on. Just finish it. We ain't got time for your conscience to work itself out."

"I'm not going to—"

Cayla grabbed the Glock and shot Paul Vickery four times.

The gunfire reverberated in the small room. The air shook with the noise. Vickery's body jerked violently as the bullets hit his back.

Will's hands flew up in front of his face. His knees pulled in like some part of his brain thought he could roll himself into a ball and stop the bullets. He waited for Cayla to turn the gun on him. And waited.

Nothing happened.

Will peered up, expecting to find the Glock staring back at him.

Instead, he saw that Franklin had grabbed the gun away. He was breathing hard, though there obviously hadn't been a struggle. "Fuck, Cayla!" he screamed. "What the fuck was that!" Franklin knelt down beside Vickery. He pressed his fingers to the man's neck. "You killed him!"

"You're welcome, motherfucker." Cayla's cigarette bobbed in her mouth. "I heard you upstairs, Shawn. You told them every damn thing that's been going on. No wonder Lonnie didn't wanna hand you over the business."

"Shut up!" Franklin pointed the Glock at Cayla. "Just shut the fuck up!"

The cigarette dropped out of her mouth. "Get that gun outta my face."

"I said shut up!" Franklin pressed the gun to Cayla's chest. "I told you to let me handle this. I told you to just shut the fuck up for once in your miserable life and let me do what I know how to do."

Cayla asked, "What're you gonna do, Shawn? Turn state's evidence? Go to the cops and tell them you're sorry?"

"Stop talking."

"You gonna shoot me in the chest, Shawn? That what you promised Chuck you was gonna do? Murder me?" Her words were strong, but she took a step back. "You know we gotta get rid of him or he'll go straight to the cops."

"He won't go to the cops!" Franklin screamed. "He's a con. He's on parole!"

Will stared down at the floor so he didn't give himself away. He had no idea why Franklin had maintained his cover.

And he would never find out.

Tony Dell pushed open the saloon doors to the kitchen. Will couldn't guess how long he'd been standing there. He'd obviously heard enough.

Tony took three steps across the room and jammed his knife into Franklin's neck.

Franklin's mouth opened. He dropped the gun. He put one hand to his throat, tried to steady the handle of the knife with the other.

And then Tony pulled out the blade.

Blood shot out of the wound like a water pistol.

Franklin went down on one knee. He gasped for air. Will could hear his breath wheezing through the open slit in his neck.

Cayla said, "Jesus, Tony, finish it."

Tony didn't want to. He was soaking in the spectacle of Franklin's death. The blood pouring out of his neck. The way his fingers quivered as he reached out for help. Franklin finally lost his balance. His whole body shifted, his knee slipping out from under him. His shoulder hit the floor. Blood pooled around his head. His fingers kept trembling. A pungent odor filled the air. His big chest rose for one last breath that he would never let go.

And then it was over.

"Damn," Tony whispered. "I think he shit hisself."

Cayla slapped Tony on the back of the head. "How many times do I have to call you? I swear to God, I thought Shawn was gonna arrest me outside the hospital. I told you he wasn't right with this."

"You wanna stop your yapping and thank me for risking my neck to get here?" Tony wiped the knife blade on his jeans before shoving it into his boot. "They's twenty squad cars set up on the other side of the highway. I had to take the back way."

"Well, poor you." Cayla picked up her still-burning cigarette from the floor. She grabbed Franklin's Glock and tossed it into the kitchen. "Take care of Bud and bring my suitcase. If we gotta go the back roads, I'm gonna be late for my flight."

Tony said, "Shit, you don't gotta get there four hours ahead. That's for them, not you."

"You ever been on an international flight before?" she demanded. Tony's expression gave him away. "Just be quick, and don't forget to bring my suitcase." She opened the door, but didn't leave. She walked over to Will and jammed her fingers into his front pocket. He kept his body as still as he could. She pulled out the keys to Sara's BMW. "Might as well drive there in style."

Tony slapped her ass. "Hell yeah, baby."

Cayla gave Will a nasty look. Her voice went from her usual high-pitched singsong to a witch's snarl. "Make it hurt, baby. This asshole cost me thirty grand."

She slammed the door behind her.

In the silence, Will heard a clicking sound. He realized it was the breath stuttering in and out of his mouth.

Tony shook his head. "That gal is a piece of work, lemme tell ya."

Will said nothing. Twice now, he'd seen what Tony Dell was capable of. Watching Eric Haigh get stabbed, all Will could think was that he never wanted to go out that way. Now that he'd seen the alternative, he wasn't so sure.

Tony breathed out a heavy sigh. "Get up, Bud. I ain't gonna kill you on the floor."

Will struggled to get on his knees. Finally, Tony grabbed his arm and yanked him up. Will tried to pull away, but it was no use. His hands and feet were tied. He was trapped. He was going to die in this house, on this floor, beside Paul Vickery and DeShawn Franklin.

The only thing that brought him any peace was knowing that Benjamin was safe in the attic. He had Will's phone. They would trace him. They would take Benjamin to his brother. Both boys would be home soon.

But Sara would have nothing. Will was still legally married to Angie Polaski. The courts wouldn't care that Will hadn't seen her in months, that he'd hired a divorce lawyer to track her down. His wife had all claim to him—not just his body, but his memories. Angie had grown up with Will. By virtue of proximity, she knew more about him than anyone else on earth. She was his Pandora's box that only opened when it was time to mete out pain.

Sara had Will's dog, his toothbrush, and whatever clothes he'd left in her apartment.

"Welp." Tony slid the knife out of his boot. "Might as well get this over with." He held it up for Will to see. He'd obviously picked up the trick from the redneck. And as it had before, the trick worked. Will felt his gut clench.

Tony smiled at the effect. "You scared, Bud?"

Will tried to summon Bill Black. He couldn't let himself die a coward. "Go ahead and do it, man. Don't drag it out."

Tony had always been contrary. He lowered the knife. "I guess you pissed somebody off real good." He indicated Will's face. "Got two black eyes, broke nose. I know Junior didn't do that to you."

Will swallowed. His throat was still hurting. He thought about the whiskey Sara had forced him to drink. She was right. It had made him feel better. Everything she did made him feel so much better.

Tony asked, "Who tore into you, Bud?"

Will knew Tony wanted an answer. This wasn't part of the killing game. "The cop. He caught up with me last night. Sucker punched me." He looked at Paul Vickery. "Guess he won't do it again."

Tony laughed. "Thass a good'un, Bud. I guess he won't." He used the knife to clean under his fingernails. The blade dug into the skin under his thumb. Instead of flinching, Tony watched the blood bead up. "Where'd you get that fancy car?"

Sara's BMW. Her registration was in the glove compartment. "Stole it off a woman in the cafeteria."

"That right?"

"She left her keys on the table. I went out into the parking lot and pressed the button until I found it."

"That's a good trick. I'll have to keep that in mind." Tony hefted the knife in his hand, then started flipping it end over end. "I was wonderin' about somethin', Bud." He glanced over his shoulder as if he wanted to make sure they were alone. "I ain't queer or nothin', but I seen you done some grooming." He explained, "Back at the club, when Denny made you pull your shorts down?"

Will shook his head. "What?"

"Seems to me, a man don't groom hisself like that unless he's doin' it for a woman. Am I right?"

Will swallowed again. He couldn't accept that he was going to die talking about his genitals.

Tony kept flipping the knife. "Cayla talked me into shavin' my balls once. They itched so bad I near 'bout scratched 'em off." He shrugged. "I guess it's better what you did?"

Will couldn't tell if he was asking a question or making an observation.

Tony caught the knife by the handle. He smiled, like he'd just figured something out. "You're still sweet on that lady up in Tennessee, ain't ya?"

Will tried to summon up a Bill Black answer, but then he remembered that this was exactly the kind of death a man like Bill Black would face. "Yes," Will said. "I'm in love with her. That's where I was heading—up to Tennessee. I don't want my kid growing up without his daddy."

"That's what I thought," Tony said. "You was just trying to make her jealous, wasn't you? Going out with Cayla like that."

Will nodded. "Yes."

"You came here to tell Cayla that, right? That nothin' was gonna happen?"

"I know she's your girl, Tony." Will grasped for an excuse to explain why he was here. "I heard at the hospital they were looking for her. I came here to tell her that she might wanna lay low for a while. I was looking out for her in case you couldn't."

Tony's jaw twisted to the side as he considered the excuse. Finally, he decided, "You're a real gentleman, Bud, lookin' out for her like that. I always knew you was good." He paused. "What's this about you leaving town?"

Will tried not to flinch as he swallowed. "I was heading up to Tennessee right after I checked on Cayla for you. There's nothing in Macon for me."

"That right?" Tony asked. "You was gonna skip out on your parole?"

"Heat's too much around here. Too many dead cops. Just a matter of time before the pigs try to pin it all on me."

"You could always turn."

"I don't snitch on my friends. And I won't—" Will cut himself off before he started begging. Tony liked to hear people beg. "I wanna see my kid grow up. No reason for me to ever come back here again."

"That's real sweet, Bud. I bet you woulda made a good daddy."

"It's all I ever wanted," Will lied. There were too many bad things that could happen to children for Will to ever want one of his own. Still, he told Tony, "My daddy ran out on me when I was a kid. I don't want to do that to mine."

Tony studied him carefully. He finally said, "My daddy ran out on me, too."

Every muscle in Will's throat strained to keep the conversation going, to create some fictional fairy tale about the woman in Tennessee, their wonderful lives together.

But Will knew it was too late. Tony was done listening. He was trying to make a decision. Will could tell by the way his eyes scanned back and forth as if he could read Will's mind.

Finally, Tony sheathed his knife back in his boot. "Be careful on them mountain roads."

Will felt his lips part. Just like that, the good ol' boy Tony was back.

"I hear Tennessee's real pretty." Tony walked toward the door, then he remembered Cayla's suitcase. He had to grab the handle with both hands. "Shit, she's got just about every damn thing in the house packed in here."

Will didn't speak.

Tony said, "I like you, Bud. It's a shame I ain't never gonna see you again." He gave Will a hard look. "Right?"

Will nodded furiously. "Right."

Tony dragged Cayla's suitcase out the front door. He didn't bother closing it behind him.

Will felt his body sway as he listened to the suitcase scrape against the porch. It banged against the concrete steps, then scratched down the driveway.

They couldn't work Sara's keyfob. The panic alarm went off, but they managed to stop the piercing siren before it got too loud. A door opened and closed, then another one. A few seconds later, a door opened and closed again.

The engine turned over. The tires screeched as Tony stepped on the gas.

Slowly, Will's body adjusted to the fact that he wasn't going to be stabbed to death. He had to lean on his hands and drag his knees behind him in order to get to the front door. He saw the brake lights on Sara's BMW glow as Tony roared out of the subdivision.

Will sat back on his heels. He closed his eyes and just breathed. His heart was pounding so hard that he could almost feel it tapping against his ribs.

Benjamin.

The boy was still in the attic.

Will didn't want to call for him in case Tony changed his mind. Besides, Will's hands and feet were bound. He couldn't exactly run up the stairs and catch the kid when he jumped down through the hatch.

And there were two dead bodies down here. Benjamin had seen enough bad things to last him a lifetime.

Paul Vickery was lying on his side. The gouge in his head had stopped bleeding. His wrists were bright red where the twine cut into his flesh.

Will pressed his hands to the floor and dragged his knees, thinking he was moving like a caterpillar. It was hard to believe that he'd told the boy that football joke just a few hours ago. He was probably at Grady Hospital by now. So was Sara. She was safe. That was all that ever really mattered.

Will stopped beside Vickery's body. He checked the man's pockets for his cell phone. He found a wallet, a set of car keys, and a handful of change, but no phone. Will patted Vickery's chest. There was something hard underneath his shirt.

Vickery groaned, and Will jerked back like a snake had tried to strike.

"'Uck." Vickery pulled down the gag. He cursed a few more times as he loosened his collar. Will could see the black Kevlar vest underneath his shirt. "What the hell happened?"

"You got shot." Will checked Vickery's back. Four flattened bullets were lodged in the vest.

"By you?" Vickery asked.

"No." Will sat back on his knees again. "I saw you on the road talking to Tony Dell last night."

Vickery blinked, like he couldn't understand. "No, you didn't."

"White Honda. You were pulled up by Tony's truck."

"Do you know how many white Hondas there are on the road?" Vickery tried to roll over onto his back. "Why didn't you tell me you were a cop?"

"I was too busy getting the shit kicked out of me."

Vickery chuckled, like it was a fond memory. And then he looked at DeShawn Franklin and his face fell. "I trusted that bastard with my life."

Will didn't say he was probably right to. "Where's your phone?"

"Front pocket." Vickery tried to reach down, but the twine stopped him.

Will knew the pocket was empty, anyway.

Reluctantly, he crawled over to Franklin's body. The blood had stopped pumping along with his heart. The wound in his neck had slowed to a dribble. Will tried not to shudder as he searched the body. His wrists being practically glued together didn't make the task easy. An eternity passed before he found the phone in Franklin's shirt pocket.

Will backed away from the dead man before he even looked at the phone. By necessity, he held it in both hands. His thumb swiped the screen. Instead of a keypad, a microphone icon flashed up. The red button below it was flashing. There was a clock counting off the seconds, and below that, a flat line like on a heart monitor.

The line bobbed up and down when Will told Vickery, "I think he recorded us."

Vickery shook his head, but didn't answer.

Twelve minutes, twenty-three seconds. That's how long the recorder had been running. Franklin must've started it when Will woke up from his Taser fugue.

Vickery said, "You gonna call somebody or what?"

Will pressed the red button. The timer stopped. He wasn't familiar with the phone's operating system, but they were all pretty much the same. He touched his thumb to the icon of a house. He touched the symbol with a telephone receiver. The keypad rolled up. Will dialed Faith's number. He rested his hand on his face as he waited for the connection to go through.

She answered on the first ring. "Franklin, what is it?"

"It's me," Will told her. "I'm at Cayla's house."

"Will?" Faith's voice trilled up. "We've got sixty cops combing the woods for you. We can't pinpoint your phone."

"You need to put an APB on Sara's car. Tony Dell and Cayla Martin stole it. They're headed toward the Atlanta airport, taking the back roads. International terminal. She's going to Germany."

Faith didn't bother to cover the phone as she shouted orders to her team. As soon as she finished, she asked Will, "What about Benjamin?"

"He's safe." Will looked at Paul Vickery. He still didn't trust the man. "What about the other thing?"

"They're at Grady. Sara called over an hour ago. They're both fine."

Will felt relief flood his senses.

Faith said, "The boy started talking in the ambulance. His name is Aaron Winser. Amanda was right. His parents live in Newfoundland. They were going through a bad custody battle. The father was on a fishing trip. The mom thought he'd abducted the boys. The police were about to arrest him." Faith seemed to realize she was talking too fast. She slowed down her words. "The parents are on their way to Atlanta right now. Jesus, Will. You had me scared to death."

"Hold on." Will couldn't stay on his knees any longer. He didn't want to sit down, so he pushed himself up against the wall. Vickery's eyes tracked his every movement. They both heard sirens in the distance.

Will asked, "How far out are the cruisers?"

Faith said, "Five minutes, tops. Call Sara."

"She's probably busy."

"Don't be an idiot."

Will heard a click as she hung up the phone. He glanced at Paul Vickery. The man was still on his back, his elbows and knees bent at an uncomfortable angle.

Vickery asked, "You gonna help me here? This hurts like a bitch."

"It certainly looks painful." Will felt some give in the twine that was digging into his ankles. After a few unsuccessful shuffles, he hopped toward the kitchen.

"Where're you going?" Vickery shouted. "Come back here!"

Will didn't stop until the saloon doors flapped behind him. He leaned against the counter to catch his breath. And also to catch himself, because hopping around was harder than it looked.

DeShawn Franklin's phone had gone back to screensaver mode. The picture showed two little girls dressed in Mickey Mouse ears. Will didn't want to think about someone telling the man's nieces what had happened. He swiped the screen and dialed Sara's number.

She was used to getting strange calls on her hospital phone. Still, her tone was strained when she answered, "Dr. Linton."

Will said, "I'm okay," in a voice that sounded exactly the opposite.

"Are you sure?"

"Yeah." Now that he had her on the line, Will felt it all start to catch up to him. Sara had literally saved him by the short hairs.

"Will?"

"Everything's fine." He made his voice stronger. "I'm just a little tied up at the moment." He stopped himself from laughing at his own joke, mostly because he was pretty sure Sara wouldn't find it that funny. "I don't know about your car, though."

"Sweetheart, do you think I give a damn about my car?"

Will hoped she still felt the same when she turned on the news and saw her BMW being tracked up I-75. "Are you at the hospital?"

"I'm at home. Denise gave me a lift while Amanda interviewed the boy. She's going back to Grady to stay with Aaron until his parents are there. Did Faith tell you?"

"Yes." Will closed his eyes. He liked thinking about Sara being safe at home. "What are you doing?"

"Lying on the couch. I was going to take a shower, but I feel like I've been run over by a truck. I'm too sore to move."

Will thought about the night before. "Sore from me?"

"A little," she allowed. "When do you think you'll be back in Atlanta?"

"I'm driving back tonight." Will decided at that moment that he would quit his job if that was the only way to make it happen. "I'll call you when I'm ten minutes out." He covered the bottom part of the phone with his hand, an easy task considering there was no daylight between his wrists. Still, he lowered his voice, telling Sara, "I want you to fill the bathtub when I call."

She sounded surprised, but said, "Okay."

"When I get there, I want you to get in the tub with me."

Her "Okay" was very different this time.

"Then we're going to talk."

Her voice changed again. "Just talk?"

"I'm going to answer every question you ask me."

"Every question?" she repeated. "The water will go cold."

"We'll keep it warm," he told her. "I mean it, Sara. No more secrets." Will looked out the kitchen window. He saw a police cruiser kicking up dust in the distance. His resolve started to slip. Will felt like he was stepping out onto a tightrope. His hands were so slick he could barely hold the phone.

Still, he managed to say the one thing he should've told her in the first place. "I trust you."

Sara didn't speak, but he could hear her breath through the phone.

Will felt his throat start to tighten. He should probably hang up. He wanted to hang up. But he asked, "What do you think? Does that sound good?"

"Baby." She sighed out the word. "I think that sounds like the perfect way to start the rest of our lives."

17.

FIVE DAYS LATER

Lena sat across the table from yet another Internal Affairs investigator. Brock Patterson's black-and-white ensemble reminded her of the woman who'd investigated her the week before. Lena wondered whether there was a departmental dress code or if they all secretly worked night shifts at Olive Garden. If their pay was commensurate with Lena's, it wasn't a stretch.

"Detective Adams?" Patterson said. He'd obviously asked a question. Lena had stopped paying attention when she'd figured out the repetitive code to his interrogation. Every twenty minutes, he reset, asking the same questions he'd asked before, but using different inflections, different phrasing.

When did you find the boy?

You found the boy when?

Where was the boy when you found him?

The boy. Aaron Winser. He was safe now, but they were all too terrified to say his name on the record.

If Lena was being honest, she never wanted to think about the boy again. Not out of spite, but out of self-preservation. She'd spent four days rehashing every horrible detail of the shooting gallery—the dead bodies, the cold fear that sat in the pit of her belly when she stared down Sid Waller. And then the worst part, the part that she'd left out during the first investigation—finding the boy.

Lena still had nightmares about pulling back that panel in the basement, seeing those two terrified eyes staring back at her. Aaron's pupils had been black as coal, set in a field of reddish white. He hadn't said a word when Lena lifted him out of the hole. He'd felt so light. Like a blanket. Lena had cradled him in her arms, cooing to him. She'd never had a maternal bone in her body, but with Aaron, it came naturally. She stroked his hair. Kissed her lips to his dry forehead. Her hand on his back felt the rapid thump-thump-thump of his heart, and she thought of her little bean, forever captured on that ultrasound file she kept on her computer at the office.

"Detective Adams?" Patterson said. "Could you please focus?"

"Can't you just look back at your notes and write down what I told you the first time?"

"The first time you were interviewed or the first time you told the truth?"

Point taken.

Lena sat back in her chair. It was uncomfortable by design. The room was cold, painted cinder blocks with scuff marks around the vinyl baseboard. She stared at the mirror behind Patterson, wondering who was watching. Her last run-in with the rat squad had taken place in the conference room. Lena guessed with Lonnie Gray sitting in jail, the whole force was being treated differently.

There was a half-empty bottle of Coke on the table. Lena took a long sip before putting it back down. "Tell me why this happened."

Patterson's mouth turned down. He looked like the living embodiment of a frowny-faced emoticon.

Lena said, "No one will tell me why Jared and I were attacked. Was it because of the boy? Did they think I knew where he was?"

Predictably, Patterson wouldn't yield. "It's my job to ask the questions."

"Is it really my job to answer them?" Lena asked. She was sick of not knowing. It was all she could think about. What had she done to bring this down on them? What stupid mistake had she made? What asshole had she pissed off?

She told Patterson, "My husband was almost killed. I was attacked in my home. Don't you think I deserve to know why?"

"My colleague is investigating the attack. As you know, you and I are here on a different matter." Patterson had the poker face of a banker denying a loan. "Your cooperation would go a long way toward—"

"Toward what?" she interrupted. "I wasn't involved in any of this. I did what my commanding officer told me to do."

"You lied under oath."

"Did I?" Lena smiled. She'd been too careful for that. The first investigator hadn't asked about the boy. As far as Lena knew, there was no law that said you had to volunteer information.

Patterson sat back in his chair, obviously trying to mimic her relaxed demeanor. "We're both on the same side, Detective Adams." He tried to sound reasonable, though they both knew he had skin in this game. He'd be looking at a big promotion if he could weed out a few more bad cops, and the man had made it clear from the beginning that he didn't trust Lena. "We just want to make sure the case against Mr. Gray holds. It seems to me we share the same goal here."

"Mr. Gray," Lena echoed. No one was calling him Chief anymore. No one was laying claim to him at all. "My goal is to get back to my husband. He's better, by the way. Thanks for your concern."

Patterson tucked his chin into his chest. He did this whenever Lena pushed back, a physical manifestation of hitting a brick wall. He let out a short puff of air, then stacked together some papers on the table. "I'll be just a minute." He stood up. "Feel free to take a bathroom break if you need one."

Lena gave him a salute as he left the room. He was obviously going to confer with whoever was behind the one-way mirror. She guessed it was Amanda Wagner. The deputy director would count arresting Lonnie Gray as a feather in her cap, though the truth was that Will Trent deserved the credit. He was the one who'd risked his life.

He was also the one who'd kept Lena from killing a man.

While Lena was no stranger to having blood on her hands, taking on the two rednecks who'd broken into her house had been different. If she thought about it too long, the bloodlust came back. She could feel it boiling up into the back of her throat. Her muscles tensed. Her hands clenched. Even standing in the ICU over Jared's bed, Lena had struggled with the impulse to go one floor down and finish the job on the monster who'd wanted to kill her husband.

Not that he'd succeeded.

By some miracle, the doctor said that Jared was going to make a full recovery. He was looking at a few months of physical therapy, but his otherwise good health and youth had been on his side. Of course, now the same two things were working against him. Jared had been home less than thirty-six hours and he was already going stir-crazy—staying up too much, moving around too much, getting in her business too much.

She was tempted to send him to his mother's. Lena didn't hate the woman as much now, maybe because Darnell Long was the only reason Lena had a functioning kitchen. Fortunately, Jared's mother seemed to understand that their truce was only as strong as the miles between them. She had already made one trip back to Alabama. If Lena was lucky, Nell wouldn't return to Macon until the trial.

Not that Lena thought there would be a trial. Just this morning, Fred Zachary, the second shooter, had taken a deal in exchange for giving up the rednecks at Tipsie's. The rednecks weren't talking, but it was probably just a matter of time before they decided to play ball.

That left Tony Dell, and Mr. Snitch had made it clear he didn't want a deal. He admitted to being on the street the night Jared was shot. He admitted to stabbing Eric and DeShawn to death. He corroborated everything DeShawn had told Will Trent about Big Whitey and Sid Waller. Basically, he'd thrown everybody under the bus, including himself. It wouldn't be long before someone decided Dell should stop talking. Lena figured he was planning his own suicide. The fact was that Tony Dell had nothing to lose.

The Atlanta police had caught up with Dell and Cayla Martin outside the international terminal at Atlanta's Hartsfield-Jackson Airport. Dell was obviously a psychopath, but he was also a survivor. He'd known the gig was up. He'd raised his hands and gotten out of the car.

Cayla Martin wouldn't go so easy. She'd jumped behind the wheel and tried to outrun the police. Unfortunately, she'd run in the wrong direction. Lena wondered what was going through the nurse's mind when she saw the shuttle bus speeding straight toward her. According to the accident report, there were about two seconds between the time Martin tried to turn the wheel and the head-on collision. Lena knew what it felt like when you thought you were about to die. Two seconds was an eternity. Martin wasn't wearing a seatbelt. Probably another second passed as she flew headfirst into the shuttle bus and snapped her neck on one of the seatbacks.

Lena couldn't help but think that the sweetest part of that story was not Martin's brutal death, but the fact that Sara Linton's sixty-five-thousand-dollar BMW had been turned into the world's most expensive Rubik's Cube.

Laughter tickled Lena's throat as she pushed herself up from the chair. She started pacing the room, forcing herself not to count off the steps because she already knew the space was twelve feet

across by ten feet deep. She looked up at the camera. She smiled,
though she felt the snarl in her teeth. She wanted to get through
the pile of paperwork on her desk. She wanted to check on Jared.
She wanted to go home and do the things that made her feel like a
normal person: clean the house top to bottom, do the laundry,
tend to her garden in the front yard. Winter was just around the
corner. Lena should probably pull out the petunias, but she didn't
have it in her to let anything die just now.

She'd been to too many funerals lately.

DeShawn Franklin's body had been unceremoniously cremated
at a facility outside of Macon. Other than the mortician, Lena
was the only person in attendance. His sister didn't want her children there. His ex-wife wouldn't speak his name and his current
wife wouldn't show her face in public. Jared hadn't wanted Lena
to go, but he didn't try to stop her, either. She had made a lot of
mistakes in her life. She figured DeShawn had tried to do right at
the end. He'd turned on that recorder on his phone. Lena didn't
know everything that the recording had captured—nobody at the
station did—but apparently, DeShawn had given Will Trent
enough evidence to bring down Big Whitey's organization. That
detail alone earned DeShawn one pair of clear eyes watching him
go to his maker.

Eric Haigh's interment had been markedly different. The state
had cleared him just before the burial yesterday morning, so he'd
been given a proper send-off with officers in dress uniforms and a
full police escort. Lena guessed she wasn't the only cop there
thinking that the last funeral they'd all attended was Chuck
Gray's. Lonnie's son had died of leukemia three months ago. Lena
had cried at Chuck's ceremony—not because she liked Chuck,
who was the kind of spoiled asshole you'd expect of the chief's
son—but because she'd felt so bad for Lonnie Gray.

She imagined Lonnie was feeling very sorry for himself right
now. He had an excellent law firm fighting the charges against
him, but as smart as Lonnie was, he'd made one enormous mis-

take. Lena figured it was arrogance that had brought him down. Lonnie never considered the possibility that the GBI would seize his home computer. Even without the murders, kidnappings, and trafficking, the state had found enough child porn on the chief's hard drive to send him away for a hundred years.

Stupid, sick bastard.

Last month, Lena had run a 10K with Lonnie. They were raising money for leukemia research. Lonnie had thirty years on her, but he'd beaten her to the finish line. Lena relished the thought of his strong heart ticking away as he marked off prison time for the rest of his miserable life. She hoped some big, nasty con did to Lonnie Gray exactly what he'd done to Marie Sorensen and all those other poor kids. Lena hoped they did it to him every second of every day until Lonnie fell over from exhaustion. And then she hoped they picked him back up and started all over again.

Lena wanted to think Lonnie's imprisonment would help Marie Sorensen's mom and the Winser family sleep better at night, but she knew from experience that some demons never went away.

The door opened again. Patterson stood with his hand on the knob. He didn't enter the room. He looked highly annoyed, which told her everything she needed to know.

Lena said, "I guess the rat didn't get his cheese."

She didn't wait for Patterson's response. She brushed past him, flashing her teeth the same as she had for the camera. Lena knew that she shouldn't push it, that she hadn't gotten away with anything, but anytime you left the rat squad with your badge intact was a reason to celebrate.

Lena felt her smile abruptly drop when she saw Denise Branson standing in the hallway. She had known that Denise was in the building, but Lena had prayed like hell that she would never have to see the woman again. Not that Lena had ever had a prayer answered before in her life.

Nor had she ever seen Denise Branson so obviously uncomfortable. It was hard to look at. She shuffled from one foot to another. She wouldn't look Lena in the eye. There was an air of humiliation about her, as if she'd been beaten down so many times over the last four days that she'd forgotten what it was like to get back up.

Patterson said, "Ms. Branson?"

His tone had a snarky edge to it that Lena didn't like. If the man had kept silent, Lena probably would've never spoken to Denise again. As it was, she asked the woman, "You need a bathroom break?"

Denise was obviously surprised by the question. Still, she nodded, and they both headed toward the one place Brock Patterson couldn't follow them. Lena saw the disappointed look on his face as the door to the ladies' room closed.

Denise got right to the point. Her voice had the practiced tone of somebody who was used to apologizing. "I'm sorry. I've got no excuse for what I did to you."

Lena prompted, "But?"

"No buts." Denise seemed resolute. There was none of her usual self-assured swagger. "I misled you about the boy. I dragged you into this without your knowledge. I've got the rat squad looking at you when you didn't do anything wrong."

Lena asked the question. "Is that why they tried to kill me and Jared, because they thought I knew where the boy was?"

Denise shook her head, then shrugged. "I don't know, Lee. It doesn't make sense that they'd go after y'all instead of me."

Lena kept coming to the same conclusion. She was a dog chasing its tail. "Who else did you tell about the boy?"

"Friends. People I could trust."

"I thought I was a friend you could trust."

This time, Denise had an excuse. "I thought I was protecting you."

"That's a lie," Lena said. "You didn't trust anybody at work. Not me, not Lonnie. You knew something was wrong. You thought there was a mole, and you thought it could be anybody from the top down."

Denise let out a heavy sigh. She looked like she couldn't muster the strength to argue anymore.

Lena asked, "Did you suspect Lonnie was Big Whitey?"

"I don't know," she admitted. Lena could tell from her expression that this was the truth. "It seemed odd that Big Whitey was getting tipped off. I thought maybe it was one of Lonnie's secretaries or somebody on your team."

"Or me?"

Denise's gaze settled somewhere behind Lena. "I didn't think so, but the stakes were too high for that kind of risk."

Lena studied Denise Branson, thinking not for the first time that she was looking at herself five years ago. The old Lena would've absolutely tried to go it alone. She didn't trust anybody. She didn't lean on anybody. She never asked for help. She thought there was only one person in the entire world who could do things the right way. Even today, all those tendencies were still there. Lena spent a good deal of her time battling her baser impulses. Sometimes she won. A lot of times she still lost. She consoled herself with the knowledge that at least she was trying.

Lena said, "I heard Lonnie was in the mayor's office when they grabbed him. Took him straight out the front door of city hall so God and everybody could see him."

Denise grinned, obviously familiar with the story. "That blonde chick's the one who arrested him. Agent Mitchell. I bet she kept her foot up his ass the whole time."

Lena didn't doubt it. "If Lonnie was half the man he claimed to be, he'd find a way to kill himself, save the courts the trouble."

"Give me a damn shiv, I'll do it myself."

"Get in line." Lena blew out a long breath "I can't waste anymore of my time on that bastard. How're the boys doing?"

Denise's face lit up with something that could only be described as pure joy. "They're good, Lee. I put Aaron in his mama's arms myself. He's surrounded by family. He's back with his brother. It's gonna be tough, but they've all got each other."

Again, Lena got the strange sensation of looking at herself. All those balls juggled in the air were worth it when you managed to keep them going. Watching them fly brought a bigger rush than any drug on the street. Of course, the high never lasted. No one could keep juggling that many balls for long. The first time one of them dropped, you wanted to die. The second time, you felt bad. The third and fourth times, you just found another ball to throw up into the air and moved on.

Lena had dropped so many balls in her lifetime that she'd lost count.

She told Denise, "I forgive you."

Denise looked surprised, then wary. "Why?"

"I have no idea," Lena confessed. She was living proof that second chances worked, but she'd never been able to extend that courtesy to anyone else. Losing Jeffrey Tolliver had taught her a lot of things, but the possibility of losing Jared had floored her.

Denise asked, "You wanna think about it?"

"No." Lena offered the naked, unadorned truth. "DeShawn and Eric are dead. Lonnie turned out to be Satan. Paul's put in an application for the Atlanta PD. Jared almost died." Lena felt a lump in her throat. She left her little bean off the list, but the memory was still raw. "I guess I can't afford to lose anybody else."

Denise was still skeptical. "It's probably my fault you and Jared almost got killed. I could've gotten you fired. It's only through the grace of God that those assholes in IA believe your story."

"You think they believe me?" Lena laughed. "The only reason I'm not on the street or in a jail cell is they can't prove anything." She walked to the sink and turned on the faucet. The water was ice cold. Lena bent down and drank from the tap.

Denise said, "I've been a bad friend to you. I know that." Her voice went low. "And I know you've been going through some things. Before all this, I mean."

Lena turned off the faucet. Denise wasn't the only one with trust issues. It had never occurred to Lena to talk to anybody about losing the baby—not to Jared, not to Denise, not even to herself. Truthfully, it felt like too much of a failure, something she should be ashamed of.

And even if it didn't feel that way, Lena wasn't about to pour out her heart in the women's toilet at the police station.

She told Denise, "It's all right. It's something I had to go through on my own."

"I get that." Denise wasn't one to sit around gazing at her navel, either. "I'm here if you want to talk, though."

Lena looked down at her hand. It was resting on the sink instead of pressed to her empty belly. She wondered if that's how it happened—incrementally. The nurse from Dr. Benedict's office had been right about one thing: it didn't go away, but it got different.

Lena let out another long breath. She looked at the mirror over the sink, thinking she'd aged about twenty years since this all started. "Jared's been bugging the shit out of me. I could use an excuse to get out of the house."

Denise caught Lena's gaze in the mirror. "Me, too."

Lena waited.

Denise cleared her throat. She struggled to speak. "Her name's Lila. We've been dating for a while."

Lena didn't push it. "How long is IA gonna keep you here?"

"Long as it takes."

"Call me when you're finished. We'll go to Barney's."

Denise looked away. The beaten-down expression was back. Barney's was a cop bar. She obviously didn't want to be seen by the men she used to command.

"You know what?" Lena grabbed a handful of paper towels.

"As far as I can tell, you were the only cop on this entire force who saw something was wrong with Lonnie. You saved that kidnapped boy's life. You kept him hidden and safe. You made sure he got home to his family. You gave Marie Sorensen's mother a face to the name. You took a vicious predator off the streets. You wrapped all of this up in a pretty bow for the state to untie." She tossed the paper towels into the trash. "Am I right? You did all that?"

"That's one way to phrase it."

"As far as I'm concerned, that's the only way to phrase it to any asshole who asks."

Denise shook her head. She saw where this was going. "IA isn't gonna see me as a hero, Lee. They're gonna fire my ass as soon as it hits the chair."

"Then you tell them you'll go straight to whichever news station will take you. Hell, go to the nationals. Go up to Canada. Tell them what you did to save that boy, and then let the Macon PD explain why they fired you for it." Lena laughed at the thought. "If they need somebody to corroborate your story, give them my number."

Denise stared openly. "You are one crazy bitch. You know that?"

"Maybe." Lena rested her hand on the door, but didn't open it. "I've been exactly where you are right now too many times not to know how to dig out of it."

"You really think that's gonna work?"

"Never underestimate the modern police force's aversion to bad publicity," Lena said, thinking she should put that on a plaque by her office door. "Don't let them hit your pension. That's what they'll go after first. Don't let them bust your rank to anything lower than detective." Lena smiled as she thought of something. "What do you think Paul's odds are getting onto the Atlanta PD?"

Denise smiled, too. "White male, ex-military? They'll roll out the red carpet."

"Either way, I'll need a new partner."

"Little salt and pepper?"

"More like *Chico and the Man*." Lena held open the door. Her smile dropped for the second time that day.

Will Trent was leaning against the wall. His face was a mess. Black and blue bruises were punctuated by dark red spots that were about the size of a grown man's knuckles.

Lena told Denise, "Call me about that beer."

"You got it." Denise didn't look at Will as she headed toward the interrogation room. Patterson was standing sentry in the doorway. He glared at Lena. She resisted the urge to stick out her tongue at him.

Will waited until Denise had shut the door. He told Lena, "I see Jared's out and about." She must've looked confused, because he said, "I just saw him go into the locker room."

Lena felt her jaw clench. She was going to kill Jared. After all her stupid husband had survived, she was going to strangle him with her bare hands.

Will nodded down the hall toward Denise. "She going to be okay?"

"What do you think?" Lena asked. She wasn't being belligerent. The state would have a lot of sway in Denise's case.

Will said, "I think the department has enough bad press without pissing off somebody like Denise Branson."

Lena wondered how much Will had heard standing out in the hallway. "She seems ready to take her medicine."

"In my experience, people like that don't generally stay down for the count." He stared his meaning into her. They both knew Lena had a habit of rising from the ashes.

"Right." Lena looked at her watch, though the only thing on her immediate agenda was to drag her idiot husband home by the collar. "I'll let you get back to work."

"I'm already finished. I was waiting to talk to you."

Lena felt dread flood through her body. "About what?"

"To tell you that you were right."

She laughed, thinking this was some kind of joke. "Right about what?"

"The attack. IA wanted me to wait until you were cleared to tell you."

Lena wasn't laughing anymore. "Tell me what?"

"It wasn't your fault. The reason those two men went to your house that night was because Jared said something at your doctor's office."

Lena couldn't make sense of the words. It was like he was speaking Japanese.

Will explained, "Cayla Martin was filling in for one of the nurses at Dr. Benedict's office while you were there. She overheard Jared talking about Big Whitey."

Lena's mouth didn't just open in surprise. Her jaw practically grazed the floor. Cayla Martin. The name had sounded familiar when Lena first heard it three days ago, but she'd never in a million years put it together. "I thought she just worked at the hospital. That she was Tony Dell's stepsister."

"She did part-time work at Dr. Benedict's office." Will spoke carefully, like he was explaining it to a child. "Cayla overheard Jared telling you that Lonnie Gray was Big Whitey."

"No." Lena felt a dry laugh scratch her throat. The conversation sounded more and more like a really bad joke. "He wasn't serious."

"Cayla felt differently. She told DeShawn Franklin, who said it was probably nothing, and then she told Lonnie Gray, who put out a hit on you and your husband."

None of this made sense. "How did she—"

"Cayla was dating Chuck Gray before he died of leukemia. She was close to Lonnie. Or, as close as two people like that can be." Will put his hands in his pockets. "You want my personal theory, I think she was just one of those women who likes stirring things up."

Lena felt her head shaking even as her brain tried to process the information. She remembered the doctor's visit. She remembered Jared talking shit. And she remembered taking him seriously for just a brief moment before dismissing his theory like she dismissed every jackass theory that came out of his mouth.

All she could manage was, "I don't believe you."

"Why not?" Will asked. "It's the truth." There was no smile on his face, no indication that he was about to reveal the punch line. "It wasn't your fault. I wouldn't say it was Jared's fault, either. It's just something that happened."

Lena pressed her back against the wall. She'd been racking her brain trying to figure out where she'd gone wrong, what she'd done, and in the end, she was completely blameless. "I just assumed . . ." Lena shook her head again. She was turning into a bobblehead doll. "I thought it was something to do with work."

"That's a reasonable assumption," Will agreed. "We all thought it was work-related. But it wasn't."

"We were . . ." She let her voice trail off. Lena couldn't say the most startling part of all: On the street, you expected bad things to happen. They had been in her doctor's office. Lena had thought they were safe.

She told Will, "I don't even remember meeting her. I've seen her face all over the news and it never even crossed my mind." She felt a jolt from a distant memory. "I think she even called me on the phone."

Will said, "If it helps any, you've really annoyed my partner. She's spent her professional career saying there's no such thing as coincidence."

Lena kept shaking her head. She'd never believed in coincidences, either.

"So," Will said. "Any questions?"

Lena could only think of one. "Does Sara know it wasn't my fault?"

He hesitated, but told her, "Yes."

Lena didn't even try to fight the smile on her lips. "And she knows that you're down here telling me?"

"Yes."

"She didn't try to stop you?"

"I should head back to Atlanta." Will pushed away from the wall, obviously uneasy with the subject. "I'm glad everything worked out for you and Jared."

She couldn't let him leave. "Why didn't you just call me? Or email me?"

He gave her a knowing look. "You always come out better when we're off the record."

Lena didn't have to ask for clarification. Her memory flashed up that night in the house when she'd held the hammer over her head. Jared was bleeding out on the floor. One man was already dead. Even now, the bruise on Lena's knee was still tender where she'd dropped her full weight onto Fred Zachary's spine. If she thought about it hard enough, she could hear the crack of bone echoing in her ears.

Georgia's Castle Doctrine law provided that any man or woman could use deadly force against an intruder so long as they believed their life was in danger.

Will Trent knew just as well as Lena that Fred Zachary had no longer been a threat.

He gave a slight bow, his only acknowledgment of the truth between them. "Until next time."

"There's not going to be a next time."

"Lena." He sounded almost wistful. "I really hope you're right."

Will kept his hands in his pockets as he walked away. Lena remembered the first time she'd met him. With his three-piece suits and mild manner, he was more like an undertaker than a cop. In Lena's quest to learn from her mistakes, Will Trent was up there with the big life lessons. That undertaker had almost sent her to prison.

And not without good reason.

Lena gave Will enough time to leave the building before she approached the interrogation room door. She listened carefully, but couldn't hear anything. Denise had a quiet voice and Brock Patterson had the dulcet tones of an ancient nun. Lena pressed her palm to the door as an act of silent solidarity. So many times, Lena had been on the other side of that door. So many times, she'd known in her heart that no one was waiting on the other side.

"Hey."

She spun around, surprised to find Jared behind her. The shock wore off quickly. "You dumbass. What are you doing up here? How did you—"

He kissed her in a sloppy way that was meant to shut her up.

Lena scowled as she pulled away. He was wearing blue sweatpants and a bright orange Auburn sweatshirt. His bandages were off. His hair stuck up like a duck's ass in the back. The scalp had Frankenstein stitches that had already been documented on several Facebook pages.

She asked, "How did you get here? You're not supposed to be driving."

"Estefan picked me up to come see the new Harleys."

"Estefan," she muttered. The two had half a brain between them. "You need to go home."

"So, take me home." He wrapped his arms around her waist.

"Jared."

"Take me home." He grabbed her ass to get her going. Lena slapped away his hand. Cameras covered almost every angle of the building. She imagined the front desk sergeant was pressing *record* at this very moment.

She said, "You should be at home asleep right now. You were in the hospital. You almost died."

"I'm not sleepy."

"Bullshit. You can barely keep your eyes open."

"I wish you couldn't keep your mouth open."

She gave him a sharp look, but she took the hint. Lena had spent enough time with Nell to know the kind of wife she didn't want to be. She was all for putting a man in his place, but Jared's father was so neutered he probably sat down on the toilet to pee.

Jared leaned on her as they made their way toward the front exit. "These bikes are gonna ride awesome, babe. There's push buttons on the bags, they've all got the 103 power pack . . ."

Lena tuned him out. She let Will's revelation roll through her mind. Cayla Martin. Dr. Benedict's office. No matter how hard Lena tried, she still couldn't recall meeting the woman. She was just one of those faceless people who blended into the scenery.

Jared didn't remember her, either. At least he hadn't commented the one time he'd watched the news with Lena. Cayla Martin's face had come on-screen and he'd turned off the TV before the story could run.

Unlike Lena, Jared didn't seem interested in finding out why they'd been targeted. He was too focused on being happy that the shooters hadn't succeeded. More likely, he thought it was Lena's fault but didn't want her to feel bad about it.

Lena had no problem letting him live in blissful ignorance. Since Fred Zachary had made a plea deal, there would be no trial. There would be no testimony explaining why two men had been sent to kill Lena and Jared. There was no reason for Jared to ever find out that he'd been at the root of all this evil. As forgiving as he was of others, he did not easily forgive himself. Lena was much more accustomed to living with guilt.

Not that she'd ever felt guilty for lying to her husband.

They finally reached the front lobby. Jared stopped walking. He put his hand to the wall to help keep his balance. They both knew they were in a camera blind spot. Every cop in the building knew how to stay off film.

Instead of doing something lewd, he told Lena, "You smell a little sweaty."

"Thanks a lot." She punched him in the shoulder.

He smiled sweetly. "Have your eyes always been brown?"

"Have you always been an idiot?"

He stopped smiling. The creases at the corners of his eyes didn't completely go away. "I want to try again."

Lena felt her face flush. He didn't have to tell her what he wanted to try again. "Do you think that's a good idea?"

"Hell no." He laughed. "That didn't stop us the first time."

Lena couldn't respond. She wasn't sure how she felt, whether or not she was ready. Last time had been an accident. To do it on purpose seemed like tempting fate.

"Lee." Jared took her hand. He'd been doing that a lot lately. Lena kept waiting to feel annoyed, but mostly, she found herself appreciating the solid feel of his hand, the tight grasp that told her he was going to be all right.

He said, "I want a baby with you. I want to make a life together. A family."

Just hearing the words made her want all of it, but Lena was too afraid to answer, too terrified to get her hopes up again.

Which is why she said, "Okay."

Jared grinned like a fool. "Really?"

"Yes." She said it again just to make sure. "Yes."

He kissed her, his mouth lingering longer than usual. His hand cradled her face. Jared looked into her eyes. His thumb traced where his lips had been. "And I want to rip out the kitchen because my dad did it wrong."

Lena's string of profanities was muffled by a trumpet of motorcycles pulling into the parking lot. She could see them lining up through the glass doors. Six Harley-Davidson police-issue bikes gleamed in the sunshine, courtesy of Sid Waller's stash of money in the basement of the shooting gallery.

"Hot damn!" Jared sounded like a frat boy at a pool party. He hobbled toward the parking lot, grabbing the back of a chair, the door handle, anything he could use to propel himself toward the bikes.

Lena shook her head as she took a key out of her pocket. Weapons weren't allowed in areas where prisoners were kept, so there was a row of lockers by the front door. She slid her key into the correct lock. Lena had never been the type of woman to carry a purse. She had shoved her messenger bag into the tiny locker so many times that the canvas was worn where the metal edges scraped into the material. Out of habit, she did a quick inventory of the bag, making sure her Glock was inside, her wallet, her keys, her pens.

Almost as an afterthought, she checked the outside pocket for the postcard. There it was—stamped and ready to go. Lena had been carrying the postcard around with her for three days, putting it in her bag, sticking it in her pocket, tossing it onto the dresser. Now, she pulled out the card and looked at the photograph of downtown Macon. "Thank you for visiting the Heart of Georgia" was written across the top in a curly yellow script.

Lena flipped the card over. The address was the same one she'd written years ago on an envelope she'd mailed to Atlanta.

The letter.

Lena knew that she'd always placed too much value on Sara Linton's opinion. For years, Lena had let the blame for Jeffrey's death shadow her every move. She was so low at one point that she had to reach up to touch bottom. Lena had written the letter to beg for Sara's forgiveness, to seek absolution. She'd structured her case the same way she would present an investigation in court. She'd testified to her own good character. She'd laid out the evidence. She'd highlighted the inconsistencies. She'd expertly spun the divergent facts in her favor. Lena hadn't been writing an apology. She had been begging for the return of her very soul.

The postcard was different. Two words, not three pages. Giving something, not asking for it.

The truth was that Lena had recovered her soul on her own. When she looked at her life now, all she could see was good. She was good at her job. She was good to her friends. She had married a good man, even if he talked too much. They would eventually have a child together. Maybe more than one child. They would raise their family. They would suffer through Nell's visits. They would have birthday parties, Christmases, and Thanksgivings, and no matter what Sara Linton thought about Lena's choices, she would always know that she had done the right thing.

Virtue was its own absolution.

There was a mail slot by the lockers, a brass plaque with the words U.S. MAIL engraved in bold print across the top. Every day around lunchtime, the woman in the front office collected the outgoing mail and took it to the post office. One of the perks of working at a police station. Especially if you liked long lunches.

Lena stared down at the postcard. For just a moment, she thought about tearing it up. She couldn't bring herself to do it. Lena was fine. Sara was the one who needed forgiveness. She was the one who couldn't let go. It cost nothing to release her.

Lena angled the postcard into the mail slot. She held on for just a second, then let it drop into the basket below.

Outside, a motorcycle revved. Jared was straddling the bike. Estefan was behind him because he couldn't hold it up on his own.

Lena hefted her bag over her shoulder as she headed toward the door.

Toward Jared.

Toward her life.

She smiled at the thought of Sara reading the postcard. The message was simple. Lena could've just as easily written it to herself—

You win.

Acknowledgments

I feel very lucky to have some really great folks on my team, among them Angela Cheng Caplan, Diane Dickensheid, and Victoria Sanders. Thank y'all so much for being the glue that helps hold this thing together.

As always, much praise goes to my editors, Kate Elton and Jennifer Hershey, for their insight and generosity.

Yet again, Dr. David Harper was very helpful with the medical details. He's kept Sara from killing lots of people over the years, and I appreciate his continued guidance. I owe eternal gratitude to the fine agents at the Georgia Bureau of Investigation for answering what I am sure seem like crazy questions. I promise I am only asking how to commit crimes in service to story. Chip Pendleton, MD, is a great doctor and even more generous adviser on all things Grady. I thank you, sir, for your ribald sense of humor and—more important—your time.

To Beth Tindall at Cincinnati Media, aka Webmaster Beth, aka my good friend: thanks for sticking with me all these years, and for not letting me use too much flash.

To all my publishers around the world and the good people who work on my books: I so appreciate your support. To my readers: I continue to be grateful for your kindness and all the cat photos you post on Facebook.

To my daddy: thanks for always being there even when I was young and stupid.

To D.A.: thanks for promising to be there when I am old and wise. I am sorry that only one of those things is happening.

ABOUT THE AUTHOR

KARIN SLAUGHTER is the *New York Times* and #1 internationally bestselling author of *Criminal*, "Snatched" and "Thorn in My Side" (e-book original novellas), *Fallen, Broken, Undone, Fractured, Beyond Reach, Triptych, Faithless, Indelible, A Faint Cold Fear, Kisscut*, and *Blindsighted*; she contributed to and edited *Like a Charm*. To date, her books have been translated into more than thirty languages. She is a native of Atlanta, Georgia, where she currently lives and is working on her next novel.

www.karinslaughter.com

ABOUT THE TYPE

This book was set in Sabon, a typeface designed by the well-known German typographer Jan Tschichold (1902–74). Sabon's design is based upon the original letter forms of Claude Garamond and was created specifically to be used for three sources: foundry type for hand composition, Linotype, and Monotype. Tschichold named his typeface for the famous Frankfurt typefounder Jacques Sabon, who died in 1580.

Van Buren Public Library
115 S. First Street Box 405
Van Buren, IN 46991